I0748057

THE SHADOW PRINCE'S RUIN

Dark Companions #2

K.A. Merikan

This is a work of fiction. Any resemblance of characters to actual persons, living, dead, or undead, events, places or names is purely coincidental.

No part of this book may be reproduced or transferred in any form or by any means, without the written permission of the publisher. Uploading and distribution of this book via the Internet or via any other means without a permission of the publisher is illegal and punishable by law.

Text copyright © 2024 K.A. Merikan

All Rights Reserved

http://kamerikan.com

Cover design by

Trif Book Design

https://trifbookdesign.com/

CONTENTS

CHAPTER 1

HAWK

Do sardines ever get canned with sardines that previously tried to shank them, so they're stuck together for years, until the Grim Reaper opens the container and devours them both? I've been at death's door five times, so I guess I'm long overdue a hot date with Hades.

Today, I am that unlucky sardine, and the guy who almost succeeded at killing me two months ago glares at me from across the van. The two guards escorting us to another prison sit close to the doors at the back, discussing something in low voices. Both Samson and I are cuffed to the floor by our ankles and wrists, too far away from anyone, including each other, to cause any damage.

I should resent being treated like some rabid beast, but let's be honest, I deserve it. If my cuffs had any slack, I'd be wrapping the chain between them around Samson's neck.

With no one here to make sure protocol is followed, the younger of the guards, a cute blond with a canine protruding from the line formed by his otherwise straight smile, turns on his cell phone and flashes his colleague something. They both grin.

"What is it? Redheads? Cumshots? Gay?" I ask, letting my gaze linger on the young guard's eyes. I would do him in a heartbeat, even if he is a bit too muscular for my taste. But then again, nobody's perfect.

A low grunt echoes between the truck's steel walls, and the guard stuffs his cell down his pocket. The daylight sneaking through small barred windows offers me a flash of his horrified expression as he stutters, "No, that's... my kid. Jesus Christ, Coleman, shut the hatch to that filthy mind of yours! I'm sure you can find a dick to suck in your new cell."

Damn right I can. I've had enough going on in the face department to get down and dirty with pretty boys back in high school, and at thirty, I'd be even more of a catch if I hadn't been unfairly incarcerated. Green eyes and tattoos can make a guy forget such minor details as a murder conviction. I've actually had several marriage proposals by mail.

Samson looks up with his bloodshot eyes. "Getting antsy? Not fucked anyone since your last hole sold you out?"

I don't know why he's baiting me, because neither one of us can reach the other. We're stuck like two eunuchs at an orgy.

"I don't come and tell," I tell him in a steady voice, because the reality is that between suffering from an infection and barely recovering from this bastard turning my stomach into a pin cushion, I'm not in the mood for procuring blowjobs. At least while in hospital, I got the great news of being STD-free.

"You should be dead!" Samson snarls and spits at me, but his saliva pathetically falls next to my shoe.

I smirk. "With that kind of aim, no wonder you have no kids waiting for you out there."

Samson lowers his voice. "Next time I'll aim my knife for your fucking dick. If you survive that, at least you'll get to live your shittiest life."

One of the guards scowls at us. "Can you two shut it? You'll both be in the can for life. Why make yourself even more miserable?"

I hold Samson's gaze, until his blue eyes are my sole focus, his scarred jaw and the narrow nose that would have been so easy to break, only a blur. "Or maybe *magic* will save me again, and I'll end up with an additional inch between my legs. Who knows?"

Samson raises his ass a few inches off the steel bench as if to lunge at me, but the chains don't let him do shit and he just struggles against them as I laugh.

One of the guards gets up. "That's enough—!"

The driver starts honking. There's a screech of tires and gravity suddenly shifts, throwing us around like a bunch of trainers in a washing machine. I grab the bars my chains are attached to, and they prove to be a blessing as my long brown hair flies in my face, obscuring most of my vision. The guards, who were sitting without seatbelts, get smashed against the metal walls, just two sacks of bones and flesh.

The tumble ends in a sudden collision, and I tense every muscle, holding on to the handles by my seat as two bodies fly past me and land on the wall separating this compartment from the cab with a dull thud.

The seatbelt that held me secure now digs into my stomach, reminding me of the ordeal I've been through since the shanking, but I open my eyes, trying not to succumb to the sense of nausea pooling in my stomach as the world comes to a halt around me.

The scent of blood is tart in the air as I take in a bloodstained face. The young guard with the protruding canine has his eyes open, but there's no life behind them anymore. A bundle of keys shines by his belt, and I grab them, elated that they're close enough.

My mind explodes with promises of freedom, of an escape from the madness of spending the rest of my days behind bars and thick walls, so I ignore the grunting close by and skim through the keys, locked in a state of absolute focus.

Only when I slide the right key into the padlock keeping me chained do I spot a booted foot twitching helplessly.

Fuck.

I look up to spot Samson, blood dripping from his nose and off his bald head. He's choking the life out of the other guard. I have sympathy for the guy, but my much bigger concern is Samson grabbing the dead guard's gun.

I open the padlock and pull on the chain.

He aims my way.

I rip one hand free.

He shoots and... misses.

My ears ring from the loud bang, but I grin like a madman and launch myself at Samson, flinging my leg his way. The firearm goes off again, and I feel a rush when gun smoke-scented air swishes all too close to my head, but then my foot collides with the fucker's head. I slam it against the wall with all the strength I have. The pistol clutters to the floor as Samson attempts to grab my calf, but I flex my entire body and kick his face again and again, seeing red as the side of the truck dips at the impact.

"Don't even need a shank!" I yell at him, consumed by my fury. The need to end him is so much greater than even finding out if we're hanging off a cliff.

I know it's done when he stops moving, his head a stew made of bone, blood, and brains. I'm heaving as I take in the destruction around me. The floor under my feet is uneven, and one of the walls is bent out of shape. I glance through the bars between the back and the cab to confirm that the driver isn't moving either.

Am I like a cat? Was this my sixth life granted?

Shock slowly leaves my body, replaced by a weakness in every limb, and I stare at the carnage around me, exhausted as if I'd been digging graves all day.

What. The. Fuck.

Not that I'm complaining.

A switch flips in my head and prompts me to free myself from the remaining cuffs and chains. For all I know, the cops are already en route, and as lucky a bastard as I am, opportunities like this one don't just fall into a prisoner's lap every day.

I'm meant to spend the rest of my life in prison, with the possibility of parole coming only once I'm old and hopeless. I don't fucking deserve that. So maybe I've made mistakes, and disagreed with the law many times, but my intentions have always been good, and I should get a second chance.

Today, this damn sardine is swimming free.

I'm about to climb out through the wrecked back door, but then go back to pick up the guard's wallet. It's not like he's gonna need it. I'm sorry for him, but it's not my fault fate had this freak accident in store for him.

A quick browse through his pockets leaves me with some cash, mints, and two condoms. I leave the phones, too worried there might be some tracking apps on there that I don't know how to disable. I've been in the can for five years, and technology has never been my strong suit.

I emerge into the setting sun, blinded by the blood-red sky. The first inhale of fresh, wood-scented air makes my head spin, and when I look around, taking in the brilliant green of the leaves, freedom seems within reach.

I thought I would never again smell the earthy, damp aroma of the forest, but trees are everywhere within sight. Figures. This is Maine.

The transportation truck fell off a small cliff, and shouldn't be visible from the road, so there's a chance its failure to arrive at its destination might not be discovered for another few hours.

I'm in the north, I know how to stay off-grid. What's stopping me from crossing into Canada? Worst-case scenario, I get caught. What can they do then? I've already got a life sentence wrapped around my neck like a noose. And since I'm not taking the gun with me, nobody can even claim I'm armed *and* dangerous. I'm so tall every bed I ever owned was too short, and I'm strong enough to knock a man out with a single punch. Don't need a firearm to make grown men piss their pants.

I climb a cliff covered in enough bushes to give me leverage and then.... I start walking. It's a marathon, not a sprint, so I keep a steady pace as the sun sets behind me. And when a vehicle approaches? I hide in the bushes. Easy. Simple.

Walking wherever I want and the absence of a schedule I'm obliged to follow are like a rush of the purest cocaine. Elated, I can barely feel any fatigue by the time I encounter a road sign informing me of a town two miles ahead. Problem is, I'm still wearing bloodstained overalls, and unless I come up with a way to make myself look like a regular citizen, my freedom might be very brief.

I must be the luckiest bastard out there, because there's a clothesline on the property ahead. I snatch some clothes, which all smell fresher than the air after a storm, and they don't fit half bad, even though their owner must be shorter than me, judging by the length of the sweatpants. The poor bastard's neighbor even left a pair of muddy work boots outside waiting for me.

I dispose of my bloodied shoes and clothes in a pond and keep walking. Going by the guard's watch, it's getting close to ten p.m., but I haven't gotten far enough to consider rest.

I need energy, I need calories, I need food to fuel me through the night.

And the universe really is on my side tonight because, I spot a green neon sign that makes me salivate.

Best Burgers Bonanza.

"Yesss, baby..." I whisper to myself and walk faster, lowering the stolen baseball cap over my eyes. After years of enduring prison grub, this is my Holy Grail. I'll be eating two—no, *three* fucking juicy burgers and more fresh, crispy fries than a high school football team after practice.

And who knows, maybe luck will strike me a third time today, and I'll even get laid.

I do have two condoms.

CHAPTER 2

SYLVAN

I *hate* the human realm.

I hate daylight for giving me sunburn. I hate seeming incompetent at every step, just because this world is new to me. I hate having to tuck my pointy ears under a cap. I hate the scratchy fabric of my uniform at Best Burgers Bonanza. I hate that the silver collar around my neck blocks my access to shadowcraft (as meager as my skill is). I hate that I am an elven prince, Sylvan *fucking* Goldweed, and instead of getting the respect I deserve as a royal, I'm stuck flipping burgers for a pittance.

Am I really supposed to live like this for *fifty* years? Two months into my banishment and I'm already on the verge of killing someone when asked for extra ketchup.

I don't know what's worse: that after a few years in the human realm my body will begin to deteriorate, 'grow old' as if I were some soulless beast or animal, not an elf. Or that, while I am stuck here, being of no use or significance to anyone, life at the Nocturne Court carries on. Soon enough, my connection with it will wither, and even my own mother will forget me. All the progress I have made in alchemy will be in vain after fifty years of new developments in the craft.

I will never prove myself.

I will amount to nothing.

I will forever be the most useless Goldweed prince who ever lived.

"Hey, man! Is the ice cream coming or what?" yells a teenager with the complexion of scorched earth.

If I stay here long enough, will my smooth skin also erupt with spots?

"Apologies, the machine is broken," I lie, because I will not be cleaning it *again*. It's almost ten at night, and from then, the restaurant will only be open for drive-thru customers. I can't wait for the bunch of rowdy adolescents occupying the booth at the back of BBB to disappear from my sight.

I would have told them to get out in more blunt terms, or even not accepted their order ten minutes before closing time, but I've been reprimanded for my *attitude issues* several times already. I can't lose this job with no other plan for survival. Because how else am I to earn my keep in a world so strange and unfamiliar? Lord Kyran did me a favor by securing a meager room and work for me, and if I'm ever to earn his forgiveness and have him end my banishment prematurely, I cannot openly scorn his gifts.

Resigned to my fate, I take hold of a broom and approach the booth, since I've been told cleaning up is a universal and polite way to send patrons home. I've only been here two months, but all the manual labor has already made my hands rougher, and exhaustion sends me to sleep as soon as I lie down, but I am safe, and as long as I keep my head down—

"But just look at that short king," a raspy voice says, and one of the teens in the booth flashes me a smile. He's wearing a loose pink T-shirt and clothes that are flashier than those of the other males at the table. A rubber bracelet featuring various shades of blue and green jitters on his wrist as he waves at me. "He just appeared out of nowhere this spring," he adds, never taking his eyes off me.

"You should ask him out," a young girl says, slurping her milkshake and poking the guy with her elbow.

I throw daggers at them with my glare. For some humans, my looks have been a huge point of interest, but entertaining that is the last thing on my mind. The flashy guy shifts to the edge of the booth, while all his friends watch on, munching on the last of their fries.

"Will you be going to Black Tree High once the school year starts? Or are you home-schooled or something?" he asks as the girl snorts so hard milkshake comes out of her nose.

They are all *repulsive*. I couldn't care less about their appearance since they're over-grown children, but everything about their attitude, demeanor, their lack of manners, and basic respect for others is so agitating to me that if I had access to shadowcraft, I would have—

What? My talent for wielding shadow is so painfully underdeveloped I couldn't dream of using it to teach all of them a lesson even if I didn't have a power-blocking collar around my neck. Then again, I could grow sharp claws out of shadow, and if I made sure to slice through an artery...

I straighten up, trying to seem taller, which is pretty futile and we all know it. No wonder they are mistaking me for their peer, because at five-foot-two, I'm hardly an imposing figure.

"Is there a reason for this questioning?" I ask, then make a point of taking a long glance at the burger-shaped clock on the wall.

One of the boys rolls his eyes at his friend and pushes a cold fry into his mouth. "Jeez, aren't there other guys willing to suck your dick on that—"

"Grindr," the Milkshake Girl says and sucks on her damp paper straw again.

"Yeah, that."

I don't know what 'Grindr' is, but I am most definitely not about to suck anyone's dick. Especially not some rude, childish fuck's. Still, I sense my cheeks warm, and my pale complexion surely reveals that I'm blushing. The flush is an absolute abomination on my face, and doesn't accurately communicate my feelings on the matter *at all*.

The guy in pink groans. "But he's so cuuuute."

"I would *strongly* disagree," I say through gritted teeth, clenching the broom harder. "You do not know me, and you have no idea what I am capable of. A child picking roses in the moonlight is 'cute'. A bunch of newborn bats feasting on coralberries are 'cute'. A moth desperately hitting a window to get to light is 'cute'. I resent the very notion of being anything like those pathetic critters."

They stare at me, then all erupt with laughter at the same moment. Mockery hits me like sour rain, and as fury boils under my skin, I consider whether the broom in my hands could do some damage. If I tried really hard, I could make at least one of those children bleed for disrespecting me.

But before I can make my move (and lose my job for it), Kurt, my co-worker, steps close and puts his hand on my shoulder. "You flirting with underage boys again?" he asks, winking at me.

I want to yell about how incorrectly he's interpreted this pathetic situation, but one of the girls speaks first.

"Oh, how old are you?" she asks, as if that meant anything.

"I am twenty-five, if you must know."

Pink Boy makes a face as if I've declared I eat roaches. "You're *old*? Like... what? You really got a baby face, man. I need some skincare tips asap."

I raise my chin. At least when he's sitting and I'm standing, I can look at him from above. "It might be too late for that in your case."

Kurt spins me around and gives me a gentle shove toward the registers. "Carla asked for some help in the kitchen before she leaves. I'll close the doors."

Kurt is an acceptable specimen. For a human. While younger than me, I do have to begrudgingly admit that despite his lazy disposition and a tendency to wear his hat backwards, he knows the workings of Best Burgers Bonanza like the back of his hand.

The teens are debating my supposed rudeness in low voices. Well, they deserved everything they got. Just last week, the same damn group was asking me whether I was an 'albino' because of the fairness of my hair. Yet another concept I wasn't aware of since it doesn't exist in the Nightmare Realm. They must have spent at least half an hour debating whether an albino can have dark blue eyes like mine. It's maddening. And as much as I appreciate Kurt coming to my aid, seeing them finally get up after they ignored me for half an hour feels like yet another insult.

I swear, one day I will lose my patience and blood will be spilled on the mint green tiles of Best Burgers Bonanza.

Carla, the manager's assistant, waves at me in passing, already out of her work uniform. "Remember to check every door and window, and don't forget to switch on the alarm," she says, as if she believes me feeble-minded.

"There, all done," Kurt informs me, pulling off his polo shirt on the way to the lockers. "If you forget how something works, just call me. I won't go to sleep until you close the shop."

I wish I could dismiss him, say I never forget anything, and that I don't need help, but in my first week here, I spilled the frying oil, set off the alarm twice, and accidentally defrosted a whole batch of burgers too soon. I've been humbled, and Kurt was always there to pick up the pieces. I may have cried myself to sleep after that first week. If there's anything I hate more than my banishment, it's being inept.

"Thank you, I appreciate it."

He also got me a phone on which I can receive messages from our boss, and didn't ask for any payment. I truly am lucky to have him as my guide, as infuriating as it is that I need one in the first place.

Soon enough, both my co-workers are gone, and I walk around, checking if everything is working as it should. I have a notebook with drawings and diagrams I can compare all the gauges and switches to, but I find it punishingly hard to remember all the settings, since I don't understand their purpose.

Everything makes so much more sense in the Nightmare Realm. You want swamplight? Harvest mucus off the right type of frog or snail in the bog. The rules around it are simple too. The closer the harvest is to the full moon, the brighter the light will be. Then, all you need to do is put it in a lantern and set it on fire. You will get beautiful, stable green light that produces no heat, and is safe to be used even by children.

The array of multicolored plastic switches which I have to handle every day? A madman's folly. I've been trying to learn about their inner workings. There is a spark, power travels down a cable, ending up in the painfully bright lamps above the tables, but how it manages to set them alight still eludes me. It won't stop me, of course, from judging all electricity as crude, and aesthetically unappealing.

I could easily learn all about it if I had the time, but understanding the people around me and their culture takes precedence. To function in the human world efficiently I spend a lot of time plowing through their books and watching television in my spare time.

And I've been yelled at for removing one of the sockets off the wall to find out how cables work, so I won't be doing *that* again any time soon.

Just as I open a book on the history of crime detection in the human world, a raspy voice croaks in the headphones I'm wearing. "Meat time," a man says, and I sigh before heading for the drive-thru window.

"Good evening and welcome to Best Burgers Bonanza. Can I take your order, please?" I recite the formula I could repeat in my sleep.

"Ah! Hello! I'd like a Super Bonanza meal with coffee, a cheeseburger with extra pickles, a set of Cowboy Sliders with chicken, and a Marshmallow Sundae. Oh, and the cookie special."

I tap everything into a machine as I've been taught, even though it would have been much more convenient to write it down on a piece of paper. I tried to convince my boss about that when I first arrived, even showing off my neat handwriting, but to no avail. Apparently, if I do it on the machine it logs it... somewhere, so their taxes are counted automatically. Why would they *want* to pay more taxes? I don't know and didn't ask.

"Anything else, sir? We do have a special offer which would allow you to get an extra portion of fries for just fifty cents with your sliders."

The man laughs, and his rasp buzzes in my ears so intensely I find myself curling my toes. "You convinced me. Bring it!"

I do smile at his cheerfulness, even though I'm instantly embarrassed that talking someone into additional fries gives me any sense of achievement.

"It will all be ready in a few minutes, please approach the window to pay," I say, because my manager has taught me payment comes first, as some people may take the food and run.

"Coming right up," the customer tells me, and I'm about to walk off to throw the meat into the fryer when thudding footsteps resonate in the drive instead of the growl of a motor engine.

I pop my head out just in time to see a towering beast with long, thick arms. Since arriving in the human realm, I have faced men and women who far outgrow the average elf. They are stockier by nature, and distinctly hairier, but the giant standing before me in a black hoodie, joggers, and with a baseball cap pulled low over his eyes must have forgotten to stop growing.

When our eyes meet, his jaw goes slack as he cocks his head, staring at me as if I were made of gold.

I lick my lips, unsure what to do for a moment because he is a bit intimidating. I end up clearing my throat as I eye him.

"Sir, you must come in a vehicle to use the drive-thru. Otherwise, you are causing a risk to everyone on the road."

This seems to wake him up from whatever realm his mind drifted off to, and he looks around the empty asphalt. "There is no *everyone* here. Just us," he says and his mouth stretches into a smile. As he tips his chin higher, the glow coming from above catches dark stubble, an element of appearance in some human males, which I've become unwillingly preoccupied with. It makes them look somewhat... beastly.

I hesitate, once more glancing behind him, at the empty road. "If I bend the rules once, I will be obliged to do it again."

The stranger licks his lips before stepping closer, about to reach inside through the window, but he stops himself in the last moment. "Nah, I'm a gentleman. There's no obligation to do anything."

He is most definitely no gentleman, but I don't want to argue for the sake of the argument. He's been friendly enough. "I will agree this one time, but I warn you that it cannot become a precedent." I discreetly assess the width of his shoulders. He's... massive. It gives me that tightness in the throat and moths in the stomach, like when I used to take sneaky glances at the royal guards, sometimes even taking my walks at a time when they were likely to bathe in the pond.

The stranger grins and winks at me. "Don't you worry. I'm real good at keeping secrets. Maybe I could buy you a drink? Or a cookie?"

My neck gets hot under the silver collar. "I do not need to be bribed. I made my choice to serve you out of my own free will. Are you paying cash or card?" There's a tension between us I can't fully pinpoint, but it's making me nervous.

The man snorts, shakes his head and bites his lip as he looks at me with a half-smile. "Okay, I'll just be frank. I can't take my eyes off you, and I want to talk to you a bit more. Do you want that cookie?"

I stare at him, dumbstruck. "I am not female," I say, because I've learned the hard way that some men approach me because my delicate features confuse them about my gender.

"I know."

Heat rises up my neck. I wish I was more experienced in these things, but matters of the heart have never been my priority.

But also, what is he thinking? That I, Prince Sylvan Goldweed, will fall at his feet because of a handsome smile and thick arms? Unless... Dread pools in my heart.

"Did they pay you to come here and agitate me?" I ask harshly.

The man pulls up the visor of his cap just enough for the light to catch the green of his eyes. He has really long lashes, which make his masculine face even handsomer. "Who's *they*? I just came in for food and got hungry for more than that."

That is blunt. Since getting banished to the human world, I've been busy establishing myself and finding my feet. The possibility of being intimate with someone hasn't even occurred to me. I'm out of my depth and resort to what I know—shutting down a situation before it can overwhelm me. I despise not being in control, and this man is most definitely trying to pull the reins out of my hands.

"I'm afraid you can only buy food here. You must pay or leave." I cringe on the inside at my own voice. Could I not have been nicer about it? More flirtatious? I bet I'll be lying in bed tonight and coming up with hundreds of answers better than what I just said, but it is what it is.

The man deflates, but his smile doesn't falter completely. "Sure. As I said, no obligations," he adds and opens his wallet before placing paper bills and some change in front of me. As I take the money, he steps away from the window, triggering a motion-activated light that would have long ago switched on if he drove a car.

This time, it's me who stares, because the stranger's handsome exterior and gravelly voice both pale in comparison to the beauty of the shadow he's casting. Blacker than the depths of Grief Ocean, it radiates power I have never before seen concentrated in a single human's darkness. It's like a beast forced into a cage too small. Not only is it so potent it seems to pulse, but slim dark tendrils extend beyond its edges like abandoned children desperate to find a home. His shadow isn't just more powerful than any I've seen. It's feral and ripe for plucking, like he's been bound to an elf before, but their bond was severed death.

"Wait!" I say, even though I know he will be awaiting his food anyway. I'm frantic and desperate to not lose sight of him. My heart pounds ever faster. "Are you... someone's Dark Companion?"

He blinks but steps back to the window. "Ooh, is that some new slang I missed? I could definitely be your *companion* tonight. And we could do dark, dark things," he says and winks at me.

He has no idea. Since I arrived among humans, I've not seen anyone whose shadow was accessible like his, practically begging for connection. I could bind his shadow to mine *right now*, and he'd be none the wiser. With such power as my crutch, I'd no longer be my family's weakest link, the laughingstock of the Nocturne Court.

I reach out, expecting the shadow tendrils to accept the invitation and curl around my fingers, but they remain in place, as if I didn't exist.

That's right, the collar around my neck prevents me from using any shadowcraft.

I let out a helpless whine, which soon morphs into a sigh when the huge hand squeezes mine, encasing it in a warm, cozy cocoon.

"In case I wasn't clear enough so far, I think you're the prettiest twink I've seen in... forever."

I've heard that word before, and while I'm not certain what it means, paired with 'prettiest' and the way he looks at me, I'm guessing he's attempting to compliment me.

My fingers sizzle under his touch, and I breathe a little too fast as I glance from his eyes, to our fingers, to his shadow begging to be claimed. I don't know how yet, but I *will* get the collar off and bind him to me.

My life would change completely if I had a Dark Companion like him. Banishment be damned, I'd claw my way back to the Nocturne Court somehow.

Only now I truly register what he meant and blush even more furiously. He thinks I'm pretty?

"I finish work in an hour. I'll just get you your food, and… will you wait for me?" I ask, squeezing his hand, but at this point I'd be willing to break the rules and close early just to make sure he doesn't wander off anywhere.

"Hell yes. I'd wait on this curb for a week for a pretty thing like you." He lets out a raspy laugh and pulls out a little square wrapper from his wallet. There's a ring-like shape inside, but I have no idea what that might be. "You have a place?"

He… doesn't? Right. He doesn't even seem to have a car. I have no idea who he is, but the packet looks a bit like the condiments we serve with takeout orders, so I'm guessing it's food (?). I'm not used to spontaneous decisions, but if I let a shadow like that slip out of my grasp, I'll never forgive myself.

But maybe this is a good thing that he wants to accompany me home? I'll be able to keep an eye on him. Speaking of which… is that blood on his knuckles?

I swallow, wondering if I'm making the right choice, but I always overthink things, and this is simply not the time for that. I nod. "It can be arranged. A place where we can enjoy *this*," I point to the wrapper. "Together." I smile, glad my ears are tucked under the cap, because they tend to twitch when I'm nervous.

There's a sharp, lustful glance in the man's eyes as he rubs my hand with his thumb, and when he steps away, letting go, for a moment I stand still, his food and my obligations forgotten.

Many shadow-wielders say meeting one's Dark Companion can feel like a strike of destiny, but when I look at this massive human whose name I don't even know, I don't feel that at all.

This isn't happening *to* me. I'm taking destiny into my own hands.

CHAPTER 3

HAWK

For the past five years, cheap prison versions of Thanksgiving and Christmas dinners have been the best fare I could hope for, but with a bit of money in my pocket, I can now get whatever I want. Succulent chicken. Smoky beef patties. Fries that are actually crispy, and even ice-fucking-cream.

For the first time in years, I feel sated after a meal, and as I rest on the curb behind the restaurant, waiting for my one hundred pound dessert, smiles don't leave my face.

So maybe it's reckless to stay around here so soon after I went off the radar, along with several other people who are now dead, but if I were a cop, I'd be searching for a fugitive someplace more sensible than a fast food joint in the town nearest to the accident site.

Or I'm just excusing the insatiable need to put my dick in that pink mouth.

To say I'm mesmerized would be an understatement. Maybe I've just gotten used to guys being rough around the edges back in prison, but Sylvan (going by his name tag) is so pretty I can't think straight. Talking to him is like encountering a fairy tale illustration in real life. His wrists are delicate like meringue, and his skin reminds me of the palest peach.

I stand by the locked door to the restaurant so I can get a glimpse of him sooner, and at one point he gave me a sweet smile from behind the counter. I'm twice his size and killed a man hours ago, but he makes me melt like the ice cream I've just eaten. He even gave me extra sprinkles. Cuteness is my kryptonite, and he's got it in spades.

My heart skips a beat when he emerges from the back of the kitchen without his uniform. He's dressed in a button-up black shirt and dark jeans, and the color only emphasizes how pale he is. I didn't see much of his hair when he wore a cap, but it's now visible, and he's combed it nicely. He wants to make a good impression, which is adorable, because by the end of this night, his white hair will be matted from rubbing against the sheets.

When our gazes meet through the glass pane in the door separating us from one another, his expression is somber, as if he were about to make a life-changing decision. Which I suppose he is, considering he's about to sample my cock. I'm not the poetic type, but his eyes are something else. Like sapphires covered in frost, and the fact that his lashes are also very pale only makes that first impression sink deeper into my brain.

As soon as he steps out though, one thing becomes undeniable.

He is *tiny*.

The top of his head doesn't even reach my shoulder. He could bury that pretty face in my chest hair without even leaning down. I could pick him up, bridal-style, and carry him off so he doesn't need to tire his small feet, without breaking a sweat.

My dick twitches at the thought of all the things I can do to him, and I'll definitely need more than two condoms for *that*.

He offers me a curt smile, as if he wasn't a tiny thing about to have a fuck fest with a guy most people would cross the street to avoid at this time of night, and turns around to lock the restaurant.

"Oh shit," I mumble as my gaze drops to his ass, showcased by a pair of jeans. I can barely resist the temptation to drop to my knees, drag the denim off him, and eat his ass right here, in the faint glow of the lamp installed above Best Burgers Bonanza's back door. He would shiver, bite his lips, cheek flat against glass, and push back, begging for more. And those two steps would work perfectly to make up for some of our height difference, allowing me to rail him from the back as he holds on to the door handle.

I have not fucked an ass this fine—scrap that, I haven't had *any* ass since my arrest—and I sure fucking hope he has more condoms where we're going, or I might just be irresponsible.

I place my hands on his hips and lean in, nuzzling the back of his head. What's that smell on him? It's fresh like droplets of rain on leaves, and I find myself kissing the side of his neck before tasting the skin, which smells as though he's just taken a shower.

How? Do they provide such facilities for their workers? Something must have changed for the better while I was in jail.

The way he gasps and freezes in my grip makes my cock stiffen. "A-apologies it took so long, I had to clean the ice cream machine, and it is an ordeal."

"I would wait for you until morning, pretty boy," I say and pull his hips against mine, so he can sense my arousal. His hair is soft like duckling down, and barely reaches his ears, giving me a good view on how pink his nape is getting—

I glance back to his ears, only now registering their pointy, elongated shape. *What?*

He turns around in my grip, blushing profusely. "This is not an appropriate place," he whispers breathlessly. "I don't even know your name yet."

"I can tell you my name, but only if you never tell anyone," I whisper and guide his hand to the front of my pants. His touch is uncertain, but it still sends a shockwave down my legs and sets off explosions of pleasure in my skull. I can't wait to see those slim fingers around my cock. They'll make my dick appear even more impressive.

"Oh. I—that is... sizeable," he utters, not looking up anymore. "And I agree to keep your name to myself."

Something about the way he speaks turns me on too. So proper. I want to ruin that prim exterior. I want to make his pink mouth spill filthy words to me.

"It's Hawk, like the bird. And what should I call *you*?" I ask, sandwiching him between me and the wall with his hand still resting on my dick. I can't help myself. I lick the top of his head, right through the parting, hair and all.

"Sylvan. My name is S-sylvan," he says, but his voice breaks a little at the end.

I'm a bit of a dog. When I sense prey, all I wanna do is chase.

At this point, I'm hard enough for my brain to be scrambling. Do we really need a 'place'? Could he not go down on me here? There's no one around.

Sadly, he pulls away his hand and presses my stomach. I flex it so he can sense my muscles.

Fine. I've waited for over an hour and can wait a bit more. "Where's your ride, baby?"

He clears his throat and slips out of my grasp, but makes sure I follow. He points to a... bus stop down the road lit by a yellow lamp. "Just down here. It shall arrive soon. I was hoping we could set some ground rules, because there might have been a misunderstanding."

I follow him like a dog, salivating already. I swear to God, he is the hottest person I have ever touched. "Sure. You want to have a safeword, or something? Soft and hard limits? I'm good with that."

He glances back at me and despite the flush, his blue eyes are bright and attentive. "I'm not sure I understand, but you have something that is of no use to you, yet could change everything for me." He looks behind me, but there's nothing there but asphalt.

"I do?"

"Your shadow. It might be ordinary to your eyes, but I see it for what it is." Sylvan sighs and extends his hand until his fingers are covered by my shadow. What I'm focused on is that he places his other hand on my arm.

I want more touch. I want skin to skin. I want it *now*.

Even though all this shadow stuff sounds a bit cuckoo.

He meets my eyes. "Have you ever had a near-death experience? It's not unusual for a shadow to swell in force when a human is dying or filled with despair."

I stare back at him as my mouth dries, but I offer him a smile and shrug. "Who hasn't, am I right? I'm like a cat, and still have three of my nine lives left."

He nods, sizing me up with that inquisitive gaze. "That does explain a lot. Was one of those times almost drowning in a river?"

I shift my weight as a phantom eel twists in my guts. This question is setting off alarm bells as I suck in air, remembering a dream about tar-black water flooding my mouth, and the huge face of the moon staring at me from the sky as a shadowed creature loomed above the surface and reached for me.

I don't want to entertain this anymore.

"Are you like... into all this New Age stuff?" I ask, placing my hands on his hips as I look down at him, drinking in his marble-like complexion, the huge eyes like moonlit lakes, and narrow, pouty lips.

He cocks his head with the tiniest frown. "Have you noticed my ears, Hawk? I am—"

The bus swoops in next to us a bit too abruptly, but the quicker we board, the sooner I'm in his bed. Sylvan huffs in frustration, but goes in first, giving me the best view—his ass in jeans.

My instinct is to push my face against it and lick the denim, but I can't be a menace on public transport if I want to reach his place at a sensible time. I lower the visor of my baseball cap and pull up the hood to ensure that any strands of hair that might have come loose from under the hat remain hidden.

I'm pleasantly surprised to hear that he's paying for my ticket and swiftly follow him to the back of the bus, past the lone other passenger sitting at the front.

"You were saying something about your ears," I remind him as we sit down just before the vehicle moves. The light's off, but I can see the outline of their unusual shape. He must have had some kind of cosmetic surgery to get them like this, and probably wants to show off. I'm more than happy to indulge him.

He looks straight into my eyes. "I'm an elf. I've not told any humans about this. I shouldn't really, but it is important for you to understand. I'm not just *some* elf either, I am a prince of the Nocturne Court."

Oooh, role play! I can go with that!

"Really?" I ask, feigning surprise, already in my role. "I thought elves only existed in fantasy books!"

I must have done something right because he grabs my hand, and I feel as giddy as a schoolboy. We're even in the back of a bus, like where I got my first blowjob, on the way home from a school trip. So many fond memories.

"No, we are most definitely real, but for reasons into which there is no need to delve in, we live apart from your world. What you need to know is that your shadow is very special, and it would be my greatest pleasure and honor to claim it." Sylvan strokes my palm with his thumb, sending a spark of arousal straight to my dick.

"I'm sure we can work something out," I say and place my hand on his thigh before moving it up, closer to his groin.

I can't get enough of how fast he blushes, how his eyes widen a little. I can almost sense his skittish heartbeat.

"Is that what you would like in exchange? My body?" he whispers the last words, and his grip on my hand becomes stronger.

Hook. Line. Sinker.

I slide my fingers between his thighs, and my toes curl at the warmth I sense. "There's nothing I want more, Your Highness," I whisper and pull his hand up to my lips, because I am committing to this role fully.

Those pointy ears of his twitch, and that has to be the cutest thing I've ever seen. When I press my knuckles against his cock, I sense it stiffening.

He lets go of me and unbuttons the top of his shirt, revealing a slim silver collar covered in dark engravings, no doubt part of his elf-persona-thing. "Do you see this abomination?"

I nod, already tempted to grab it, because I'm certain he's wearing it for a reason.

"Until I get it off my neck, I cannot bind your shadow to me. But I know of a grimsmith who can take it off. I fear I am not as capable in your world as I would wish to be, so I only toyed with the idea of paying him a visit. Do you know of a town called Boston? That's where he resides."

That's... elaborate for a sexual fantasy, but whatever gets this beauty off. "Oh, the legendary Boston Blacksmith. Yeah, I heard of him, my prince. We can go see him."

When we pass a green neon sign mounted on the roof of a bar, Sylvan's eyes glisten like two crystals. He grants me a nervous smile and ever-so-slightly presses his crotch against my knuckles.

Fuuuuuck. I'm so horny for him I could hump him on the crusty leather seat of the bus.

"It is settled then. Once I claim your shadow, you may use my body."

I chuckle and slide my arm around his shoulders, leaning closer as I trace an eight over his bulge. "Oh, I definitely want to sample you tonight."

His composure crumbles, and he blinks several times. I'm not sure what his role-playing game is about exactly, but he's definitely hard.

"What do you mean... 'sample'? While I may not be of substantial size, I assure you I will give you pleasure. Are you questioning my capabilities?"

I chuckle, losing myself in the game. It might be a bit too complicated for a dumb brute like me. "It just means I don't want to wait until we're in Boston," I say and slide my thumb along the back of his ear. It twitches against my finger in the cutest way.

He strokes the front of my hoodie. "Well, we don't always get what we want at a moment's notice, do we? Sometimes, patience is required. Until then, I welcome you to stay with me. My accommodation is less than ideal as I live with my landlady, but it should be fine if we are discreet. I do not wish to be parted from you."

I'm so confused by the push and pull he's doing. Maybe he wants to play the role of a ravished prince, so he's being coy? I can work that out when I'm in his bed.

"And how far is your palace?" I ask, staring at his mouth, but the moment it opens, I lose all interest in the answer and lick the seam of his lips.

Also, I need to go to Canada, not Boston, but what's a little detour?

Sylvan gasps, and I take the opportunity to deepen the kiss. Oh, and what absolute fucking bliss this boy is. Pliant like marshmallows, a little shy when my tongue meets his, but he doesn't push me away. His trembling fingers settle on my sides as I *devour* him.

All the pleasure centers in my brain light up like a Christmas tree because he is exactly what I love, yet what I've been denied for years. I want my dick inside him so bad I might just come in my pants from this kiss. He smells like mist in the morning, his mouth is so warm and inviting, and when I push his knees farther apart, he opens up without question.

I am going to ravish this elven prince tonight, and then, maybe wait out the manhunt for me in his basement. Or something. He's not going to report me if I treat him right.

I push him back a little, just to try my luck. I shouldn't be drawing attention to myself, I really shouldn't, but he is temptation personified.

Just as I consider a blast from the past and going down on him back here, the bus comes to an abrupt stop.

My beauty slides out of my embrace all too quickly and adjusts his hair. He doesn't shy away from holding my hand as we make our way to the exit, and it gets me all mushy inside.

He glances at me from under the long pale eyelashes. "You are a very fine kisser," he whispers with a little smile, and I can't wait to show him what else I'm *very* good at.

CHAPTER 4

SYLVAN

So... that was my first kiss.

I'm still a bit overwhelmed, because all of Hawk is overwhelming. From his size, to his confidence. No one has ever treated me the way he does, and I'm not sure what to make of it, because the mix of compliments and disrespect is disconcertingly arousing. He dove in for a kiss as if it was his birthright to fondle a prince.

I push my hair into place, stealing glances up his towering form.

"If you go to the back of that house," I point to the place where I'm staying, "there will be a tree you should find easy to climb to get to my room. You must *not* be seen," I emphasize, because my landlady has made it clear just how much guests are not allowed.

He grins in that endearingly frank way only lowborn people do. There's no need for him to put up a face, hide his true thoughts and feelings in order to obfuscate reality in service to a greater goal. He can show me what he really thinks, and in that moment, jealousy is like a splinter causing a painful infection under my nail.

He's big like a wild beast I'd never dare face on my own back in the Nightmare Realm, yet if I want to seize the power of his shadow and reclaim my rightful place at the Nocturne Court, I'll have to be braver than I've ever been.

The street is quiet at this time of night, as humans love their sun to bits and avoid coming out when it's absent from the sky, but to my eyes, it's light as day, and I easily pick up details of the small homes erected on both sides of the road.

I hate everything about this place.

As someone who grew up between the intricate walls of a palace, with its gothic architecture, awe-inspiring art, and gardens kept up by the most skilled groundskeepers, I find this human town painfully unimpressive. I have seen pictures of grand buildings and awe-inspiring mountains with snow-capped peaks that *supposedly* exist somewhere in this world of gasoline, concrete, and plastic, but while there is nature here, the uniform lawns and lone trees are nothing like the grand gardens of the Nocturne Court. Even the woods I've seen from the windows of my bus seem young and underdeveloped in contrast to the ancient forests of my realm, with their twisted trees, mossy ravines, and beasts that could take one's life within two seconds.

In the elven realm, even the simplest folk from the villages inhabited by craftspeople and farmers have an appreciation for detail and beauty that seems absent from this lesser reality where utility always seems to triumph over sensuality. Though even the most useful of mundane items here appear to be flimsy and set up for failure, as if there was no point in repairing them once they inevitably break.

I wasn't allowed to bring many things and was instructed that the Nocturne Court fashions would make me stand out too much, so I'm stuck in jeans and an acceptably elegant shirt, but at least I got to take a few pieces of jewelry with me.

I'm deep in my thoughts when the beast in front of me makes a deep bow, throwing one hand to the side. "My prince, I will do as you ask. Nobody will even know I exist." He grabs my hand with his massive fingers, and kisses my gold ring. It only reminds me how overheated I got when he pressed his tattooed knuckles against my cock. I can hardly believe what I've already let him do tonight.

"The neighbors often watch what's happening, so it's better if you stay behind. I will give you a signal from the window," I say and turn around, slipping out of his grasp.

All I can think of when I start walking toward the house I'm staying at is that he's watching me. Even though our arrangement is still flimsy, all he wants for his shadow is my body. *My* body. Not something I've ever been praised for, yet he seems insatiable for it already.

I don't have to worry about this deal yet, as nothing will happen until I get the collar off. Until then, I hope to become more acquainted with him, which will hopefully make the... process easier.

But I'd be lying to myself if I didn't admit that his touch was welcome. He is exactly the type of man I'd imagine when lying awake at night, unable to sleep because my mind is troubled by too many thoughts. I drift off into a fantasy where I don't have to make important decisions that can decide my fate. Under a man like that, I could stop thinking altogether for a while.

For now though, my mind works like a household of servants before an emperor's visit, and my heart is already beating faster as I open the door of Mrs. Moor's house. She is an unpleasant woman, and I've been wondering how to stop being her lodger since the day I arrived.

It is unfortunate that I don't seem able to earn enough money to afford living anywhere else, as the new Lord of the Nocturne Court set me up here and is, apparently, supplementing my room and board. No matter how many additional hours of work I take on, my money never stretches far enough. It doesn't help that I do struggle a little to understand how financing an acceptable pair of shoes costs so much. I'm used to getting the finest garments without even needing to ask for them, as I represent my family.

Or *used* to.

The back of my neck burns as I open the door with a key and enter the house as quietly as I can. Mrs. Moor is almost always asleep past midnight, but she insists on sleeping with her bedroom door open and can be awoken by even the faintest noise. Sweat is already beading on my back as I use both my hands to lock up and then remove my outside shoes. She always insists I use slippers inside, but I am not risking any footwear so late and climb the stairs holding them in one hand.

I'm relieved to hear her snore, because the last thing I need tonight is getting berated about my rent being late. How can she not understand that I will only receive payment at the end of the week? It's unreasonable for her to treat me this way, yet what am I now if not a pauper, lucky he isn't forced to sleep in the streets?

All my skills in alchemy, potions, and powders, are irrelevant in this world, and every day I am reminded of how little I know.

With a sigh of relief, I close the door of my room behind me and turn on the light. It's what the man selling it to me out of his garage called a 'lava lamp'. It cost me a whole dollar and fifty cents, but I couldn't resist its green and yellow glow that so reminds me of swamplight. Sometimes, I sit at night and watch it, amazed by the moving bubbles.

I make sure my surroundings are tidy, because Mrs. Moor likes to do unexpected checks, but everything is as I left it. The room is smaller than my former housemaster's closet, but beggars may not be choosers. I have a reasonably comfortable bed, a desk, and a wardrobe, each piece of furniture in a different color. No embroidered canopy, not a single sculpture, and no intriguing taxidermy on the walls.

I haven't decorated much, because deep down I hope the Lord of the Nocturne Court will end my banishment prematurely. The new plan of going to Boston makes that seem like a good choice. Still, I like to be in control of my fate and will establish with Mrs. Moor that I shall come back after my trip. After all, it's good to have a plan to fall back on, if the best possible outcome does not happen.

I climb over the bed to reach the window. For a moment, I worry that Hawk might have given up on me, but he emerges from behind the shed where Mrs. Moor keeps the lawn mower she insists I use once a week at least, transforming the grass into a uniform carpet resembling what I can see in all the neighbors' gardens.

Moonlight, is that man big! He might be the tallest and broadest person I have ever met, which is intimidating but also does something funny to my insides. I ignore the insistent sensation and wave at him, prompting him to approach the tree. The leaves growing level with my window shake, as if a beast was using the trunk as a back scratcher, but moments later his eyes meet mine, and he swings his foot through my window, already leaning over the emptiness separating him from safety.

Does this man have a death wish?

I hold back a yelp and grab his hand to save him from falling were he to wobble. But his life must be worthless to him, because he pushes his other leg away from the tree and grabs the side of the open window, pulling himself in.

Unbelievable! If he fell down and died, his shadow would be lost forever!

My heart is beating out of my chest, yet he just gives me a cocky grin.

"Mrs. Moor is sleeping downstairs, so we must refrain from loud noises," I say, all too aware he has not let go of my hand.

His fingers are so long, so thick, and the meat of his palm—almost as hot as his tongue was. He towers over me like a bear standing on two legs, and when he sweeps me close, I sense the fresh sweat and laundry detergent, my whole body pulses.

"So... where is your shower, my princeling?"

"Oh... I do not mean to be unaccommodating, but after a whole afternoon and evening surrounded by greasy fried foods, I must wash, and Mrs. Moor might notice if two showers are taken. She startles awake sometimes, and we cannot rouse her suspicions."

I glance down at his knuckles, once more wondering if the stains are dried blood. He ate with those hands though. Surely this is just my imagination playing tricks on me because of my worry-prone disposition.

He removes his baseball cap, releasing a flood of thick, dark brown hair that reaches a bit past his shoulders. It's frizzy, likely from being stuffed under the hat without much care, but I barely keep in a whine of appreciation, because the locks somehow make him appear even more handsome. Beastly. Which I shouldn't like. But I do.

"Let's shower together," he says, startling me into a stupor.

My finger reaches my teeth but as soon as I realize I'm about to nip on it, I stuff it into my pocket. He cannot see how nervous he makes me with his casual suggestions.

"T-together..." I repeat, desperate to give myself more time to think.

Hawk hums, and as he takes a step toward me, I cannot resist falling into his eyes. They're green, like a field full of moss and fern and flecked by lightning bugs. "Yeah. It would be only fair for me to see what I'm getting in this bargain, since you already got to assess my shadow," he says with a confident smirk.

My brain is overheating, then melting, because he's right. I owe this to him.

But I don't even have a servant dress me at the Nocturne Court because of how inadequate I feel in my body. My older brother never spared me any mockery. He might have been a reed, where Hawk is a sprawling oak, but he was tall, elegant, wide-shouldered. Me? I am a frail branchlet, broken off from the grand Goldweed tree prematurely.

I stare into Hawk's eyes without blinking. He doesn't seem set on humiliating me, and he kissed me with the fervor of a man on his wedding night, so...

I take a deep breath and grab his hand. I must be brave. I owe this to the Goldweed name. "Let us do so," I say and pull him along.

I can't remember ever being this *aware* of another man's presence, but Hawk's closeness burns me even in all the places where we're *not* touching. He is surprisingly quiet for someone of his size, but the moment I lock the door behind us, revealing the white tiles covering every bit of wall and floor, nervousness replaces the worry that we might be overheard.

Hawk grins. "A walk-in shower. Hell yes! I haven't been in a bathroom this nice in ages," he whispers, and I decide not to point out that my bathing chamber at the Nocturne Court was larger than Mrs. Moore's living room and featured a whole garden of medicinal plants.

I guess this tells me something about him, as did his lack of car. If he is poorer than the average human, talking him into becoming my Dark Companion should be easier.

In the bedroom, we had the soft green glow, but here, the stark white light is almost blinding, and I am painfully aware that he will get a good look at *all* of me. I don't want to be a coward anymore, I want to be a man my mother won't deem unworthy of even saying goodbye to.

Yet I pause, stiff as a dead tree when faced with a man Hawk's size in close quarters. I stare down at his shadow, so alive with the need to be bound. He's not a shadow-wielder, so he cannot see it, but its darkness is like a void, as if he were standing in thin air over an endless chasm. If I step in, will I fall?

I clear my throat. "I would just like you to take into account that despite my size, my body can offer many pleasures." I cringe, regretting my wording already. Damn it. I should have been more enticing. More flirtatious. More... *something*.

Hawk blinks, already, opening the zipper at the front of his hoodie. He cocks his head and cups the side of my face with that massive hand. "Hey, I know I'm a big, scary-looking guy, but you can breathe, okay? I'm gentle as a lamb."

Only when he says that do I realize that my breaths have been shallow. I inhale and nod.

"It's just that the situation is quite peculiar. Indeed, I've never seen a man like you."

Thinking becomes much harder when he takes off the hoodie, revealing his strong body covered in not only tattoos but also thick, dark hair that reaches his wrists. I touch his forearm, too curious for my own good.

The deer etched into his flesh where I choose to place my fingers seems to flinch at my attention, and a little shiver goes down my spine as the dark hair tickles my skin. And there's so much more of it within reach! On his chest, over the pile of bones marked with the words *RIP Grandpa*, and the left pec, where four paw prints sit as if the small animal that left them was there moments ago.

"A man like me?" Hawk asks, unbuttoning the top of my shirt.

"S-so *hairy*," I utter in amazement even though I tremble with nerves as my own skin is revealed inch by inch. I've been taught to be reserved, to think my words through, but everything about the body in front of me defies logical analysis. "May I?" I ask, hovering my hand over his stomach, and when he nods with an amused expression, I press my palm to the coarse hair and thick muscles.

The tips of my ears burn, and I'm losing my mind. He is lust personified, and I'm powerless. We're not even doing much, and I'm already getting hard.

Even his scent, while tart, as if he's been working all day, is not unpleasant, and when he leans closer, I'm initially too brainless to react in any sensible way. Then, he picks me up by the butt, my growing erection presses to his stomach, and he's licking my cheek as I lose my footing and frantically hold onto his shoulders.

"You're so damn beautiful, you know that?" my hairy monster says before effortlessly spinning around and... carrying me into the shower.

Suddenly, I'm at his eye level, all too aware of just how easy it is for him to manhandle me when I don't have my shadowcraft for even an ounce of defense.

"Am I?" I whisper. Then, in a bout of absolute madness, I steal a quick kiss from his lips. I can't get over how hairy his face is. It... scratches me, since the short dark stubble feels like boar bristles.

I find myself with my back to the tiles inside the shower, his hands firmly planted on my ass, his torso between my legs, our mouths so close together I could kiss him again and again, but as I struggle to make up my mind, he dives in first and rubs his scratchy cheek against my neck before kissing it. "You're like a prince from a storybook, with such fine fingers and wrists, such a pretty face, such big eyes..."

I smile as my heart pounds faster. He's making me so much less nervous about my body. I slide my fingers up his nape and into his long hair. Some of it is tangled, coarse to the touch as if he lived in the wild. Who is this man with a shadow so exquisite the Lord of the Nocturne Court would envy me my Dark Companion?

His appreciation loosens my tongue. "I've been told my size will always be a hindrance." An understatement of the vile things I've heard from my mother and siblings about my height and underdeveloped shadowcraft.

But he's already shaking his head, frowning as if my words enrage him. "No way. There's nothing you can't do," he rasps, gently rubbing his body against my bulge, and when I whine, he captures my mouth with his lips, blocking the noise.

I have always considered my mind to be my greatest asset, if not the only one. I'm someone who thrives in the world of alchemy, books, and court intrigue thanks to his brain. The sole reason I was caught meddling in an assassination was because my late sister had the not-so-smart idea of writing down our plans in her diary.

I prided myself on being unapproachable and uninterested in matters of the flesh, far too busy in libraries and labs. Hawk is turning me into someone else altogether. I whine and curl my toes, overwhelmed by the ease with which my body responds to a man between my legs. Maybe I'm not as driven by logic as I thought, and I don't know how I feel about that.

It's as if I've only ever had salted oatmeal, so how could I predict that a bite of apricot-stuffed pork would turn me into a glutton?

"You really like what you see?" I mumble against his cheek, all too aware of how needy it sounds, but I have to know where I stand with him. Though currently, I stand nowhere, because my feet dangle in the air.

Hawk's groan sounds like one made by a wolf waiting for its meal inside a cage. He puts me back on the floor yet keeps me against the wall, leaning over me, rubbing his stubbly cheek against mine. I rise to my toes as pleasure courses through me like lightning. "You're so elegant, and dainty, and I want to see all of you. Naked. I want you naked, princeling," he says, cupping my face and locking our lips in a short but intense kiss that leaves my head spinning.

With my mouth still burning, I refuse to make any more excuses for myself. If he decides I'm not to his liking after all, I will strive to offer him something else for his shadow. But... I do hope he likes all of me. I'm still aware of the size of the beast I felt in his pants, but looking at the size of me, he surely cannot expect me to match him in that department.

I kind of like how he calls me princeling too. It could seem patronizing, yet feels affectionate on his lips.

I dare a smile when I unzip my jeans. My mind says: *This is fine, this is perfectly natural, and ordinary, and we're all only flesh vessels for our souls,* but my stomach clenches, my chest aches, and my mouth is suddenly too dry to utter a word.

He whistles, and as I anxiously look up to check his reaction to my pale, naked body, the sight of fire burning through his forest green eyes brings a relief so immense I can barely think. He licks his lips, staring between my legs, and then shoves down his joggers revealing... oh, dear moonlight...

He is magnificent.

As he kicks the pants out of the shower, he's left naked, covered only with tattoos and hair. I stare at his thick manhood, surrounded by a dark thatch of curls. His thighs are as muscular as a horse's. A massive, scary centipede is inked on one leg, and a snake on the other, but my attention is still focused on his masculine attributes as he grins, placing his hands on his hips. "And you? Do you like what you see?"

I steal another glance at his cock. Long, hard, thick... an absolute masterpiece. I want to feel how hard and hot it is so badly I'm no longer my logical self.

The smart me wouldn't even *be* in this bathroom, knowing the temptation might prove too much, knowing that if one is trying to trade one's body, one shouldn't be giving it away.

"Yess..." I hiss and wrap my fingers around his cock. Not doing anything else, just *feeling* it. I lean forward and press my face between his hairy pecs with a groan. I can imagine feeling safe here. "You look incredible. The sheer *size* of you..." I mumble against his skin. I never imagined I could turn into some lust-filled imp, but here I am, inhaling his sweat as though it's an aphrodisiac.

I whimper when he shoves down my pants and underwear, and they pool around my feet until he kicks the garments away, leaving us both naked and touching. My brain's roasting in the heat of the desire I'm allowing myself to answer, and as the first drops of water hit my skin, I remove my socks. But then I'm all his, and he's kissing me, touching me, until it's almost too much.

His fingers awaken my skin in new ways, and even though I try to match him, growing bolder in the way I stroke and knead his flesh, it's clear he's leading the way. He even grabs some soap and spares my body no attention with it. When he slides his fingers between my ass cheeks, I have to bite back a yelp, and stiffen against him. I've never been in a situation like this, and I'm painfully out of my depth.

On one hand, I've already allowed too much, on the other, I have to put a stop to this at some point. I'm just not sure where that point is. Allowing him inside my body? Making him come? I know about all these technicalities. I'm inexperienced, not stupid. But reading books about sex is very different from pressing my skin against the thickest, juiciest cock I've ever seen. Only now I spot that right above it he has a tattoo stating *Kiss Me Here,* and it sparks an avalanche of utter filth inside my head.

I already see myself on my knees, servicing him while the shower rains on us, blinding me and tickling the top of my head as I obediently suck on Hawk's prick, eager to make him happy, desperate for him to like me even more.

"I bet this pretty little hole is just made to take my dick," he rasps, dragging his finger through my crack and teasing me.

No one's ever spoken to me that way. No one dared to approach me so shamelessly, and now that he's here, rubbing my skin until it sings with pleasure, I find it hard to resist when he pours soap into my hands, and then brings them to his balls, telling me exactly how to wash him there. My mouth dries as I wait for my turn to touch his cock, and when he guides me there, I almost feel like I'm about to come myself.

My face is on fire, but I don't want this to stop. His words are filthy, but full of adoration. For once, I feel as if I'm the prize.

I don't know what to say, but I still stroke his hard dick with my soapy fingers. It feels like getting to know his prick, and I appreciate that more than he can know. I'm an overthinker and if I am to allow this beast inside me one day, I most definitely need to get acquainted with it first. I want to know what he likes most, how much pressure makes him moan, and how fast he likes to be stroked. I watch without even blinking, taking in every detail in the bright light. How dark it's getting, how veiny it is, and how it reacts to my touch.

"You look so damn tasty," Hawk rasps as I roll my thumb against the tip of his dick. Before I can answer, the tip of his finger enters my anus ever so slightly, making gentle circles, as if it wanted to get acquainted with my body too.

His eyes change, darkening further, and as I weigh my words, too aroused to decide whether I should tell him off for touching me there, he spins me so I face the wall, and then... his nose dives between my buttocks.

"Oh!" I yelp, paralyzed with my hands against the tiles. I have this terrible tendency to freeze when shocked. Oftentimes, I imagine all the things that might happen, so I have a response at the ready.

This wasn't an option in my mind at all.

"Yess..." Hawk groans, sending a shiver down my legs. "Pink, lovely, and fuckable, just like I imagined."

Before I can come up with anything to say, or what I even think, for that matter, he spreads my buttocks with his massive hands and *licks* me.

Taint to the bottom of my spine, his wet tongue drags over my pucker, making me moan and sizzle with lust. I don't need any more reassurance about how much he likes me. I arch his way with a moan, eager to be his meal, even though I know I shouldn't allow him to sample this much of me. I was supposed to show him my body, and instead, I'm losing my grip on reality.

"Oh fuck..." I whisper, flattening my cheek against the wet tiles as fire sparks down my legs, and then up my back, culminating in an explosion inside my skull. He squeezes my ass, rubs my thighs, and then teases my pucker with the tip of his nose before breathing in my scent with a low grunt. I'm on fire. And while a part of me is ashamed of being in this intimate position with a perfect stranger, I also relish the chance to be with someone who deems me worthy of their attention.

Back home, I never knew how to approach the men I was interested in. They were all, without exception, uncomfortable pursuing a royal, and I never learned how to invite them to my bed, which left me in a permanent sexless limbo.

But Hawk isn't intimidated by my status, nor by the bargain we're going to soon make official, and as he plays with my hole, teasing it and entering it with his tongue, my muscles relax, ready for... something.

Something I know I shouldn't be allowing if I am to keep even a shred of myself to bargain with.

I'm a panting mess. Wet, with my cock dripping pre-cum, flushed as if I've stayed out in the sun, and with my legs spread open. The tickle of his stubble on the insides of my buttocks is driving me up the wall, and it's hard to deny how badly I want more. How I want to be under him. How I want him to take charge of my body.

It's everything I've been taught is a weakness. I should be in control of the situation, I should be predicting the moves others may make and anticipate what reaction I should have to them.

"I'm... I..." I whisper like some beast in heat, unsure what I even want to communicate. That I'm so aroused I might come at any moment? That I'm afraid taking his cock will hurt? That I think he's the most mesmerizing man I've ever met?

Frankly, I don't know what I want, and a part of me needs for him to make all those decisions for me.

He teases me in fast, frequent licks while drawing on the skin between my thighs, and I bite the inside of my cheeks to keep in the noise growing in my throat as my blood is saturated with ecstasy. Soon, I see a glimmer under my eyelids, like during that one party with fairy dust, which I awoke from in the cold garden.

I rock my hips, stabbing myself on my future Dark Companion's tongue, and each swing my cock makes through the hot, damp air feels like a caress bringing me closer to finishing. I whine, reaching down to touch myself, but Hawk slaps my hand away and grabs the base of my cock, squeezing it hard enough for my brain to stall.

"Not yet, pretty prince," he whispers before nipping my buttock. He rises behind me without warning, and then pulls me close, so his hard cock presses to my back.

My mind is a blank slate. Instead of scheming and plotting, all I want to do is... purr. As if I'm one of Mrs. Moor's cats and just want to be petted.

"No?"

My self-control is on the brink of dissolving altogether. Hawk only makes any thinking harder when his fingers find my nipples and pinch them gently. I'm ashamed of how much I want my hole teased again, but he kisses my nape and whispers.

"Wait for me in bed."

I want to protest, say that I planned for him to sleep on the floor, but I nod and walk out of the shower on legs like seafoam.

"But... you will come, right?" I ask, glancing at the thick shadow he casts on the wall. It turns toward me, black and pulsing, and I hear Hawk speak.

"Give me three minutes, princeling. I'll soon be back to serving you. And yes, I will *come*."

CHAPTER 5

HAWK

There's so many things people don't value enough until they're no longer accessible, but I'll never again take warm showers for granted. For the first time in years, I can just relax and massage my scalp with fresh-smelling foam as warm water drips down my body and washes away the fatigue of half a decade. I get to brush my teeth in peace, and hell, I even use some face cream. I'm not quite renewed yet, but it's a start, and by the time I switch off the water, I'm ready to *serve the prince* all night long.

At this point, there's probably a manhunt out for me, but it's not like anyone's gonna search for me in a random guy's bedroom. Maybe an escape north is going to be easier if I wait out the initial rush of attention? I wrap a towel around my hips, pick up our scattered clothes, and peek into the corridor. Thankfully, I can't hear or see any indicators that Sylvan's landlady... who's probably his mom, awoke so I return to his room, rolling my bare feet over the wooden floor.

It's showtime.

I can't believe I had enough self-control to send him to the bedroom after rimming him so thoroughly, but I want to savor him. His body is more perfect than I could have imagined, a work of art sculpted in pale marble. Sylvan is so malleable too, putty in my hands. When his cheeks flushed pink, pointy ears twitching, I could have eaten him alive. I want to squeeze, pinch, hear him moan, see him lose his composure until he's a beautiful mess, begging for my dick.

I walk into the room engulfed in green illumination coming from a lava lamp in Sylvan's hands and the moonlight behind him.

I came in cocky and ready to jump right into bed, but I stall at the picture he makes.

Pretty as a fairy tale prince, he's sitting on the bed. The moon looms high in the sky outside and shines through the fabric of... is that a ladies' nightgown? Despite being black, the garment is so thin I can see the outline of his body under it, and I wonder if he's still hard behind that raised thigh, or if he was naughty and jerked off.

"Is that... like... a nightdress?" I ask, careful not to ruin the mood, because if he wants to play the *princess* next, I can go with that too. All I care about is that he's beautiful, willing, and seems as amazed by me as I am with him.

Sylvan pulls on the frill at his wrist. "It's a night*shirt*. For sleeping. I was able to bring it with me from the Nightmare Realm. It's made of frailweave. Is this unusual for you?"

Aah! That's right, men in the olden days wore those really long shirts to bed. I've seen it in a couple of movies my ex made me watch with him. Sylvan is more committed to his role than I thought. Is that even his real name, or did he choose it because being called an ordinary one, like Greg or Owen, would have ruined the fantasy for him?

I smirk and meet his gaze as I drop the towel to the floor. "I'm a simple man, princeling. I like sleeping naked."

I love the way his eyes zero in on my dick. He might speak fancy and be all demure and shit, but deep down, he's a greedy, filthy boy who invited a man off the street to his bedroom. I *see* him.

"Oh. And... you do not get cold?" he asks as if we're not about to get down to business. The flush is back on his white cheeks and I want to *lick* it.

I'm not always into the innocent act, but his take on it is so unpretentious and real.

"Not if I have a pretty thing such as yourself to keep my cock warm," I say, placing my knee on the edge of the bed and taking the lamp out of his hands. I can already imagine a whole lifetime of sleeping with my dick between his—

No.

This is a short-term thing. Maybe even a one-and-done. I'm on the run from prison and can't be losing my head over a pair of pretty blue eyes.

His breath hitches, but he places his elegant hand on my thigh, seeming amazed by the hair there.

"I can see your point. I've not had the pleasure of sharing my bed before."

I used to be like that too, always looking for a fresh ass, never wanting to get tied down, and rushing out of someone's bedroom right after sex. With a face like his, and enough recklessness to invite a guy like me over, I bet this bed is a high traffic area.

I place the lamp on the nightstand and grab Sylvan's ankles, yanking at them to bring his ass to the edge of the bed. If this prince wanted to be treated gently, he wouldn't have picked a tattooed brute.

His gasp makes my dick hard in an instant, and the motion forces his shirt to ride up all the way up his thighs. Maybe I do prefer it to pajamas. Easy access.

"Can we... kiss again?" he asks sweetly, reminding me of how he complimented me about being a good kisser. It makes pride swell in my chest like I'm a dog getting a treat.

I grin, leaning over him, my hips between his open thighs. "You want these lips? Take them, baby," I tease, focused on his flushed complexion. It's like cream with a bit of strawberry jam mixed in for color, and I wish to have a meal like him every day of my life.

No looking out for guards, no stench of unwashed bodies, and no weird prison politics mixed up in who you fuck.

Just a pair of sweet eager lips, a guy who smells like a meadow at midnight, and his pure, unadulterated adoration for my dick.

Sylvan wraps his arms around my neck before delving in for a kiss. The fabric of his shirt is soft as clouds, and I can't wait to be inside him, because I *know* it will feel just as heavenly. He might be initiating the kiss but remains a bit shy about it, leaving room for my tongue to play with him. He tastes of mint and some other herb, and I enjoy every second I get to explore his warm, wet mouth. Maybe I should fuck it first? Drive my dick deep between Sylvan's pink lips? Just imagining them spread around my cock makes me rock-hard.

I hum, crawling on top of him. He's now locked in the cage of my body, and as his limbs curl around me, pliant and needy, I grab my dick and rub it up and down the seam between Sylvan's buttocks. He gasps into my mouth, and I respond by nipping his tongue, ready to rock his world.

His eyes fly open and he pulls away from the kiss, pressing on my shoulder. He's flustered. "Oh. I... don't... we..."

I watch him, even though all I want is to dick him down, but then it dawns on me what this is about. As much as I'd love to do him raw, I'm not about to make a fuss about a condom when I'm getting such a treat on a silver platter.

I reach into my joggers, but when I show him the wrapper with a question on my face, he frowns.

"You wish to... *eat* now?"

I glance at the package and it's apparently strawberry daiquiri-flavored. "I mean... I suppose you can lick it too," I tell him and open the wrapper before pulling out the pink condom. The air fills with the artificial aroma of fruit, but I ignore it and shift closer. "Want to put it on me or—"

Sylvan takes a deep breath, looking no less confused than before. He must know I want to fuck his ass. He was practically begging for it in the shower.

"I'm not sure I follow. Do you not *eat* condiments on other food items? That is... an object."

It's like being splashed by icy water. "Do you know what this is?" I ask, showing him the rubber as hope dies inside my chest, because. What. The. Fuck?

This can't be part of his role play. That would be too weird. I think.

He's growing exasperated and despite me kneeling between his open legs, he crosses his arms. "I cannot know *everything*!"

Shit.

Shit. Shit. Shit. Shit.

"Are you... over eighteen?" I ask, trying to remain calm, because this is too fucking weird. I like them cute, but I'm not in the market for sheltered kids! If he says he's five hundred or something like that, I'm out, because that's exactly what a teen with an overactive imagination and fake elf ears would say.

Sylvan huffs. "I am twenty-five. Do *you* know how to harvest coralberries? Or when to milk a seagoat? We all have matters we're ignorant about."

I roll my eyes and slide from between his legs, because this is damn ridiculous. "Can we pause it with the role play for now? Real talk, okay? Do you know what sex is? Do you know what I wanted to do?"

He turns to look at the moon as if it's very interesting to him, and pulls down his shirt. "Of course I know what sex is... but I may not know all the details, so no, I'm not sure what that thing in your hand is. I've not yet had the pleasure to..." he drifts off.

He's a virgin.

Honestly? I'm not that surprised, considering he's just tried to distract me by mentioning 'sea*goats*'.

I drop the condom to the floor and exhale, glaring at him. "Do you know what anal sex is? Were you sheltered, or something? How do you not know what a condom is? When I showed it to you back at the restaurant, what did you think I was suggesting, if not fucking?"

Sylvan's lips tremble, he scowls, but he still won't meet my gaze. "I don't know! Eating something. I thought it was a condiment. They come in those tiny packets, do they not? I *know* what anal sex is, and I understood that's what offering my body means. It's something... I would like to explore in the future, but we haven't bonded yet, and we won't be able to for as long as this thing remains around my neck." He pulls on the silver collar abruptly.

Is this his roundabout way of saying he's not ready for anal?

I count to five and grab his hand. "It's not a condiment. It's a latex... sheath you pull on your dick to prevent pregnancy and STDs. I don't have any—they had me tested—but when people don't know, they can use condoms. Is this you telling me you never had sex with anyone and missed all and any sex ed?"

His hand is clammy when he squeezes mine. "I've just... not had the opportunity." His pointy ears twitch again and again, like nervous puppies.

I exhale and peek in his eyes as hope awakens inside me again. Maybe the whole elven prince shtick is just his way of dealing with shyness? He seems sane enough otherwise. "But you... you want to have sex with me, right?"

He nods in an instant, and I appreciate the enthusiasm. "I want to wait with giving my body to you fully until our bond is made, but we can—I would *like* to do other things until then."

If he's a virgin and not all that well-educated about sex, he's probably just scared. I can work with that.

"Next time, you need to tell it to me straight. Simple man, remember?" I ask, pointing at myself as I lean close enough to kiss his shoulder, uncovered where his thin nightshirt has slid off.

When he gives me a shy smile, it's like moonlight shining down on me. He is just *that* charming. So maybe I won't get to fuck him deep and hard right now. That's okay, I can live with that. And maybe I was supposed to enjoy his sexy peach tonight and move on, but I can stick around. He wants to go to Boston after all. If that grimsmith is a creep who put that weird collar on Sylvan as part of some BDSM game, I could help him deal with the bastard.

"It's true. You deserve that. You deserve to know what will happen if you allow the bond." He slides closer and slips his dainty hand to my cheek. I can't help it. Whatever the bond is for him, I want it. I've always been a sucker for cute twinks, and he's everything I could want, from his lovely feet to his hypnotic eyes like two blue crystals with whole galaxies in them.

"Are you like... very into marriage?" I try guessing as I slide my knee between his legs and move my hand under the thin nightshirt, exploring the smooth, nearly-hairless skin.

Now that I know I won't be fucking his ass tonight, my disappointment eases and I turn my mind to the other things we can do until then.

He smiles, and it fills me with unexpected relief. Only now I realize how much seeing him upset bothered me. "That's not how I would call it. I want you to become my Dark Companion. And I'm happy to exchange my body for it. Your shadow is like nothing I've ever seen, and when I get the collar off and my powers are back, I will use a strand of my hair's shadow and tie it to your darkness. That will be our promise."

Is it kinda woo-woo? Yes. But does it make me feel all gooey inside to be chosen by this absolute stunner? Also yes.

And, besides, I've seen and heard stranger things than this. If a huge percent of the population can go around claiming the Earth is flat, what's so weird about Sylvan easing his anxieties by reimagining himself as an elven prince? He must have been through a lot, poor guy.

I stroke his damp hair and wrap one hair around my finger. "Yeah? You need a strand of you inside me?" I ask, and when he nods, I pull on the hair without thinking, then roll it between my fingers, and stuff it in my mouth. When his eyes go wide, I smile and swallow, washing it down with some water from a cup on the nightstand. "There. My promise."

Of what? I'm not sure yet. That I'll take him to Boston? That I'll beat the shit out of the bastard who collared him? That I'll marry him in an ancient forest? That I'll fuck his brains out when he's ready? Works for me.

I've never been into the virginity thing, but it's kinda hot to think I'll be his first. You always remember your first.

"I can't believe you did that." Sylvan shakes his head, but he's smiling, and my hands are back under his nightshirt.

"I might be a bit crazy for you already, my little prince," I whisper, rolling on top of him and burying my face in his sweet, sweet neck. "How about we seal the deal, hm? You might not want my cock in your snug little hole yet, but do you want it in your pretty mouth?" I ask and curl my fingers around his dick. It's on the small side, but fits his body perfectly. Easier to suck too. He's hard for me already, and I love its curved shape in my hand.

Sylvan nods, sliding his warm hands up my back. I don't have to know his whole life story to be at ease with him. It's the way he looks at me, how he opens his legs for me, how he arches up for a kiss that make me feel desired.

"I don't know how much of it will fit," he whispers against my lips. "But I really want to... lick it. It has to be the most magnificent cock I've ever seen." The scarlet is back on his cheeks as soon as he says that, and I can't get enough of it. I need to fill his mouth, make him swallow, moan and whimper.

"I'll ease you into it, baby. Trust me, your mouth was made for sucking cock," I whisper and capture his lips in a kiss that has us both shivering by the time I pull away and meet his gaze.

He rocks against me, all delightful in his arousal. I must have been his first kiss as well. He's twenty-five, needy, and full of pent-up sexual frustration I'm more than happy to ease. He'll be sleeping like a baby after I'm done with him tonight.

"I'll do my best," he says so earnestly, I kiss him again.

"Pretty sure you'll enjoy yourself too, princeling," I say, drawing a little heart on his cheek with the tip of my finger. How could anyone resist this kind of temptation? "Ready?" I ask, rising to my knees.

"Yes. Please."

It's like he really is magical, because when he says that word, a whole flurry of horny ideas splashes into my mind. I already know I'll get him to beg for my dick when we get to anal fuck. I want to hear needy whimpers, see his face flush, and for nasty words to spill out of that prim mouth.

"Should I just do what I want then?" I ask, straddling his chest. His eyes, beautiful like the most expensive sapphires, widen with lust, and he licks his lips before shyly placing his hands on my thick thighs. I love the contrast of my meaty body and his pale, bony digits, and when he nods, lowering his eyelids ever so slightly, I kiss my index and middle fingers before pressing them to his lips. "I'm going to make you so wet and messy."

His eyes glaze over with lust, and there's no more of that lost lamb innocence in his expression. Without me even asking, he parts his lips and licks my fingers, gaze firmly planted on my cock. So what if he's still a virgin? He just needed the right guy to pluck him.

"Ooh, you sweet, pretty thing," I rasp, shifting my hips forward, so my dick sways right in front of Sylvan's cute face, hypnotizing him as I grab the pillow and stuff it behind his head, so he's in a more convenient position.

I glance back with a smirk at his nightshirt all the way up his hips and his needy cock. I'll make him wait until I'm sated.

I grab the sides of his face, lowering myself but keeping my cock just out of reach as I stroke it. "Now I just need to decide if I want to flood your mouth with my spunk or come on your flushed cheeks. Decisions... decisions..."

Sylvan lowers his eyelids, hiding those gems he has for eyes behind a curtain of white lashes. He can't find his voice though, and I don't blame him, because he seems far too preoccupied with my dick to think.

"Tongue out," I say, to test the waters, and when he rolls it out like a red carpet, I wipe the moisture gathered at the tip on its soft, pink surface. He is pliant. Obedient. No wonder he got himself in trouble with someone who welded a collar on him.

His hot breath tickles my skin as he makes deep exhales through his nose.

"You're a good boy already, but I'll make a good cocksucker out of you. Your body will be mine after all. I need you ready," I whisper as I rock my cockhead over his wet tongue. I'm in fucking heaven. He is delightful.

There's something irresistible about a man unable to help himself in the face of arousal, and seeing his eyes roll back, his cheeks darken, takes me to the highs of anticipation. I keep touching myself as I rock my hips, dragging my balls over that innocent face, and I gasp when he opens up, licking my sac.

"You are a natural, prince. Who would have thought a *royal* was so into licking another man's balls..." Because why not? If that's his fantasy, I can lean into it. Kinda hot to be the brute who ravishes this snow-white princeling.

I love the little whine he makes. It sends arousal all the way to the tip of my dick until I drip pre-cum on his face, yet he never takes his mouth off my balls.

I even have to calm him down when he starts sucking on me too firmly, but once we ease into it and he starts exploring my balls with his tongue, I grin, staring at the pale hair between my thighs. "What would your mother, the queen, think if she saw you like this? It would be a real scandal, wouldn't it?" I continue, prodding at his fantasies.

He stills, hesitating for a moment. "Definitely, if someone knew we're doing this before we're bonded," Sylvan mumbles, happily pressing his nose to my balls. He moves his hands up my thighs as if he also can't get enough of touching me.

I grin and tighten my thighs over his head as I give myself a moment to just feel his touch and enjoy it. I did have oral sex in prison, but it wasn't like this, not with a pretty twink who's never done a wrong thing in his life and has no ulterior motives. "That's it, you want that cum served hot, don't you?"

He makes a dreamy sigh and trails his flattened tongue over the underside of my dick, all the way to the head. Be still my heart, because my cock sure won't be.

"I want to taste you," Sylvan whispers, sounding a bit shy again, which combined with the fact that his mouth is on my dick makes me want to plow those pink lips and come right now. His fingers tremble, their movement is slow, but inch by inch, he still finds his way to my ass. Bold. I like it.

"You want me to push in, little prince?" I ask, rocking my hips. We both gasp when my cockhead taps Sylvan's open mouth. I change my position, because the answer to this question is painfully obvious in his hazy eyes. Resting both hands behind my lover's head, I hang over him with my cock hovering above his greedy lips.

"Why do I even ask?" I tease as I slide my cockhead in. "Isn't your body mine to use after all? However I like. Whenever I like." Okay, okay, maybe only after that bond he's talking about but I've already made my promise, and the idea makes me horny. I push my cock in farther, until it fills his cheek, and I'm treated to the most personalized porn ever. I rock my dick in for good measure, poking at the inside of his flushed cheek again and again.

Sylvan moans and squeezes my ass, but he's not intent on stopping me in any way. He *wants* to be my toy, my hot, wet fucksleeve.

And I want him to be that too.

Who would want a treasure like him for only one night? He might be mad, but I'm certainly not.

"Suck it. Gently, really savor how I taste. I want you to remember it in detail, so you can imagine it even when you can't take it in your mouth, no matter how desperate you get," I whisper, watching him hollow his cheeks.

And fuck, yes, his warm, smooth mouth feels so perfect around my dick. In an ideal world, I would never pull myself out and remain forever encased by this pillowy comfort.

Every now and then as he sucks, he looks up into my eyes as if to ask if he's doing it right, and if that isn't just precious, I don't know what is. I see no reason to spare him praise when he's being such a good boy.

"Ah... That's it, keep your mouth nice and open for me," I say as I push my cock in deeper, getting him used to the sensation. I let out a grunt every time he sucks harder, letting him know how much I appreciate his horny mouth. Judging by the way his gaze slides from my face and down my body, I'm confident he's enjoying the show too. Still, I ask.

"You like what you see, hm? You like a big, muscular dude who could fold you like a pretzel and split you open? I know boys like you. You're just dying to satisfy me as many times as I want." I babble, pushing in harder. I stop the moment his throat convulses around me, and withdraw gently before he can choke.

Damn, he's *so* hot.

He lets out an incoherent whimper that only spurs me on. Despite the tears pooling in his lovely eyes from the strain of taking my dick, he's not tapping me to pull away or signaling for it in any way.

No. He wants me to fuck his mouth. He's been waiting twenty-five years for this after all. For a big fat cock tickling his tonsils.

I rock my dick into him at a steady pace and reach back to find his cock not only hard but twitching at my touch. There's a pool of wetness from all the pre-cum he's been dripping on his stomach.

"That's how horny you are?" I ask, barely squeezing his cock, because I don't want him to come yet. "Painfully stiff just from sucking my dick? Can you taste my juices already?"

I let go of him when his cock twitches in my hand, desperate for release. Too bad. I want him hot and needy when he takes my load.

Locking my eyes on his, I bring my damp hand to my lips and lick his pre-cum off. Damn. It's so smooth to the taste. "You better get me off, or I'll never let you come," I whisper and make another push with my hips, this time, I don't immediately withdraw after hitting his gag reflex, and when he squeezes my thighs, I shush him in a gentle voice. "Breathe. I know you want to let me all the way in. You want to bury your nose in my pubes and close your lips around the base as I plow in," I add, massaging his neck as he coughs, blinking away tears.

And still, no pushback.

I want to keep him.

He makes a few needy moans of confirmation and I sense him shifting under me as he slides his hands to the small of my back. He's so aroused he can't stay put, so I need to ground him.

I grab the sides of his head and drill into him. Slowly at first, but then, as he gets used to the pressure at his throat, I go faster. Every time I drag my cock over his soft tongue, a shiver of pleasure goes down my spine. Lust pools in my balls when I watch my dick stretch his lips.

"That's it. You're gonna be so good at this," I rasp, stroking his pointy ears with my thumbs. "You'll take my load twice a day, won't you?" I tease as I speed up my thrusts into his hot mouth.

His hum sounds like confirmation but also travels up my shaft, and all the way to my insides as I ease him in. Hot vapor fills up the space between my ears instead of brains. "I'll play with you whenever I want, and you'll be too into it to stop me," I say, shivering at the plunging noise inside his throat.

Fuck. He is irresistible. I want that collar off and to really make him *my* boy.

"We'll be driving down the road, and I'll just pull your head down if I feel like it," I fantasize out loud and he whimpers in response, but I'm going for it now. I'm fucking his face in earnest, holding onto his ears and taking no prisoners.

I'll be coming in his mouth and making sure he swallows every last drop. My heart beats faster with every second, and I feel so alive. I feel *free*. For the first time in five years I feel truly in charge. Anything I did behind bars was a pale shadow of my new reality. My wings were clipped and claws cut off. I'll never allow it again.

Tears roll down his cheeks, but he's holding onto my ass for dear life and clearly doesn't want me to pull away for more than the inch that allows him to breathe. I smile and pet his head as I ride his face, ready to let go of shame and all the bad things that happened in the past. This is my lucky day, and I will make something out of the chance it offers.

My balls smack his chin, and the heat that's been cooking inside them rushes up my shaft, erupting inside Sylvan's mouth.

"Swallow. Take it," I order him, focused on his messy features.

His eyes go wide, and he chokes a little but doesn't push me away. He takes a deep breath through his nose, and after the initial shock, he sucks and swallows like he was made for it. I grunt in bliss as I make a few last thrusts, filling his mouth with more cum every time. It feels like letting go of years of pent-up rage and resentment. I thought I'd moved on after a year or two in the can, but I only sense the true relief now.

"You like that?" I rasp. "A full belly of my cum..." I smile in satisfaction and pull out a little so my cockhead still rests on his tongue.

I let go of his pink ears, leaning over him as he swallows what I gave him despite the tears running down his cheeks and the mess of saliva on his chin.

"You're so fucking beautiful, you know that?" I utter without thinking and grab a folded piece of white fabric with a golden trim. I use it to clean his face, starting around the eyes, so I don't get cum in them.

I'm sorry to be out of his mouth, but I know I've overstayed my welcome when my cockhead becomes too sensitive. He sighs when I pull out, half-lucid when he stares at me. Then at the fabric.

"Oh no!" he whines and limply pushes my hand away. "Not this one! It has my family crest!"

I look at the already stained handkerchief, noting the letters *S. G.* and a stylized octopus locked inside an oval crest adorned with seaweed. I shrug. "We'll just wash it, my prince. No problemo," I add, dropping it to the bed as I lean in to kiss him.

I'm very aware that he's still hard and horny out of his mind, but he's so *cute*. Little prince with his pointy ears and embroidered handkerchief.

Sylvan takes a deep breath and strokes my stubbly cheek as we kiss. "Your cock tasted delicious," he whispers against my lips. I'm pretty sure he's exaggerating when it comes to flavor, but my chest fills with glee either way.

"How do you think I'll like yours?" I ask and kiss my way down his chest, already pushing his legs open. My mouth waters when his dick pokes the underside of my chin, and I grin when Sylvan puts both his hands across his lips. Heat radiates from his body as I rub my nose up and down his shaft, drinking in his musky essence, but it's already twitching in response to my touch, so I take it in my mouth before my princeling can start begging.

His thighs make the best ear muffs when they close around me. He tastes… good. Great even. Salty, without a hint of bitterness. I stroke the soft, hot skin of his legs as I take all of his cock in with ease.

I barely move my head twice before he shoots his load, hips rising off the bedding. He's muffling his moans, but I still hear him panting. I glance up to see his back arched, his flushed chest and stiff pink nipples. Even sweaty, he smells only of the fresh scent of soap and his own aroma that's like nothing I've ever sensed on a man. I'm no poet but it's like moonlight seeped into his skin.

"Perfection," I mumble, crawling back up with my lips tasting of him. He's still trembling, gasping for air as I cradle him close and kiss his cheek.

It feels good to lie down to sleep together.

So damn good.

He's so tiny in my arms I already feel protective of him. He's lovely, absolutely lovely, and doesn't even pull down his nightshirt, so I can be his big spoon and press my dick to that pretty peach.

I kiss the back of his head like he's my kitten. Kiss the pointy ears, cuddle him to my chest, overwhelmed by how much I've missed someone so sweet in my embrace.

I can make a little detour to Boston. Why not? And then take him with me to Canada. After all, he doesn't seem to have a lot going for him here. An evening shift at Best Burgers Bonanza, no car, and a room he claims to rent even though I think he's just hiding that he lives with his mom.

I know what my family would say, but it's not kidnapping if he agrees to go.

CHAPTER 6

SYLVAN

I start, unsure what's going on. A massive arm is wrapped around me, and my first thought is that I'm being abducted, and I need to—

But then I remember. Not just who I'm with but what I did, and the naked body of a man pressing against me makes it abundantly clear. At night, I even got undressed to feel him closer. I'm a little embarrassed of how I lost control and handed myself over to carnal pleasure. It's not the way I usually act, but Hawk opened me as if I was a clam to be devoured raw.

I would describe our sex as *transcendent*.

Never have I felt so at peace with losing control. He awakened a side of me that has lain dormant, forgotten among important matters like trying not to lose my life to court intrigue or attempting to find a way of proving myself useful and worthy of respect.

But there it is. The need to be hugged.

My heart is a little tender, as if it got bruised by all the manhandling last night, but I find comfort in hugging Hawk's massive arm and curl deeper into his embrace, pressing my back to his hairy chest. I'm so excited for him to become my Dark Companion. Not just because his shadow should allow me to complete feats previously unheard of, but also because... well, the sex was incredible.

Not everyone's Dark Companion bond is intimate in nature, so I am beyond lucky for this human to be such a good match for me. I don't know yet how I will use my future power to restore my position at the Nocturne Court, but I know my return from banishment will be spectacular.

Once the Lord sees our combined might, he will have to welcome me back. My mother will never again call my shadowcraft crippled. And with a man like Hawk at my side, the courtiers and servants will no longer gossip behind my back about how I won't ever find a suitable match. They might whisper about what goes on in our bedroom, but at the end of the day, the power of Hawk's shadow will remain a convenient excuse for why I, the last prince from the Goldweed bloodline have tied my life to a man who is so clearly pursuing *me*, not the other way around.

When Hawk hums and tightens his arms around me, I'm struck by how foreign this is. I have never before procured any lovers, paid or otherwise, so this whole thing feels new, and not just in the carnal sense. I haven't been touched like this in a very long time, since my nanny was scolded for coddling me many, many years ago. She never hugged me again thereafter, and while I have shaken people's hands, or given them pats on the back, physical touch has become intimidating over time.

Not with Hawk. Not anymore at least.

His body produces almost too much heat for my comfort, but I bear with it, because I want to keep enjoying his touch until he's awake. I even kiss his knuckles, wondering if his tattoos have any meaning.

After the frenzy he got me into last night, I almost regret that our deal means we have to wait with anal, because even though I'm a little frightened, I wonder—

The door swings open, making my heart stop, and I suddenly can't breathe.

"How many times have I told you about splashing water around everywhere?" Mrs. Moor yells, but the moment her eyes land on me and Hawk, she *screams*.

Behind me, Hawk starts awake too, backing away from me and removing the comforter from my naked body in the process. I try to protect my modesty, but it's no use when Hawk cries out, falling into the gap between my bed and the wall, wrapped up in our only covering like a body prepared for burial.

"How dare you fornicate under my roof?" Mrs. Moor shrieks like the evil witch character from a cartoon I saw a few days ago. She might be an average human woman in her forties, with short blonde hair, but her soul is as ugly as a creature from the deepest sea. "I was doing you a favor, but you're a pervert like my ungrateful son! Out! Out!"

I grab the only thing left on the bed, a pillow, and cover my crotch. I am *mortified*. If I didn't know any better, I'd assume I was bitten by a despair, and now I'm living my worst nightmare while my physical body slowly dies from the beast's poison. All that's needed to complete the picture would be my mother shaking her head, and my dead brother saying I don't need a pillow this big to cover my privates.

"Mrs. Moor, please, it's a misunderstanding. You must allow me to explai—"

"There is nothing to explain! There is a man in your bed! I thought I was helping out a polite young man in need of a Samaritan's hand..." She takes a deep breath and squints at me. "You have ten minutes to gather your things and *leave*. I will not support your perversion in *my* house!"

And worst of all is that the disgust in her gaze mirrors a look I've so often been given by my family members.

Underdeveloped.

Useless.

Not fit for the position I was born into.

A failure. And it doesn't matter that her reasons for being angry are utterly ridiculous.

She storms off, leaving me with scattered thoughts and goosebumps all over my skin. Nausea rises in my throat, but before I can consider running off to the bathroom, the bed shifts away from the wall, and Hawk rises from the floor, wrapped in the comforter as if it were a hooded cloak.

"What the fuck is her problem?"

My breath is ragged, and I can't speak, because my throat is too clenched with panic. I've just lost my lodgings in an unfamiliar world.

But even though my body wishes to shut down, I get up on weak knees and throw away the pillow, fighting my instinct to hide. Hawk has seen me naked and had no complaints, so there is no reason to get coy now. I am a Goldweed, and I *will* survive this. Somehow. I must.

"Her son's gay, and so she's taking out her unreasonable hate on me," I say and start moving even though I can barely breathe. I need to gather the few possessions I have. That is my priority, and if I can focus on the task at hand, I will be able to ignore any feelings trying to crawl out of my chest.

"Some people really shouldn't have children. My parents weren't great, but they tried," Hawk mumbles, crawling back onto the bed and shedding the comforter. I can't bear looking at him now, so I pull on a fresh pair of underwear and glance around, relieved my belongings are so few and far between that I might succeed at packing them all within those ten minutes the evil witch of Blackwood has allocated for it.

But then my gaze settles on the trunk servants carried in when I first moved here. Hope leaves my body. There's *no way* I can carry that thing.

"What should we grab?" Hawk asks behind me, and the sound of a zipper tells me he's getting dressed as well.

How is he so calm about it? I'm guessing it's because it's not his life falling apart. I hoped to come back here after Boston to plan my way back to the Nightmare Realm, but it wasn't meant to be.

I stuff my journal into my bag, along with some writing supplies, clothes that may be useful, my jewelry. It is only then that my mind registers his question.

He said *we*. Like this is somehow his problem.

"Do not fret, this is not your burden," I say with my chest tight.

He pulls on his hoodie, his body completely hidden under the fabric as he cocks his head. "What do you mean? We've got to stick together. Just tell me what I can do. Is everything in this room yours?" he asks as I open the trunk marked with my family crest and stare at all the things I haven't bothered to unpack, since they would have made me stand out too much.

The fine silks, the heeled shoes which make me that little bit taller, and most of all, my books on alchemy. If I leave them here, Mrs. Moor will likely burn them.

"Fuck!" I let myself lose patience as I try to choose one or two to take with me. I needed two servants to lift this damn trunk. "I don't have that much, the bare bones of this room belonged to her son. But I can't leave the books behind. Is there any chance you might lift this with me?"

He frowns, shuts the lid of the trunk, and then, like a madman, grabs the handle on one side with both hands. I roll my eyes, about to tell him it's no use, but then my luggage leaves the ground, and Hawk exhales. "What the hell do you have in there? Rocks?" he asks as he places it on the bed. "Do you have rope? Will be easier if I can tie it to my back."

I stare at him for a moment, but I appreciate his ingenuity. And strength. "Yes, I think this could work." I pull off the rope tying the curtains, then watch him fashion it into a strap while I finish dressing in the drab human clothes. It has to be said that they will be comfortable for travel. I don't even know how far away Boston is.

It doesn't take us long to grab every single item I own, including my lava lamp, and the ugly human toothbrush made of white plastic. I'm numb as I assist him with tying the trunk to his back. He looks like an overgrown turtle but still smiles at me in encouragement, as if this is all nothing. "Just one thing. I want to be discreet. Can you distract her so she doesn't see my face?"

After years of surviving intrigues at the Nocturne Court, I expect the worst, and worry he's trying to rob me without witnesses, but that's absurd. We made a deal that is beneficial to him. Surely he wouldn't leave without me.

This must be about him spending a night in my bed. I've learned in unpleasant ways that many humans have an issue with same-sex relations. Mrs. Moor ranted to me about her son the day I arrived, and as little love as I have for Lord Kyran's Dark Companion, I don't envy him his mother.

If Hawk doesn't wish to be seen with me, I will oblige even if it stings after the night we spent together. "I will do my best."

He gives me a thumbs up and waddles forward, keeping both his hands on the walls of the hallway, likely to avoid hitting them with the trunk. My stomach is in my throat as I step toward the stairs and listen to the angry sound of the TV Mrs. Moor spends lots of time watching in the kitchen. For a moment, I'm paralyzed by the desire to avoid confrontation by heading straight for the exit, but I've promised to protect Hawk's identity, and I shall not disgrace myself by going back on my word.

Two exhales later, I run down the stairs and head into my hostess's beige kingdom. After two months in the human world, I am aware they don't consider whites and pastels to be mourning colors, but knowledge doesn't change the way the washed-out tones around me make me feel. It doesn't help that the sun seems particularly bright today.

Mrs. Moor glares my way, cradling her favorite mug as if it were a weapon she might need to use against me if I lash out. "Keys. I don't want to ever see you again."

I put the keys on the counter. "I can't say it's been a pleasure, Mrs. Moor." There. Why not tell her what I think before leaving? I wish I had the courage to confront my own mother, but I've been banished for five decades, and I feared I might need her support by the time I return to the Nocturne Court, weak, gray, and wrinkled like a prune.

But who am I kidding? My mother is a woman so intimidating only Lord Kyran himself dares put her in her place.

I stiffen when Mrs. Moor shoots up from her chair and swats my arm. "How dare you? No wonder your family chose to abandon you," she spits out, pursing her mouth in an angry grimace.

My superior elven hearing picks up the click of the door on the other side of the house as Hawk leaves this ugly place. The relief of it doesn't make the stabbing pain of her words any less hurtful, but she has already kicked me out. I no longer have to prostrate myself before her.

"Amusing, coming from one whose own son chose to forsake her."

Her eyes go wide and... she grabs my arm. Something I have not accounted for from a middle-aged human lady. "My *son* chose to abandon all morals I raised him with and became another man's house boy, so I am glad I will never see him again!"

"Unhand me!" I yell when she shakes me. I have no qualms fighting a woman in her prime, but it doesn't feel right to hit one who is not, so I'm trapped in a cage of my own manners.

She scowls, lets go, and goes straight for the sink, as if she doesn't want any residue from my sweat on her palms. I don't bother staying to exchange any more angry words and storm to the exit, upset that I'm so weak she was able to shake me in the first place. My shoes are black slip-ons, so I just stuff my feet into them and step outside, facing Hawk who... waits for me in front of Mrs. Moor's open car. The sun makes me squint and lower my head to avoid most of its burn, but there isn't much more I can do to protect myself from it.

"All done?" he asks and approaches the passenger seat, opening it in a familiar gesture. Back home, servants would also put stairs in front of a carriage, but cars don't come with such conveniences and require one to fold their body without care for decorum.

"I... yes, but... I am sure Mrs. Moor is not in the mood to lend us her car."

Hawk chuckles and gestures inside, so I slide into the seat, hating how unbecoming that must look. I want him to appreciate my royal demeanor, but how can I remain dignified in a world not made for it?

The sun is already hot on my skin, so I put on a wide-brimmed hat of straw or some similar material and zip up my hoodie to protect myself from its touch as much as possible. I don't want to make a fuss, and while I attempt to spend as much of the day as I can indoors, today that will be impossible. I have to bear with it.

Hawk climbs into the driver's seat, and when he closes the door behind him, I feel as though we're both stuck in a giant oven. At least my things are safe in the trunk, which my promised placed in the back seat.

My *promised*. Should I even call him that before I tie my shadow to his? I suppose we did make a promise.

I expect the familiar noise of the starting engine, but Hawk just releases the handbrake, then moves the stick, and the vehicle rolls forward, down the gentle slope of the driveway.

I swallow and my stomach ties into knots. "We're stealing this car, aren't we?"

Hawk chuckles as we roll farther down the street, still with the engine off. "Well, yeah." He grins at me from behind dark-lensed glasses and only turns the key in the transmission when the vehicle comes to a halt. "But don't worry, I know a place where we can have it repainted and re-licensed. And they might get rid of that collar for you too," he says while my world is crumbling!

"It cannot be taken off by human means. We need to go to Boston. Also, what is the punishment for stealing a car if we are caught?" I'm no stranger to bending the law and scheming, but if I am to one day be executed, it will not be for petty theft.

As we speed up, leaving behind the life that's been forced on me, Hawk chuckles. "Ah, don't worry, just a few hours in the stocks. Nothing we can't survive," he says cheerfully, as if being mocked and having rotten produce thrown at us was nothing. "And as for the collar, why not try? Trust me," he says and places his hand on my thigh.

His touch chips at my resolve, and I sigh. "I suppose it would be unreasonable not to try."

Hawk grins and leans in to kiss me, the road ahead forgotten. It's so new for someone to casually show me affection, I don't know what to do with it or how to express my appreciation. I stare into his eyes, mouth dry, then something flashes in the corner of my eye, and I yelp.

"Watch the road!"

He hits the brakes, and we come to a rapid stop right before the intersection. I manage to brace myself and avoid hitting my head against the dashboard, but Hawk seems un-bothered as he reaches past me, stretches the safety belt, and then locks it across my torso. "Road trip!"

It's me this time who steals one more kiss before the light turns green.

I need to be bold if I intend to escape my banishment and take him as my Dark Companion. I might be jumping into the abyss of the unknown, but what is life without a bit of risk?

CHAPTER 7

SYLVAN

I shudder with humiliation when my stomach growls again, not only making my insides tremble but also cutting through the buzz of the engine. Unbelievable. At this rate, my promised might decide I'm gross and unworthy of his time.

I pretend it didn't happen and instead focus on the paper map as the vehicle shakes on the uneven road. "Go right," I say, sinking deeper into the seat. Hawk insisted on traveling down the least frequented routes we could find, so I have to remain alert and tell him the way. Fortunately, map-reading is a skill that doesn't differ much across the realms.

There are dense woodlands wherever the eye can see, but the road we are about to enter is covered by asphalt instead of gravel, which will be an improvement.

"You okay? Don't know about you, but I really need coffee," Hawk says as I shift away from the sun's rays darting inside through the window. After Hawk told me black clothes absorb the heat of the sun, I changed into Mrs. Moore T-shirt. The new garment is white, with flowers printed at the front, and hugs my body, unlike most of the shapeless garments the humans seem to prefer. And while I do feel less hot now, my skin is pink and burns from too much exposure to the damn star hanging in the sky.

Hawk, on the other hand, seems unaffected by the bright glow and whistles happily when he points at a road sign. "Gas station! We might just get some food!"

"How are you this cheerful when we have so little?" I sigh in exasperation, fanning myself with the map. I'm not made for this weather, but I refuse to show him all my weaknesses. I'm already worried the only reason he's talking about food is because he heard my stomach growling. Then again, yesterday, he did eat enough for four, so maybe someone his size needs more nourishment.

"See, I never had much, sweet cheeks, and now that I have a car, a boy at my side, and enough money to buy gas and lunch, I feel that's plenty," he says, winking at me.

I suppose he cannot understand how difficult it is to lose one's rights and status, so I bite my tongue and adjust Mrs. Moor's pink sunglasses, which help me deal with all this brightness, but I still try to focus my eyes on shade.

It takes us another fifteen minutes to reach the isle of civilization buried in the endless sea of trees. As young as those woodlands seem in comparison to the forests surrounding the Nocturne Court, I'm surprised by their vastness all the same. A small home with laundry hanging in the garden stands on one side of the large parking lot surrounding the gas station. There's just two more cars around, other than ours, and a single truck parked in the very back of the lot, which makes it less likely for anyone to identify our stolen vehicle.

Hawk is rummaging through the glove compartment as I slide out, stretching my legs and seeking refuge in the shade. He emerges moments later, with the bottom of his face covered by a fabric mask featuring a cartoon bear and hearts. Between that, the baseball cap, and the huge shades, he's unrecognizable. Save for his sheer size of course.

I consider my words, but I am no stranger to conflict, and he doesn't seem skittish. "Are you ashamed to be seen with me?" I ask, standing straighter even though my ridiculously bright top doesn't lend me any dignity.

"Why would you think that?" he asks and offers me his hand.

Now it's me who hesitates if it's appropriate to walk hand in hand, but I eventually allow it. "The mask confused me." I do wonder if I can afford a better hat myself. I left the straw one in the car, too embarrassed by how it looks, but now I worry about getting blisters on the parting in my hair.

The air smells faintly of gasoline, but the nature around us, and the elusive aroma of the hot ground overpower it as we walk toward the shop. A family with two teenage kids sits by a wooden picnic table at the side of the building, all eating hot dogs, but when one of the young girls nudges her sister, staring straight at us with a small smile, I feel self-conscious.

Since coming to this realm, I have learned that some humans have an unhealthy focus on other people's love lives, and their attitudes toward men and women who prefer their own gender vary in ways I find unpredictable.

A giant bear carved in wood flanks the door to the gas station on one side, but at least the interior is pleasantly cool. I wonder how far my twenty dollars and thirty cents will stretch. I will need to study all the prices before I make my purchases, as I've learned the hard way that the tax added at the counter can inflate the cost substantially.

"I need to assess the offerings," I tell Hawk as I slip my fingers out of his grasp. He does have such nice hands. Thick, warm, slightly hard to the touch in places.

"Sure," he says as we enter the small shop which has everything. A claw machine stands in the corner next to tourist brochures, but there's also basic groceries, and even a small selection of hot foods on offer.

The proprietress of the establishment zeroes in on us with a frown, and Hawk releases the raspiest, most unhealthy-sounding cough I've ever heard. She clears her throat, appearing flustered, and grabs a remote before raising the volume of the small television mounted behind the counter.

I struggle with some of the foods in the human realm, so establishing which ones might be to my liking is difficult. I don't like when they're too greasy or too spicy, but also too mushy, like porridge. I also dislike soup, but only if it's hot. Warm drinks are acceptable as long as they don't have *bits*. My co-worker at BBB introduced me to cold tomato soup, gazpacho, one time, and I appreciated him for it. He had made fun of me for being a picky eater, but then also made a game out of trying to find foods I like, which was kind of him.

If I were to say what I *do* like, it's things that are salty and crunchy, like pretzels, natural cereal, all types of waffles, hard vegetables and fruit, but also crispy meats. I also love milkshakes and smoothies as long as they're completely blitzed, which I discovered while working at BBB. The Nocturne Court also offers a whole variety of sea foods I enjoy that don't exist here.

Oh and bat wings. How I miss crispy bat wings with grief salt.

Even beginning to explain my tastes can become awkward, so when pressed, I do just eat what's offered and bear it.

I begin to rummage through the shelf filled with packaged snacks, looking for something that has the chance to appeal to me. I discreetly squeeze some bags to check if the food is hard or soft.

Close by, Hawk lets out a laugh, which he then follows with more coughing. "Look at this. Perfect for a prince," he says, showing me a children's play set featuring a tiara with fake blue gems, a plastic necklace, and a scepter topped with a heart.

I've been in the human world long enough to recognize that while plastic can sparkle, it is easy to destroy and of little value.

I raise my eyebrows. "Truly? Is it?"

Hawk stalls, and while I can't see his expression behind the mask and shades, he seems somewhat deflated. "Well, you have no crown, and doesn't every royal need one?"

"I have a crown. Back home. I chose not to take it so it's safe."

It's like he's pointing out that I have nothing. I put my foot on the bottom shelf and use it for leverage to climb toward the top shelf where I can already see the massive jar of my favorite pretzels.

The edge I'm holding on to digs into the flesh of my fingers, but then two strong hands close on my waist and lift me, so I'm level with the familiar packaging.

"Hey!" I yelp in panic, feeling like a child's toy in his grip. I grab the pretzels anyway since I *am* already up here. "I was managing!" I mumble when he casually puts me down.

"You might have slipped."

"Then I would have suffered the consequences of my own actions, as is appropriate." I glance to the side and, of course, the cashier is snooping on us. "Are you trying to humiliate me?"

"Why are you upset?"

The fact that I can't see much of his face only frustrates me further. "Because I am perfectly capable, and you are suggesting I'm not."

Hawk spreads his arms and leans over me. "Jesus, I was just trying to help. What's your problem?"

"Do not hover over me like I'm a child." We need to establish some boundaries, even if it's unpleasant.

He takes a step back, showing me his palms. "Fine, I won't be spoiling your shopping with my help," he says and storms off toward the counter, leaving me to contemplate the food in my arms.

I'm pretty sure I upset him, and now that fact is hanging over me like a dark cloud. I may have learned about customer service at Best Burgers Bonanza, but dealing with my promised, my *lover*, is proving much more challenging. I wish I could just already *have* the experience.

I flinch when he buys his food and stomps out. Should I apologize? I'm the one who's feeling patronized.

With my jar of pretzels and a bag of carrot sticks, I approach the shopkeeper. I'm torn about how to make amends to my promised, but then I spot a pin with a hawk among other wildlife-themed decorations. I have to give up on the carrot sticks to afford it, but I hope it will make him smile. It does have *Hawkward* written on it, and everyone likes a good word game.

"Crazy how even with all the modern technology, someone snuck into the MET and just snatched that thing. So many pricey paintings in there, and only this antique gets stolen? Bet some rich fuck made a special order. Like it's not enough that the elites harvest blood for their face masks," the shopkeeper says, resting her chin on the heel of her hand.

I follow her gaze to the television screen, and the pin almost drops from my hands as I face a picture of the greatest of the missing Nocturne Court artifacts, the Sunwolf Crown. Lost in the aftermath of the Night of the Bloodknife, centuries ago, it was thought to be gone forever, yet the powerful relic I've so often seen in a fresco at the back of the throne room stares at me from the screen with onyx eyes. Shaped like the skull of a huge wolf, yet molded to rest on a human's head, it has crystal teeth and symbolic sun rays shooting up from the smooth part meant to rest on the wearer's scalp. It's made of solarin, not platinum and gold, and much more priceless than the TV presenter discussing the *"bold robbery"* could ever know. She claims it's been found by archaeologists in Mexico just two years ago, and I cannot believe it's been in the human realm this whole time.

So many times, my mother has mentioned that if only one of us Goldweeds claimed it, the Lord of the Nocturne Court would fear us enough to share his power. But if I could put my hands on such a prize and offer it to Lord Kyran, my banishment—

"Breaking news! The missing truck moving two dangerous prisoners has been found. It seems that the driver lost control of the vehicle, but one of the convicts murdered the other survivors in cold blood and seems to have escaped, so remain vigilant. He is dangerous," a presenter speaks as I hand over all my cash. The shopkeeper's gaze trails down my top in a way I can't decipher, and as she opens her register to deposit the money, I raise my gaze to see a familiar face on the screen and I can no longer think about the Sunwolf Crown.

"If you see this man, do not approach him, he may be armed. Instead, alert the sheriff's department." The person on the TV reads out a phone number as I stare at Hawk's likeness. He looks much more imposing in the picture, without even a hint of smile, and the harsh lighting isn't doing him any justice.

But I shouldn't be considering whether his depiction is handsome or not when I've just learned he has escaped prison *and* murdered several people.

My mouth is dry, and only a moment later do I hear the woman point to the few cents of change she put on the counter.

"Y-yes, thank you. Good day." I turn, hugging the plastic jar of pretzels like a lover.

This can't be happening. My Dark Companion. Wanted.

And much more dangerous than I ever expected. Am I really such a bad judge of character? Am I naive?

I walk out of the shop and stand on its porch, sucking in air as I attempt to get to grips with this new reality. So this is the reason why he didn't want to be seen by Mrs. Moor. So this is why he's wearing that stupid mask. And he's told me nothing, because he likely believes he can toy with someone as inexperienced as me.

He has no idea who he's playing with. I'm Prince Sylvan Goldweed, and even with the damn collar around my neck, in a world so new to me, I am capable of—

"Hi there, it's a nice day, aint it?" a male voice says, and when I spin around, I'm faced with a man who's taller than me but not freakishly so, and who's watching me with a smile behind his neatly-trimmed mustache. He's relatively young, though with some creases at the eyes, and he offers me a friendly nod.

I take a glance around, but Hawk is nowhere to be seen. The car is still there though, which means he hasn't abandoned me.

"If one considers sunshine nice," I say with the tiniest nod back.

He laughs, shrugging. "You're funny. That your lunch and dinner?" he asks, pointing at my pretzels.

"Sadly. Everything is vastly more expensive than it should be."

The stranger sighs, and his gaze slides down my chest. "My truck's parked behind the building. If you need some cash, we can make that happen."

That piques my interest. Finally. My luck changes. "That would actually be very helpful."

His brows rise, and he clicks his tongue, stepping off the porch. "This way. You're looking nice, by the way."

As we walk together, I compliment his mustache in return, since a man who wants to give me money deserves that much.

CHAPTER 8

HAWK

Is this guy for real?

I planned to hide from Sylvan and make him miss me for a couple of minutes, but instead I overheard a conversation that had my jaw on the asphalt. The boy only gave his first blowjob last night, so either he was this greedy for more and didn't yet get the memo that I claimed him, or he was so utterly ignorant about what he agreed to.

Anger burns in my chest as I watch Sylvan follow the trucker (quite a handsome guy, I gotta admit), but the moment they disappear from sight, I sneak behind the building and dash past the trash cans, toward the large truck, where they are both headed.

I hate that despite my frustration with Sylvan, he looks like an absolute snack in the cute top. Is it really so wrong that I tried to help him at the store? I wasn't trying to poke at his fragile ego.

It's hard to even consider that little spat though when the guy leading Sylvan opens the back of his truck and *my boy's* eyebrows rise. I move a little closer, just enough to hear the exchange. A part of me wants to barge in there already, but I need to be smart about this. I need to know where I stand.

And maybe, just maybe, I'm a little pissed off about Sylvan claiming he can take care of himself, so I want to let him try.

"Inside?" he asks in that cute accent of his I can't pinpoint.

"Inside sounds perfect," the trucker says, and his hand makes a little circle over Sylvan's ass.

"Excuse me! Please don't do that," he says and takes a step back.

That's when it becomes painfully obvious that Sylvan didn't come with this trucker to satisfy some desperate need to suck more dick, and my feet carry me from behind the bushes, straight into the bastard's personal space.

"Hey, hands where I can fucking see them!"

The trucker's gaze darts between me and Sylvan. "I… don't know what this is about."

"Sure you don't. I heard everything!"

"Look, no court will ever convict me for solicitation, because we haven't discussed anything like that," the trucker says, wrapping his arms across his chest, all smug. I need to wipe that expression off his filthy face.

I slam my forehead against his so fast my sunglasses fall to the asphalt, and I drag my damp mask down to glare at Sylvan as the bastard falls over, holding onto his face.

"I thought you didn't need my help," I grumble.

He takes a step back, hugging that damn jar of pretzels as if it's a shield. "What are you doing? What 'solicitation'? He wanted to give me money! And in the position I am in, accepting charity cannot be beneath me."

The trucker is still scrambling at our feet, so I focus on my social cue-challenged boyfriend. "'Charity'? He didn't want to just give you money. He wanted to pay you for getting him off!"

Sylvan licks his pretty pink lips, eyes wide as if I told him there's a third ear growing on his forehead. "I am not a harlot," he chokes out, but I can see that his world is crumbling.

"He thought you were, and you just walked off with him. What if I didn't notice?" I growl, but as panic passes through Sylvan's features, the trucker pulls himself up by grabbing the open door into the cab. He's bleeding from his nose as he faces me, but I know I'm fucked when he freezes.

"You're that escaped—"

I have never been a thinking man. But I unlearned it even more in prison. My fist collides with his face before I can think, and he collapses to the asphalt, knocked out cold.

"Fuck…" I mumble.

Sylvan adds his own, "Fuck!" and runs his fingers through his hair. "I didn't know. I didn't… know," his voice starts to tremble in a way that sets all my nerves on high alert. "I'm not stupid. I just didn't realize—" He takes a deep breath, but a tear still spills down his cheek.

My insides wilt, and I place my hands on his shoulders, stepping over the trucker. "Of course not! Nobody knows everything, and how were you to read the signs when you're an elven prince trapped in a different realm, right? But that is why you need my help."

He rubs at the tears, but at least he's not shoving my hands away. "You don't understand. I must know how to handle all matters. I cannot go through life expecting others to catch me if I fall."

I notice that he flinches when I squeeze my hands on his pink shoulders. He can't be… sunburned, can he? The summer isn't intense yet. "It's not reasonable to avoid help when it makes sense to accept it, like when you're too short to reach the top shelf."

He hates it, I can see it all over his face that facing the truth is like having to bite into a lemon. "I don't like being incompetent," he says through gritted teeth.

At least we're getting somewhere.

"And you're not. But everyone has their strengths and weaknesses."

"I don't feel I have any strengths lately," he says and moves his foot to avoid getting the blood from the trucker's nose on his shoe.

This sounds like a longer conversation, and we need to get going.

I exhale and give him the keys to our car. "Look, get ready. I'll just quickly make sure he doesn't send the cops after us."

Sylvan cocks his head at me with an unreadable expression. "Don't… kill him."

I frown and glare at the man lying on the asphalt. "What? Why would I kill him?"

Sylvan spreads one arm to the side. "Because you killed several people just *yesterday*." At least he has the decency to keep his voice down. "I saw you on TV. You are being hunted. And *you* talk about trust? You told me you're as tame as a lamb, and this is what I find out?"

I still, meeting his intense blue eyes. God, they're beautiful.

And what can I possibly say in my defense? I might not have straight up lied, but I did omit the truth about my situation. "I wanted you to like me."

He rubs his forehead as if all of this is an inconvenience. He's not running away, nor throwing his snacks at me in an attempt to distract me. He's either got some balls on him, or he's that deranged. Either way, I'm taking that as a good sign.

"By the way," I add, seeing that he isn't yet throwing any more accusations my way. "I only killed *one* guy yesterday, and it was because he literally shot at me and almost killed me two months ago before that! Look!" I lift my hoodie at the side to show off the scar where he shanked me. Though I'm also hoping to distract his morals with my abs.

Sylvan points to the trucker. "Do you need help?"

I shake my head. "No, get ready to go. I'll make sure it takes him some time to free himself. And no, I will not kill him just because he wanted to sample you," I say and drag the dude up.

Sylvan turns around, but then hesitates and gets back to me. He pulls out the guy's wallet and takes the cash out of it. "He deserves it, right?"

Wow. I might have found myself a real gem.

"Smart boy! I would have slapped your butt if I had any hands free," I say and haul the limp body into the cab, which is a feat of strength even for me. Lifting weights is way easier, even much heavier ones. But limp bodies? Unreasonably difficult.

After what Sylvan just did, I'm pretty sure he's not about to drive off and leave me behind. Though I don't think he knows how to drive even if he wanted to do that.

I roll the trucker into the sleeper cab, tie him with a bit of hauling rope, gag him, and block the compartment from the outside to give us more time. I then jog back to the car where Sylvan is already waiting with a pensive expression.

I grin at him and open the back door to pull out my gift for him. I place the small plastic tiara on his head as soon as I'm in my seat. "For my fair prince."

He sighs but doesn't protest the gift nor take it off. He pulls something out of his pocket and presents it to me, looking up with the biggest, bluest puppy dog eyes I've ever seen.

"Sorry for making it *hawk*ward," he mumbles as I stare at the pin with the bird of prey.

It takes me a long moment to realize that he's gotten me something too, and I find myself melting. My boyfriends would usually try to give me sex, or cologne, or some other thing you could offer just anyone. This? This tells me he's *trying*. "Best gift I've ever gotten," I mumble and take it from him before pulling off my hat and attaching the pin to the crown.

He doesn't shy away from me when I kiss him, and then we drive off before anyone else recognizes me. I'm kinda buzzing that Sylvan knows these things about me and still dares sit with me in the car. Could he be... *The One*?

Sylvan takes a deep breath and rubs my forearm. "I ask you to disregard my tears. It is only a physical reaction. I am much tougher than I look, and I need to know the truth. Why were you in prison, and where are we actually going?"

I exhale and entwine our fingers as soon as I can. I don't like talking about the biggest mistake of my life. In an ideal world, I would just wipe my memory and never need to acknowledge it again, but I'm not going to have that luxury, so I suck it up and speak.

"My friend was abused for years by his father and uncle. I should have thought about other options, but they were evil people, and the world is better off without them," I tell him before taking a deep breath as the sun blinds me when the road changes direction. "We're going to visit my family, because I'll probably never see them again."

Sylvan chews on that for a while, his perfect doll face a mask of absolute seriousness. "I guess some people deserve to die."

Heat buzzes in my chest when I glance his way, because this is exactly how I feel, and aren't common values the most important thing for two people starting a relationship? I smile at him, and while his never-ending dedication to the elf prince persona is starting to be a bit concerning, he seems sensible overall. Maybe it's... like that defense mechanism thing I've heard about during a talk in prison? Maybe he's trying to deal with something traumatic that way, and if he starts feeling safe, all will return to normal? I consider my options, and when silence stretches, I clear my throat and continue, making the decision to play up to his madness. After all, whatever story he tells me will be a regurgitation of reality.

"Could you tell me more? About *your* family and the place you're from?"

His frown only deepens, but he looks no less beautiful, even though his nose and cheeks are a little sunburned. "I guess we are both criminals, so why not."

He groans and starts struggling with the lid of his pretzel-filled jar. I wish to tear it out of his hands and help him, but I can't do that when driving. I try to think of a way to say it that won't hurt his self-esteem.

"How about we stop here?" I ask, slowing down when I spot a bunch of empty picnic tables. As soon as we're out, I can open the jar for him under the pretense of grabbing some snacks for myself.

I'm surprised at how intense his scowl is.

"I cannot do this anymore!"

"Do what?"

"I cannot just sit under this scorching demon of a star!" When he points to the sky, it becomes clear he means the sun. "Even this ghastly shirt didn't help. If anything, it made my reaction worse. My arms ache from the touch of all this brightness, and I refuse to get devoured by it."

"That's a bit... dramatic. If you had told me at the station, we could have gotten sunscreen. Did you always get burned so easily? Are you one of those people who are allergic to the sun?" I ask, passing the picnic tables. It's been years since I've been out here, but I used to spend a lot of time in these woods. I know a place that could work better.

He huffs and pokes his tiara. "I suppose you could say I'm allergic to it. But I figured I have to bear it. No point in burdening you with my inadequacy."

"Aren't we bonded? Didn't you say I'll be your companion?" I ask, increasingly frustrated.

"Dark Companion," he corrects me as if this was the most important issue to focus on.

"Exactly. Shouldn't you trust me? Shouldn't you lean on me? Why would you be in pain for no reason?"

He takes his time to consider it and I can't believe it's so hard for him to comprehend. "I accept your argument. I will try to be more open about my struggles so that you may alleviate them if you have the means to."

"Thank you. It will make me feel better," I tell him and brake as we pass an old, overgrown road I still remember. I go back, and then turn between the trees, driving over weeds growing through cracks in old asphalt. The place I'm now taking Sylvan to was the perfect spot for discreet dates when I used to meet up with a guy who lived around here.

I can only hope it hasn't lost its charm.

CHAPTER 9

SYLVAN

We stop in front of a white building topped with a tower which has a cross on top. We're in the middle of a forest, with pleasant shade from the dense trees around us, and the church is no doubt abandoned, going by its state and that of everything around it.

It's similar to the place Mrs. Moor took me to when I first arrived in the human realm. The experience made me politely decline the next invitation. We don't worship any gods in the Nightmare Realm, even if there is a sentiment of making offerings to destiny, the belief that our ancestors watch over us, or respect for the moon and its unknowable influence.

I, for one, am a man of science and believe that with enough work and research, one day we will understand all the intricacies of the world surrounding us. There are rules to everything, even if we don't understand them.

"Are you... religious?" I ask, as based on my conversations with Mrs. Moor, the subject of belief can be a tricky one.

Hawk snorts as he stops the car in the dense shadow of a massive tree that will soon start poking its branches through the top windows of the abandoned church. "We did have a tree for Christmas, and Grandma made us wear cross necklaces, but honestly, if there's no belief attached to it, that's more like carrying an amulet for luck, isn't it?" he asks and gets out of the vehicle.

I nod and follow him out. I clear my throat and give him my jar, in an attempt to follow through on my words and ask for help. "Would you be so kind as to open it for me?" It's very different from handing something to a servant, often even without a word, as helping is what they are there for. This is like asking an equal, which means admitting I am in fact incapable of doing something myself. Showing such vulnerability isn't something I'm used to, nor have been taught to do, but Hawk seems happy when he unscrews the lid and offers me the pretzels.

"We can wait out the worst of the sun here. This place has been abandoned for years, so I doubt anyone will come around, other than maybe kids trying to drink or fuck in peace," he says and grabs a blanket from the trunk along with a bag of shopping. He approaches the door of the church as I put one crunchy snack in my mouth.

I'm so unused to someone *wanting* to do nice things for me.

"I need to change out of this," I take off the flowery top that didn't help against the sun at all. "I am done being something I'm not."

Hawk smirks and whistles at my half-naked body. For once, I'm not self-conscious. He's seen me and told me how much he likes every bit of me. I might not be convinced, but he is and that's what matters. Just like he might not appreciate how incredible his shadow is. Even now, it seems to yearn for me, reaching out with helpless tendrils.

Not long, my love, not long.

As I pull out a silky, midnight blue shirt out of my trunk, I feel his eyes on me, and I do not resent it. In fact, I may have arched my ass up a bit higher for his viewing pleasure. He sighs, and I can hear him shifting, as if he can't make up his mind whether he should be a good boy or go with his gut.

"In an ideal world, I'd push you against this car, pull down those pants and rim you until you're nice and relaxed. And then—"

A flush hits my cheeks, but I'm starting to feel more confident in these matters. I smirk as I crawl back out and put on the shirt. "And then what?" I tease, meeting his gaze head-on even though I am *covering* my body, not offering it.

In this heat, I won't wear a tight vest or jacket over the shirt, the way I usually like to, but I still tie the fabric at the collar into a delicate bow around my neck.

He swallows, following my movements with his gaze. I might be inexperienced in the ways of romance, but seeing him this taken with me is awakening new doors, to rooms I didn't know existed.

"And then, I would slowly, gently drill you open with my cock and make you beg me to never stop," he tells me in a dark voice that has my balls tingling.

I extend my wrists to him in a silent request for him to close the skull-shaped clasps on there. "And yet, you have to wait." It's much easier to be so cool and collected *before* we're actually touching, because last night, the sexual frenzy overpowered me completely. When he crawled on top of me, spread my legs, lifted my shirt... I was his in an instant.

His fingers are thick, so he struggles with the small fastening, but I give him time, and when he succeeds, he offers me a triumphant smile.

"Good things come to those who wait, they say. But I hope we won't need to wait too long, because I might just go crazy," he tells me, massaging my hands.

"I intend for you to be my Dark Companion by the next full moon," I whisper and pull him down for a little kiss. It's for the better that he's a killer. He will fit into my world with more ease. I turn to the church. "We can enter? It's not someone's property?" I ask, but I get my answer when Hawk grins at me then slams his boot against the rotting door several times.

Finally, the door swings open, inviting us into the embrace of shadows.

"If you don't tell anyone, I won't," he says and holds the door for me, as if he sees worth in serving me. I'm greeted by a cool damp scent, which relieves the burn on my skin as I step inside and face a wooden floor covered by all manner of scattered items, from books to furniture and artificial flowers. At the very end, behind two rows of identical benches, the floor is elevated, and on the stage is a pulpit, and behind it—a kind of piano.

"I used to come here with my ex," Hawk tells me, taking a deep breath as he rolls out the checkered blanket and places it in the middle of the floor, away from the rays of light streaming through the windows above.

Based on the television shows I've seen I decide he means a former lover. "Are we close to where you lived then?"

He shrugs, resting his hands on his hips and offering me a somewhat tight smile. "Yes. It's not far."

When I sit down, movement catches my eye in the hollowed back of the pulpit. I lean in when I spot the culprit—a large brown spider with long legs. I reach out to it with a smile and look back at Hawk when it crawls on my hand.

"Look! He's so cute and fuzzy."

He blinks, stiffening as he sits on the blanket, but then his face brightens. "I think this is only the second time I'm meeting someone who actually likes them."

"They're lovely. With their many eyes, the delicate webs they create, and you can often use their parts or venom in alchemy. Which, I admit might seem grim, but such is life. Death is often just around the corner." When the spider starts walking faster, I let it back into its shadowed hiding place in the pulpit. "Like over there," I point to a rabbit carcass in the corner which is now just a pile of bones with mushrooms growing inside it. "Nothing goes to waste. The beast is no more, but it fed a different kind of life."

Hawk bites his lip and lies down on his side, facing me. The nearest ray of sunshine falls behind his head, its glow a sharp contrast to his dark hair. "You're really different," he says after a moment of silence, and reaches out to stroke my shoe.

I sit down, feeling such relief without the sun on my skin. "To understand me, to understand my family, you need to know where I'm from. And where I will take you." I smile at the thought of bringing him with me, already my Dark Companion, so no one can take him and his shadow away from me. Of course, his presence will put a target on my back as well, but it's a risk I'm willing to take to finally *be somebody*.

He shifts closer and, after a moment's hesitation, places his head in my lap. "I want to know everything," he declares, and his forest green eyes peek at me, shining with flecks of gold.

I stroke his long dark hair and watch his lids shut. "What will be most striking to you from the very beginning, is that we don't have the sun. The day is illuminated by moonlight, and the night is like the darkness under your eyelids. We, the elves of the Nightmare Realm, appreciate the shadows, but it will take you a while to get used to the change. My world is dangerous, filled with unimaginable beasts, ancient plants, and we, at the Nocturne Court, live on the shores of a violent ocean, also known as the Sea of Sorrows. But the realm is also beautiful. Like that spider." I point to the pulpit, then grab a pretzel to feed Hawk. "Once you learn to live in its web, you can appreciate how intricate it is, and how to survive within it, instead of struggling against it. And you will have as much time to adjust as you wish, because you will not age."

"Really? There will be no twink death for you?" Hawk laughs, chewing on the pretzel as he winks at me and pulls one of my hands to his chest.

I stroke him, amazed that I'm invited to touch this gorgeous man and that he seems to want me as if I were as tall and strong as my older brother was. "What is that?"

Hawk clears his throat. "Well... it's when a guy who's kind of boyish when it comes to looks grows out of it. Just a joke, babe. I'm sure you'll always be hot."

I shake my head. "At twenty-five, I'm in my prime, and unlikely to change, unless by injury, or curse. Unless I'm forced to stay here for the remaining length of my banishment. Fifty years." I shudder at the mere thought of it. "But if I am lucky and determined enough, I will get this collar off soon, then make you my Dark Companion, and we will find our way back to the Nocturne Court. I am not sure how I will convince my Lord to allow it, but I hope that when he sees your shadow, bound to mine, he will realize I'm worthy of a place at his side. You see, I'm only a minor prince, from a side branch of the family, but as royals, we have obligations to the Realm.

"There is a monstrous creature called Heartbreak, and every few years, or sometimes in longer intervals, it will approach the shores and threaten our people. It's like no monster you can imagine. Unlike a lion or shark," I try to mention animals he might know, "it is like a mountain in the sea. Giant, ancient, I believe, without consciousness. It cannot be killed. It is like a storm. But it can be chased away, and that is what the royals and any knight with a Dark Companion is supposed to help with. And yet..." I take a deep breath, unsure if I should tell him about this, but when we get to the Nocturne Court, an unfriendly soul will surely tell him all about my cowardice. "The last time it approached, I saw its towering form on the horizon, its bulging flesh, its sheer size, and I just couldn't face it. The Lord and his Companion managed to push it back, but my brother died in the attack."

Hawk's eyes open, and he gives my hand a tender squeeze. "I'm sorry. It must have been terrible to lose a sibling. I can't imagine."

I entwine my fingers with his. "I lost all three of them in close succession two months ago. A brother and two sisters. But while I feel more alone than ever before, you have to understand my family has never been like the ones in your television shows, unless the show is *The Sopranos*. One of my sisters was executed for attempted murder, the other died trying to get a Dark Companion of her own and failing, while my brother died fighting Heartbreak. He also betrayed Lord Kyran. As the younger brother, born with neither strength nor talent for shadowcraft, I was always groomed to support my siblings, especially my brother, who was supposed to take over the Nocturne Court when the opportunity arose. I am boring you with all these Court politics, surely. What I'm trying to say is that my family isn't close. We've been like a den of vipers, together only for convenience. Now, only my mother remains, since my father is in exile as well. I might replace what my brother had been to her, but I have to come back with *power*. Your shadow is that power."

Hawk whistles. "Wow, and I thought *my* family was messed up." He exhales and rolls over, so he's facing my stomach with his head still in my lap. "Don't repeat that to them, obviously, but I didn't really miss them when I was in the can. I do love them, in a way, but I'm not worried about losing touch with them. I know they're not the worst family one can have, but I think I was my worst self whenever I was around them. Which, I guess, is me saying that I can go wherever you want to. I'm on the run from the law and have nothing to go back to. I need to be somewhere outside police jurisdiction."

His hair isn't the silkiest, but it's long, dark, and smells nice. I enjoy stroking it as if he were my pet beast, a little rough around the edges. "I promise you I will not be a coward again. I will not run away when we face danger. As soon as I have your shadow, I will protect you." I lean down and kiss him. He might be twice my size, but he doesn't truly understand what might await us when we enter the Nightmare Realm illegally. I don't want to scare him with the whole truth, but everyone needs someone they trust, and I want us to be that for each other. He's already promised himself to me, and I shall not fail him.

Hawk grins, nipping my lips when I try to pull away. "Right back at you, princeling. Me, and my mean, muscular shadow, are ready to protect you too. Nothing's gonna happen to you if I can stop it. I just hope your mom isn't going to kick me out the moment she sees me."

I snort, imagining my mother's face at the sight of him. "Oh, I have no doubt she will criticize my choice, but she will respect it when she sees your shadow. And it is my *choice* to share my bed with you as well, whether she likes it or not." It only now strikes me just how stuck I was under my whole family's boot, always knocked down a peg whenever I dared stick my neck out.

"Hmmm, they can try to stop me from sharing your bed. Not gonna happen." Hawk chuckles, and as he rolls his face against my crotch, the vibrations from his hum awaken all my senses. "Big, dirty human leaving his hot cum inside a beautiful prince like you. Such a disgrace," he mumbles, kissing my cock through the fabric.

I gasp, and my fingers still in his hair. I should chastise him for saying such things, but the excitement they awaken in me is so visceral I'm embarrassed. I've been taught that only the powerful deserve respect, yet here I am, aroused by him talking to me so crudely.

"I probably shouldn't allow it..." I say and bite my lip.

"Not allow what?" Hawk whispers, rising to his knees. He grabs my legs and pulls on them, and then I'm on my back, staring at the paint cracking on the ceiling above. A wave of intense heat stabs between my legs when Hawk spreads my thighs with a raspy laugh.

"This," I whisper, placing my hands on his shoulders. "I shouldn't allow *this*. You on top of me. A human prisoner on the run. And here I am, a prince, spreading my legs for you."

My breath becomes shallow, and I can't get enough of him. He is so handsome with those green eyes and cocky smile. When he takes over control, I'm nervous, guilty, but oh so relieved. We're entering dangerous territory with this game of words, but it's too tempting. Like a delicious scent I follow without knowing what awaits me when I find its origin. A beautiful rose bush, or a venomous snake hiding within it?

Hawk lowers his hips to mine. I gasp when our manhoods touch, and slide my arms around his neck, overcome by need unlike anything I ever felt. The way he pursues me and takes the reins is the most powerful of aphrodisiacs, and as heat courses through my body, we start grinding against one another.

His teeth glint when he smiles. "But it feels so good. I bet you're just embarrassed that someone might know, but behind closed doors, you would get on your knees and service me every time I asked."

I shiver, but he's not done explaining what he means and slides two fingers in my mouth, stroking my tongue and pressing down on it with a soft sigh.

"Just like you swallowed it all last night. I can't wait to pop your cherry and use your ass too."

Fuck. I want it. At this point, I won't be stopping *him* but myself. I moan and suck his fingers, shamelessly rocking my hips. My cock presses against his through our clothes, and all I can think of is what it would be like for that thick tool to thrust into me.

When he nips my neck, I moan louder and grab his wide shoulders, because it makes me feel as though he is feral, and I have to tame him.

"You know it's true. You want to be taken like *I'm* the prince, and you're my concubine," Hawk whispers, rolling his tongue against my flesh. As his skin warms, the scent clinging to it, fresh yet earthy, intensifies, and I realize that this must be what a predator smells like when it's about to mate.

He slides his fingers out of my mouth to untangle my bow and reveal the shallow collar around my neck. I'm panting, rocking against him, becoming a mindless animal with his body on top of mine. I've never been this aroused before. Sure, I've experienced attraction, but Hawk makes me forget who I am so that I can become flesh led by instincts.

"I did trade my body after all. It will be yours to do with as you please."

A shiver goes down my spine when I think of it. Of him deciding he wants me during a ball, taking me behind a thick curtain to quickly satisfy his needs, then leaving me dripping with his cum.

It's so lewd.

So undignified and unworthy of the last drop of Goldweed blood.

But as I imagine him taking me in rough thrusts, a virile animal in need of breeding his partner, my hole spasms, and I wrap my legs around him. Pulled by an unstoppable impulse, I kiss his lips, and he cradles me with those big arms.

"Ohh fuck... you know exactly what to tell me," he whispers and squeezes my sensitive nipple. "I will make it my job to never leave you unsatisfied."

"Ah... you're so... heavy. I love it," I mumble, rubbing myself against his thigh in a motion that might be enough to make me come soon. I slide my hand between us with a gasp and cup his crotch, frantic with the excitement of having access to a man like him.

And it's not just about how attractive he is. Hawk makes me feel safe to express my needs, even when they're embarrassing.

I whine in protest when Hawk pulls away, and even try to drag him right back, but when he unzips my jeans, I understand what he wants and help him drag the pants off. They keep hanging on to one of my feet, but the fabric is no longer in the way as Hawk shoves his own bottoms halfway down, revealing his amazing dick. He spits on his hand, rubs the saliva over his cock, and then pulls both my legs to his shoulder. In this position, they're squeezed together, but I only understand his purpose when his hot shaft prods the backs of my thighs.

"I want to come inside you so bad," Hawk rasps, a deep flush covering his face as he shoves himself into the tight heat of my thighs, and his cockhead emerges from the tight cleft between my legs, pointing at me. I can sense the hot, pulsing shaft against my skin.

It's mesmerizing.

"Not yet," I mumble, even though I want him to push inside me with every inch of my body. But I promised myself to deny him this one thing, afraid that if he gets it before we make our bond, he might not stick around. I don't believe he would, but this tiny thread of control is keeping me sane. "But I want you here…" I say and lift my shirt to show off my stomach as a target for his cum.

Hawk's eyes roll back as he thrusts into the warm pocket between my thighs, and the next time his dick peeks out, it pokes my sac, sending an electric current through my body. Contorting with my back rising off the blanket, I let out a shameless howl and encourage him loudly, even though my skin is already burning from the friction of this fuck.

"I want you to smell of me."

Such an animalistic idea. I would have scoffed at it if I wasn't just as feral. I reach for my cock, desperate to come, but he pushes my hand away and wraps his own around me instead. He starts pleasuring me at the same pace in which he's fucking my thighs. I won't last long. I watch him, so powerful over me, his hand so massive on my prick. I like feeling fragile next to him. He holds my legs up with ease, and our eyes meet when I moan.

"Yes… Hawk! Yes!" I whine, rubbing my ass against his hairy thighs.

"When you finally let me inside you, I'm not going to let you out of bed for the whole night," Hawk rasps, his gaze intense as he works his hips, rubbing the inner sides of my thighs raw. I imagine him rolling me over for another round every time I try to leave our future bedroom, and thinking about being *taken* by this beautiful beast pushes me over the edge. I cry out, tensing as he keeps plowing my legs.

My eyes roll back, I arch my spine, desperately reaching for his shoulder. It's as if he understands me without words and grabs my hand, leaning forward and fucking my thighs faster. I squeeze his hand as he milks the last spurts of cum out of me, leaving me a boneless mess. I don't even care about staining my shirt. I have another one.

As soon as he senses I'm done, he lets go of my cock and pushes his slick fingers between my buttocks. I'm too tired to protest, but I don't have to worry. All he does is press the tips of his digits to my throbbing hole.

"So hot and needy, I bet. It's gonna be so snug on my dick," he mumbles right before his cum shoots onto my chest and stomach, a few drops even reaching my face.

He is perfection when he comes. Lips parted, cheeks flushed, eyes on me. There's a desperation on his face, as if he couldn't decide where to look and which part of me to kiss, but then he dives forward and gathers his own cum from my belly. Overwhelmed, I moan at his touch, and respond to his kiss. The world is a flurry of color, and when his slick fingers return to my buttocks, rubbing the cum into my flesh, I can't bring myself to stop him either.

I shiver when one of them penetrates my insides, carefully rubbing the hot seed into my walls.

He's not pushing it in deep, but the digit is thick and I'm still panting from my orgasm. I shouldn't allow this, but the thought of having his cum inside me is too tempting to resist.

Maybe I'm not as smart as I thought. Maybe I'm a dumb animal desperate to be bred.

The little moans I'm making don't sound like the cold and collected Prince Sylvan Goldweed I always saw myself as.

"Do you like it?" I whisper, overcome by a wave of shyness now that the urgency of sex has dissipated.

He lifts himself enough to meet my eyes and removes his finger out of my hole. I'm convinced we're done for now, but Hawk gathers the remaining cum from my belly, only to bring it to my opening and continue massaging his seed into my insides.

"This is the loveliest hole I've ever seen. So tight and responsive to my touch. I *need* to mark it."

I lick a drop of cum off my lip and lift one of my legs to his other shoulder so he can freely watch the sticky mess he's creating. I know this is all a sexual frenzy, I know this can happen, but I have the same instinct as the one he speaks of. I ache because he's not bound to me yet.

"Can we just stay here a while longer?" I whisper and reach for a pretzel.

"Of course," he answers in an instant, his gaze on the finger playing with my hole.

I could probably ask him now whether I can brand my family crest on his forehead and he'd say yes. I guess this is also a kind of power. One that I never before knew how to wield.

CHAPTER 10

HAWK

The past five years in a cage of steel and concrete did not make my memories of home fade. The cops would question my family, possibly watch the property too, awaiting my arrival, but this is far from the first time a Coleman has been on the run from the law. My family has had quite a bit of experience with that throughout the past century, so I keep away from main roads and approach the woodland at the back of the vast property. It's getting dark, but I keep the car lights off as I move down the gravel road only ever used by the forest service. And us.

My eyes are strained from trying to find the spot I'm looking for. Back in the day, I remembered it by heart, but fortunately two of the trees close by remain marked, and I sigh in relief when I spot them. Soon enough, we will both get something to eat, and pillows to rest our heads.

Not that Sylvan needs a bed to fall asleep.

He looks so precious with his head against the window, curled up under a flowery blanket. His lips are parted, as if he's already inviting more kisses, and his pale lashes lay against his sunburned skin. He reminds me of a white moth. Fragile, nocturnal, beautiful, but a little scary.

I'm already regretful about having to wake him up. The guy's been through so much in the last twenty-four hours yet stood by me even after finding out I'm on the run from the cops. If that's not a good sign for our future, I don't know what is.

I believe at least some of what he told me about his family is grounded in reality, so I'm not surprised he escaped to la-la land after experiencing such loss.

I stop the car and listen, to make sure no other vehicle suddenly appears on the road. When I'm satisfied with the silence, I get out and dive between the trees, taking a lungful of fresh pine-scented air. I used to hate this part of the process, the need to exit the vehicle, push through bushes that never failed to scratch me or leave a spider in my hair, but now I relish the touch of leaves, and the crunch of old needles under my feet. Moments later, the hidden gate is open, and I drive through it, then carefully mask all traces of my presence. I even kick the gravel about to hide tire marks before returning to Sylvan, who hasn't woken up throughout any part of the lengthy process.

My family and I haven't always been on the best of terms, and none of them has ever set foot in any of the jails and prisons I've been in throughout the past five years, but they are blood. I can count on them when it matters.

As I make my way down the narrow road leading to the family property from the back, I hope the privilege of being one of the Colemans extends to me even now. After all, we have a code.

It takes around twenty minutes for the vehicle to approach the familiar compound, leaving behind the dense woodland and entering the clearing. A light comes on in one of the cabins, making me think they might have installed a motion sensor. Moments later, another window lights up, this time in the biggest house on the property, the one I know so well. The one my parents live in.

I lean over to Sylvan and push some hair off his forehead as I kiss his lips. If I have to wake him up, I want to do it gently.

Even after a whole day, he smells so fresh, like the rain, and dew on dense grass, and as I slide my finger over his pointy ear, his eyes open.

"Where... what?"

"We'll be spending the night here," I explain and kiss him again, but he pushes me away, sucking in air as he raises his hands, staring right past me.

I exhale and look over my shoulder, straight at the barrel of a shotgun pointed at us from behind the window.

"Have I really changed so much, Wolfie?" I ask, and the gun lowers, revealing my older brother's face.

Wolf shakes his head. His hair is just as dark and shaggy as mine, but much longer. "Fuck me..." He takes a good long look at Sylvan. "No. You haven't changed at all from what I'm seeing."

I shrug and open the door, shaking Wolf's hand as I step out. "I take it you already heard—"

"Did you abduct him?" my brother asks, leaning close as he whispers, and I feel my cheeks burn. "When did I ever do that kind of thing?"

Wolf rubs his face, blinking his eyes awake. "What am I supposed to think? You're on the run from prison, and you show up here with some snowflake-looking kid." His voice is lowered, but I still worry Sylvan might hear him as he gets out of the car from the other side.

"We just have... similar goals," I mutter as a familiar silhouette appears on the porch alongside numerous other Colemans watching us from their homes.

This is exactly what I always tried to flee from.

"Is it him?" My father asks.

Wolf shrugs. "Sure is. And he has company."

I pull Sylvan close as soon as he's within reach and wave, acknowledging everyone. "Don't you worry, I won't stay long... but I do need to swap this car for another." They'll know what I mean.

Sylvan pulls on my shoulder so I lean down, and only then he whispers into my ear. "Do not tell them about my origins. They will not understand."

This is actually for the better, because I'd have a hell lot more trouble explaining that my new boyfriend is an elven prince.

All the Coleman men are tall, but my father? He's like a bear. About my height, but much broader around the middle, and with a much hairier face than mine. When he approaches, Sylvan steps back, and it makes me feel so protective of him I'm struggling against the need to pull him into my arms for a cuddle. Where he's a toothpick, my dad is an oak tree.

"You better tell us everything and quick," Father says with deep grooves appearing on his forehead. There are only a few lights around, but I still spot some new silver in his hair.

Before I can speak, Wolf decides to fill him in. "The kid's also on the run."

I don't even get to clear up the misunderstanding when my other brother, Fox, butts in. "What? You brought your prison boy toy?"

"There's nothing to see. Go to sleep!" Father hisses and looks around the cabins making up the compound. My brothers' wives are visible in the windows of their respective homes. Leah's even holding a child young enough for me to not have met.

This command makes me relax, and I rub Sylvan's shoulder as the other members of my family retreat into their homes, surely back to forgetting about my existence.

"We just need a different car," I repeat. "We'll be on our way soon."

Father crosses his thick arms on his chest, and as he studies me, I'm struck by the realization that at this point it's like staring into a mirror revealing what I'm going to look like in twenty years.

I'm happy to conclude it won't be too bad.

"The police were already here, looking for you," Fox adds, combing his shaggy auburn mane with his fingers.

"You'll need to go before dawn," Father mutters.

I nod, disgruntled by how this is going so far. I don't want Sylvan to see me for the black sheep I am. "Wolf, do you have the steel cutters?" I put my thumb under Sylvan's collar to show him what needs done.

Fox wraps his arms on his chest and whistles, showing off the big gap between his front teeth. "The plot fuckin' thickens."

I sense Sylvan swallow against my finger. "I don't think it will be possible to cut with regular tools."

He's got no idea that he just said the magic words to trigger Wolf's ambition and can-do attitude. "Doesn't look that thick to me, I'll handle it."

"Since when are they collaring inmates?" Fox asks, and I clear my throat.

"I actually... just met him yesterday. He wanted to go with me."

Father rolls his eyes, slouches, and spins on his heel, heading for the house. "And now you brought him here! Did you lose what little was left of your brains?"

I swallow when Wolf smirks at me, then pull Sylvan along, not trusting myself to meet his eyes. We came here for a new piece of junk. Is that really so much to ask?

"I didn't kill the guards—" I say on the way toward the porch.

"Shame," Father cuts in and walks right into the living room I spent so many evenings in.

"Hawk!" my mother yells and pulls me into a big hug. At least someone's happy to see me, even though she never visited me in prison either. She's still in her pajamas and robe, long silver hair scattered over her shoulders. "I'll make you two some food. Who is this?"

Sylvan makes a little bow with his head and gives a stiff smile. "My name is Sylvan."

I hate the look my mother exchanges with Dad, but I ignore them and lead Sylvan to the sofa. "Those are my parents. And he is my partner," I say, because while I've known him for about twenty-four hours now, I have no intention of parting from him in the near future. After all, I promised him my shadow, and all that weird shebang.

And he is super-hot.

Wolf grunts and steps right back outside "I don't want to be around for *that* conversation. Lemme get the tools."

Dad is the first to lose it, and slams his fist against the table so hard Sylvan flinches. "Your 'partner'? This is exactly why you always get in trouble. You get a lucky shot escape, and you find yourself a new boy to fuck up your life on the same day?"

"Is that why you never visited?" I ask, meeting his gaze while Mom makes some noise in the kitchen, maybe unwilling to listen to this painful and embarrassing conversation.

"So you're gay. I get it. In a way," Father says, towering over us as he makes a convoluted gesture, likely meant to express how little he can imagine being attracted to another male. "But I don't understand why you stupidly threw away your life for a pretty face. He wasn't even blood. Who does that?"

Sylvan clears his throat and I'm already dreading how my dad will react to anything he might say. "We already share a bond that will soon be deeper than any blood relation can be."

He looks like a diamond in mud on the beat-up leather sofa. He radiates beauty, and if only I manage to keep him, I will get to bask in that glow.

Fox sits at the table with one foot on another chair and raises his eyebrows. "Oh, so he's crazy. Now it all makes sense."

"Fuck you," I growl and squeeze Sylvan's hand, because he might not live quite in the same world as everyone else, but there's logic to his actions, and when we reach Canada, maybe I can find help for him there?

Father shakes his head. "Nothing to say? The boy who put you behind bars is living a cushy life now. Last I heard, he bought a house on Fire Island."

Free as a fucking bird and likely barely remembers me.

I rub my face. "Are you two done?"

"I will never be done," Father growls as the soothing scent of cocoa reaches my nose. "You don't do those things for people who can ditch you. Only family is worthy of sacrifice. And you don't understand because you won't have children, and you always wanted to leave us too. I'm surprised you even bothered to come over."

"'Cause he needs something," Fox *helpfully* adds, and if I wasn't holding Sylvan's trembling fingers, I might be strangling my brother just about now. Does this mean Sylvan's already making me a better person?

"I can assure you there will be no *ditching* anyone," Sylvan says in a confident voice that doesn't betray nerves the way his hand does. "Sometimes, you have to trust destiny, and it has brought us together for a reason. He will be mine."

I know how it sounds to their ears, so I'm not surprised when Fox cackles like a hyena, and my father drags his massive hands down his face.

But I fucking love it. My heart tingles as if it were pumping champagne instead of blood. So maybe I have a weakness for pretty boys in trouble, and maybe it's easy to impress me, but who wouldn't want to feel special once in a while?

"It's your own life you're fucking up again. You are an adult," Father says as Wolf enters the room with a pair of steel cutters. "We will get you the car, but you will be on your own after that. If this fancy little shit fucks you over, don't you run to us for help."

"He won't," I say, trying to control the anger flooding my veins.

As I turn to Sylvan, ignoring my father, I notice his expression has changed from the tense attempt at a smile to a cold glare. His pale pink lips have tightened into a tense line, and his blue eyes could cut my father in half if Sylvan really did wield magic. It's a glimpse at a new side of him, but I'm not sure which one is the mask. The sweet smiles and innocent blushing, or the icy promise of cruelty?

His focus is gone the moment Wolf stands between him and my father with the cutters.

"Okay, lean your neck back against the sofa," my brother instructs, eyeing the collar. "Is this some new kind of tag? Like an ankle monitor, but fancy?"

I shrug, hoping Wolf will decide he understood me and deal with the damn shackle. As the huge tool touches Sylvan's neck he squeezes me harder with his sweaty hand, and I kiss the tip of his head as Mom enters bearing two mugs. One's my favorite, huge and featuring a hawk mid-flight, the other is one of hers, with a view of the mountains.

"Are sandwiches all right?" she asks, offering me the cup of chocolate.

"Can you toast it for him?" Because I learned on the way about Sylvan's preference for all things crunchy. Yet another adorable feature.

"Sure thing, sweetie," Mom says and pats my shoulder before disappearing into the kitchen again.

"Please be careful," Sylvan says, breathing hard when the jaws of the cutters close on the band around his neck.

Even though nothing bad will happen, and he'll get a scratch at best, it still unnerves me to see him so vulnerable next to my brother. He really needs me. I can be important to him.

The thought alone makes my heart beat faster.

Wolf squeezes the cutters, making an unpleasant sound reminiscent of a screech, but the metal won't budge. He tries again, and several violet sparks pop into the air as if in warning.

Wolf pulls back with a frown. "The fuck?"

CHAPTER II

SYLVAN

"**S**top it! That's enough!" My skin is burning where the purple flames fall, and I shoot to my feet, brushing my chest in an attempt to shake off the sparks. What if they set me on fire? Hurt me? Scar me for life? What if Lord Kyran already knows I tried to remove the collar without his permission?

"I told you it's no use," I yell as the tool clatters to the floor.

Wolf shows his teeth as if he really is his namesake, but it's Fox who speaks from his armchair.

"This is what happens when you try helping whinging children like him. You should have learned that from your last boy toy."

Hawk slams his mug on the table, and some of the hot chocolate spills down his fingers, onto the wood. "Shut the fuck up! I'll never see you again, and *that's* what you have to say?"

I straighten my back to seem at least that little bit taller among these damn giants. "Why should I cower and not speak my mind when I am more informed in the matters of my own collar?" I'm so frustrated that I can't even explain to them what it is. No shackle forged by a grimsmith, from the royal Umlaris Band, which has the power to contain the force of Sunlight, to the most ordinary dream bracelet, can be removed by sheer force.

Wolf waves the cutters in front of me. "What fucking 'matters'? I've been working with metal half my life when you'd struggle to even use these."

Hawk rises and shoves his brother back. "Don't get in his face!"

"Or what? He won't put out later?"

"Fuck. You," Hawk growls, and while I can sense he wants to leave my side and go after his brother, he refuses to budge.

I place my hand on his back, because knowing he's so close calms me down. I've never had someone stand up for me this way. When I made the impulsive choice to speak my mind, I was prepared for a smack from this uncouth man, but Hawk is there, like a wall of muscle. If I had access to my shadowcraft, I could have surprised Wolf with razor-sharp claws for the insolent way he speaks to me and my promised. I might not have much talent for shadowcraft, but I learned to use what little I do have to its maximum potential.

But with the collar still firmly around my neck, Hawk's sturdy presence is the only thing between me and Wolf's brute force.

"Truth hurts," Fox laughs, not even caring to get up.

I loathe the way they're trying to humiliate my man in front of me. It reminds me of all the times my own siblings picked me apart for anything from my size, to my lack of love life, and my puny shadow.

"Nothing you say matters," I say, eyeing Wolf with cold fury. "How dare you insult your brother! Soon enough, we will be gone to enjoy a life of immeasurable respect, cherished for our bond, and wanting for nothing while you rot in a house in a forest, forgotten by all within a century."

I barely get to finish the sentence when someone grabs the collar of my shirt from the back, so hard he lifts me and the fabric rips. "Listen here you little shit!" Hawk's father yells. "We have everything we need here, and as far as I understand, you're homeless and wanted by the cops!" The fabric digs into my flesh, choking me, and I freeze, because I can't expect Hawk to confront his parents for someone he's only just met.

But he spins around, grabs his father's hand where it's holding me, and stares at him above my shoulder. "Let go. He's mine."

A hot shiver trails down my spine, and as it darts farther, it almost feels as if Hawk is teasing my hole with his fingers again.

I shouldn't be finding this moment arousing, but when his father lets go of me with a huff, I fall into Hawk's embrace, ready to fulfill his every wish. This submissive side of me is a shame to my family, but I can't help how I feel next to a man so big and strong.

My brother would have called me an embarrassment to our bloodline, and if he weren't so afraid of Mother's wrath, he would have labeled me a bastard to boot.

Hawk's father huffs like a bull about to charge. "Don't run your mouth if you can't handle the consequences, *boy*. And you?" he says to Hawk. "Let's go get you a car before I report you to the cops myself!"

Hawk glances at me, sliding his fingers through my hair as his mother steps out of the kitchen carrying a whole tray of various sandwiches. "Go on, boys. There will be plenty of food left when you're back," she says and sits on the sofa, right next to the spot I previously occupied. She's old in ways elves never get to be, unless they're banished to a short existence in the human realm, but her eyes are kind, so I settle next to her and nod at Hawk.

"All right," he mumbles, watching me from above. "I'll be close."

When he leaves with his father and both brothers, I release a deep sigh to ease some of the tension coiling inside my chest. I cannot believe I was just grabbed like that. I'm aware my position in this world is one of irrelevance, that my title means nothing here, but knowing this and being confronted with the physical reality of that fact are two different things.

I grab a crispy sandwich that smells quite nice, of salty meat and cheese. "Have you heard that the Sunwolf Crown was stolen in New York City?" I ask in an attempt to make some small talk while we wait.

Hawk's mother stalls, but then shakes her head. "I... don't believe I've heard anything about that. We don't get that much news here, you see. Only found out about Hawk's escape from a neighbor on the radio."

"Ah, a shame," I say, wracking my brain for more things to say. My mother always chastised me for making conversation partners uncomfortable with awkward pauses, but just thinking about it makes me *more* nervous and prone to speaking out of turn. "Your son has been most gallant to me." A bit of a stretch, but a compliment always goes down well.

"Yes, Hawk's a very good boy. Always was. Even if a bit rough around the edges. I didn't expect him to turn out gay, to be honest," she says and pushes the cup of chocolate closer. "Drink it. It'll make you stronger."

"Will it?" I ask in amazement and grab the cup. The drink is warm, but if it's an elixir of strength, I am willing to endure the unpleasant heat on my tongue. The beverage is way too sweet, but I close my eyes and gulp down the whole thing in one go, not caring about manners. If I am to survive another day in the sun, I'll need the energy this nice woman so lovingly infused into the contents of my cup.

"So... what is really between you and my son?" she asks, pulling the folds of her robe more tightly around her. "Did you... correspond with him while he was in prison? If he brought you here against your will, I can help you. Hawk can get a little... overenthusiastic when his heart guides him."

I bite into the crispy sandwich to give myself a moment to think, but it doesn't seem like she's intending some elaborate trap after trying to soften my attitude with a sweet drink. "Oh, no, if I am a victim, then it's only of my own impulsivity. Hawk is special to me." Because I can't even begin to explain to her that when he becomes my Dark Companion, both our lives will change for the better. "We may have met just last night, but I have never felt so much tenderness for anyone before."

Saying it out loud fractures me. My heart beats faster, my cheeks flush at the memory of the filthy things we did together, and moths flutter in my stomach when I think of his protective attitude, but... *But*. We *did* only meet last night. Can I really trust someone, a human at that, just because my body yearns for him? Because when I see his shadow, I want to step into it and bathe in its thick darkness? Because I crave a bond that'll ensure I'll never again be lonely?

Am I like a fish which has lived all its life in a bowl, and now that it's been set free into the ocean, can't see the threats, too blinded by delight?

My hostess sighs, peering at me with a gaze that reflects many of my own fears. "You do know he was convicted for double homicide? And that he is on the run? I want all the best for my son, but if the two of you are found together, you will be tried for assisting an escaped convict. I don't think prison is the place for a boy as delicate as you."

"Prison..." I wonder out loud to give myself time to think. Surely, it won't come to that? I don't even know what human prison looks like. I assume it's no pleasure palace, just like the dungeon under the Nocturne Court is not a place I'd like to be trapped in.

But do I have any choice? I could always abandon Hawk, but even though I haven't tied my shadow to his yet, the thought of doing so repulses me. Not just because I'm so greedy for the power he'd offer me as my Dark Companion. He is risking a lot for me, and I have given him hope by offering him a place at my side in the Nightmare Realm.

I am a prince of the Nocturne Court and my word counts for something. If he could challenge his own father for me, then I shall stand by him too.

I squeeze my eyes shut for a moment as fatigue settles over me, reminding me how long the past day has been. But I can't doze off when my promised's mother is talking to me, so I clear my throat and take another bite of the crunchy sandwich. "I am taking this leap of faith, and so far Hawk has proven himself to be a man of strong conviction when it comes to me."

She licks her lips. "I love my son, but you seem like a gentle soul, so I have to warn you that he has an insatiable appetite when it comes to men. Don't put all your eggs in one basket."

Jealousy greener than swamplight flares up in me at the very idea of Hawk turning his attention elsewhere. "He will *not* have another."

She stares at me incredulously, and gives a soft laugh. "How would you stop him? You would do yourself a favour settling on someone more like yourself," she says, and I find myself massaging my eyes, struggling to stay awake.

Was I not supposed to be strengthened by the sweet concoction? My tongue feels so heavy when I try to speak. "He is... who I want to..."

It's too late when I recognize I've been duped. As I tilt to the side, Hawk's mother is there to catch me and settle my head on a pillow.

"This is for your own good, sweetie," she whispers just before I'm taken by a dark fog.

CHAPTER 12

SYLVAN

I smell wood, stale fabric, and something sharp and biting... spirit? My limbs are heavy as bags full of gravel, and my head lolls from side to side in a world that seems filled with slime instead of air. The uncomfortable sensation on my tongue feels like the obvious consequence of whatever potion I've been given, but as I try to move it and swallow, it becomes clear there's cloth in my mouth, and that it's tied to my head.

Panic sets in as my eyes open to near-complete darkness, but when I try to move my hands to find out where I am by touch, I discover that my whole body is bound.

I'm trapped.

My wrists are fastened behind my back, my ankles are tied together, and I'm attached to the insides of this soft coffin by a belt strapped around my waist.

This can't be happening. Could they know who I really am and seized me for the bounty on my head? If Lord Kyran installed spies around me at Best Burgers Bonanza, then I am already a known fugitive.

I attempt to make a sound, but the gag rests so deep in my mouth my whine comes out muffled. I would have tried knocking on the walls, but every surface around me, including the lid I just pressed my forehead to, is cushioned.

I'm frantic with worry, but will not let myself be overcome with it. I am a Goldweed and my life cannot be snuffed out like a candle.

Think. Think. Think.

It's then that something crashes outside my prison, making me flinch with fear, but the sound of the familiar gravelly voice soothes the cramps inside my abdomen.

"I ask again, where the hell is Sylvan?"

I want to embrace Hawk's words, let them wrap around me and know that everything will be all right from now on. I utter a whine, but as he keeps questioning his family, it becomes clear that the same thing that keeps their voices dull is muting mine.

"I told you, honey," his mother says. "I couldn't keep him here by force. He left as soon as he realized he had the chance. You're delusional to think a boy like that would stay. He was probably too afraid to tell you, since he knows who you are."

My heart sinks. They're trying to get rid of me. Like *I'm* the problem. Like *I* could somehow hurt Hawk's future prospects. Helpless anger fills me with fresh determination and I move my bound legs around to feel for anything that could help me escape. Elves have superior vision in the darkness, but even I can't see anything in this coffin.

"He wanted to go with me," Hawk insists.

"Oh, I'm sure he did want something, just like that last pretty face, who you chose to drop your whole future for," Hawk's father interjects.

There's a moment of silence, and then Hawk speaks. "Why would you fucking say that? You forgot about me for five years, so you don't get to judge me now!"

"Oh I will speak my mind, because you're literally here to ask for my help."

Hawk's mother clears her throat. "At any rate, you need to go. Maybe it just wasn't meant to be? You'll have an easier time without him. Find yourself a nice boy with a clean slate. Someone who won't know you're wanted."

I hear stomping nearby, so I shuffle around, but I'm barely making any sound, and humans' hearing isn't even as good as mine.

"For the right guy, I'm sure you're a catch, son," Hawk's father says as if to soften the blow of his harsh words. "But you have to face the facts. Sylvan left. And Kevin testified against you. You need to make better choices, and that should start tonight. Focus on yourself and get across the border."

It pains me to hear that they hound him like that. I don't really know that much about Hawk, but the darkness of his shadow tells me he's not had an easy life. He doesn't deserve to be lied to about me when I most definitely *want* to go with him, and make him mine.

My foot hits something hard and my heart skips a beat. I tap it several times, but the noise isn't loud enough because of the rubber soles of my shoes. Where are steel buckles when one needs them?

"Sylvan would *not* leave. So this is your chance to tell me the truth. What have you done with him?" Hawk growls, and I squirm at a series of noises that follow.

"Please, stop wrecking our home!" his mother shouts, with an edge of rage to her voice, but he doesn't seem to listen, and the next thud sounds as if he were trying to break through."

"I know he's still in the house! I know *you two*!"

I stall, taking it in. He believes in me so much? Over his own blood? How foolish of him, yet how sweet.

I roll the mysterious item with my feet, from one corner of my trap to the other, and I'm pretty sure I hear some splashing, as if it's a jar with liquid inside. For a moment, I consider whether I can smash the glass somehow, use it to cut the binds on my wrists, but then it hits another jar and my heart soars. High-pitched noises are easier to notice, so I put my hope in the clinking glass and grab the jar between my feet to repeatedly slam it against the other one.

The shooting pain of a cramp is replaced by an icy sensation, then a burn as the liquid spills over me. The tiny space I occupy fills with the absolute *stench* of potent alcohol. It's so intense I could get drunk on the fumes alone, and having to inhale through my nose isn't helping. I rattle the broken glass with my legs anyway, because I'm not giving up.

Not on myself, and not on Hawk!

The voices outside my prison go quiet, and then, the box containing me rattles, as if a huge bassal has captured it with its jaws in an attempt to reach my flesh.

"Wet... how do I fucking open it?" Hawk roars to an echoing silence.

"Just calm down!" his father yells, so I rattle the glass with even more fervor despite pain shooting up my leg.

I don't like to admit to weakness, but I am frightened. If Hawk had left me, would they have disposed of me? At this point, I'm not sure what might be worse—being murdered or turned in to Lord Kyran as a proven fugitive. But I don't get to entertain this empty worry for much longer, because something clicks, and then light hurts my eyes as the lid above me opens. Hawk is only a dark silhouette at first, but I recognize the width of his shoulders and take a deep breath of fresh air, released from the pungent trap.

I look up at him, unable to extend my arms, but he's leaning down to unbuckle the belt tying me to the interior. Relief floods me from the tip of my head to my toes when our eyes meet. I've never felt this way before. Someone has my back just because they want to, not because I will be useful to their cause.

We've just met, and yet he believed my intentions over his family.

Despite what he's been through with this *Kevin*, his heart is so open. It makes my own crack and let in his light.

His mother's whisper is barely audible to me, but I still hear it as Hawk removes the wet gag from my lips. "He should have been knocked out until morning..."

Maybe I would have been. If I were *human*.

"What the fuck is wrong with you?" Hawk snaps as his big, warm hands cradle my head and wipe away my sticky drool. He's tense as a storm cloud ready to burst, but while he's addressing his parents, his gaze remains focused on me when he pulls me up and against his chest. It is only then that I realize they'd locked me inside their sofa.

What kind of people have a trap like this in their living room?

"It was for your own good!" Hawk's father yells, but doesn't dare approach. "This boy will be your downfall! He will talk to the cops!"

"My hands are tied," I whisper, curling against Hawk. I try to ignore the ache in my leg, where glass cut into it, but I'm still dripping blood.

He frees my hands, and when he starts rubbing the red marks around my wrists, where the string dug in a bit too tightly, I'm overwhelmed by this display of care. I've once again faced my own fragility tonight, but Hawk's not only here to have my back but also won't be swayed from believing in me.

I couldn't have hoped for anyone worthier to have as my Dark Companion.

"Are you okay? How many fingers do you see?" he asks, showing me three.

"Three," I whisper and as soon as my arms are free, I wrap them around his neck. I want to bask in the safety of his hold. I love feeling so small next to him. It's as if he can hide me from the world and I won't even feel shame over needing his protection.

"I'm talking to you, Hawk!" His father steps closer, looming over us like a malicious giant ready to take my savior away. But my promised pushes his arm under my knees and lifts me as if I were a cat, not a grown man.

"First aid kit. Now," he demands, placing me on a large table.

His father raises his hands. "It's barely a scratch. I wash my hands of this!"

But Hawk's mother brings what he asked for without meeting his eyes. I bite my lip when I look at the gash above my ankle where glass slashed through my jeans. She stands aside and doesn't say a word when Hawk cleans my wound. Even though it hurts so much and I'm bleeding, the wound is shallow enough to not need stitches.

I fight not to flinch when Hawk presses a bit of gauze to the cut, and wraps my leg with fresh dressing. I bite the inside of my mouth, but two fat, shameful tears still slide down my cheeks. Why am I a wimp who cannot control this physical reaction? My brother would have laughed in my face. No wonder even my own mother didn't think I'd amount to anything.

I take a deep, shaky breath, avoiding Hawk's gaze, but instead of rolling his eyes at me as anyone else would, he cups my cheeks and kisses the tears off my skin.

"It's okay, the cut is shallow, and nothing will happen to you on my watch."

I nod at him, unable to gather any sensible words to such a display of affection. I'm not used to it. I'm not used to relying on anyone else or them actually caring. I'm not even sure I deserve it until I prove myself worthy.

But this human I only met yesterday, a human who allegedly killed people in the past, is there for me, even at the cost of familial bonds.

"Look, we wanted to make this easy on you," Hawk's mother says, but he doesn't acknowledge her in any way and carries me toward the open door. A moth flies in, as we exit, drawn to the very light we leave behind. I shut my eyes when I spot Wolf watching us from the balustrade he's sitting on with the shotgun resting in his lap.

"Respond to your mother," Hawk's father demands, but his words are also left unanswered as my promised carries me away from the duplicitous people who tried to force us apart.

Too choked up to speak, I squeeze Hawk's shoulder when he fastens my seat belt in the new car he swapped out for the stolen one.

He smiles and gives me a tender kiss on the lips.

"Where are you going?" his mother walks closer to the car and doesn't even spare me a glance.

Hawk's fingers twitch on my shoulder, and he snaps back, "To the fucking Nightmare Realm. The cops definitely won't find me there. And you won't either, so don't even try," he says and slams my door before walking around the car to slide into the driver's seat.

Wolf shows him the middle finger from the porch, which I've learned is a very rude gesture in the human world. Hawk doesn't waste a second to respond in kind. He starts the car with a rumble of the engine, and I can just about see the sky turning a bit orange above the trees.

"I'm so sorry, Hawk," I whisper when he drives off fast enough for the dirt to rise behind us.

"No. *I'm* sorry. I swear I didn't think they would do something like that," Hawk says through clenched teeth as we dive between the trees.

I look down to the bandage around my leg, struck that I'd gladly be hurt again if it meant getting to feel Hawk's caring arms around me and receiving tender kisses while he assures me I will be 'okay'.

I slide my hand to his on the wheel. "But you were there for me. You believed I wouldn't leave you."

He glances my way for only a moment, switching on the headlights to illuminate an overgrown track with branchlets smacking the vehicle from both sides as we pass through. The golden glow only reveals what's close, but I'm not scared of the shadows and brush my thumb across his palm.

Hawk clears his throat. "Of course not. You need me to get you to Boston."

"No. I need *you*. For reasons both selfish and tender." My heart beats a little faster at that confession. From the moment I met him, I've been thrown into deep and treacherous waters, but I'm learning to keep my head above the surface, and I haven't drowned yet, so that has to count for something. And maybe... I'm actually enjoying this swim.

His mouth quirks, and he takes one hand off the steering wheel to place it on my shoulder. "You're surprisingly forgiving. Most people in your situation would have asked me to leave them in the nearest town," he says, but the sentence feels unfinished, almost as if he wants to ask, *Do you want that?*

"You might think a prince like me must be refined and sheltered, but I'm no stranger to violence. Do I tremble too much when I shouldn't? Yes, but I know I need to be tough if I am to survive back at the Nocturne Court. You are my promised and I will see to it that you become my Dark Companion. I'm willing to forgive a lot, though I would appreciate you not taking advantage of that."

"Only in the ways you'll enjoy," Hawk tells me with the flash of a smile. "Don't worry, babe, I've got you."

My insides flutter with glee, despite the pain in my leg and the stench of alcohol. I'm glad I'm not the driver, because I would have crashed the vehicle into a tree, too absorbed with the spark in his green eyes.

"Hawk? Would it be too much to ask for you to share more with me about this 'Kevin'? Why were your parents so wary of me?"

The temperature in the vehicle drops, as if I've climbed into the massive freezer at the back of Best Burger Bonanza and laid down on a bed of beef patties. But if we are to be life partners and succeed at returning to the Nocturne Court, we need to trust one another, so I stay firm and keep looking at him.

He tries to wait me out, but when that doesn't happen, air leaves his lungs in a loud puff. "I... didn't really want to talk about it. You'll think I'm a naive cock-whipped idiot."

I don't always understand all the wording humans use, but I get the gist of what he means. "Oh? I will not judge you." When he gives me a skeptical glance, I decide I need to give as much as I intend to take. "When I was not even twenty, I was assigned a guard who made my heart race a little too much. I would often find excuses for outings just to spend more time with him. I thought I was finally doing something of my own, unbound by my family's wishes. Maybe even going against them. I allowed him to lead the way to a tavern known for its disrepute, because I thought something might happen between us.

"When he led me to a private room, promising sweet little nothings, my mother was waiting for us. I was being tested and failed. She planned the whole thing just to show me I cannot trust men based on my heart's fancy. I know what it's like to be proven naive." It's been years, yet my cheeks burn when I recall this story.

"What the fuck?" Hawk growls, squeezing my shoulder. "Can't believe I'm saying that after what just happened, but your family might be even more messed up than mine!"

I sigh. "That might be a fair assessment," I say and focus my eyes on his face. I have humiliated myself in front of him. It is now his turn.

"Fine," he mutters and stares ahead as we pass through the woodland, in the dark silence of the upcoming dawn. "So my parents were wary of you, because they know what kind of guy I like, and I've done some real stupid shit for boys much less pretty than you. Like Kevin," he says and hits the brakes as we face a barrier of wood and steel, mostly overgrown by vines.

Hawk opens the door and leaves the vehicle without a word. I watch him open the obscured gate, then drive the car past it, and then close it again while I wait, stewing in never-ending anticipation. I hate Kevin already.

The sky's pink now, and we both look at it as my promised joins me in the car. I worry I might have to force him to go back to the previous topic, but as we start rolling along a gravel-covered road, he speaks.

"You know I'm on the run, right? Well, I ended up in prison because Kevin kept telling me his father and uncle were treating him horribly and he had the bruises to prove it. Every time he'd come to me crying I felt this savage, unstoppable rage. I offered we could move in together, but nothing was ever good enough. He feared them and said he'd never feel safe until they were gone. So I... made them go away."

I nod, despite having to fight my jealousy. "And you don't wish to... reunite with him?" I make myself calm on the outside, but still start biting my nails.

Hawk laughs. "With the guy who called me a monster during the trial? He claimed I planned everything and that he had nothing to do with the deaths, as if he hadn't pleaded for me to take care of things," he says in a voice soaked with bitterness. "He just used me."

I stroke his thigh, wishing I could climb into his lap and hug him. "I can see why someone could want a man as powerful as you on their side. It is his loss that he renounced you."

"No shit," Hawk mumbles with a scowl. "It's embarrassing how I was ready to save him when he just collected evidence to give the police as soon as I was done. But I was serious. I just wanted to help him. To take care of him. I always..." I squeeze his thigh when he gives me an unsure look. "I might not look it, but I like cute things. I have a soft spot for pretty boys, and I always wanted to be a hero for the guy I was with. My family accepted it, begrudgingly, but they didn't get it. I no longer fit in. I was a problem. A hindrance, always wanting things they didn't see as important. My brothers were fine sharing the same space, I wanted a place of my own, just *something* of my own. So I built myself a little cabin when I was around thirteen, and then got this cute little kitten to keep me company. He wasn't the family pet. He was *mine* and mine only. But then, a hawk stole him, and that was that," he finishes in a grim voice. "Believe me, the irony is not lost on me."

I see him in a new light, and the more I know, the more I realize how much about him is still hidden from me. I have so much to still learn about Hawk.

I realize I even stopped biting my nails, and instead I trace my fingers over his muscular thigh. "I can be yours, and yours only. If you killed for me, I would have helped you hide the bodies."

He stares at me and chuckles. But before I can get upset over him not treating me seriously, he offers me his pinkie. "Promise?"

I've seen this kind of thing on the television so I hook my finger with his. He's being playful, but I mean my words with all my heart. "Promise. And I will promise you so much more on the day we make our vows under the full moon. You will bind your shadow to mine, and as I agreed, my body will forever be yours. But I already know I will offer you so much more. Not every Dark Companion becomes their partner's lover, but I would like us to be that. It is not an attachment of convenience for me."

Hawk exhales, and his fingers weave through mine. "I really want to believe you, princeling. Some would say I should have learned my lesson. Apparently not. My family would have laughed so hard, but I like that you're so passionate about this."

I smile at him. "I've never been as impulsive as I am around you, but I like it. You unleash me from the shackles in my own mind. And it doesn't hurt that I can't stop thinking about the night when you finally come inside me," I whisper the last words, afraid that he might not like the way I worded it, but his hand squeezes mine more firmly.

"Oh, you're such a tease! But that's okay. We need lube anyway, and we don't have any," Hawk mutters, chuckling to himself as we reach a crossing and turn right, headed toward the rising sun. "So now a quick dip to Boston, and then we're out of here. For good."

I clear my throat. "I was thinking actually... I have seen reports on television about this object called the Sunwolf Crown. Though it's probably in the human realm under a different name—that's irrelevant. But if it's the real thing, and I don't see why it wouldn't be, finding it could mean the end of my banishment. It used to belong to the son of the first Lord of the Nocturne Court. I do not wish to bore you with the details of its use, but if I brought it to Lord Kyran, he'd have to be grateful enough to restore me to my former position at court. It was stolen just two weeks ago from a place called New York City. Do you know of it? Could we go search—"

"No," Hawk tells me with finality to his voice, even though his gaze is almost apologetic. "I am already taking a huge risk by driving you to that blacksmith. If he's the only person who can take off that thing around your neck, then so be it, but I can't go back to prison and spend the rest of my days in a cage."

I'm disappointed, but I nod. He knows his world better, so if he says it's too risky, I have to trust him. I raise his massive hand to my lips and kiss it. "You will not. I will not allow it. You will become my Dark Companion, we will go to the Nocturne Court together, and see what we can gain thanks to the power of your shadow. Lord Kyran will not be able to dismiss such an asset."

Hawk swallows, watching me for the longest time. But then his hand squeezes mine, and the car speeds up, carrying us toward destiny.

CHAPTER 13

HAWK

It's been a long day.

Such. A Long. Stressful day. Driving into Boston in broad daylight would have been damn risky, so we waited it out, moving to the south of the city along small roads. I did get a bit of shut-eye after we hid the car in a woodland, with Sylvan keeping watch, but it wasn't nearly enough after already missing sleep on the night my useless fucking family tried to part us.

My boy might be a bit crazy, or a tad too invested in Dungeons and Dragons, but I feel protective of him. While many would have called my decision to linger in the very area where I'm known as a fugitive as suicidal, I can't say no to his pleading eyes.

I don't know what kind of metal that collar is made of, but my brothers couldn't get it off, and the sparks they accidentally created left several purple burns on Sylvan's skin, scattered over his throat like dark stars in a faraway galaxy.

I considered telling him that, but he doesn't seem to be that much into sci-fi, so I settle on calling them pretty, which seems to ease his anguish about his perfect skin being ruined.

In any case, if that grimsmith guy can free him, I'll help make that happen. I even know the name of the bar he's supposed to frequent, but I've only been there once, many years ago. It's somewhere on the outskirts of town, but the exact location keeps eluding me.

"Hawk! Look!" Sylvan exclaims and squeezes my forearm. It's warm, but I'm stuck in a hoodie to hide my tats. It wouldn't matter that much, but I mourn every missed opportunity for his soft fingers on my skin.

Soon, I tell myself. *Soon.*

I hoped he spotted the bar, but instead, I stare up at a massive billboard advertising the *Biggest Pretzels in Massachusetts!*

"Are you… hungry?" I ask, wondering if I'm stupid or just self-destructive. I should not be in Boston. I should not be thinking about getting him pretzels. I shouldn't have even hit on him in the first place. And yet, here I am, basking in the glow of his attention.

I've never even *seen* a boy this fine.

Any time tears glisten in his beautiful blue eyes, I feel this primal need to do anything I can to stop them from falling down his cheeks. Seeing him squirming in pain from the wound on his leg had me on the verge of going ballistic on my whole family. The only thing that stopped me was that I wanted to take care of his leg and get us out of there.

"I would very much love to try them. Can we afford to? I have some money left, and soon enough, we will not need human coin anyway…" His growing smile lights up the car, and my heart beats faster.

I smile, even though deep down I know this means he's out of touch with reality. I'm fine with being reimagined as a hot barbarian to his elven prince, but there is no denying our situation. Still, everything inside me wants to soothe and please him, so I press a small kiss to his head as we dash past the billboard. "I suppose we could ask about the bar while we're at it."

Sylvan claps his hands together, looking excited like a kid at Christmas, his pointy ears twitching. He rises in the seat and stares out of the window in anticipation of the giant pretzels. After five years in the can, just being in the presence of such an adorable creature makes me melt. It doesn't hurt either that the attraction between us is sizzling louder than a donut in hot oil.

He changed into a different shirt when I was napping, since my dad tore the collar of the other one. This top is black, loose, with almost the entire back covered in lace revealing milky skin, as if to tease me. Elaborate frills cover half his hands, starting at the wrist, and I'm amazed that the outfit didn't get wrinkled. Must be some fancy new fabric.

I took the initiative at my parents' place and repacked his stuff from the unmanageable chest into a massive bag for me and a smaller backpack for him. Do I think it's ridiculous to be taking all those books and trinkets with us? Including a *lava lamp*? Yes. But when I thought about him crying over losing his precious possessions, I knew I couldn't leave them behind.

"How thrilling!" Sylvan says as we approach the cafe-gas station-shop with a giant pretzel display at the front. "They cannot possibly expect one person to eat that," he points to the display. "A whole family wouldn't be able to."

As he glances my way, a chuckle rolls out of my throat, and I pull him close, so *happy* to be here with him. Maybe I'm not destined to escape the law after all, but what time I have, I want to spend with him, enjoying his eyes on me and feasting my own on his amazing body, soft lips, sapphire eyes.

"This one might not be edible. Let's see what they have inside," I say and put on the same face mask that obscured my identity at the first gas station. It's nothing special, just a bit of printed cotton, which happens to smell of stale lady perfume and has a bit of a pink stain left by the lips of Sylvan's former landlady. But it works.

"You prefer sweet? Salty?" I ask as we stop in front of the shop's bright windows. It has seen better days, as there are cracks on the blue and brown walls. A part of the neon logo mounted on the roof keeps blinking, but our vehicle is the only one within sight, other than an old van at the back, which likely belongs to the owner.

We'll get some crunchy snacks, ask for the way to the bar, and be on our way.

Easy-peasy.

"As long as it's not too sweet, I would like to try both," he says with all seriousness, as if this decision is of great importance.

He stretches when he gets out of the car, and even standing on his toes, he's so... tiny. I love how big it makes me feel next to him. If we weren't trying to avoid attention, I'd pick him up and carry him inside for the fun of it. I'm a fugitive with only a few bucks to my name, yet to him, it seems I can offer so much more. He's impressed by my size, my strength, excited to get a pretzel, and even my not-extraordinary driving skills are amazing to Sylvan.

He walks into the shop first, and I notice he's limping a little. I hope his leg doesn't hurt too much, but we will get to take care of that eventually.

The elderly lady behind the counter looks at us from behind thick glasses. Her hair is like a cloud of cotton candy, though white rather than pink, and she's wearing a T-shirt depicting her with two huge iced pretzels.

"Oh, hello! You're just on time. I was about to close for the night," she tells us with a winning smile and already picks up a small paper bag, ready to serve us.

There aren't many pretzels left at this hour, but I'm drawn to the one smudged with lashings of cheese.

"Thank you, madam, we will not be long. What is cinnamon?" Sylvan asks, stunning us both into silence.

The shop owner meets my gaze, clears her throat, then turns back, only to return with a steel container filled with brown dust. "It's a nutty spice."

"May I try it before I make my decision? I don't like spicy food."

I fight the urge to put my arm over his shoulders. "It's not hot, if that's what you mean."

"Ah, yes, in that case, I might like some."

As soon as I spot him lifting a whole spoonful of cinnamon to his nose, alarm bells ring in my head and I pull him away. "It can be dangerous to inhale it."

He stills, and I swear he was about to just eat a whole spoon of cinnamon to the cafe worker's wide-eyed terror.

Sylvan puts down the spoon after smelling it from a good distance. "Oh. That is indeed good to know."

"Well... what can I get you?" the owner asks with a smile glued to her lips as she puts the container to the side. One of the pretzels, sprinkled with bits of salt, is the size of my pecs, but the others appear to be a more manageable size.

"The big one, the one with cheese, and... one with cinnamon?" I ask, glancing at Sylvan, who offers me a fervent nod and rolls on his heels, as if he can't contain his excitement.

It's so damn cute.

And it pisses me off that were I straight, and he—a girl, I could have cuddled him now without drawing attention. But it is what it is.

I place a banknote on the counter, and after a second of hesitation, grab some lube and condoms too from an area with basic medicines and cosmetics. "We're looking for this bar... it's called The Rusty Stallion."

She doesn't look into my eyes when she scans my items. "It's two miles down the road or so, but I'm pretty sure it's been closed for a few years now, and found no buyer."

My mouth goes slack under the mask, but I nod and join Sylvan, who's helping himself to some water from a fountain in the corner. "That guy we're looking for... you sure he'll be there? This lady says the bar's no longer open," I tell him in a low voice.

Sylvan smells his cinnamon pretzel and his pointy, sunburned ears twitch like he's a happy kitty. "It might look that way, but I know a way in, don't worry."

I get myself a cheap coffee from a machine, because I'm pretty sure this will be another long night, and we sit at a small table.

"How do you know he'll be in? Do you have a number we can call?" I ask, pushing my foot between Sylvan's. The chair's narrow and keeps digging into my flesh, no matter how many times I shift around in it, so I just accept my fate and focus on the positives—like Sylvan's sugar-dusted smile.

His eyes light up when he bites in. "Oooh! Very good. I will miss this when we leave. Not too sweet, the dough has a bit of crunch at the edges—Yes, the grimsmith. If he does have a phone number, I don't know it. But it's where he works. I very much doubt he will be anywhere else than at his workshop." Sylvan leans closer and lowers his voice. "He was banished almost thirty years ago before I was even born, but my family finds it important to know of people like him."

Of course they do.

Because Sylvan is a prince from a royal line that's been attempting to take over the throne of the Nocturne Court for almost a thousand years, blah, blah, blah—

"You can tell me if he's an ex, or something. People don't always have sex within BDSM settings," I try to encourage him to speak the truth.

He looks genuinely insulted, but why else would he be wearing a collar welded around his neck? Sylvan *must* have been up to something to end up in this position, and the innocent ice prince face can't fool me. I'm not judging him for it either. I just need to know what to expect so that I can protect him better.

"I'm not sure what 'beediesem' settings are, but he and I were most definitely not involved in any way. I don't even know what state he is in after thirty years in the human realm. I dread to imagine it, really, but last time I heard of him, he was alive, even if banished for life. You see this?" He points to a tiny engraving on the collar. Increasingly disgruntled, I nod. "This is the Nightweed crest, a brand of the Nocturne Court's Lord. If I enter the Nightmare Realm without taking it off, I will be hunted. The grimsmith, Tassarion, has one like it on his skin, as he is never allowed back. Frankly, I find it an injustice to be sentenced to fifty years, when it's my brother who schemed against Lord Kyran—"

"Can you be very honest with me this one time, Sylvan?" I ask, and when he lowers his chin, staring at me, I go on, content that I have his attention. "Do you actually believe any of this, or is this some kind of full-time role-play situation?"

He goes still, doesn't even chew, and his pupils grow wider as if I've dropped a splash of ink into the dark blue. "Hawk. Are you saying you've not believed me all this time?" Sylvan swallows and clenches his jaw.

I don't *want* to confront him about it, I really don't, but what the fuck am I supposed to do when my life could be on the line? I might have picked a better moment for it, but it's not like I can reverse time now.

"You claim to be an elf from another world. How can I believe that? I thought we're... acting out your fantasy," I mumble, leaning back as his mouth trembles. I hate how disappointed in me he looks, but that expression is soon replaced by a growing frown, which... yeah, does make him resemble an offended royal.

"How dare you? I have given you my body. We have made promises! It will be full moon in the Nightmare Realm *tomorrow*, and you're questioning my intentions? Worse, you don't even believe in them?"

I hate how the mask muffles my voice, so I pull it under my chin and lean toward him. "Look, you're great, but I have no reason to believe all this fantastical stuff, do I? You wouldn't be the first guy to believe he's something he's not. This dude in my prison believed he was taken by aliens every night, and *that* was a load of shit."

Sylvan gets up, probably to look at me from above for once. Fire dances in his blue eyes, but we need to talk about all this sooner rather than later. "Did you make your promise to become my Dark Companion because you thought it to be of no meaning?"

I clear my throat and take note of the shop owner glaring at us. "I figured you liked me as much as I liked you."

"'Liking' is of no consequence, Hawk! You are on the cusp of pledging your shadow to me. Binding your life to mine. Our mutual attraction and shared desire are only a lucky twist of destiny."

I'm the one who should be angry, but when I sense the scorch of his disappointment on me, it's like being lashed.

I have such a weakness for him.

"Look, I will believe when I see proof, but you gotta admit it's kinda difficult, no?"

Sylvan is so flushed his whole face is rosy, but his voice is like ice. "Fine," he grits out through his teeth. "But until your shadow is bound to mine, my body is not yours to toy with. I will not be made a fool."

Despite my best intentions, I roll my eyes, because he'll be under me before we work out the level of his delusion, and we both know it. He's drawn to me just as much as I am to him.

"Why are you like this? I'm not trying to cheat you. In fact, I asked this question because I feel you're too deep into the whole elf thing, and I'm worried!"

"Because my whole life I've not been taken seriously, and here you are, my *promised*, doing the same!"

I get up as soon as I see his eyes glazing over.

"Sylvan, I do take you seriously, but would *you* believe me if I told you we could live on the moon, without seeing any proof?" I ask and reach out for him, only to have my hand brushed off.

"Don't!"

I flinch, feeling as if he's struck me.

"Is there a problem?" A male voice asks, and I freeze, looking over Sylvan's head, straight at one of the two cops buying fucking pretzels.

When did they even enter? I was so wrapped up in Sylvan, I didn't notice. I feel my face flush as the colors of a police car loom on the edge of my vision, and my hand darts to my mask, but the other cop zeroes in on me, taking a sharp inhale.

"It's him!"

Fuck.

Fuck. Fuck. Fuck.

This will be the most costly fucking meal I ever consumed.

CHAPTER 14

HAWK

Years of staring at the world through bars, years of concrete, steel, and men in identical uniforms flash before my eyes. The reek of the toilet in my cell might be only a memory, but right now it overpowers the fresh aroma of pretzels and coffee. And when I dash forward, grabbing a chair as I let the weight of my body carry me forward, all I can see is a future in a cage.

A future I should have done more to avoid.

The cops reach for their guns when I collide with them, swinging the seat of wood and metal. I hit something with a dull slam sounding like a head being stomped to death, and the force of the collision reverberates over my makeshift weapon, echoing in my muscles. The policewoman stumbles back toward Sylvan while the male cop's eyes go wide. I face the muzzle of his 9mm SIG Sauer, but the chair pushes his hands up before he can pull the trigger. My stomach tightens at the burn of gunpowder, but when the bullet whistles in my left ear, I know we won't get another chance to scramble out of this mess. I need to put my full force into it *now*.

I twist the chair without mercy. Bone cracks as the cop's arm gives in under the pressure of steel, but he only falls when I slam my forehead against his face. I've smelled enough blood to know everyone's is the same. Whether it's a cop, an accountant caught doing financial crimes, or a ruthless killer. Inside we are all just meat and will break with enough pressure.

At least the old lady cowered under the counter and doesn't intervene.

The female cop is dazed, she's holding her head with one hand, but points her gun at Sylvan with the other.

He raises his hands, pale as snow, and shifts toward the counter. "Please, no, I was abducted! I've got nothing to do with him!"

It hurts worse than being stabbed with the dirty shank that should have ended my life weeks ago. As soon as she looks at me, assessing who the threat is, Sylvan grabs the container of cinnamon and throws the brown powder in her face. She starts coughing, the cloud of spice hovering around her like angry bees.

That's my boy.

For a moment there, I was sure he'd turn on me after our argument, but he runs right to my side.

"Lucy! Stay down!" the male cop yells. At least he's not being a hero. Good for him.

I kick his gun away and pull on Sylvan's hand. It feels so good in mine, as though I was always meant to hold it.

"W-we... n-need... assistance..." the woman chokes into her radio, but I don't listen.

I would slash through as many bodies as it would take if it meant freedom for myself and Sylvan, but at this point, the police know there's a problem, and nothing I'd do here can change that.

"Get in," I bark, sliding into the driver's seat, and I back out of the parking space the moment Sylvan's door closes. A car comes to an abrupt stop and hits its horn when I dash onto the street, cutting him off, but keeping our heads down is no longer a concern. Not with our survival on the line.

There isn't that much traffic at this time, and the darkness aids me, making other vehicles easy to spot by their headlights as I speed past stoplights and change lanes on my way to—

"The pretzel woman. She'll tell them where we're headed. Fuck," I grit through my teeth, slamming the wheel as my stomach sinks.

What the fuck should I do?

"Go there. Trust me. Go to The Rusty Stallion," Sylvan says with so much conviction I struggle to question it.

I don't have the time to reconsider. We're speeding down a straight road, and I'll either trust that my deranged twink elf boyfriend knows some secret hiding spot at this bar, or straight up ignore him and drive on in hopes of losing the cops.

I have a few heartbeats to make that decision, because we're approaching the place and fast.

I only spot the old rusty road sign due to the bright mustard ad right next to it. A part of me wants to trust my own instinct and run like a mouse fleeing a bunch of cats through an unfamiliar labyrinth, but when Sylvan places his hand on my thigh, the decision is made for me.

The wheels squeak, and the air fills with the odor of burnt rubber, but I slow down enough to make the turn without rolling and drive through the deserted parking lot. A broken tent, that's likely no longer occupied, leans against an old van, but the surroundings of the bar could be the set for the next post-apocalyptic movie.

I know it's futile at this point, but I refuse to park out in the open and drive behind the building to the faint roar of police sirens in the distance.

Our only hope is that Sylvan's friend is actually a squatter in this abandoned bar and that's why my sweet, if deluded, boy believes we will be saved here.

As soon as we burst out of the car, Sylvan grabs his bag from the back seat. It's ridiculous, but I'd rather waste a few seconds on taking the massive one too instead of using the time to argue with him. It's so heavy it might be useful as a shield or weapon, if push comes to shove.

We stop in front of a tall wooden door covered in metal studs, which makes it look strangely medieval and out of place in this back alley. The carving at the top is in some language I don't know, but if Sylvan's friend is into this whole pretend-to-be-elves game, he might just help us.

I pull on the handle, but the door won't budge, so I knock on it with my fist, desperate to find out how doomed we are.

Sylvan runs his fingers over the wood and nail studs. "Wait. I've got it... I think... I'll open it."

But the police sirens are getting louder. We don't have time for whatever he's doing.

"We need to go. Come on," I say, pulling on his arm as my gaze darts around the industrial buildings around us. "If we don't switch cars, we'll be sitting ducks!"

But Sylvan pushes at me, his face scrunched with anger, as if he genuinely doesn't understand our situation. "No! We need to go through here!"

Do we now?

I don't think so. But I take two steps back, and then bulldoze through the door. A part of it breaks as I stumble into dusty silence.

My arm hurts from the force, but nothing is more painful than the sight of the empty back room, which hasn't seen a person in months. Boxes covered in dust, a few broken bottles on the floor, spiderwebs in every corner, and when I flip the light switch, I notice there's no light bulb in the only lamp.

I failed. Myself. And Sylvan too, by following him on this wild goose chase based only on his sweet but clouded mind.

I'm going to die today, because I will *not* go back in the can! If the cops start shooting, and they fucking will, I'll cover Sylvan, so at least he'll know I meant it when I said I care. Maybe he will miss me when I'm gone.

Still, I pull on Sylvan's hand, because there might be a safe place to hide inside. "If they spot you, raise your hands, and slowly go down to the ground," I instruct him despite the bile rising in my throat, because I was the one who pulled him into this. I barged into his life, made him cover for me, and even drew him into my family's clutches, which left him with an injury.

"No!" Sylvan digs in his heels and pulls me back toward the door like some stubborn mule. "I need to open the door correctly."

I meet his determined blue eyes. What do I have to lose at this point? The sirens are ever louder, and I slowly turn numb to what's to come.

I won't be able to run any farther.

"Do you really like me?" I ask, following his lead, back outside. If I am to die because I went to Boston at a pretty boy's request, at least I want to know this much.

Sylvan pulls the door closed in front of us, and his fingers are back on the studs in the wood. His expression is unreadable, but oh so serene in the light of the neon at the end of the alleyway.

"I do. It frightens me how much."

I can barely hear him over the sound of the sirens but my heart sinks when a car stops close by with a screech of tires. I swallow when a colorful glow pulsates around us, letting me know we've been caught.

Sylvan turns to the door, and when he presses on one of the nails, it gives in under his touch, like it's a button. He then presses another, and another, seemingly at random. One at the bottom, one by the handle.

He huffs, gets to his toes, attempting to reach the top of the door. "Lift please?"

"Get out with your hands up," shouts a cop from the other side of the bar as blue and red keeps coloring everything beyond the shadow of the building.

Sadness drizzles into my heart, but I do as Sylvan says and bury my face in the delicious valley of his spine as I raise him off the ground. He smells like dew first thing in the morning, and I hope the mystical river I dreamt of last time I was dying will this time carry me someplace good.

"I had fun with you," I tell Sylvan as more police cars arrive, and the request for me to give myself up is repeated.

Maybe I should listen? But what would be the point of that?

Sylvan presses the metal stud as soon as he can reach it, and something... clicks. He pushes the door open, and when I put him down, he tugs me inside and locks us in.

The siren and the usual noise of the city disperse, as if this place is perfectly soundproofed. I suck in air, ready to search for a hideout, or maybe even a weapon, but the aroma inside, thick with the smokiness of a fire and some exotic spice, makes me stall.

And is that... a carpet under my dirty combat boots? My hand finds Sylvan's, and I stare straight at the flames dancing in a fireplace worthy of some medieval castle.

I've never been this confused in my life.

Where is the dust? The dirty boxes and broken bottles? And should the back room of the old dive bar be this spacious in the first place? It sure as hell should not feature a ceiling of thick wooden beams, nor the heavy furniture decorated with elaborate carvings and fur blankets.

"What the fuck?" I mutter, staring at a horned head mounted above the mantelpiece. It appears vaguely human at first but is twice the size of mine and has a wide, gorilla-like nose.

Sylvan gets to his toes and covers my mouth with his hand. "Stay still and silent," he whispers, as we hear footsteps, and cops slam their fists on the door.

We're dead. We're so fucking dead.

I glance into the window leading into the alleyway, and I swear there wasn't one there before, but I can see a cop. Fog covers the glass, but he's there, staring straight at us. And yet... also somehow right *through* us.

I flinch at the crash of breaking wood and the shouts that follow, but while the sounds echo all around me, they're dull, almost as if they were coming from inside a massive fridge.

Are the cops... looking for us in the building next door? They might still find us here, so I look around in search of a weapon or hideout.

A few candles are scattered over a thick wooden table in the middle of the room, their green flames casting light over an unfinished letter written with a quill and ink instead of a pen. But then my gaze rests on a huge axe with an engraved blade, and I head toward it, ready to pluck it off the wall.

"I think we're safe," Sylvan says, exhaling behind me. "I need you to stay here. You cannot be seen by Tassarion before I get this collar off."

He's not phased to see me cradling the axe, which is actually way heavier than the replicas I've held in the past a couple of times, but calling our situation safe is plain ridiculous.

"Oh, so it's *him* who is the problem? There's cops everywhere around us," I whisper.

Sylvan drops his bag on the grand leather sofa and runs his fingers through his silvery blond hair. "I will explain later, you can hide behind that." He points to a suit of armor worthy of Sauron from *The Lord of the Rings*. Massive, covered in spikes, and yet somehow regal.

What is this place? I want to ask, but he's already headed for a door on the other side of the room.

"I will be fine," Sylvan says, looking back at me. "But we can't allow him to see your shadow."

Which to me sounds like alarm bells. This *is* his ex, and this ex will be so jealous he needs to be appeased before seeing me.

In these circumstances though, I have to let Sylvan take the lead. I still wonder about the door though. Sylvan knew some secret buttons to enter, but... how did it happen? Did I not notice when we were outside that he led me to a different entrance? Was I too frantic to pay attention?

I squeeze the wooden handle in my hands as he opens the door, letting in the smell of hot iron. I'm mesmerized when an orange glow deepens the shadows on Sylvan's determined face, but the moment is cut short when a male voice asks, "Who are you? What are you doing here?"

CHAPTER 15

SYLVAN

I hold my head high as I step through the threshold. Built in a circle around the dark shaft of the hearth, the forge has runes and magical symbols carved into the floor and walls. Some of them emit the faintest red glow, and as I enter, inhaling air that's hot and sulfuric like dragon breath, the steady tap of metal against metal stops.

My knees feel like marshmallows when I face the tall form of the grimsmith, who regards me from his place at the massive anvil.

"Who are you? What are you doing here?"

I'm struck how very out of place he seems in this elven forge. Tall and broader in the shoulders than a member of my kind ought to be, he reminds me of the old quarry workers who congregate at Best Burger Bonanza every Friday after work. The fire deepens the grooves marking the spots where his skin folds whenever he emotes, and seeing them makes me doubt it's the man I seek in the first place.

"Tassarion?" I ask, keeping my voice steady only thanks to the training a life at the Nocturne Court has given me.

"Who's asking?" the smith says, approaching me in slow steps. His bare chest glistens in the glow of the fire, and I follow a drop of sweat until it reaches his leather kilt. Over his heart, a dark brand marks him as banished. It's the crest of the Nightweeds, a kelpie on a shell in a circle of seaweed.

I meet his dark eyes, mustering all the royal dignity I've been taught to carry myself with. "I am Prince Sylvan Goldweed." I recoil when he pushes back some of his dark hair and I get a glimpse of his ears, cut short where they should become pointy. A symbol of his banishment being permanent.

How barbaric.

"Ah, the one sent here to grow old and stale, just like me?" Tassarion asks as an ugly grin stretches his lips. I struggle to keep my eyes on him. I have seen plenty of humans with wrinkles, but they look so unnatural on an elven face it makes my blood pump faster. Is *this* the future Lord Kyran wants for me?

"I have so much sympathy for your plight. It has only been two months for me in the human realm, and I already sense it seeping my life force. I cannot begin to fathom what you have been through. I know I'm lucky that my banishment is not meant to be permanent."

Tassarion shakes his head. "I heard all about it. Fifty years. You will be a husk by the time you're allowed to go back. Time doesn't stop just because you're a royal."

I clasp my fingers in front of myself to fight the urge to bite my nails. "That is why I'm here. I need to go back, and I need my shadowcraft. You're the only one who I know of who can take off this collar." I unbutton my shirt to show him the contraption on my neck.

Tassarion steps closer to inspect it. "And why would I do that when I've been left to rot here? Your family has been greatly diminished." From up close I realize he even smells more like a human now, of musk and salty sweat.

I swallow when he slides his fingers under the collar and runs his thumb over the crest etched into it. "You owe my family the favor. I wasn't even born yet when you were banished, so there's nothing I could have possibly done for you, but my mother fought for you. Lord Arsen wanted to execute you for experimenting with Sunlight fire, but thanks to her intervention, you were banished instead."

The grimsmith leans against the wall, but at least he lets go of my collar. "After thirty years here, I'm not sure if that was a favor or a curse," he says bitterly.

"And yet here we are. You are alive, and if you play your hand right with me, you might still have a chance to come back to the Nocturne Court. My mother and I are the only Goldweeds left, and I don't even toy with the illusion that I may fight Lord Kyran for the throne, but I *will* have power at court. I have new means to redeem myself. And when my position's reestablished, I will do what I can to bring you back. Lord Kyran was only a child at the time of your transgression, so it will not be that difficult for him to forgive you once he sees how useful you could be."

Tassarion lets out a raspy laugh. "You? I've heard your talent for shadowcraft is the most insignificant in generations. On top of that, you took part in a plot to assassinate Lord Kyran. He will want nothing to do with you."

I drown the urge to lash out, because I need his help and I'm in no position to fight a man twice my size. Story of my life. Always forced to pull back. "He knows my siblings were most at fault, and as for my talent or lack thereof... I have a plan. Do you not wish to be part of a future in which the son of your tormentor is cut down?" *That* is a fantasy I indulge for his pleasure, because I will get rid of the collar by any means necessary.

The grimsmith rubs his chin, assessing me from head to toe, but then walks over to his tools with a smirk. "I have plans of my own to find my way back to the Nocturne Court, but I do owe your mother a favor, and an enemy of my enemy is my friend. I will have use for a Goldweed ally. Come here, princeling."

I hate how patronizing it sounds. When Hawk calls me that, his voice is filled with affection, but from those parched lips it's nothing short of condescending. But I won't gain anything by expressing this sentiment, so I approach his collection of tools and eye the unfinished dagger resting on the anvil. It's no longer red-hot, but seeing it brings me back to the moment when the damn collar was first closed around my neck. The thought of hot tools once more working so close to my skin has my stomach dropping, but I can't get my life back otherwise. Who wouldn't trade off a moment of fear and discomfort for freedom and a new chance at life?

The tools of Tassarion's trade cast deep shadows on the walls, but both of ours are gray, mine even more faded than the smith's. This mirror of my form has always been a source of great shame, and even the simplest of peasants could easily spot my weakness at a glance.

But that won't matter any longer when I can use what little shadowcraft I possess to bind myself to the hollow darkness of Hawk's shadow. It will make up for everything I lack, and the Nocturne Court will be forced to respect me.

"Sit," Tassarion commands as he pulls several vials out of a cupboard. He might have been here for decades, but unlike me, he was allowed to keep his shadow powers, and jealousy eats at me. I watch him form a long needle out of nothing, then dip it into each of the bottles. He lets the shadow spill onto a set of cutters, and runes marking the tool awake with a blue glow.

I can only imagine what his shadowcraft was like at the peak of his power, before the human realm exuded its crushing force on him.

"Lean your head back," he instructs, and I'm painfully aware of the lack of any pleasantries. He's making a point of not using my title. One day, I will get even for it, but I suppose the life he's been forced to live is punishment enough.

I expose my throat to him.

He snorts with laughter and taps his fingers where the purple sparks bit into my skin. "You were trying to get it off with human means."

"An attempt as good as any," I groan.

"My tools will do the job, but they're old, and like me, not what they used to be. They might scrape you, but that will be much worse if you flinch. Are you sure you wouldn't like to be restrained?" I sense the smirk of satisfaction without even looking at him. And no, I most definitely don't want to be anymore at his mercy than I already am.

"I will manage."

Tassarion shrugs and picks up the glowing cutters. When I sense their hot radiance so close to my skin, my thoughts drift to Hawk, who's still waiting for me in the other room. His distrust still hurts, but if he wants proof, I will be able to deliver it to him the moment the collar is off. I imagine him holding my hand in his overgrown paw, and that reduces the fear coiling in my guts like a snake.

But when metal slides against flesh, burning the side of my neck, I utter a frantic shriek.

I stay still, despite the tears pooling in my eyes and my heart beating out of my chest.

"Just the other side now," Tassarion mutters, and I might be wrong, but I have a feeling he's being careless on purpose. He wants a royal to suffer, and I'm the closest thing he can get.

I don't dare to nod and wait for more pain, watching his lips quirk as the umbrasteel burns my flesh the second time. It's an excruciating sensation, similar to a stab, but I squeeze the armrests, and by the time the collar rolls off me and clatters to the floor, I know it was worth the pain despite the humiliating tears in my eyes.

I'm as free as I can be.

"That wasn't so bad, was it, princeling?" the smith asks, casting a shadow over me as he leans forward.

I'm still catching my breath, exhausted by fear and the tension lingering in my muscles, so I respond by shaking my head and try to focus my gaze on the unnatural face looming above.

Something about it makes me uneasy, but before I can make up my mind as to why, the door slams into the wall, and Hawk barges in, the engraved axe high above his head. "What the fuck are you doing to him, you freak?"

Tassarion grabs a dagger off the side table. "And who in all hells are you, huh?" he snarls but then his tone changes, and he steps a bit closer to my promised. "E-exquisite…" he whispers.

"It's fine, Hawk, I'm fine," I say, even though I'm still a bit dazed by the pain burning the sides of my neck. I don't know what this is about. I just need to rest for a few seconds before we can go on and enter the Nightmare Realm, leaving behind this in-between place.

Tassarion ignores me, so I look up, forcing my eyes open, and my stomach drops when I spot Hawk's long, tar-black shadow. It's almost reaching the smith's feet.

A split second is all it takes for Tassarion to pull a strand of hair-thin shadow from his head. He reaches toward my promised's darkness, luring in one of the threads always pushing out of the edges. He squeezes both in his right fist.

"No!" I scream, stumbling forward, but when the grimsmith opens his palm, his shadow is already one with Hawk's.

I'm breathless as fury rises inside me, scorching every ounce of good will and kindness I ever possessed. How dare this washed-out criminal steal my promised in front of my very eyes, using my moment of weakness against me in a way so perfidious?

I spin my shadow into a lash and send it at the bastard, but after not using shadowcraft in months, it makes barely a ripple.

CHAPTER 16

SYLVAN

It's like watching my future vaporize and disperse into nothingness in front of my very eyes. Hawk's shadow was the only means of earning my way back into Lord Kyran's graces and back to the Nocturne Court. To lose it means being stuck in the human realm until I become a husk of my former self like Tassarion has.

But when Hawk approaches, attempting to stand between me and the dancing shadows, as if he believes himself capable of protecting me from a user of shadowcraft, the fury inside me turns green. Perhaps there are more humans out there, who escaped the River of Souls and have a shadow dark as the depths of Grief Ocean. Perhaps I could tie myself to someone else, but that person would not look at me the way he does, wouldn't be so dependable, patient and loyal. They wouldn't be so ready to place himself between me and danger. And I sincerely doubt their touch would feel as addictive.

I peek out at Tassarion from behind Hawk. "What have you done?" I say through clenched teeth, still in disbelief over what has just happened. "Release him!"

The grimsmith shrugs and wraps his arms on his chest, but his pale shadow remains close to his feet. It's nowhere near as strong as it must have been at the peak of his craft.

"You're a prince of the Nocturne Court. You know the bond is unbreakable."

I step out from behind Hawk and put my hand on the axe to let him know I've got this under control, even though I definitely don't. I must remain confident if I am to deal with this lowlife.

"You're a master of grimsmithery. If someone can break such a bond, it's you." I flatter him in an attempt to sort out this mess.

Tassarion shakes his head with a smug smile. "No one can do that, not even the Lord of the Nocturne Court. I will make much better use of his shadow than you ever could. Besides, look how his shadow calmed down." He points out that the wild tendrils around Hawk's darkness have settled. "It was begging to be taken."

Hawk stares at him, then back at me, lowering the axe as confusion colors his face pink. "Can someone tell me what the fuck is going on here? I'm all for weird kinks, but this is me using my safe word. I feel like I'm in the *Twilight Zone*!"

A low rumble leaves Tassarion's mouth and shadows carry him across the floor, as if he were gliding on one of those mobile walkways I've seen at the mall.

"You shall see today. It's Full Moon in the Nightmare Realm, and I'm willing to break the rules of my banishment to make you my Dark Companion," the smith whispers.

Dark tendrils slide over the walls in a gleeful dance, and Hawk's mouth drops open as he inhales, going tense. "What was in that coffee...? Was it... spiked?"

My heart is hot and cold at the same time. It's not just about the potency of Hawk's shadow anymore. This is an affront to the Goldweed name.

Nobody takes what's mine.

I stand in front of Hawk. "Stay back, he's dangerous," I say because while Tassarion's shadowcraft is diminished by the years he spent in the human realm, neither of us knows the extent of his powers. I'm only glad Hawk isn't his Dark Companion yet, because if he were able to use Hawk's shadow freely, I'd be helpless against him. He would have choked the life of me within seconds, and since I'm banished, he wouldn't even be punished for it.

"I sure am. And I'm not giving up on an opportunity like this." Tassarion extends his fingers to his face. "I will treat you well—"

Hawk leans back as if he were about to be touched by a limb swarming with maggots and slaps the hand away.

That's it.

I lose it. This bastard is not allowed to even *look* at Hawk, let alone speak to him.

I launch myself at Tassarion with a primal screech. I don't care how strong the bond of their shadows is. I will break it.

I have the advantage of the grimsmith not expecting my physical attack, so I pounce at him. He's leaning forward, still surprised by Hawk's rejection, so I target the first thing I can get my teeth on and bite his cheek.

My opponent roars, grabbing at me, as if he couldn't decide whether he wants me off or not. As I cling to him, my shadow is cast on both of theirs. I search for a weakness in their new bond, a place where I can cut it, or some reassurance that the threads are somehow slipping free at least, but there's nothing. They are one. Welded like the fucking collar was on me.

Hawk's no longer mine, and the anguish of that fact makes me clench my jaws until I taste blood.

The smith roars, and when a push doesn't get me off, I feel a dire force pry my jaws open. I let go before any of my teeth can crack, but a punch sends me stumbling to the floor with copper on my tongue and stars spinning around my head, along with the whole room.

Hawk's silhouette is a comforting dark figure, but before I can fully recover, he drops the axe and dashes behind Tassarion, twisting his arms back. "Sylvan! Are you okay?"

Tassarion snarls at Hawk in fury. "I'll teach you how to behave!"

Even his throat is red and the veins on it protrude from under the skin.

I know what to do.

I know how to break their bond.

My shadow gathers over my fingers, and I shape it into razor-sharp claws. I may not have much talent, but I've learned how to make the best of it.

Tassarion's shadows try to grab my foot, but I leap forward and slash his neck without mercy.

Blood splashes onto my face and spills down his bare chest as his dark eyes lose focus. I've gone straight for the jugular, and he's already collapsing. Hawk lets the smith drop into the red puddle. He steps back, staring at me with eyes the size of necropearls, but his shadow grows unruly again, trembling and pulsing as Tassarion dies at our feet. I've never killed anyone with my bare hands before, but I don't regret a thing.

I wipe my face with the sleeve of my shirt and spit out excess blood as the crimson flood reaches the tips of my shoes. All I care about is my promised, and as soon as the thread connecting the stolen shadow to Tassarion snaps, I'm there to snatch it.

"You're a real life psycho twink," Hawk mumbles, watching me, as if he isn't sure if approaching me is the wisest of decisions.

I pull a wooden stool close and stand on it so we are face to face as I kiss him. I stare right into his eyes, and slide my hands to his stubbly cheeks. "No one is taking you away from me. Not him, and not even the Lord of the Nocturne Court."

CHAPTER 17

HAWK

I stumble with relief when the sticky, unfamiliar sensation in my mind disappears. For a moment, I could almost feel the blacksmith's flesh without touching it, and when he told me he would *treat me well*, a sense of nausea overcame my entire body. Now, the intrusive sensation is gone, but I still cannot shake off what I've seen.

Shadows danced over the walls as if they'd been images cast from a projector, but I can't see any device that could have been their source, so how the hell did that happen? I half-expected them to rise off the floor like some freakishly realistic 3D projections and attack the cops, who should definitely have broken into the bar at this point. Then again... how could a space as tall as this forge be hidden inside a random single-story building on the outskirts of Boston? How did I not see the smoke from the massive fireplace, when it has to go *somewhere*?

Sylvan grabs a wooden stool and steps over the fresh corpse, as if killing this stranger caused him no discomfort. When he puts it next to me and climbs on it, I'm too scatter-brained to realize what he's doing until his lips are on mine, sharing the taste of the dead man's blood.

I should be disgusted, or unsettled at least, that this sweet boy has a killer in him, but when he cradles my face and tells me I'm his, I let the moment carry me and roll my tongue against his.

The tips of his... claws dig into my skin, and the very real pain makes me accept the truth. He cut the guy's neck with tar black claws that grew out of his fingers. The shadows moved at their own accord.

Either I'm in the middle of a mental breakdown or he *is* really an elven prince.

He was special to me before, but I see all of him now, and believe the unbelievable.

"Oh, my darling, I'm so sorry," he says when two drops of blood drip down my face. I'm not sure if he cut me accidentally, or if it's the blacksmith's blood, but I'm too high on adrenaline to register pain well. Sylvan pulls back, and I see the claws melt, slide down his hands and then join his shadow, leaving behind just his lovely, if bloodstained, fingers.

I should think he's an absolute psycho and run the other way, but who am I to speak? I've killed people for the man I thought I loved too.

No one has ever wanted me this much, no one's ever chosen *me*, fought for *me*.

No one but this tiny cutie who has to stand on a chair to kiss me.

"This is... real," I mumble, settling my hands on his hips as my gaze wanders over the massive hearth, the rune-covered walls, and the pointy ear, which doesn't bear a trace of surgical scars. "The world of the elves, are we in it already? Is that why the cops didn't follow us?"

He strokes my hair with so much tenderness I want to both cuddle him and fuck him like a maniac. I've never felt so wanted.

"I told you it's real," Sylvan says and kisses me again, without a hint of resentment for my lack of trust. "The house is protected by a powerful illusion, so the police can't enter, we are safe. But we're not in the Nightmare Realm just yet. We will go there soon though. And since the bastard did take off my collar, I can bind your shadow to mine, as I promised." When he raises his hand in an elegant gesture, I'm not imagining things, a dark thread rises from his shadow and wraps around his finger.

I blink, then pinch myself, but the image doesn't disappear, defying everything I know about the world and its physics. "Holy hell... you're a magician."

Sylvan's smile is sweet despite the bloodstains on his face. "Of sorts." He gives me a dreamy look from under pale eyelashes as he pulls another thread, this time from my shadow, into his hand. "It's called shadowcraft, and I might not have much talent for it, but with your shadow tied to mine, my power will be so much greater. He tried to take you from me. But I'd rather die than let that happen." He twists the two threads in his fingers into a tidy bow, then squeezes it.

When he opens his hand, they form a single, uniform thread connecting our shadows. I'm flooded by a sense of warm anticipation so very unlike the repulsive shackles of my brief connection with the smith.

I swallow, pulling Sylvan close, until I can sense his heartbeat where our chests touch. My head is spinning a bit as the scenery blurs around his serene features. "But I didn't agree. How could he just...do that? I thought it needed to be mutual.

Sylvan kisses me again, and his arms cradle my head as we embrace. "Your shadow is so potent. I think it's because of your near-to-death experiences. But it's also vulnerable. I don't know why, but only the shadows of those drowning in the River of Souls are like that——desperate to attach themselves. Yet I found you in the human realm, in my path. Any shadow-wielder can bind a shadow like yours to theirs, and your consent would have been irrelevant. The bond can only be made with one human, and it cannot be broken. Other than by death.

"Your precious shadow on the other hand can only be used once you become a Dark Companion, and for that to happen, you will need to make a vow. It cannot be forced, though I have heard stories of lies and coercion. Even stories of a shadow-wielder killing the person they bound to them when the human wouldn't comply under any circumstances. That will not be our case though, will it?"

Sylvan's voice is sweet in my ear, as if we were in bed already, whispering filthy promises. "I will take you to the Nightmare Realm, and under the cover of my shadow, you will vow to be mine as the full moon gazes upon us. Body, soul, and shadow. And as promised, my body will be yours." He backs out enough to look into my eyes with such softness, I can't believe he's a killer even though a body is at our feet. "But in truth, Hawk, you already have my heart as well."

He's such a temptation. A never-ending sundae with fruit, whipped cream, and copious lashings of sauce. I can barely think when he's stroking me, peering deep into my eyes, making such sweet promises.

Nobody ever wanted me like this, mutually and without shame. For good.

It's addictive, and when I slide my hands down his body, taking hold of his ass, he whimpers in excitement.

"Are you saying I can just have this? Escape the law, and then live forever married to a prince?" rolls out of my mouth as I push my nose into his fine dew-scented hair. Now I know why he always smells so gloriously. He is not of my world.

I love the way his breath quickens. "You can have *everything*. Is it so bad that I don't want to wait until you're my Dark Companion?" His whisper is raspy, but it's his words that throw gasoline over the fire inside me. "Some say that it shouldn't be done. That it's coercive…"

He's so precious.

"I only want you if you want me, my prince. But I don't think it's a secret I'm daydreaming about your body," I tell him and knead his buttocks.

Sylvan nuzzles my cheek. "I don't want you. I *need* you. I need to know what it's like to be under you, to please you, to be a vessel for you." His voice trembles at the end in a tone that awakens my most feral instincts.

He might be powerful, magical, and a prince, but he's a little shy about the things he wants from me, and that only turns me on more.

"You literally murdered a guy for me. That's commitment," I rasp and slide my finger up and down his crack, pushing on the fabric to tickle his hole through it. He's so responsive.

Sylvan shivers and bends his spine when he pushes his hips back, and I nip his upper lip, captivated by the ecstasy painted over his features. "You want to be my 'vessel', huh? That can be arranged, pretty thing." No rubbers it is then.

"Now?" he asks, kissing my neck.

The mix of needy and vulnerable is intoxicating. Just like when I first saw him and couldn't look away, couldn't leave despite it being such a stupid thing to do while on the run from the law.

But now I can have him, and arousal dances in my veins when I slide my hands down his thighs, feeling them as I kiss my way along his jaw. I intend to savor this. "'Now' what?" I tease and lick the side of his face, making him moan. "What do you want from me, princeling?" I'm pretty sure I know, but I want him to say it. I want to see him blushing when he admits he wants my cock.

Sylvan squeezes me tighter, and now that I know he really is a prince, I wonder how he got here. Not why he got banished, that can wait, but how did he get to be twenty-five and a hapless virgin when he's so adorably fuckable.

"I want you on top of me," he says, hiding his face in the crook of my neck.

I spit on my fingers and grab his jaw with my other hand as they dive into the back of his pants, headed to the center of his heat. I remember rubbing my cum into his hole, but now I'll do much more than that.

His eyes roll back when my damp fingertips slide over wrinkled flesh, and I lick across his open lips still stained with blood. I want him to lose himself. I want him to scream, twist, and arch in my arms until he's so pumped out I'll have to carry him wherever we're going next.

"Are you too embarrassed to ask for the things you want? For my cock diving deep into your needy hole?" I ask, making him tremble with my words.

"It's... I shouldn't ask for that. I should be the one in control. But I don't want to," his voice turns into a whimper when I press my finger against his opening. My dick will fit so snugly in there. The only one he'll ever have, because there's no way I'm ever letting go of this gem, not when he wants to keep me for good.

"What would all the other royals think if they knew you want to be fucked like this and filled with cum until that's all you can think about," I say, dipping my digit into his opening so rapidly he slides one knee up my hip, begging to be taken away to my den of choice.

I can do that. I'm more than happy to take charge.

The little moan he makes reverberates over my skin like a ripple on a lake and goes straight to my dick. His gentle fingers tighten on my arms, and my mind fills with memories of the previous times we've been together. Of his mouth so full of my dick he had tears in his eyes but wouldn't tap out. Of his pink pucker slathered in my cum and clenching against my fingertip. Sylvan's beautiful face flushed, eyes glazed over, lips trembling when he came.

"Please..." he whispers, shifting his ass against my fingers in a way that makes me imagine him dancing in my lap just as passionately.

I slide my finger out and grab him with both hands. He somehow immediately knows what to do and curls his limbs around me as I stumble forward. I kick away the stool, walk over the smith and head for the open door. A part of me wants to have him on a desk full of tools, which would clatter to the floor while I have my way with him, but this will be his first time, and I want him to be comfortable.

"You might not believe it, but I never fucked a prince before," I hum, kissing him again as he attempts to rub himself against my body.

"First time even for you then." Sylvan nips on my ear.

He's my perfect choice. Not because of his royal blood, but he's what I was always drawn to. Sweet but with spice. A kitten with sharp claws. Fragile, but determined.

Is it a little deranged that I'm impressed by how easily he killed a man? Just for standing in his way? Sure, but it's a testament to how much he wants me, and that's my catnip.

His pretty face and slender body drew me in, but his intensity is what makes me stay.

I put him down on the large leather sofa in the first room, already missing the hardness of his dick against me. I love seeing him from above, it makes me feel even bigger. So small, but freckled with blood, Sylvan makes the loveliest picture, and I can't wait to *ruin* him.

He's already unbuttoning his shirt, and I don't miss the way his eyes stray to the bulge in my pants.

I might take my time preparing him for what's to come, but I will not be patient about seeing him naked. Determined to feed my eyes on his pale flesh, I slide his shoes off, and then grab his pants, tugging them down his legs.

"Oh, I've never been with anyone hotter. That's almost better than being with a prince," I say and drop his clothes on the floor before opening his legs to glance at his stiff cock. It's straining the front of his simple black briefs, begging for my attention.

His gasp goes straight to my balls, and when I look at his parted lips, I wonder if I shouldn't have him suck me first. He was so eager to please me when he did that. And he even said that he doesn't want control. I can most definitely take over.

"Some people say it hurts?" Sylvan says, and the flush on his cheeks would make my dick hard if I wasn't ready to go.

I let out a dark chuckle and lean over him, gorging myself on his clean scent. He might have expressed worry, but when I climb on top of him, he accepts my presence and unfolds for me, begging for attention.

"It can, but I'll get you nice and ready, so you can relax when I take my big hard dick," I say, pulling his hand down my pants, "and push it inside you."

His lip curls, and he takes a deep inhale as he cups my cock. I see the desire pooling in his eyes, glazing them over. This flower wants to be plucked. "I can take it. I think. I want to."

He's adorable as he mindlessly strokes my dick as though he's petting a cat.

"Of course you can, my sweet prince. And I shall use your royal body as often as you want to," I say, shoving my joggers down to reveal his hand stroking my length. My girth makes his elegant fingers appear even more delicate, and I wish to suck on them all. "Or rather, as often as *I* want, because your flesh will be mine. These thighs, stomach, this chest," I continue, moving my palms up his body. "Even these lips," I add, pushing my thumb on his tongue. "Oh yes. I just might use them most. Every day before you attend your royal duties, you'll be leaving with a belly full of my cum."

His eyes grow wider, and when he sucks on my finger, my dick twitches in his grip. He's so pliant. Nothing turns me on more than a gentle beauty like him getting railed and filthy. He's even trying to take his underwear off with one hand, just to not let go of me with the other.

"You want to give it a quick try?" I rasp, leaning toward his face, so he knows what I'm suggesting. I can see lights come on in his irises, and as he nods, trying to pull me close, I climb up and pull his head up by the hair. He opens up, I slide in, and it's fucking glorious.

"Ohh, fuck me, I swear you have the best damn mouth," I mumble, shifting forward to sink my length deeper into that wonderful, velvety channel. "Must be because of all those big, important words you're using. Who would have thought a prince could be such an accomplished cocksucker."

His mouth full of my dick, and I teasingly prod with the tip of my tool on the inside of his cheek. Even his ears have turned pink, and I'm confident he loves the teasing, because he's inching his fingers toward his own cock even though he barely managed to pull his underwear down his thighs. The big blue eyes looking up at me are the picture of innocence, but it's a facade. He wants to be dicked down, and I'm the man for the job.

I love how my pants push on the underside of his chin, trapping him for me as he swallows, lost in his own world, as if anything beyond the space between my thighs ceased to exist.

"I want to see you like this every day, calming yourself down by sucking on my dick. Your tongue was made to lick my balls and gather my cum," I rasp, gently thrusting as our eyes meet.

He's such a stunner. Such an absolute hottie. I can't believe I get to touch him, and he wants to make me his... well whatever the title might be, I'll be important.

He's unsure and experimental in the way he sucks on my cockhead, but oh so enthusiastic. I'm more than happy to be his plaything another time and indulge in the adoration in his eyes, but now that I got the green light, I want to fuck him. I want him moaning my name when he finds out how good it feels to have his prostate stroked. I want to hold his lithe body against me when he comes and feel him shiver, ass pulsing on my dick and milking it.

I chuckle at the disappointment and longing on his face when I pull my cock out of his mouth. I still tease his bottom lip with the tip. "What are you made for?" I ask, stroking his silvery hair.

"F-for licking your cock," he whispers.

I nod. "Damn right. But also for stroking it," I tell him and curl his fingers around my saliva-damp shaft before pushing in and out of his fist with a gleeful grin. "And for taking it up your tight little ass. You want it so much you can't wait a day longer."

Sylvan touches himself absentmindedly, so I stop him with a gesture, because I don't want my virgin boy to blow his load too early. His chest is moving so fast already, his pink nipples like two stiff peaks.

"Is that bad? It's so glorious, I find it hard to think about much else." He leans forward to kiss the tip of my dick, and this time it's me who needs to be out of his soft hand if I want to come deep inside him instead of now.

I laugh and descend his body, kissing his face, his neck, his lovely pale chest. I bite his nipples until he's gasping for air. "It's you who said it's unlawful, or something. But I want it *now*. I want you now. I would have had you in a back alley behind Best Burgers Bonanza if you let me," I whisper as I soothe him with my tongue and find the lube in my pocket. Now, my pants are useless, so I kick them off and continue my journey down, rubbing my stubbly face over creamy flesh.

Sylvan starts gasping when my face gets closer to his cock, but I'm not taking any risks, so I just blow air over his shaft and suck on the flesh of his thigh.

"Please..." he once again moans out that unspecified request and spreads his thighs wider for me. His fingers roam over my shoulders, so I take off my hoodie. I want to *feel* him wherever he decides to touch me.

He's so pale against the dark leather. Like the moon against the night sky.

I will tear this moon down and eat it as if it's a meringue.

"I promise you'll be satisfied or I'll die trying," I tell him and squeeze a large dollop of lube into my hand before grabbing his leg and placing it on my shoulder. Sylvan gasps, watching me as I bend him in half, but then my slick hand touches his opening, and his eyelids flutter as if they were dancing butterflies.

Yeah, I *can* be a poet. Sometimes. Can't help myself with someone as pretty as him.

Other times, I can be a dirty-mouthed fuck, if that's what my boy needs.

"That's one pretty pink hole. You've not even fingered yourself?" I tease as I slide a finger inside him, and oh, how deliciously the muscles tense around me. He's a sight to behold spread open like this. He must have the best ass I've ever seen. A soft, round little peach I loved eating.

"No," he gasps when I fuck him open with my thick finger.

I don't even know where to look because that dick hungry hole is my personal porn, but his face getting redder by the second is worthwhile competition. He's bent in half, ass available to me however I want it.

"But you still know this is what you want, don't you? A man taking control and getting what he's owed? Getting off inside you?" I rasp and watch him nod. "Like you're not a prince but some servant kept for pleasure, available whenever I need to come. Mouth, ass, wherever I like. I might just come over these lovely nipples. What do you think?"

I'm half-lucid with lust when I push another slick finger in and stretch him open. My dick is throbbing with the need to have a go.

Sylvan nods, panting, his cock leaking pre-cum all over his tense stomach. "Yes. I will be yours to use. However you like. I could kneel and open my mouth so you can jerk off into it. It's even fine if you miss. I just want to satisfy you."

He is perfect.

I grin. "Oh, baby boy, I'm gonna give you the ride of your life." He's so compact I can easily reach his cheeks even in this position, and I make him suck my thumb as I rail his ass with my fingers. The moans and whimpers are music to my ears, and I'm getting lost in this strange room filled with the smell of fire and his arousal.

We're kissing, grabbing at each other, and the gentle crackling in the fireplace provides the most otherworldly soundtrack to the insanity of what I'm doing. I never before considered things like marriage, but I want to take him as mine and claim him for good.

I love how pliant his muscles are around my digits, how they stretch when I curl my fingers and roll them at the mouth of Sylvan's hole. My dick is stiffer than it ever was, and it's muddling my mind as I take a whiff of his hot skin before pulling myself to my knees.

He blinks, once again touching his stiff cock, but this time I'm not making him stop. He's been such a good boy.

"I'm going to fill you up now. Focus on it. Focus on how my cock feels inside you, on how much pleasure you're giving me," I tell him, playing on the sexual fantasies he's revealed. I lick sweat off my lips as I spread him open and drizzle more lube over my cock, and then onto his exposed hole. It glistens as I once again rub the clear gel in. But I can't wait anymore and grab my dick, aligning it with the tight ring that will suck me so lovingly.

I pull his ass higher, so I have easier access, and push in with a grunt as I hold on to his trembling thighs. I want to go easy on him, so it's only my cockhead for now, but it takes all my restraint to not go in balls deep. Stars seem to flicker under my eyelids from the desire I feel right now, buried in his sweet ass.

Sylvan's panting, moaning at my every move, his eyes rolling back, hair spread over the leather. I could come from just looking at him. A dream come-fucking-true.

The most gorgeous guy spread open with my dick and moaning, "more…"

His words, whispered with such soft abandon, go right to my head, like a vodka infusion drank straight from the bottle, and I shift my hips to push inside him that bit farther.

"You like that? You like being used by a big, strong man like me?" I ask.

He swallows and bites his lip, meeting my eyes. "I… I like to feel… overpowered," he whispers the last part, but I hear him loud and clear, so my hand trails from over his face, and to his slender neck. It's stained with specks of the smith's blood. My lovely little monster.

I don't squeeze, just let it sit there so he knows I could as I make a hard thrust that makes him cry out.

I come to a standstill, buried almost all the way in his heavenly body, but I don't want this to be painful for him, so I wait, my toes curled and teeth clenched as I fight my instinct to *fuck*, to move my shaft in and out of the tight sleeve of his flesh until I'm spent and my balls run dry.

"I could do this at any time," I whisper, grinning when my words make his dick twitch and release clear liquid onto his stomach when I fold him farther. "You're so much smaller than me. So much weaker…"

His tense muscles ease a little around my cock, so I'm guessing that's his arousal flooding his body. "Yours. All yours," Sylvan moans, and even shifts his ass against me in a needy motion.

He wants me to move, to thrust into him.

I want to do that.

But the position with one of my knees on the floor, the other on this stupidly shallow sofa isn't great for vigorous movement, and *someone* needs to be practical, because he's already half-lucid, grabbing my forearm and stroking the hair on it.

I watch his face when I pull out and it's filled with so much disappointment and confusion I almost let out a chuckle.

"I want you on hands and knees," I murmur, and before he gets the chance to answer, I pull him off the sofa in one swift tug.

CHAPTER 18

SYLVAN

I can't believe the ease with which he carries me off the sofa, but my mind is too fuzzy to think, and I go from the utter shock of him pulling out to the softness of a fur rug in front of the fireplace. I touch my cock, moaning when pleasure sparks inside it and trails down to my empty hole, but then Hawk's kneeling beside me, and he rolls me to my stomach in a single move. Before I can think, he pulls me up to my hands and knees, and shoves my thighs apart.

A low grunt escapes his throat, and I shiver, sensing his gaze on my naked body. I know I'm short, and thin, and my shadowcraft is close to none, but as long as this one man wants to see me like this, touch me, satisfy himself using my body, I'll be happy.

The heat of the flames caresses my side as I stretch like a cat, whimpering when Hawk's heavy palm rests between my shoulder blades, only to trail down, to my hips.

I can't believe I've been waiting for this for so long and needed banishment to find someone who can fill the void inside my heart. And my body.

I moan when his slick cock rolls up and down my crack, but then the head pushes in, once again opening me up. The stretch stings, but it's not nearly as painful as I feared. Perhaps I'm a glutton for punishment, but a part of me relishes in the discomfort, as if it's yet another layer to the overwhelming sensation of that big, wide cock filling me. A price to pay for the pleasure of having it deep inside me.

I may still be new to this, still adjusting, but I couldn't have dreamed of a better lover. Hawk responds to my illicit fantasies, making me comfortable to indulge in them and show him that sexual side of me. For once, I don't have to be guarded and in control.

For him, I'm a pliant body with open legs and an available hole, and I don't question it. I don't overthink.

In this place, I'm even free to moan as loud as I want. There's nobody here to laugh at me for soiling the Goldweed legacy by submitting to someone else, a human at that.

I arch my ass up higher for him, and I've never felt more alive. I lose myself in him, enjoying how he's pushing my body to its limits. On this soft fur, I'm just an animal, indulging in the most primal form of exchange.

He's a beast in human form, and I'm powerless against him.

I whimper and fall forward when he bottoms out, and his balls slam mine. I can't even begin describing the sensation of being taken like this, but as invisible fire dances over my flesh, I writhe and coil, guided by the strange mixture of pain and pleasure unlike anything I ever felt.

My secret dreams, the same ones I've left unspoken for fear of shame befalling my whole family, materialized in the form of a tall, hairy man, who grabs me as if he has every right to it, and fucks me like an animal desperate to plant its seed in a willing mate.

I chose him for his shadow, but right now I'd have given myself to him forever even if he didn't cast any at all.

"Oooh, fuck, wish you could see this, kinky prince," Hawk rasps as his hips slap my buttocks over and over, and his cock slots back in, massaging my pleasure spot. "Your ass jiggles every time I thrust in."

I want to answer, but I'm left speechless when he pulls out altogether and holds my buttocks wide open. It only lasts a moment before he buries himself back in, making me scream when his dick slides against my prostate. "How does something so long even fit inside you? Maybe your hole's magical too?"

He grabs my sides with hands so massive they almost wrap around my waist when he squeezes. "Fuck..." I utter, at a loss. "Fuck..." I never thought sex could feel this intense. I now see my wildest fantasies were like touching through glass. But he not only stimulates my body with his sheer physical force. The things he *says* make me shiver and gasp. I want to be his plaything forever.

"That's how you like it? Exactly what you wanted?" he asks, chuckling, but in a way that seems satisfied rather than condescending as he speeds up, riding me as if he were ready to finish. Oh, how I want him to. But also, I want this to keep going, because the friction of his thrusts makes me feel so incredible inside.

I can't decide, and with raspy moans escaping my chest over and over, I can't bring myself to answer his question. He's entering me like a machine, tirelessly and without an end in sight, but as his hands squeeze my flesh, and a raspy noise tears out of his lips, I know that he's coming.

Heat shoots deep inside me, pulsing in every bit of my body.

I felt the connection to him when I bound our shadows, but now it intensifies. I sense his heartbeat quickening. It throbs like it wants to *reach* me. When we're so close, it seems to beat against mine. Will he feel that too when he becomes my Dark Companion?

For now, all romantic thoughts slip back into the gutter when he lies on top of me. Hawk is so heavy his weight pushes me down. My knees slide apart, and I'm left to take his final thrusts. My ass is sore, but I secretly love it, moaning every time he pushes in, planting his seed.

"So cozy inside you..." he murmurs against the back of my head as he slides his hand under me and grabs my cock. "Feel all that spunk? It's gonna be dripping down your legs." He licks my ear to its very tip.

When he starts jerking me off, I writhe under him, excited by how I can barely move with his whole weight on top. It makes me breathless, as I rock my hips between his hand and jabbing myself on his pulsing dick.

I think of all the cum he's pumping inside me, how I let him use me, manhandle me, overpower me... And then he once more shows me his force when he wraps his massive hand around my neck.

I cry out, coming harder than ever, and when my ass clenches on Hawk's softening cock, it only intensifies my orgasm. I squeeze the soft fur of the rug in my hand, rubbing my face against it to muffle my noises, but it's no use. I moan. Shout. Scream so loudly it leaves my throat raw, and he holds me through it, whispering dirty and sweet words alike.

How I'm his moonlight prince.

How I'm his tight warm cumhole.

Somehow, both seem appropriate.

I don't know if it's the shadow bond or love, but it feels real damn close.

His heartbeat slows, as does his breathing, and he stretches, finally slipping out of my body. But when I expect him to pull away, he grabs me and wrestles me to the rug alongside him.

"Hell yes," he mumbles, cuddling me close.

I settle into his embrace, too tired to fight him. Never before him have I felt so comfortable with another person. I'm not ashamed that he saw me unravel or of the things I told him in the heat of the moment. I rest against him, catching my breath.

I know it's silly, but after having sex with him, I somehow feel more like my own man instead of the family pushover. With a smile, I tune into the heartbeat that resonates within his shadow. I ache a little, but I'm so satisfied.

It's also a relief for my collar to be off, and I revel in access to my shadow. Toying with it is like meeting an old friend. In a moment of goofiness I cannot explain, I form several tendrils, no thicker than fingers, and let them pet Hawk's back.

He stirs, blinking as if he was about to fall asleep, and glances over his shoulder.

"They're not much," I explain, "but you deserve all the cuddles I can give."

How sappy, my inner voice says. *Are you even a Goldweed?*

But is it really so bad to enjoy another person without an ulterior motive? To want to give more than I get?

Hawk stares at me. "That was you? Jeez, I thought a giant spider ran over me," he mumbles and pulls me close to his chest, burying his face in my mane.

"Um... thank you? For, you know."

Why are you so awkward? Why?

I cover my face and take a deep breath, trying to focus on the pleasure still settling in my body instead of picking apart what I've just said.

"For my amazing sexual skills?" he asks, chuckling, and pushes on my forehead to make me look at him.

My face flushes with heat, but I nod. "Yes, that. It seems we are..." What? A good fit? It would hardly explain how I feel about him right now. He seems so relaxed and casual while I scramble to make sense of everything that's happened between us since our first meeting. "Like... I'm a locket only you could open." Sappy. Again. But what if that's what my feelings for him are? All mushy like fermented coralberries. Maybe I have to become at peace with that, and allow him to be my weakness.

Hawk bites his lower lip, grinning. "I definitely seem to have the right key, don't I?" he asks and kisses my forehead before urging me to rest my head on his chest. I've never heard a more beautiful heartbeat than his, and the intimate nature of the gesture settles me a bit.

"But you really shook my world too. So damn pliant, so excitable, so pretty," Hawk says, stroking my bare skin. "You feel okay?"

After a bit of hesitation, I wrap my arm around him and push my face between his furry pecs. "I'm just... a little overwhelmed with everything. But you make me feel safe, like you're where I belong. You not only gave me so much pleasure of the flesh, but also a closeness of the souls unlike anything I have ever known."

Don't cry. Don't cry. Don't cry.

Hawk grins and looks straight at me. "Aw, you're so sweet. But give me time, and I'll do my best to be the knight in shining armor you deserve. You do have knights in that other world, right?"

I snort, cuddled up under his arm. It's like he brought the sunlight with him and I thought I hated it but melted anyway. "We do indeed have knights. Who knows, maybe with how strong and broad you are, you might become one someday." I imagine him as my personal guard, and my stomach flutters with excitement. It's too soon to think so far into the future, I know. Still, I see him at my side at court, and while his size would only emphasize how small I am, I love imagining how impressive he'd be in armor. The first human guard at the Nocturne Court? I'd have to check the history records to make sure that's the case.

Hawk hums and kisses my forehead with a silly smile. "You may call me Sir Hawk."

I can be soft with him, and it's so new I'm still adjusting to it. I let the tendrils of shadow slide over his back, then all the way to his neck and cheek. I don't *feel* his skin through them, but I can sense the touch.

"And are you ready to serve the Goldweed cause?" I kiss his hairy pec with a smile.

Gasping, he nudges the shadow tendrils with his finger, and smiles when they wrap around the digit like a baby's hand. "As long as that doesn't make me the villain. Kinda like the idea of being the good guy for once," he says, winking at me.

I look up at him with my most innocent expression. "Do I look like the 'bad guy'?"

Hawk stalls, his mouth falling open as if he's gotten lost in my eyes. "Damn, I think I would have burned cities to the ground if you looked at me like that," he mumbles and leans forward, pressing his mouth to the little shadow tentacle I created. "You said you were banished? I assume you did something people didn't like."

I groan, pushing one shadow tendril behind his ear to stroke him. "I may have taken part in an assassination plot against our Lord. Though, in fairness, at that point he was still a prince, and my intentions were noble. Me and my family, we considered him a rake, a wastrel, and someone who would doom us all if he gained the position of supreme power. And the plot wasn't even my idea." I had a better one, that would have most likely succeeded, but maybe I don't want Hawk to know that about me just yet. "My involvement wouldn't have been revealed if it wasn't for my sister's diaries. A farce really."

Hawk frowns. "So you, like... committed treason."

"Well, we all make mistakes in life, do we not? I do not wish to kill him anymore. That does have to count for something, right? I reluctantly admit he will make a fine ruler, and all I want is to get back into his good graces so I can return to my rightful position at the Nocturne Court. Now, with a Dark Companion." I kiss him under the collar bone.

Hawk clears his throat, and while I understand his hesitation, he must get on board with my plan or everything will be lost. "And you think he'll just forgive you? Is that possible?"

"I was but a marginal part of my family's plan. And when our cousin got seriously hurt during the assassination attempt, I saved his life. This is why I was banished rather than executed, and not even permanently. I'm sure when the Lord sees us together, me as the master of your shadow, he will see the value of keeping us around."

Clearing his throat, Hawk lets his gaze wander down my chest. "So... what will be my role in this? You connected our shadows. What now?"

I pull on the thread of shadow that connects us and show it to him with a wondrous sigh. "This means you are meant for me. My promised. We're only hours away from the full moon in the Nightmare Realm, so as soon as we're there, we will make our vows, and you will forever become my Dark Companion. Then, I will be able to wield your powerful shadow and not be forever doomed with my own, which is like clouds where yours is obsidian. To say I cannot wait to feel that force within me is an understatement."

Hawk pulls on my knee and moves it to rest on his thigh, entwining us even more completely. Oh, how delightful it is to be wanted this way.

"So it's like a real wedding? And people will know that I'm your Dark Companion? It's not just a secret thing between us?" Hawk asks, nuzzling my cheek. His breath is so warm and comforting, I stretch, enjoying it on my skin.

I let several shadows lock around him like an embrace and stroke the stubble on his face. It's still such a new thing to me. "Um, yes, it is most often called a wedding, and we will be considered married, even though that bond isn't always a romantic one. I do hope ours will be. And you will not be a secret. Once we get to the palace, I will show you off with pride." So everyone can see the kind of shadow the 'shortest elf in the Realm' has taken. No one will laugh at me then.

Hawk's face brightens, and he strokes his stubble, smiling at whatever fantasy his imagination's producing. "I wonder what made it so special. That smith guy also wanted it for himself."

I groan at the memory of Tassarion's hands so close to Hawk. I should have cut them off while he was still alive, but that wouldn't have been reasonable or as easy as slashing the right artery in his throat.

"Scholars disagree on what it is exactly that makes a shadow grow in potency, but there must be a pattern of despair in a person's life for that to happen," I say softly, because this might bring up some terrible memories for Hawk. "And there is always a near-death experience, of which you said you had several. How did that happen?" I don't ask just to study him. I want to be close to him, I want to know everything about him.

He transforms before my eyes. Gone is the easy smile, and his eyes dart to the ceiling as his breathing quickens, only to slow, as if he were trying to calm himself down. "Despair is a strong word. Everyone has bad moments."

I stroke his back and kiss him. "If you tell me how you got so close to death, I will be able to look for patterns." Parts of him are still like a deep ancient forest, impossible to penetrate, but I want to create paths that allow me to understand him better.

Hawk exhales and strokes my back, but his eyes remain fixed on the wooden beams above, as if he didn't trust himself to meet my gaze. "You've met my family. They're all about kids, and living simply. I was confused when it turned out I liked boys. Our little community started feeling more and more like a prison after that. So I got into fights a lot, and one time I almost died when one of my older cousins tried to teach me a lesson by choking me.

"When I woke up, it was clear I might not have survived, so I decided to go out and look for what I wanted. I went to a normal school and met boys like me. I was already big and strong at the time, so people quickly learned not to bother me about being gay. And I was real popular, invited to parties and that kind of stuff. And at one of those parties I ended up taking drugs, but I didn't know what I was doing and took too much. Almost died again."

So he was the outcast of *his* family as well, just like I was the black sheep of mine.

I sense that closeness of souls again, the conviction that I'm not alone in this universe of many realms. And that I can take away his sorrow too. I want him to drown in me and stay submerged for as long as his heartache lasts.

"The way I see it, I had a fairly average life. The world is hard on everyone, sometimes because you lack something, sometimes because you're different. But I kept trying to find my own happiness, independent from my family. It didn't work out well, as you know," Hawk adds with a bitter chuckle. "Next brush with death? I wanted to show off for my then-boyfriend and did a backflip while standing on a tree branch. I thought I'd just land or grab onto the branch instead of falling, but I did fall on my head. It's a miracle I'm alive. Then, I ran from the cops, just before my arrest. It was a crazy chase, but I felt so betrayed by my now-ex that it didn't seem to matter if I died. But I didn't. I crashed and had a few broken bones, but all is now healed.

"And the last time was two months back, give or take. Another inmate tried to kill me. Apparently, it's a miracle I survived that. They have no idea how. Maybe I'm secretly a cat and still have five lives left? Unless we count the accident of the prison van, then that's four to go," he adds, stretching his tense back in an effort to appear casual about something that's so clearly difficult for him. He finally meets my gaze and shows me a pale scar on his abdomen. "See? Already all healed up. It's weird."

"Why did he try to kill you?" I ask, trailing my fingers over the scar to see if there's anything unusual about it. Hawk has many prominent marks on his body, and I hope not a single one is ever added.

He shrugs and swirls his fingertips along my spine. "We never liked each other, and I made a joke he took real personally. He got my cellmate to lead me someplace private and attacked me when I was about to get a hand job. Kinda stung being betrayed like that. I always stood by the guy, but clearly he didn't like me back the same way. Or was just offered something more valuable than my life," he adds with such bitterness in his voice, a drop of it could spoil a whole barrel of cherin.

There's definitely a pattern I'm seeing about betrayal, and I can only hope he will give me his trust regardless. "Did you... love him?"

Hawk swallows. "I wouldn't have killed for my ex if I *didn't* love him. As for the guy in prison... not sure if it can be called being in love, but it sure was as close as I could get to it in that place. I trusted him."

"I killed for you. Do you trust me?" I look into his soulful green eyes, worried that I might be coming off as needy, something my mother could always spot and prod at.

Hawk smirks. "I think you killed the smith both for me and yourself, but it's a good start. Do you think—" He stalls, swallowing as I process the burn of his first comment. "Do you think you *could* love me?"

It's like being struck by an arrow dipped in a blend of illegal love potions. It's him who sounds needy, and he's just as embarrassed about it as I am about my desire for affection. All at once, I *know* how wrong my mother has been to scold me for wishing someone would always have my back, because I would never fault him for wanting my love. And if *he* deserves that, why would I not? If I don't see that as a weakness in him, why would it be a flaw in anyone else?

My heart beats so fast when I press my lips to his and let emotion take over instead of logic. "Would you believe me if I said I already do?" I whisper, drowning in his eyes. If this is how I feel, why should I hide it? I already trust him more than I do my family.

When his eyes brighten, filling with stars, I know it was the right thing to say.

"You do? Really?" he asks, rolling us over, so I'm flat on the furs, and he's on top of me, stroking my cheek with tenderness someone with hands as big and calloused as his shouldn't be capable of. He presses his forehead to mine and exhales, as if I've offered him the relief of fresh water after days of being stranded at sea.

"I'd kill for you even if it wasn't to my benefit. I give you my body in the most intimate ways, and I adore yours. I care deeply for your feelings, and I want to bring you joy. I'm jealous of every man you've been with, and I'm itching to make you mine forever. If that's not love, what is?" I run my hands down his sides, half-lucid with how much I treasure him. Can he feel how fast my heart is beating?

Hawk smiles. This time it's not a grin, but a wide, honest expression of utter joy. "Nobody's ever said it to me like that. You don't know what you've just done, handsome prince from the Nightmare Realm," he whispers and holds my wrists down as his smile turns predatory. "Because now you're mine, and I'll make sure you don't even look at another man again."

The buzz inside makes me breathless. I love being at his mercy, tiny under the weight of his massive body, because I know he won't actually hurt me.

"For you, I would wade into the River of Souls, even though you would have surely drowned me. But I would see those tattooed arms, a glimpse of your green eyes, and there would have been no other for me."

Hawk strokes my face and gives me another kiss. "That's so strange, but I think I dreamed about... a girl version of you when I was bleeding out after that lowlife cut me open. I was drowning, trapped in black water with so many other people, and then this one person grabbed my hand from the shore. Hair like yours, but longer," he says, smelling it as frost spreads over my heart. "With her help, I climbed out as other people grabbed her legs and dragged her under the waves. And then I finally woke up."

It's all falling into place as I stroke him with trembling fingers. He *was* in the River of Souls. And he *has* been pulled out of it when he should have died.

"A-and... when was that, remind me?"

"About two months ago," Hawk informs me before resting on top of me with a yawn.

"Did you see her eyes?"

"Sapphires like yours. Destiny, as you said."

My heart sinks because I cannot fight the realization any longer.

My sister.

He drowned my sister.

CHAPTER 19

HAWK

Something's wrong, and no amount of sweet and salty pretzels or juice can change that. I stuff more in my mouth and rub the smith's towel over my still-damp neck as I watch Sylvan carry a wooden crate out of a little room containing all kinds of strange and fantastical things, but also perfectly normal items, like the vacuum cleaner tucked into the corner. He places it on the massive wooden bed and pops open the lid, revealing several old-timey vials of pale blue glass.

I want to say something, tell him how cute he is with damp bangs falling into his eyes, but to say that the atmosphere changed since he left me to take a shower is to say nothing.

Is he rethinking his choice to sleep with me? He sang my praises right after, so I don't think it can be that.

His excuse for not wanting to cuddle more or eat together is that he's busy attempting to find a way to dispose of the blacksmith's body. While I'm impressed by the hands-on attitude, I do wish he could at least delegate some work to me, because I'm starting to feel useless. I don't like to be idle when my boyfriend, or should I say, *fiancé*, is dragging around heavy crates.

He's also distracting me by not wearing a shirt, but that's another story.

At least I have some time to look around this in-between place that is supposed to lead us to the Nightmare Realm.

"So, what are we looking for?" I ask as he grunts, shakes the crate, and then returns to the storage room. Just like the other interiors in this strange home, the bedroom is like something I'd expect to see in a fairy-tale illustration. The headboard is a lattice of iron, and the floor—stone slabs covered with a faded rug featuring knights fighting a massive black reptile with sharp teeth and two heads. It too doesn't have a window, but at least there's a somewhat normal bathroom attached to it. After seeing the rest of the apartment, I was afraid we'd need to heat water by the fire and wash ourselves in a bucket, so seeing a tub with a faucet similar to what I'm used to was a relief.

"As a grimsmith, he not only operated in metals, but used alchemy to enhance them, or infuse them with charms. That's how the smith at the Nocturne Court made the collar that bound me. The various potions, powders, sands and oils can be combined to create the concoction that will dispose of his body. Technically, there is no particular law against killing him, but we don't want to be caught in the crosshairs of whatever business he was involved in, or attached to this if someone comes looking for him."

Looks like Sylvan is much more talkative when it comes to practical matters. I already helped him move the body into a metal tub, but when I glance at it again, I do notice something odd.

"Oh. That brand he had, you know, with the pony, it's faded." It was black like a fresh tattoo, but now only a faded scar is left, as if the ink has evaporated from the corpse.

"A kelpie."

"What?"

Sylvan pushes some hair off his forehead and looks up at me. He's so serious I can hardly believe he's the same guy who moaned and cried out under me just an hour ago, drooling all over the rug.

"A kelpie. It's a monstrous steed which tempts unfortunates to pet it. Once your skin sticks to their coat, they force you back into the ocean where they drown and eat you. In the sea, its hind legs transform into a fish tail."

"So like a merhorse?" I ask, grinning at him, and approach to offer my assistance when he climbs onto a stool to grab a large crate from the top of the pile in the back of the storage space. He still can't reach it.

He frowns at me, and I worry we'll be having the 'ask-for-help' conversation again, but he huffs, rubs his face, and gestures at the crate.

"Yes, I suppose like a 'merhorse'. The point is that the brand would have alerted the Lord of the Nocturne Court if he crossed into the Nightmare Realm, but since he's dead, the magic has faded as well. Fortunately, the brand I had was on my collar, so we should have time to get to the palace on our terms. I know of several secret entryways."

I place the crate on the floor, but then approach him and slide my arms around his waist before burying my face in his nape. Whatever's bugging him, it's high time to put an end to it. "Are you this smart, or is alchemy common knowledge where you're from and dissolving a body is as easy as boiling an egg?"

He stiffens as if he wasn't a marshmallow in my arms before.

"I... hmm... I am, in fact, *very* smart," Sylvan says, making me chuckle and kiss his head. "I know I may have seemed incompetent to you at times because of my lack of knowledge when it comes to the human realm, but I assure you I am highly educated. In fact, I know more about alchemy and specialist ingredients than most scholars at the Nocturne Court."

"Really? Why?" I ask, greedy for more information, but he twists out of my embrace and steps off the stool, popping open the crate. Inside are leather bags the size of a pound of sugar, and I reach for one, curious what they are.

"What do you mean 'why'? It's important to get any advantage you can over your opponents. And don't touch that before I read the label and tell you it's safe!" Sylvan slaps my hand away, and the rejection is much more hurtful than any physical pain he can cause. He takes a deep breath. "In fact, could you please wait outside this room? I need to focus."

I open my mouth, wanting to protest and tell him that he isn't being fair, but I know from experience that nothing good ever comes from pushing another guy into a conversation when he isn't in the mood. Still, it stings to be pushed away right after the amazing fuck we shared, and a conversation where I gave up on all posturing and told him how I felt.

I've often been told that I get too intense too fast, and that it pushes guys away, but I couldn't help myself after he pretty much confessed that he loves me.

Come to think of it, his demeanor rapidly changed after he decided to shower, and *that* was right after I told him the stupid dream I had. Was he upset by something about it? Should I have lied and claimed I saw *him* in my dream, not just someone with similar features?

I was only honest with the guy who claims he wants to get hitched within the next twenty-four hours.

I'm about to say all that and many other things, but I watch him browsing the labels with focus all over his face and decide against it. I retreat like a scolded dog.

I hate that he has so much power over me.

And yet, all I still want is to prove to him that I can be useful for more than my shadow and dick. I can help him find more ingredients and bring them to him, I can rummage through the smith's place and find who knows what.

I go back to the living room and glance at the unfinished letter, in case it contains some information important to us, but it's all cryptic bullshit addressed to *Lord Kyran's eyes only* about him having something *of importance*, and that he *will negotiate* only with the Lord himself.

Sadly, the letter is unfinished, and since Tassarion's body is stuck in a tub, it never will be, so this plan he had is as dead as him.

I rummage in the living room and find some trinkets in a small box hidden inside a suit of armor. I hate myself a little for thinking one of the dark rings studded with what might be precious gems would fit Sylvan's dainty finger, but I still take it.

I grab a sturdy silver sword off the wall, in case I'll need it where we're going, but as I head to the forge, I glance back at the window through which I can still see my world. The only world I know. Am I ready to leave it behind?

I might be going to a place with no plumbing, internet, or modern medicine. On the other hand, I would no longer need to worry about the cops dragging me back to prison, and could spend my days satisfying a very hot twink and lazing around in a palace.

Though right now, I feel that my boy might just resent me for reasons I don't understand. Which is a load of bullshit.

I kick the pretty cabinet standing by the nearby wall, and stall when something inside it clicks. Frowning, I look it over before getting to my knees to see... a box. It must have fallen out of some secret compartment when the position of the dresser changed.

There's nothing unusual about the box, other than it being the size of a microwave and made of rough, undecorated iron, but as I open it, my jaw drops at the sight of a mask shaped like a wolf skull.

It's made of gold or some other metal very similar to it. I'm no specialist, and it does have an iridescent sheen to it like nothing I've ever seen. Its eyes are two smooth black stones, and the sharp teeth are carved out of some kind of crystal. From the part at the very top, several thin rods made out of the same metal as the mask stick out.

I know *exactly* what to do with it.

The other items I gathered lie forgotten as I rise to my feet and tiptoe back to the bedroom with the precious mask in hand. I'm greeted by a clatter of glass containers when Sylvan whispers in annoyance and pulls a bottle out of yet another crate. But as he puts it down, no longer holding anything breakable, I put the mask on and growl as loudly as I can.

With the stones set in the fake skull's eyes, I can't see the effect my prank is having, but I grin to myself, imagining Sylvan's eyes widen, and his mouth opening up, as if he were about to beg for dick.

He yelps, and his feet tap my way. "Take it off!"

My heart drops from the tower of hope right back to the dungeon, and I let myself release the disappointment of it with a long exhale before pulling off the mask. "What did I do *now*?"

But his face is flushed and attentive. "No, no... Nothing like that," he says, growing breathless as he takes it out of my hands. "Where did you find it? Do you know what this is?"

I don't, but he looks so excited, I'd love to bring him five more.

"It fell out of a cabinet. What is it?"

He turns it over in his hand, runs his fingers over the smooth surface. "Hawk... This is the Sunwolf Crown. He must have been the one to steal it from that New York museum. This... this changes everything." Sylvan stares up at me with eyes glistening a bit more than usual, but then gets to his toes and kisses me. It's like soothing balm on a sunburn. "I'm sorry I've been absentminded. And I'm sorry for yelling at you. Putting it on could have been dangerous for you, but fortunately it seems that's only the case if you do it in the Nightmare Realm."

I swallow and stare at the strange mask with a shiver running down my body. "Dangerous for me how?"

Sylvan runs his fingers through his hair. "Whoever puts this on, will become the Sunwolf. This artifact is ancient and was lost to our realm over five hundred years ago after the killing of the first Lord of the Nocturne Court during what was called the Night of the Bloodknife. This is what I wanted to look for in the city of New York. You see, it was thanks to this very artifact that Lord Larkin Nightweed was able to stay in power for hundreds of years. We don't know how it was forged, or by whom, but he had it created for his favorite son. The mask took away the prince's talent for shadowcraft and turned him into a creature that was half-beast, half-elven, the Sunwolf. The metal is infused with the power of Sunlight, and when the crown merged with him, he gained the ability to devour shadowcraft and even shadow itself.

"It might seem inconsequential to you, but that power terrorized all of Lord Larkin's descendants, in every branch of the family. The Sunwolf was able to strip shadow-wielders of their craft, and the threat of its power hung over the whole court like an axe. In the end, the princes and princesses decided to overthrow the Lord, but the Sunwolf needed to be dealt with first. There are many accounts of how it happened, though most claim the mask had to be cut from his face. But after the Night of the Bloodknife, the Sunwolf Crown was gone. Never to be seen again, until now. Someone must have felt it was too valuable to destroy, so they just hid it in the human realm."

My face heats. "There's a letter in the living room, addressed to that Lord Kyran you keep mentioning too. You think he wanted to sell him the mask?"

Sylvan runs his fingers over the golden rays at the top with a smirk. "I recall him saying he had 'plans' to end his banishment. This is what he must have meant. If he presented the Sunwolf Crown to Lord Kyran, it would have been a great service to the Nocturne Court. Perhaps he hoped my cousin would end his banishment."

Sylvan glances toward the bathtub where we placed the grimsmith's corpse, and as the green light of the torches colors his cheeks, I have to say he looks a little... evil. Okay, maybe *sinister* would be a better word for it, and while I don't hate it, I'd rather his anger never turned on me.

I think back to all the ways Sylvan brushed me off in the past hour, and as I watch him turn the mask in his hands, I finally voice my question. "Is there a problem? Between us? You've been all strange since we fucked. Hope you're not planning to get rid of me now that I found this for you. I've been close to death so many times, I'm not just letting anyone bleed me out, even you," I add, laughing despite not feeling amused at all.

I hate uncertainty. I hate rejection. And most of all, I hate feeling disposable.

What if I was being naive *again*? What if he wrapped me around his finger because he needs me to make the Dark Companion vow? He did say I have to *"mean it"* for the magic to work.

Sylvan puts the mask on the bed, then meets my gaze and grabs my hand. He has such dainty fingers my toes curl at their touch. "I would never do that. I'm sorry you felt neglected. I'm not... I'm not used to being open with my thoughts, so I tend to mull over them myself when something bothers me."

I exhale and sit on the mattress, pulling him straight into my lap, because this boy cannot resist being in my arms like this, and I know it. Just seeing his cheeks flush makes me a bit calmer. "But what changed? I want to give you what you need, but I can't do that if I don't know what's wrong," I insist before stroking the side of his ass. "Are you sore? Is that it?"

I see him blushing right before he hides his face against my neck, ear twitching against my chin. "No! I mean... a little, but that's not it. I worked out why your shadow was open to bonding when we first met." He takes a deep breath. "The dream you described was not actually a dream. You've been in the River of Souls and made it out alive. You met my sister. And it's not your fault she's no longer with us. Any soul trapped in the current will fight to escape, which is why attempting to find one's Dark Companion in its waters is extremely dangerous. In her hubris, she decided to reach for the most potent shadow she could find. But then you drowned her," he finishes grimly. "Was it destiny? For you to find me after that?"

I lean back as if he's slapped me with an icy hand. Air escapes my lungs as I take him in, shocked by this revelation and unsure what to say. No wonder he doesn't know what to do about me after finding out that the guy who just rearranged his insides is at fault for the death of his sibling. I'm not close with my own family, but in his shoes, I would be upset as fuck.

"Shit, I'm... so sorry."

"I've been grappling with it for over an hour and getting nowhere." When Sylvan wraps his arms around my neck, I feel needed again. "I can't decide how I feel. If I'm secretly glad she never got you, does that make me a terrible person? But what bothers me most of all is that I thought that for once I achieved something on my own. Now I found out that my sister primed you for this bond? It's hard to stomach."

Air gets trapped in my throat as I shake my head. "Were you two... not close?" I ask, even though I've already seen how unwilling he is to accept assistance. The thing I truly care about though is that he values my presence more than hers.

"I told you my family was a den of vipers, but that hardly scratches the surface. All my siblings were cruel to me, but Elodie? She found a way to fuck me over even in death. If it wasn't for her diaries, I would have never been banished. No one would have been able to prove my involvement in the assassination attempt. She hid them in shadows that dispersed when she died. Un-fucking-believable." Sylvan takes a deep breath that tickles my neck. "But even when we fought behind closed doors, us Goldweeds stuck together. I supported my older brother in his attempts for the throne because I hoped then I'd have a sliver of their respect."

I swallow, focusing on the mature, somber expression settling on Sylvan's face. He had the elongated ears and unusually pretty features all this time, but it is only now that I sense how different he is from any other man I've known. "Why didn't they respect you? You were their sibling."

"I'm not well liked, Hawk. My family values power, and I don't have it. It's only fair you know that before you vow your shadow to me." He makes a little whimper that prompts me to stroke his hair, my own frustrations forgotten. "I'm no master of confrontation, I'm an awful duelist, terrible at flirting, shorter than most elven ladies, and my shadow is so frail that sometimes I wished it gone altogether. So I turned to books and alchemy in an attempt to make up for the lack in all other matters. I hoped that if I could prove myself useful, that if I could fight the monster of Grief Ocean, or invent an ingenious weapon, I'd finally be worth something."

I feel sad for him, and even though I don't have the knowledge to reassure him, I slide my arms around his form and hold him, offering my warmth. "Can I duel *for you*? Not everyone needs to be good at everything, right? For example, I make the worst coffee. It's always either too strong or too weak."

When he chuckles, his smile turns brighter than the golden mask next to us. "That's your only flaw? Bad coffee?"

I want to be his rock, the one he turns to when the world crumbles around him. And I want to make sure he remains safe when he's under my protection.

"I wish," I admit and cuddle him closer, gently rocking him in my arms as the unpleasant rift between us closes. "But I'm not going to make this so easy on you. Whatever flaws I have, you need to discover them for yourself."

He leans back to look into my eyes and strokes my cheek. "Well, we already know you're too attractive for your own good."

I laugh and tap his nose. "It's serving me well right now."

"Do you want to dissolve the body with me?" Sylvan asks, offering me a shy smile. "I've found the right ingredients."

Is it morbid? Sure. But it feels like being invited into his world. "I'd be honored."

CHAPTER 20

SYLVAN

Hawk rearranges Tassarion in the bathtub and pushes his hand under the water's surface. In the past, I've often worked with assistants, but this feels different. I *want* him to be here with me, even if some things would have been easier to deal with on my own.

"This one won't dissolve the body, but it will prepare the water so it's receptive to the next ingredient," I tell my lover and hesitate when I open the vial filled with purple powder. "Do you... want to do it?"

Hawk's eyes glint, and he nods, grinning at me. "And this won't hurt our skin? Don't we need gloves, or something? I know nothing about this *Breaking Bad* shit."

I shake my head and pass him the vial. "Not this one. The residue won't be a problem unless we're submerged in a large quantity of liquid. We will, however, need to be careful with redpoles," I tell him, nodding toward the jar on a nearby shelf.

"And you just know all this by heart?" He asks with amazement and spills the Doe Dust into the tub. The tiny grains melt as they meet the water, making it shimmer with a yellowish hue, which brightens Tassarion's slack features. I always thought this effect was very aesthetically pleasing.

Hawk looks at me with so much adoration my heart beats faster. Alchemy is a difficult skill to master, dangerous in the wrong hands, and contributes to so many conveniences my world depends on for survival, yet it is seen as a lesser art, something anyone could master with enough effort. It only now occurs to me that I've never been praised for knowing my way around concoctions and solutions before. It was scoffed at as a way to go around my lack of talent for shadowcraft. "Well... yes. I spent a lot of time learning about all and any ingredients, their uses, and how they interact with each other. You don't need talent for that, just time and a good memory. Now, step back."

I grab one of the massive leather gloves I found in the forge and use it to pick up the next jar. "These are live redpoles." I show him the finger-sized creatures floating in the concoction that keeps them in suspended animation. "They're asleep, but they will awake when they sense blood, and become voracious. They eventually grow into lovely frogs. It takes them about a month." I worry I'm boring him, but when he leans in with a glint in his eye, I continue. "I kept one as a pet a long time ago."

Hawk grins. "That's awesome! I always liked frogs. They taste good too!" he says but obediently takes a step back as I unscrew the jar. "You're a real brainiac, aren't you? If I were your lord cousin, I would have kept you imprisoned in some tower. Sending you out here is such a waste of the skills you have."

I blush when he tickles me between the shoulder blades. "Thank you. I know that for you all this is new and different, like electricity and phones are to me. You'd probably find even something as simple as swamplight impressive, but I won't deny that coming up with the combination of ingredients I'm using now required thought and ingenuity." I drop the redpoles into the bathtub one by one. "I do have a lot to offer, and once I have access to your shadow, my power will be multiplied so many times that my cousin will have to respect me."

When the critters dive underwater to start their ferocious dance, Hawk steps behind me and kisses the top of my head. "Plenty of things are normal in my world—building space ships, chemistry, and so on—but if I tried my hand at any of that stuff, I'd probably lose all my limbs on day one. It's hot that you're so confident in your skills," he whispers as the tub fills with red foam. "And that you're fine with everything that happened here. I've never dated any guy who wouldn't have freaked out over so much blood."

I lean back against him, calmed by his size, his sturdiness. It's like resting against a statue made of flesh. "I guess I've always had an interest in learning how things work and was excited when I could find unusual connections between them. I see no reason to be scared of a corpse. He was much more frightening when he still breathed."

"You have *that* right. My aunt's husband beat her. She tried to hide it at first, but when my father and uncle found out, they went to have a talk with him. I don't know what their real plan was, but by the end of the night he was found dead just off his porch. Twisted his neck as he 'fell'. Apparently. He didn't seem so scary when he lay cold, with flies coming in and out of his mouth."

I put away the empty jar and remove the gloves. When the contents of the tub rise beyond its brim and overflow, Hawk picks me up and steps away, making sure I'm safe.

"There's nothing wrong with righteous violence. I've witnessed my first execution at seven, but I've not killed anyone before tonight," I confess and turn in his embrace. "I wouldn't say the act of taking his life made me happy, but I've never been more furious. So much was taken from me over the years, be it by my siblings or by circumstance. You? I will not allow anyone to take you from me," I tell him with sparks spreading through my body. I cannot bear the thought of someone else having his shadow, having *him*—

"Never had anyone fight like that for me either. Is it a bit psycho that I'm getting hard just thinking about you calling me your man and cutting his throat?" Hawk mutters, carrying me out of the bathroom. He leans in, and as his hot breath tickles my ear, I barely contain a soft moan.

Oh no. I'm *very* new to pleasures of the flesh, but I fear I recognize the excitement building inside me at his touch. "Oh. I... I am flattered. But we do need to go. I would like to be in the Nightmare Realm by the time the moon rises."

I'm relieved when he puts me back down, but then his hand pulls mine to the hard bulge at the front of his pants, and I know we're not done negotiating. "I'm not sure if I'll be able to focus like this," Hawk tries, but his wide smile reveals he's joking.

Which I'm not used to. The games of my siblings were cruel when they involved me, so I've not developed a playful nature. My friendly human co-worker at BBB has taught me that not every interaction must be a verbal duel, but I still struggle to navigate the idea that this man *likes* me and wouldn't hurt me just to get the result he wants.

It's so hard to pull my hand away from Hawk's stiffening cock when I do want to pull down his soft pants and suck it. But that could devolve into hours of lost time. We don't have those.

"And I won't be able to focus until you're my Dark Companion. Would you like to keep one of the redpoles?" I ask to distract him. "Now that it's fed, it will soon grow into a frog."

He looks back to the bathroom. "Yes," he tells me with a grin, but just when I think the danger of sex is over, he pushes me at the wall and rubs his stubbly chin against my cheek. It's like being stroked by hot moonrays, but I shouldn't succumb to temptation. There's too much at stake.

"We'll indulge once we're wed, my sweet beast." I give him a kiss to ease the pain caused by my rejection and slide out of his embrace.

I know I'm disappointing him, but he doesn't complain and lets go.

I use forceps to fish out a bloated redpole, then send the others down the drain. While Hawk packs some snacks for us, I clean the now-empty tub to leave behind no trace of what's happened here. The tunnel leading to the Nightmare Realm is hidden under the grimsmith's bed, but I don't know where exactly it will lead us, so we need to be ready for camping out in the wild.

I tuck the Sunwolf Crown into my backpack with utmost care. I can already imagine my cousin's face when he sees it. There will be no other way for him. If he wants to be seen as a fair ruler, and I know he does, he will have to accept my offering. And me along with it, as well as my Dark Companion whose shadow vastly overpowers that of Lord Kyran's own husband.

I spend a moment too long searching for a button or lever to move the bed aside, but Hawk solves the issue for me by grabbing the heavy piece of furniture and dragging it away from a trapdoor with iron hinges. I don't want to shower him with too many compliments, since that would make them sound disingenuous, but I can't help the giddy smile blooming on my face as I watch him use the raw power in his muscles. He's such a beautiful animal. And he's mine.

He opens the trapdoor for me before I can ask him to, and we descend into a dark passage. Once I make use of the swamplight solution found in Tassarion's bedroom, torches attached to the wall on my left all burn with a steady, green flame, revealing a passage without an end in sight. This place reminds me of the secret corridors beneath the Nocturne Court, but instead of intricate carvings predating the castle itself, the stone slabs supporting the ceiling are marked with crude pictures and writing featuring everything from names and personal insults to images of an erotic nature.

Unwilling to let Hawk focus on them too much, I slide my hand into his and lead him forward. He carries most of our equipment but hasn't yet voiced a single complaint. I did leave some of the heavier and less valuable books in the grimsmith's living room, hidden among those he owned. I don't want to abuse Hawk's kindness, and if all goes right, I can always attempt to retrieve the tomes in the future.

"Do you think you'll miss the sun?"

Hawk blinks. "Shut up! You mean it's not there *at all*? I thought you just have very little of it, like in the Arctic Circle. Don't plants need the sun to survive?"

"Not our plants. They thrive in moonlight, or other types of light that exist underground. I'm sorry if I never explained that. Our night is when the sky is clear, and our day is when the moon comes out. But our moon is bigger, brighter than the one you're used to. You will enjoy it," I assure him and kiss his knuckles.

It's as if Hawk's been waiting for it, and he pushes me at the wall, his mouth on mine as we kiss, breathing in the cold, damp air, and the sweetness of each other's bodies. "I'll definitely enjoy seeing you naked in the moonlight."

I smile against his lips as excitement lights up my body, opening it to pleasure. A wiser man would have called these stolen moments wasted, but I can't deny myself the simple joy of his tongue playing with mine. It's only when heat pools down my stomach that I press on his chest, letting him know we can't take things any further. Memories of his cock entering me for the first time flood my brain like a sniff of fairy dust, and all of a sudden I can barely bring myself to refuse his touch. It hurt a little, yet I was too aroused to care, and now the ghost of that sensation is back, reminding me of our furious coupling.

"Hawk. We don't even know how long this trip will take. We need to save our energy. Do you think *I* am not eager to taste you? But after last time you needed a nap." I pet his cheek and give him one more kiss before pulling him along.

Hawk groans but follows me without more protest. "I love it when you talk dirty with fancy words. *Eager to taste you*," he repeats with a pleased hum as we walk on, again on the trail of green torches.

My heart grows giddy with familiarity when I spot glowing mushrooms ahead. The corridor widens, its walls no longer slabs of stone but the rough rock of a cave. Even the air's changed, now fragrant with marsh orchids and salt. It brings back fond memories of extracting oils from flower petals, a task so repetitive it becomes meditation.

More fungi appear as we follow the passage, lured by their soft fluorescent glow. Most of the mushrooms have halos of green and yellow, but the blue ones scattered in between are easy enough to spot.

"Those are Cerulean Puffballs," I tell Hawk and point them out with a smile. "You have to gather them very carefully so they don't explode, but their spores make the sweetest sleep tea."

"So those aren't radioactive, or something? Your people eat them without dying in terrible pain?" Hawk asks, grinning, but there's no mistaking the awe in his eyes for anything else. His hand remains in mine, but he's enchanted, and as the colors cast on his skin change, I too see various facets of his handsome features.

My introduction to his world was painful and unwanted, but I'm already looking forward to showing him the beauty of my realm and seeing his mouth open in amazement the way it does now.

"Those aren't poisonous. Not in the deadly sense. We don't consume them unless someone needs to be sedated. Depending on the part of the Puffball you use, and how ripe it is, you can even put someone to sleep instantaneously." I glance around this underground garden where glowing mushrooms grow even on the ceiling. "You know, I might actually harvest some. You never know when such an ingredient can come in handy."

"Didn't you say we have little time?" Hawk asks, but instead of lingering nearby and attempting to capture my gaze in accusation, he walks farther into the tunnel to sit on a mossy rock.

I'm not surprised to see him pull out a pretzel. His tall, strong body needs more nourishment than my small form ever could, and I find his voracity quite endearing. He makes such a charming picture with the golden glow of Nightbells creating a blurry veil behind him.

The food is half-way to his mouth when reality crashes into me like a violent wave onto a shore.

Nightbells.

"Don't move!" I say as I freeze, terrified of what might happen next.

CHAPTER 21

Sylvan

My mind is racing as I try to work out how much danger we're in.

"Are the ones behind me poisonous?" Hawk whispers as if he fears even the sound of his voice could bring about our destruction.

"Come back to me. Very slowly," I say, taking a deep breath. He hasn't alerted the fungi's receptors, so we still have a chance to survive this unscathed. Hawk takes dainty, careful steps, as if he were walking over thin ice, and while it makes him look like a bear attempting ballet, I'm glad he's taking my warning seriously.

I grab his hand and pull him to me as soon as he's close enough. After a deep exhale, he stuffs the pretzel into his mouth, glaring back at the shimmering golden caps of the Nightbells growing all over the tunnel in front of us.

I frown, squeezing his fingers. "They're not dangerous by themselves, but they're here for a reason. We can't pass without alerting them, as they react to movement. All their gills will start ringing at once, hence their name, Night*bells,* and then their caps will pop off in the direction of the movement."

"Like... bullets?" Hawk asks with widening eyes.

"Not exactly. Getting hit wouldn't hurt much, as it's a strategy meant to attach spores to an animal, not kill it."

"So what are we worried about? We can cover our ears and run through."

I shake my head. "Someone planted these here on purpose. What I mean when I say they *all* start ringing, is all the Nightbell roots are connected. Some elves living in the wild use them as a warning measure against predators. The roots might lead all the way to whatever's at the end of the tunnel and alert someone. It works like cables transferring electricity in your world. We'll lose the element of surprise. But then how would anyone pass through here…" My thoughts drift off as I look back at the Puffballs.

Of course.

"This is a trap. If you walk between the Nightbells, they will ring in alert, but the caps flying at you will also hit the Puffballs, releasing their spores into the air and putting you to sleep, so you can then be easily captured by whoever set this up."

Hawk squints at me. "This doesn't sound good at all, so why are you smiling?"

I lift my chin with pride. "Because I know exactly what to do. Hold my bag, please." I pull out an empty vial and a pair of small shears I took from Tassarion's workshop. I then wrap a scarf over the bottom of my face as Hawk's frown deepens.

"Are you sure this is safe, princeling? We can still go back."

I straighten up and head for the Puffballs. "Worst thing to possibly happen here is that I fall asleep, in which case, do take me back to the bedroom and try to wake me up, but I have experience with these." Which fills me with pride, because so often I'm made to feel inadequate, unable to do the simplest things, like reaching items from a high shelf. Now, I get to prove to Hawk that my knowledge can save us in more ways than one.

"Baby, please be careful," Hawk says, but trusts me enough to not intervene, which I appreciate.

I approach the Puffballs, pinch one at the stem, then cut through the delicate skin of the cap so instead of popping in my face, the spores inside can be collected. I go on, continuing the process until I have a full three vials, then get back to Hawk, presenting my bounty.

"Now, cover your face too," I urge him, already making my way toward the Nightbells. "In nature, these two are enemies, competing for resources, and so, I can do this…" My heart beats faster when I approach, because I do worry that I might set off the Nightbells. But as I sprinkle the Puffball spores over the golden caps, only the faintest chiming rings out before stopping altogether.

The golden glow dims when the mushroom I've just sprinkled darkens. The others soon follow its example.

The air that's been trapped in my lungs finally escapes my mouth, and I grab Hawk's hand with my sweaty fingers. I pull him forward with a triumphant song in my heart. "I put them to sleep," I say, proud of my ingenuity when his eyes slide over me with awe.

Hawk strokes my hair as we pass the sleeping Nightbells. "Pretty *and* smart. I really hit the jackpot with you, my prince." I'm not sure what a *"jackpot"* is, but this is clearly a compliment, and I'm sure my face is pink when I take off the scarf.

But even the sweetest compliments can't take my mind off the view revealed in front of us beyond the bend of the corridor, where the passage expands into an elongated underground chamber. The cavern is filled to the brim with endless varieties of fungi, flowers, and moss cascading down the walls. I set aflame the swamplight torch on the wall, and even more colors are revealed to us in a cacophony of underground life.

As we walk hand in hand, my nerves ease, and I sense in Hawk's fingers how he relaxes when I do.

"And those are Rotting Starlights," I point to mushrooms resembling oversized starfish, which have nothing to do with their ocean-dwelling doppelgangers. One of the fungi makes a sound reminiscent of a burp and releases bright green spores from a hole in the middle of its body. "They're harmless, but their flesh smells awful after they're harvested, unless you pickle them within a few hours. You have lots of the spores on your nose," I laugh and try to reach the green specks that look very much like fluorescent freckles.

"Mm, spores... You know a lot about those after tonight," Hawk says, and rubs my ass out of nowhere. The jolt of pleasure traveling deep inside me at the memory of his girth makes me stumble. "I just worry they haven't really taken root inside you."

My face heats, and I have to bite my lip to stifle a whimper. "No place to take root I'm afraid. Or thankfully, for that matter." I give him a nervous smile, so absorbed by the lust in his eyes I stumble over a mushroom the size of a table. Hawk catches me, of course, so I don't fall.

I don't know if no one's been here for a while, or if this part of the tunnel is left to grow wild on purpose, but the sheer *size* of the fungi here makes the mind boggle. It's like a giant terrarium, and we're just passing visitors in this space overflowing with awe-inspiring mushrooms and mosses. Patches of lilac algae illuminate the walls, lighting up in glee every time the Starlights release their spores above us. I'm sure I spotted a large, yet harmless, Gooli spider skitter away into a crevice in the rocks where a single lily of the abyss peeks out at us with its tiny black caplets.

I'm so amazed by this unique flora I almost forget Hawk is trying to bed me again.

Almost. Because the insistent way he pushes me at a large specimen of the Pearly Star makes it impossible to ignore.

I sit on the soft white cap as heat pulses in my face. I lack the words to stop him when he slides his hand down my abdomen and gently cradles my crotch.

Hawk whispers into my ear. "Maybe we should keep trying until we succeed? Aren't you mine to use now that I gave you my shadow?"

I will only have power over it once we say the vows under the full moon in the Nightmare Realm, but his words are like a spell. One that makes my tongue twist and my body incapable of standing up from the soft mushroom.

There's something about the idea of being a body available for his pleasure that makes me boil from the inside in the most delicious ways. "I've never been desired this way," I whisper, glancing up his imposing form. "But since I'm an anomaly in terms of size, maybe I will also one day be receptive to your seed." Ridiculous, but why not indulge the fantasy?

Hawk sucks in air as if he were drowning, and his eyes, colored by the green glow of sparkly moss, darken in response to my words. He's a predator eager for yet another meal, but I'm no longer afraid of his sharp claws and teeth.

"Holy hell, that's so damn hot, princeling," Hawk rasps, rubbing his hands over my body, as if he wants me to understand that I'm not in a position to say no. In fact, the faster I yield, the quicker we can resume our journey, or so I tell myself, because I know he would let go if I pushed him away.

It's me who doesn't want to stop.

A rumble leaves Hawk's lips as he nips at my cheek, and I join him when his thigh glides along my stiffening cock. "I don't know what dumbasses live in that court of yours, but it's criminal that nobody got you naked before me. Your body's made for riding dick."

I give up and slide my backpack to the ground, because we're not going anywhere until my beast is sated. "The men I like, who possibly were also attracted to me... I think my position intimidated them." But not Hawk. *He* doesn't give a fuck if I'm a prince, and manhandles me as if I were a drunk stable boy. Perhaps he even revels in the power he has over me. I feel like I'm an offering to him, and that I shall be reborn after this only to be consumed again. Over and over, because his hunger can never be satisfied.

"Really? What kind of men were they?" he asks and opens my legs wider, so he can step between them. His hands keep wandering, touching every bit of my body, as if he acknowledged no rules of conduct. As if only his desire is important when it comes to this.

Opening up about such intimate matters doesn't come naturally to me. I swallow to ease the dryness in my throat. "It's not about who they were, but what the expectations are because of my royal status."

Hawk slides his hands to my jaw and forces me to look up. "Are you saying there's expectations of the role you take up in the sack? And, as we established, you like to be *taken*."

I swallow and kiss his thumb as I place my hands over his wrists. "It's less about who does which act in the bedroom, and more about..." I have to think of how to explain something that is a social construct I inherently know, not a law, "power. Being one of the princes means that I'm of high social standing and therefore expected to be *the pursuer*. And I admit I never felt adequate when it comes to that role. It's my inherent flaw, that in matters of romance, I wish to be pursued, which goes against the expectations of everyone at court. Even my mother, as a princess of the Goldweed bloodline chose her husband and courted *him*, as he was of lower social standing.

"Were I to desire another royal... things would be a bit easier, since he'd be my equal, but the kind of men I've always been attracted to... I suppose it would have been acceptable for me to pursue a tryst with them, but I never had the confidence to make a blatant offer. Especially after my mother made me realize spies are everywhere. And how would I even go about explaining to a potential lover that I want him to ravish me on the hay in the back of the barn? It was easier to give up on such fancies."

I groan and close my eyes because I cannot bear looking into Hawk's curious eyes any longer, fearful of his judgment.

But he just strokes my cheeks with his thumbs. "And what kind of men would you have liked to pursue you?"

The way he's worded it makes my heart skip a beat. He already understands what I want better than anyone.

"Tall. Strong. Confident..." I say and run my fingers up his forearm because he is everything I've dreamed of and more. I'm embarrassed to tell him all this, but there is no way around it if I wish us to connect. "Men who don't care about my status and would instead be lured by what my flesh can offer. Those who crave to conquer my body, not gain favors thanks to my position. Men who'd grab and use me if they wish, paying little mind to manners and the decorum of courting. A palace guard, a fisherman, a hunter in the woods, who doesn't know my name, doesn't know my title, just likes what he sees."

"Ooh, I can be your hunter," Hawk whispers, and his fingers slide to my groin, making me stir with pleasure. "Just found you lost in a dark cave, hungry, tired, and unable to protect yourself. And I only demand one thing for taking you to safety."

He understands me. My heart beats faster by the second, and my face is glowing with heat. "I have nothing, so what is it you demand?" I ask, but my eyes stray to the front of his pants. I can't wait to see his stiff cock again. The Nightmare Realm can wait an hour or two.

He kisses me. Hard. With passion that makes my insides turn into goo. I'm ready to let him do anything he wants. My hole is still tender from its last encounter with his prick, but if he wants to leave his seed inside me again, I know I'll let him. I desire to be anything he wants me to be. I want him to crave me more than he craves food, drink or even sleep. I want to haunt his dreams and be the only one for him.

"I've been wandering the woods on my own for so long, and that pretty mouth of yours really caught my eye," Hawk rasps as his hands spread my thighs wide, massaging their tender flesh.

I'm already hard, lust pooling in my balls, but whenever he calls me pretty, my stomach does a backflip as if I'm sixteen again and a handsome guard winked at me for the first time.

"My mouth? What could you possibly want from it?" I lick my lips. Does this game make me a pervert? Is it wrong that I want to be desired to the point that another man is willing to break all rules to embed his cock inside me? My whole body is throbbing with need.

"Oh, I'll show you," Hawk remarks with a giddy smile, and I whimper when he gently squeezes my throat.

A moment later, he pulls my face to his bulge. I make a greedy whimper and stroke his thighs.

"I see you already have an idea," my promised says but it sounds more like a purr to my ears.

I glance up at him, tucking the bottom of my shirt into my collar to show him my stiff nipples. If it wasn't for the barrage of compliments, I would have never done that, but he makes me feel like I'm not only *"pretty"*, but worth worshiping. As if my compact size is not just acceptable but exactly what turns him on.

"You can touch me wherever you wish. I'm yours to toy with," I rasp, breaking out of character because my reality with Hawk is even more delicious than the fantasy we're weaving together.

He grins and leans down, so we can kiss again. My head spins as he squeezes my pec, then glides his hand lower, toward my stiff cock, but as I believe he's about to touch it, the hand pulls away, leaving me to wail.

"Come on, now, that's not very prince-like, is it?" Hawk teases as he pulls down his sweatpants to reveal his thick dick. "Your body is mine now," Hawk continues, drilling his gaze straight into my soul. "I can have it whenever and wherever I want, can't I? You sold it."

"I did. However you wish to have me..." I salivate at the sight of the stiff cock in his tattooed hand. I love how thick and veiny it is. A drop of pre-cum already beads at the tip, and most of all, I love that it's so hard for *me*.

"Open your mouth and show me your cock," he demands, and I oblige, pulling down my jeans to show him my excitement.

The mushroom under me is soft like a cloud, and the glowing colors swirl around us, creating a world where we can indulge in each other. And while the species I'm sitting on doesn't have intoxicating properties, my mind buzzes when my man strokes my cheek with his cock. He smells like the beautiful beast he is, and I open up, showing him my tongue, desperate for a taste, for his touch, for attention.

"Good boy, so pliant for me. Go on, show me some love," Hawk tells me as his cockhead rubs my lips, then slides into my mouth. This is only the second time I'm letting him do this, yet I'm salivating as if it were the greatest gift he could ever give me.

He pushes it in over my tongue, and it's so thick it barely fits, but I still give him all of my attention, hollowing my cheeks. I extend one hand to touch his hairy stomach and reach for my own needy manhood with the other.

"Yes. That's what I want to see. Jerk off for me," he grunts, forcing his prick in faster while he slides his hand into my hair.

I can't get enough of it. His smell, his taste, the low moans he makes as I suck him harder, all send me into a frenzy of lust. I should have been so much more sensible, said no and continued our journey, but how could I possibly deny a cock this gorgeous, hot, and stiff?

He's rough, and forceful with his thrusts, but he's also stroking me gently, and waiting for my reaction when I stir too rapidly or choke on his long shaft. I feel so very filthy when saliva dribbles down my chin and I sense it drip on my chest, but while this is shameful for someone in my position, someone who should rule over others or face humiliation, I long to be the vessel for his lust. I want Hawk to use me how he likes, to squeeze and prod me. I want to drink his cum with the same fervor I dedicated to my alchemical studies.

This human might be lowborn, a fugitive, and crude, but I adore him more than anything. I don't care if I *shouldn't* find his crassness exciting, because I love his raw hunger for my body.

With Hawk, I can be my purest self, like a diamond pulled out of a ring so it can be seen in all its glory.

"That's it, throat tight and open for me, your perfect body ready for my cum. Such a pretty little cock," Hawk mumbles and tugs on my hair, speeding up his thrusts as I stroke myself with abandon. I'm not even offended for being called little because I know he finds it attractive.

I gag a bit when the sensation of fullness becomes too much, but I'm too aroused to care. All I can think of is him watching me jerk off to the edge of orgasm. The excitement is painted all over his face just like when he pushed his dick into me for the first time, as if I'm the pinnacle of his lusty dreams.

When he withdraws, I embarrass myself by attempting to reach his shaft with my tongue. Oh, how low have I stooped, but I can't get enough of his desire for me. When I see him rubbing his cock in fast, jerky motions while the green spores float all around us, I offer him my open mouth.

His cum is hot on my face. I shiver, and when I taste it, already covered with its thick drops, my own balls tighten, and I come, twisting on the soft mushroom cap.

"Fuuuck, baby boy," Hawk rasps, offering me the head of his cock to kiss. This might be my new favorite angle to watch his prick from. I'm still panting, mouth open, when he drags two fingers over my face, gathers some of his seed, and then smears it over my lips. "I'm going to have the most delicious eternity with your greedy mouth. Tell me how much you liked having your tonsils rubbed," he teases with a smirk and heat burns me from the inside.

"I…"

He trails his finger over my sticky cheek. "You made such a pretty mess all over yourself." He points out my cum-stained chest. "Go on, say 'I'm a needy boy and I love your meat in my mouth'."

I swallow, pushing down my shirt, even though my cock is still exposed. "I'm… a needy boy who loves your meat in my mouth," I admit with cheeks on fire.

Hawk grins, then leans in and kisses my sticky lips. "That's my good little prince. I'll enjoy defiling *your royal highness* again very soon."

He lets go of my hair to grab my shoulder when my world whirs, and I'm about to fall back. My bones feel soft like the damn mushroom. I use the ripped shirt to clean myself a little, but I still smell of sex. How can I complain though, when the sight of Hawk pulling up his pants makes me salivate all over again.

"You really can't get enough of me, can you?" I utter between catching one deep breath and another.

His eyes open wider, and he's back between my thighs, a grin firmly planted on his face as he kneels to be at my eye level. "How is that surprising? You are literally the best-looking person I've ever seen. Slender, cute as a button, but deadly. You have those big blue eyes, pale hair, the little nose, ass like a damn peach, and a BJ-swollen mouth," he adds, winking when he slides his arms around me, claiming me all over again. "And you're so smart on top of that, but still chose *me*. Just thinking about you makes me horny."

I wrap my arms around his neck. "It doesn't bother you that I barely reach your shoulder?" I utter and kiss his round ear, which might be the only 'cute' thing about him.

He snorts and pulls me off the mushroom, adjusting my clothes once my unsteady feet are back on the ground. "Honey cheeks, I couldn't date if that bothered me, because I've not yet met anyone taller than me other than my dad. But I *love* that you're so compact. That I can just pick you up with one hand whenever I want to, toss you to the bed, hold down those tiny wrists. Makes me feel all big and mighty. I bet I could fuck you holding you up no problem," he adds with a vicious laugh.

My ears go hot, but I can't ponder this idea right now. We need to *go*.

I smile at Hawk, so happy that this man, this massive wall of muscle with an endless supply of energy and a shadow so dark it stands out even underground, is *mine*. He might not be my Dark Companion yet, but he belongs to me already, and I cherish him.

"Maybe one day we'll find out," I tease and grab my bag.

I'm surprised when his big hand squeezes mine almost right away. The spores are still floating around the mushroom that was the scene of our tryst as we take the first step farther down the passage. "We better, because I'm leaving everything behind for one stubborn prince."

"As far as I know, you're a fugitive." I poke his side, amazed at how easily I've adapted to closeness with another person after years without as much as a hug. "I'm doing you a favor."

He snorts and places his hand on my shoulder in a gesture that feels protective. "Yeah, but I'm leaving behind electricity, the internet, reality TV, and even chocolate. You should appreciate my sacrifice, princeling."

I smile up at him, filled with pure joy. I'm leaving banishment, I will have the greatest Dark Companion the Nocturne Court has ever seen, the Sunwolf Crown is hidden in my bag, and I've just had a spectacular orgasm. What more could I want?

"I do appreciate it. I will make sure to acknowledge that in my vows to you, and I will always be ready to meet your needs," I glance down his body and grin when he winks at me.

How lucky am I to have found him by chance in the world of humans? He is not only handsome and strong. He's proven himself thoughtful and kind, he fought for me against his own family, and he trusted me even when he suspected I might have lost my mind. He never complained about needing to carry my possessions, and made it clear that he wishes to take care of me. My heart soars every time I think about his tender touches and fond smiles.

We walk for another ten minutes before the steady row of torches comes to an abrupt end, but the final light illuminates the iron steps of a folded ladder attached to the wall at the end of the tunnel. The mushrooms have been mostly cleared around it, to create more space, but the trapdoor I see in the ceiling doesn't look like anything special.

"Is there a trick to it?" Hawk asks, and I stew in the juice of uncertainty, because while I have crossed the border between worlds, I did so using the proper channels. This is an unofficial (or should I say, illegal) route, and I don't know whether we should open the door in a specific way, like when we entered the grimsmith's home, or force our way through.

"I'll go first." I reach for the first rung of the ladder and drag it down, so I can step on it, but sigh in frustration when I discover it's beyond my reach. "A lift, please?"

Hawk chuckles, and the ease with which he can pick me up never fails to amaze me.

As I start climbing, I shroud myself in a pale veil of shadow. "It's not much," I explain, "but I might be able to hide for a moment if it's needed."

He's right behind me, and while I roll my eyes, I suppose it's best for us to not lose sight of one another.

The way up only takes a moment, and then I'm hesitantly touching the rough wood of the trapdoor, listening to whatever might surprise us on the other side. But I hear nothing, and while my stomach is shrinking from worry, I can't be a coward in front of the man who agreed to give me his shadow.

I push the door up with the same kind of abruptness Kurt once tore off my Band-Aid, and the moment warm light touches my face, the world flips, and I'm falling.

I yelp, even though I told myself I need to keep silent. To make matters worse, Hawk is right behind me with his massive backpack.

I hit fabric first, but it doesn't break our fall much when we drop to... a bed?

I panic when something moves right under me, and I'm about to stab it with a dagger I took from Tassarion's when the creature yells from beneath the fabric.

"What in the Darkmoon!?"

CHAPTER 22

HAWK

I jerk up to my knees in a frenzy, and when my toes find only empty space, the heavy backpack weighs me down. With a yelp of panic, I fall another dozen of inches, and finally stop with my eyes glued to the open hatch in the ceiling above. What I see there makes no sense, because the cave floor we stood on not that long ago is now... up there. As if the small square door is where gravity flips.

Did we fall... *in reverse*? It's not something my brain can accept at face value, but as a fabric-covered shape jerks under Sylvan, he too jumps off the massive bed we've landed on with a high-pitched shriek. That's all the motivation I need. Nothing's going to happen to him on my watch!

But as I get to my feet and am about to reach for a sword hanging on the wall, the velvet blanket uncovers the monster we've accosted, and as it turns out... it was no monster at all.

Sky blue eyes watch me from a face handsome as if it's been chiseled by one of those famous artists from Italy. He's young, with red hair styled into elaborate braids. He could be a model, if it wasn't for the scar cutting across his cheek.

"What... are you?" I ask, pulling Sylvan behind me as we both study the stranger staring back at us from a massive wooden bed with a dragon-shaped headboard.

"What am *I*?" the stranger asks, adjusting his black shirt. He has the same elongated ears as Sylvan, but his accent is deeper, more melodic. He takes us in, much less fazed than I would have been if two men had woken me up by falling on top of me from the ceiling. "It is you who crawled into my bed without permission."

"This is not what we expected, but we will be on our way," Sylvan says, but the man isn't having it and grabs his wrist.

I slap it away, and the stranger frowns at me. He stands on the bed, hands on hips, as if attempting to show off his belt made out of a variety of coins. Not that he has any pants. He wears the belt over the shirt, which is fortunately long enough to just about cover his crotch.

"I demand an explanation. You came from Tassarion's forge, and he always gives me a heads-up about anyone passing through. *And* pays for it."

When Sylvan and I both remain silent, wondering how to respond, the man continues. "There's but one explanation: Tassarion is no more."

"That's a bit far-fetched—" I try.

The elf silences me with a gesture. "Unfortunate. He and I had a good working relationship for over twenty years. Alas, what's done cannot be undone," he says and grabs the slender yet intricately decorated blade off the wall. I'm ready to dash for the nearby stool, to use it as a shield, but the man leaps onto the floor with the grace of a buck in his prime and offers us a smile. "No matter. At least I no longer owe him a debt for this beauty. Best sword I ever had. It's a pity he won't make any more weapons of such prime quality."

Sylvan releases a long sigh, but his shoulders loosen a little. "We shall bother you no more—" he tries, but is once more thwarted by the chatty elf.

"I do not advise that. You," he points to me with his sword, "are human, and you," he turns to Sylvan, "are the shortest elf in the Realm, Prince Sylvan Goldweed. Banished. Therefore you must be here illegally."

Sylvan's face turns pink. "I do not need to explain anything to you!"

The elf spreads his arms. "Where are my manners? Maybe if you know who I am, it will be easier for us to speak plainly about your predicament, Your Highness. I am Fenren, King of Smugglers, and Procurer of Things. I too walk the shadowed path, only adjacent to the law. I see no silver collar around your neck, but the purple burns on your throat tell me it has not been taken off by our benevolent Lord of the Nocturne Court. If you walk out of my tavern like this, who knows how fast the news of your arrival will spread?"

I stare at him in horror, because if he could identify us both so easily, then so can everyone else. We need to rethink this. As my thoughts drift to the possible disguises we could utilize, I take in the dark interior illuminated with just a few candles. Panels of carved wood decorate all the walls, heavy velvet curtains obscure the only window, and... gargoyles stare at us from every corner of the ceiling. This place looks like the fever dream of a rich goth chick.

I squeeze Sylvan's shoulder as he stiffens, touching the marks on his neck. "No... the grimsmith did that."

Fenren clicks his tongue and approaches a desk, which belongs here like a fist belongs in a person's eye. White, plain, and made of particle board rather than wood, it's a cheap, mass-produced item from the world of humans. Maybe even from IKEA. But on top of it is a glass of black crystal, and a decanter in the shape of a howling wolf, which contains a black liquid. Still, Fenren has a sip of it and smiles at us, as if it's exactly what he needs after such a rude awakening.

"So he removed the collar off your neck, and you removed his head from his shoulders? Naughty," he adds playfully and wags his finger at us.

I might not be the most moral of men, but even I'm freaked out by the casual way he's discussing the death of someone he apparently worked with for so many years. I've met some crazy guys in prison, and an attack might come at any moment from someone like this.

"Forgive me for meeting you in my underwear, unless..." He lets the silent proposition hang in the air as he gestures at the huge bed that would easily accommodate all three of us.

"No." Sylvan frowns and steps back, even pinker than before, but then he grabs my hand. It's so sweet that it's me he reaches for when uncertain, even though I'm only human and have no other ways to protect him than my strength.

Fenren throws a braid over his shoulder. "Ah! I see... You woke me up so abruptly I'm still getting my bearings, but it all makes sense now. It's a full moon day! And this, Your Highness, will be your Dark Companion. How splendid! A wedding at The Burning Corpse! We will provide all, as I'm sure you wish to spare no expense on a day of such great importance."

There's that stereotype about men being coerced into marriage—the cuffed groom cake toppers, bachelor parties all about losing freedom, grooms holding up signs with the phrase *save me* at the altar, but while I never gave much thought to formalizing any of my relationships, the moment Fenren presents me with the idea of celebrating my blooming romance with Sylvan, I know that this is exactly what I want.

"How does that work here?" I ask, and the elf rests on a carved stool, capturing my gaze. His shirt rides up dangerously high on his bare thighs, so I hope he is wearing bottoms of some kind, or I might have to cover Sylvan's eyes.

"Well, both here and in your world, the particulars are a matter of custom and wealth. But since you are marrying a royal of the Nocturne Court, you will have the most lavish party money can buy. We will bring out the best spirits, hire many musicians, so that the songs can flow all night without break. I will also personally see to you wearing the finest fabrics. Excuse me for being blunt," he says and points to us both, "but neither a prince nor his Dark Companion should celebrate their union in rags."

Sylvan hasn't complained about my basic outfit of hoodie and sweatpants, but Fenren does have a point. Maybe I should change into their version of a suit at least.

Sylvan raises one hand while squeezing me more firmly with the other. "No, no, no need for any of that. All we need is our vows to one another."

I stall, staring at our linked fingers. "What? But you said it would be a real wedding."

Fenren leans against the desk and finishes his drink. "That is baffling, Your Highness. Surely, you are not trying to get all the benefit yet offer your promised no public commitment? There is no divorcing a Dark Companion. This is a once-in-a-lifetime celebration. You need the rose, the candle, the lace and frills, the *spectacle*. While lowborn, every guest in my tavern downstairs could be a joyful witness. Your human deserves that much at least for what he is offering."

Sylvan's ears twitch, which I've already learned is often a sign of nervousness. While I can see that he's being prodded, it does feel kind of frustrating that he seems to want our marriage vows to be over with instead of following the customs of his own world. The choice is his at the end of the day. It's not my money, but I do give him an expectant look. Is it really so wrong of me to want a celebration?

Sylvan clears his throat and gestures for me to put down the backpack. "Until I'm back at court, I only have select items and jewelry I can pay with," he says, staring Fenren down like a dragon sitting on its hoard.

"Oh, let me see!" Fenren jumps to his feet and is at Sylvan's side in an instant, eyes glistening with greed. "We will have to make the best of what's here, and then write up a debt contract for all the other frills."

I swallow and stroke Sylvan's hand as our host pulls out a string of black pearls from a little velvet bag. "Yes, I can make this work. The best food The Burning Corpse can offer, the finest clothes, and guests to confirm that the prince treated his beloved Dark Companion right."

I know what Fenren is doing, but I am marrying a prince. Do I not deserve a bit of luxury?

But as the elf pulls out the lava lamp and Sylvan's hand tightens, I step forward. "Not this. Sentimental value."

Sylvan swallows and looks up at me with the saddest puppy eyes I've ever seen. "No, it's fine. He is right, you deserve to be treated like royalty, as that is what you will soon be." When he turns to Fenren though, it's as if he becomes a different person, the mask of dignity back on, and gaze sharp as daggers. "I need to keep a few trinkets and books, but other than that, all my possessions can be yours to keep. *But* do not think me a fool. We expect not only a celebration and lodgings, but also a guide to lead us to the Nocturne Court through the forest, and provisions for the trip. I have no doubt that someone who calls himself the King of Smugglers knows which routes are both safe and secretive."

Fenren's eyes narrow. "You strike a hard bargain, my prince. Very well," he says and shakes Sylvan's hand. The ease with which he agrees tells me he's getting paid extra handsomely for his effort, but I decide not to mention it, because this is Sylvan's moment, and I don't want to embarrass him. I'm still a bit dazed about him willing to part with all the prized possessions I'd carried for him, just because he wants to treat me.

I watch Sylvan pack some items into the smaller bag while obscuring the Sunwolf crown with a shawl. I'm touched when I see him consider the jar with the redpole, only to take that too.

Fenren claps his hands and pulls a wide-skirted robe off the hanger. The lush dark blue fabric covers his undershirt and bare legs. His feet then go into leather slippers, and he opens the door, leading us out of his room. Initially, we're in the tight channel of a hallway that likely belongs to his personal apartment, but then he takes us through a locked door, and the scenery changes.

I wouldn't call the corridor palatial, since I manage to hit my head on the first beam in the way, but it's definitely something straight from a fancy fantasy tavern. Only that the dark stone making up the floor and walls is real rather than made of Styrofoam.

I take the moment while we walk to arrange it all in my head. Everything I've experienced since meeting Sylvan is like a lucid dream and I hope I'll never wake up. I'm no longer a fugitive, and I'll be at Sylvan's side and help him however I can with his plan of regaining his position at this Nocturne Court.

He first chose me for my shadow, but we've been through so much since that fateful night at Best Burgers Bonanza. Our feelings for each other are real. I might be a toppy guy, the kind of person who wants to protect those he loves. But it's nice to be treated for once and for someone else to not just talk about their love, but to show it. Like I'm worthy of it. Like I'm not just a convenient means to an end, a big dick, or useful for my fists.

I can't wait to explore this elven world alongside my perfect little prince and taste all it has to offer. I still haven't wrapped my mind around us having a forever, and a part of me fears that it's not Sylvan but me who's having a mental breakdown and imagining things that aren't there.

As we continue past numbered doors, toward a wide arch where the corridor leads into a more open space, I hear an unfamiliar melody, the murmur of many voices, and sense the aroma of grilled meat. A woman passes us in clothes that, while black as night, remind me of the one Ren Faire I've been to. She's holding a platter with something the size of an ostrich leg on a bed of root vegetables and mushrooms. The skin on that meat looks so crispy my mouth waters.

"We will eat soon," Sylvan says and strokes my hand.

I'm embarrassed by my voracity, but it's still sweet of him to pay attention to my needs without me even saying anything.

Fenren doesn't give me any time to contemplate a snack break and steps beneath the bright light of a massive chandelier made of bone and antler.

Green flames, like the ones I've already seen in the caves, burn all over it, illuminating the mezzanine around the whole interior, and the bar below. Curious eyes begin to follow us, but Fenren is already ushering us through a door adorned with a silvery moon instead of a number.

"Rest please, and soon I will send a tailor. I have much to prepare." And even though he's a self-proclaimed king, Fenren still bows to Sylvan.

I am dazzled once more. This room is redder than the curtains in Fenren's bedroom, and an elegant black fountain stands on a table in the middle of it. Cascades of red liquid drizzle into a dish at its bottom. Going by the elegant goblets next to it, I'm guessing it's a drink, not blood.

Cushioned benches around the table invite us to sit down, but I stall halfway there, because the mirror I pass doesn't show my likeness.

I cock my head with a growing frown. "Do... humans not have reflections here?"

Sylvan rolls his eyes and steps next to me, but the mirror doesn't show him either. "Cheap trick for a vampire-themed parlor." He sighs and points to a fresco of three elves in black coats feasting on a fainting maiden whose white dress is so see-through we're treated to a view of her stiff nipples.

"Is this... a love hotel?" I ask but Fenren shakes his head and gestures to the table in the middle. "And also... there's vampires here?"

"This is but a humble inn on the crossroads. Rest and enjoy yourself, while I work my magic," Fenren says and taps one of the coin ornaments in his hair. He's handsome, though his beauty is sharp as a razor where Sylvan is adorable and juicy like the ripest peach. Does this mean we have... time to ourselves?

As soon as our host is gone, I turn back to Sylvan, only to see him... steal a fork? My eyebrows rise, and when his eyes meet mine, Sylvan frowns despite turning pinker by the second.

"What? We don't know what we might need on the way, and he took my gold and sapphire set of cutlery. It's only fair that I keep this."

The floor seems to give in under the weight growing in my chest. Has Fenren seen my insecurity and manipulated *me* into spending more of Sylvan's money? We can't know if our efforts to reestablish Sylvan at court will be successful, and if we end up spending everything we have on one party... I remember sometimes laughing at people who got into heavy debt to buy luxury items they couldn't afford. How is this any different?

I clear my throat and pull him closer. "Maybe you were right? It's a lot of money, Sylvan."

Sylvan exhales and runs his pretty fingers through his hair. "No, I kept the most important books, we have the *mask*, and your redpole. Life is harsh and will always try to pluck your riches off you. As a royal Companion, you deserve so much more than I can offer today anyway. Maybe it's for the better. The road ahead of us might be tough, and I do not wish to burden you with the heavy load."

"That's... really sweet, but I don't want your life to be 'harsh'," I whisper and pull him close, until his face is squished between my pecs. I love seeing him like this, so small, and soft, and in need of my protection. But while I've never wanted another guy to take care of me in any way, this feels good. If this blue-blooded beauty thinks I'm worthy of him, then maybe I'm more than just the scum who gave up his life for a guy who never truly cared about him?

Thanks to Sylvan, I'll get another chance, in a new world.

Sylvan settles against me with a deep sigh, and I sense his tension dissolve. He kisses my pec and rests his cheek against it. "You cannot shelter me from it all, but I appreciate it. I have never known the kind of care you have shown me. You took me to Boston at great risk to yourself, you fought your family for me, and you even stood by me when you had doubts about my identity. I want you to know you are worth everything to me. And deep down, maybe I also want others to witness my vows to the man I chose."

I'm floored. I know every normal person would have called me crazy for claiming to be in love after the short time the two of us shared so far, but I don't care. He thinks I'm special, he believes in me, and I want only him.

Wrapping my arms around him, I pull him up, and as he closes his legs on my hips, it's me who listens to *his* heartbeat and finds peace in its rhythm. "The people who ignored you and didn't see you for the gem you are are so fucking dumb."

Sylvan kisses my ear. "And thanks to you, soon even they will be humbled."

I don't have time to answer, because a woman walks in without knocking, and I have to let Sylvan out of my grasp.

"Follow me, Your Highness," she says with a bow. "You two are not to see each other until the ceremony."

"What? No—" I moan, but Sylvan chuckles and strokes my hand.

"It's a tradition that will make our union all the sweeter."

I suppose he might be right, no matter how much I resent that. I say my goodbyes with a kiss to his lips, and my chest tightens in longing the moment he leaves my sight.

I turn back to the platter of unfamiliar fruit on the table, but when my gaze drifts to the fresco, I once more wonder... *Are* there vampires here?

I don't like that nobody answered my question.

CHAPTER 23

SYLVAN

The tailors working on my clothes are so swift with their needlework my eyes can barely catch their movements, and I wonder if it's a skill they've had to master to remake stolen goods into unrecognizable outfits. Still, I've been in this tiny black and white boudoir for over half an hour now, and I'm itching to get back to Hawk.

On the other hand, it's given me an opportunity to consider the upcoming nuptials.

My stomach is in knots, so I've been refusing any food, and all I can think of is that I am about to make a bond for life with a human I've known for three days. It feels so very right in my heart, but my head is throbbing with worry. How will my mother react to a Dark Companion like Hawk? While she will surely appreciate his shadow, Hawk can be so brash, so forward. *I* appreciate his honesty, but what if it gets us in trouble at court? I will be bound to him forever after all, and therefore held responsible for his actions.

My mind stalls as I look into my own eyes in the big mirror with a little crack at the bottom. Is this really the way to think about the man who's chosen me over *his* family? Over his world?

Guilt chews on my inside, and when it occurs to me I'm about to bite into my nail, I rub my face, torn between my feelings and the insistent need for my mother's rare nod of approval. I've been conditioned to chase those since I was little.

"Having second thoughts?" asks the girl who led me here. She has bright red hair, eyes as brown as the strongest coffee, and a little mouse-shaped birthmark on her bare shoulder. At first glance, she appeared to be one of the many tavern workers, given that she's wearing a no-frills apron and ties her locks back, but she hasn't moved a finger since we entered, which tells me she might be someone of more note, even if her name, Ivy, is as common as they come.

I'm not used to speaking about my feelings. Even Hawk, who's remarkably adept at pushing my boundaries, had trouble prying open my clam-like heart.

"Only nervous. This is a big commitment, and it must be made tonight, or I will have to wait another month." Which would have been a very reasonable choice, yet the idea makes my nails itch to grow into shadow claws. Deep down, I don't want to wait another minute, let alone a month. I want to be in Hawk's arms all night and melt into him again.

But I'm stuck waiting for my jacket to be finished, and I don't even know how the preparations are going on Hawk's side, since he's of substantial size, even for a human. After spending some time in the other realm, I can't deny that they differ from us in shape—their limbs are somewhat shorter, bodies—sturdier and less agile. But even among his brethren, Hawk is a giant, and I cannot imagine there are any clothes his size at the inn. Which means they must be custom-made, which will likely prolong our time apart even more.

The seamstress adds a final button to my sleeve and steps away with a pleased smile. "Oh, that is perfection. The gold truly brings out your eyes."

By Nocturne Court standards, my ensemble would be considered simple, and not at all wedding-worthy. Fitted black pants with golden embroidery, a shirt with a lace collar, and a short jacket to go with it in the same elegant color as the night sky. Tiny specs of crystals twinkle on it like stars, but I can't stop feeling as though I should be wearing my family crest for the occasion. I have often resented my family, yet I am still a Goldweed, even if in exile.

"I cannot wait," Ivy says, throwing her hands up as she slides off the windowsill, where she's been sitting for the past thirty minutes. "I love weddings, but one with a human? That, I am waiting to see," she tells me with a twinkle in her eye.

The two seamstresses leave after saying their goodbyes, and while I am still in the presence of a stranger I need to be mindful of, at least I'm no longer scrutinized from all sides. At court, I only ever trusted my housemaster with my clothing. He's taken care of my attire since I was officially introduced to the rest of the aristocracy at the tender age of fourteen.

Only he knew the insecurity-inducing flaws that needed filling, padding, and obscuring from everyone else. The fact that Hawk has seen me naked many times already, without all the adornments, and still calls me beautiful is a revelation I can't quite believe.

I miss hearing *his* opinion about my wedding outfit, as he has spared me no compliments since the night we met. I blush just thinking about the way he guided my hand to his crotch before we even made proper introductions.

"A marriage can be dissolved, but the bond I will be making tonight, one with a Dark Companion, can only be cut by death, so you must understand why I am slightly..." I trail off, because why am I even telling her this? It must be Hawk's influence and the time I spent in the human realm. It's not like me to make my vulnerabilities known. I'd be eaten alive at the Nocturne Court otherwise.

She exhales and approaches a little wooden console, which opens to reveal cups, and bottles of wine. She fills a metal goblet before handing it to me. "No, I understand, but you don't get married thinking that it's going to be dissolved, do you? When I met my wife, she felt like a creature from a different world. Always smiled, never spared me compliments, had such an ease talking to anyone she met. Her tribe visited my village to sell dreams on stage, and I was enchanted.

"Coming from a family of warriors, I've been taught that providing entertainment is a dishonorable way to live, but she was so beautiful, so kind, and she seemed to understand me in ways my family never could. I knew I would not be permitted to return if I put down my sword, but a few days later, I left with the theater, and with my wife. It was a huge risk, yes, but I never regretted that choice."

I give her a shy glance. Neither a servant nor a royal would ever open up to me so casually at court. I have heard one of my cousins, Prince Tristan Bloodweed, chatter about inane things without shame, but never *to* me.

It's... nice. To be included, instead of treated like a shard of ice better left untouched.

I take a sip of wine. Just a tiny one, since my mother often warned me that with my stature I am bound to get intoxicated all too fast. As soon as I think about her, it hits me that she is influencing my life even now, when I'm so far away. Perhaps I'm not really afraid to make my forever vows to Hawk, but rather of her judgement?

I straighten and look into Ivy's eyes. "So... you know what it's like to leave behind all you've been taught to believe for the person you love?"

She offers me a brilliant smile. "It was the best decision I ever made. Sometimes... we are not best suited for the conditions of our birth. But there's always something beyond the bend of the road. Something that might feel perfect. Like baking cakes and watching my wife perform on stage. She changed my life forever, and I believe that human could do the same for you. The way he looks at you..." She places her hands on her breast and sighs.

I melt a little, feeling my cheeks heat up. She can see it too?

Hawk's not bound by the rules I've been subjected to, and despite the betrayals he has suffered, he opened up to me. And maybe, just maybe, Ivy was right when she suggested it's not me who has been born unsuitable for my family, but that my family that was unsuitable for me. I don't even notice the absence of my parents or dead siblings.

Yet when I think of Hawk, I miss him as if we have been apart for centuries, not an hour. My chest aches, my fingers yearn for him, and the need to make him mine forever is unbearable.

"He is... he is indeed..." The words I wish to speak are not meant for her. I need to say them to Hawk. Not in an hour or two. Now. "Ivy, I know Fenren said I am not to see Hawk before the party, but I'm sure you'd understand that—"

She smirks and lifts her palm. "Say no more."

I offer her a shy smile I've only learned since meeting Hawk. It's a vulnerable expression, yet with him I feel free to show my true thoughts in ways I never dared.

"Let me guess, you want to take a sneak peek at his wedding outfit?" she whispers with a giggle, and grabs my hand, as if we were old friends, not a royal and a tavern worker.

I let her guide me though, and it's only when we reach a door at the other end of the room that old worries flood my mind. What if there's another shadow-wielder here, and he too tries to steal my promised? An assassin could be hiding nearby, ready to cut my throat, so that I meet Tassarion's fate. They would then be free to coerce Hawk into an arrangement in my stead.

The urgency inside me rises, replacing any other fear, because as soon as I think of the grimsmith, it's not my selfish need to *have* Hawk that is most prominent. I remember the greed for power in Tassarion's eyes and the threats wielded at my beloved. I need to be able to protect Hawk from people like that, shadow-wielders who would cruelly bend him to their will. I'll only be able to do so once I have access to the darkness he holds.

I cannot wait. I need to bond with him now.

Ivy wiggles her brows with a wide smile. "You do only have this one set of wedding clothes. Don't stain them."

Unbelievable.

"It's— not like that," I say awkwardly, but I give up on trying to explain myself when she unlocks the second door and shows me a narrow and dusty corridor, which no doubt is for the sole use of the staff.

"Down there...?" I ask as she urges me forward. I sense treachery and consider threatening her, because that's what I've been brought up with, but maybe not everyone is out to get me after all? When she nods, I smile again. "I will not forget this."

I turn and boldly rush toward my promised.

CHAPTER 24

HAWK

The flowers on the table feel real, as does its wooden surface. Everything else I've touched since ending up in the tavern is sturdy and not at all made-up, yet a part of me worries I've swallowed strong hallucinogens, and am currently tripping in some random place. Pinching my skin doesn't pull me out of this strange dream either, but can I trust my senses *if* I am on drugs?

"Stay still, please," the elf adjusting my clothes says, and I stiffen as he moves the little stepladder he's using to work on the upper part of the garment. Unable to make anything from scratch on short notice, the tailor decided to use the largest outfit he could find and cut open its seams so that it fits me. The garment is designed to be one of those black goth coats that brush the floor with every step of the wearer, but it only reaches my knees, and all the spots where it needed to be widened in order to accommodate my bulk are obscured with flowy, velvet fabric in a dark blue shade draped with the aid of silver buttons.

The whole thing is like a costume to my eyes, something straight off the stages of Broadway, and while it makes me look surprisingly regal, most of the people I've known in my former life would have laughed if they saw me like this. Still, I did leave them behind, so does their opinion matter?

"I have never seen a human as formidable as you," the tailor says, and my eyebrows rise as I watch his fingers speed up with the needle. He's like a human—elven sewing machine at this point. Would his pace already be considered magic, or is this just a skill here, the same way cleaning guns is back in my world?

"You mean tall?" I ask, meeting his green eyes. He is a handsome fellow with a wide, smiling mouth and pronounced cheekbones. I would definitely swipe right if I found him on Grindr. His long black braid would be very grabbable.

He's not even looking at the stitch he's working on, as if it's that easy for him. "And broad. And awe-inspiring. I have never seen that much chest hair either."

I'm not that undressed anymore, but I do recall him blushing when I first took off my hoodie.

A part of me still worries this is all an illusion, but I choose to give him the benefit of the doubt and clear my throat as nimble fingers brush my neck. "So... do you often see humans around here?"

"No, they are very rare. I have only ever seen a few and all were exceptionally hand-some," he says and smooths the fabric of my sleeves as he steps off the ladder and circles me with a fond smile. He's nowhere near Sylvan-tiny, but still a head shorter than me and slender.

A laugh escapes my lips. "You must only be importing the best specimens."

"Only. Can you grow one of those... beards?" he asks and brushes the stubble on my cheek with the back of his hand.

I raise my eyebrows. "You do know I'm getting married tonight, right?"

The elf pulls his hand away but isn't in a rush to do so. I'm flattered by the attention, and I can barely believe I'm rejecting it, but thinking of Sylvan's pretty flushed cheeks is enough for me to dream of no one else in my bed.

"I've heard you are to be his Dark Companion though. Not all of those bonds are romantic in nature. As far as I know, royal shadow-wielders often also have another spouse."

It's like being injected with acid.

Fury rushes through my veins and makes my ears thud as I stare at the elf, imagining a reality where Sylvan chooses a second husband, maybe even a wife, so his bloodline continues. I can't believe the intense hate I'm feeling for this theoretical person who doesn't even exist.

All of a sudden, I'm angry that we're wasting time on getting dressed up instead of getting married already. The need to make Sylvan mine is so urgent, so visceral, it reminds me of getting shanked in prison. As I fell to the floor, bleeding my guts out, all I wanted was to make Samson pay with his life. That's how much I crave Sylvan's vow to me.

"He's *not* getting another spouse," I rumble in a voice so low the tailor's skin flushes as he looks up at me.

"Oh. So this is a love match? Have you known the prince long?" There is no malice in his question, just curiosity, yet I'm still buzzing with the unresolved urge to punch things.

"I know him well enough to be sure he's the one I want," I say as confidence floods me with warmth. So maybe he didn't tell me about all the intricacies of elven royal polygamy, but we've had much more important stuff to do. It doesn't have to mean he intends to marry four more elven husbands behind my back.

He'd have to kill me first.

Which is also an uneasy thought, because I have seen he's capable of murder. But that was kinda hot, since he killed Tassarion *for* me.

"Do you not worry that you might be dragged into a dangerous situation because of his banishment?" The tailor cocks his head at me, brows drawn. He's worried about me, which is... nice, if surprising.

"I'm a bit of a fugitive myself," I tell him and grin at the way he takes half a step back. "So I'll take my chances with the hot elven royal."

When the tailor says nothing, staring at me as if he were both aroused and frightened—which is quite a common occurrence in my sex life—I step past him and look into the tall, decorated mirror, which still presents me with no reflection and instead remains blurred like frosted glass. "I was told this room is vampire-themed. Does this mean you have vampires in the Nightmare Realm?"

The tailor clears his throat and opens his mouth, but then the mirror slides to the side as if someone moved it with their mind. I imagine the mirror might be the lid of a hidden coffin, and this time it's me who steps back with my palms raised, ready to meet a fucking vampire.

Dressed in an elegant velvet jacket, Sylvan stands at the mouth of a corridor that was hidden behind the mirror all along. I sigh in relief, taking in his lovely form in the new clothes. He's often serious, but his current expression still gives me pause.

"Everything... all right?" I ask, because why would he come here through some hidden passage without a valid reason?

Sylvan swallows and steps into the room. He spares the tailor only a glance. "Leave us," he says, as if we were already back at court. He's more used to servants than he ever was to flipping burgers, and I can't help but find it arousing. I love him when he gets all sweet and submissive, but there's also a confidence in him that I greatly admire.

The tailor hesitates, then bows awkwardly before leaving.

I grab Sylvan's hands the moment we're alone. "Tell me everything," I say, desperate to wipe the worry from his face and replace it with one of his beautiful smiles.

Sylvan looks up. "How marvelous you look in black. And this coat…" He strokes my forearm, and I relax a little, because if he has time to compliment me, then the world isn't falling apart.

"You don't need blue velvet to look magnificent. Honestly, if it didn't mean all those people would see your body, I would gladly marry you naked," I tell him, wordlessly inviting him into my arms.

He's so quick to hug me he stumbles and faceplants right between my pecs, but that's where he loves to be, so no harm done.

I'm guessing we have time for that too, since he's not telling me we need to run from bounty hunters, or something.

"Maybe I was born so small to fit well into your embrace," he whispers, tense under my touch.

I melt and lower myself to one knee. For once he is slightly taller than me as I kiss his hands. Any and all doubts I had about this new reality disperse, because even if this is all happening in my mind, I do not want to wake up from a dream where I'm so very wanted.

"I like that. Then maybe I was born so strong and tall so you could always lean on me?"

He makes the tiniest whimper and squeezes my hands. I swear his eyes are glossing over. And when he opens his mouth to speak, he doesn't seem able to choke out even one word.

That makes me frown. "Sylvan? Did something happen? Do I need to rearrange someone's face?"

"No, I just… I cannot wait a minute longer. And in fact, I do not wish to wait until after the reception, as is the usual way. I can't bear that you are not yet mine. So much can happen in a few hours, and if you were to be taken from me because I am unable to protect you, I would never forgive myself."

I stall, still on my knee before him as he trembles with emotion, fighting tears, as if I were a piece of jewelry anyone could just snatch off the counter. Thinking about it makes me smile, but then I remember the strange pull I felt when the grimsmith tied our shadows, and it sinks in that Sylvan's fears are in fact very real.

"You want to… skip the party?"

"No, I wish for us to make our vows now. I want you to become my Dark Companion, and for our hearts to be forever tied. I don't care for tradition, for what others may think of me, or that this moon is fake." He points to the large lamp above us, which imitates a moon glowing red. "The one outside is very real, full, and it will bless our bond whenever we choose to make it."

My heart flutters in a way it hasn't since the day I chose to kill for a man I thought I loved. That decision proved disastrous. I lost my freedom and found out he's been manipulating me all along. But Sylvan? He's wearing his heart on his sleeve, and I love that about him.

With elation radiating inside me, I pluck the titanium ring out of my pocket and show it to my fiancé. It's a trinket, really, studded with crystals. I don't think they're precious gems, but what do I know? One is clear and sparkly, one is red and one is blue. I stole it from Tassarion's workshop, and while that bastard earned everything he got, I have to admit that he had talent for this metalsmithing thing.

"Do you know what this tradition means in my world?" I ask, pushing it on Sylvan's ring finger. I frown when it proves way too loose on his dainty hand, but such things can be corrected in the future.

His pale face flushes. "My apologies, I am not sure."

I… did not expect *that* response, but I can work with it. Worse hurdles have been thrown my way in the past, so I smile, rub my face against his palm, and kiss it. "Marry me, Sylvan Goldweed. Now."

Sylvan brightens with a smile so wide and so joyful, my heart leaps. He's a beautiful elven prince, and he wants *me*. "And this ring means that?" He looks at the trinket on his finger, amazed as if I gave him a star from the sky.

"If you accept it, it means you agree," I say and rise to my feet, already knowing his answer. He wouldn't be here if he didn't want me. He wouldn't risk everything for me, nor kill for me, yet here we are. Still, I add, "please."

"I will. I do. I accept it," he says, as if he expects me to take back my offer if he doesn't take it fast enough. He's *glowing* when he stands on his toes and pulls me down by my elaborate cravat for a kiss. His lips are so soft, so welcoming, and he said yes to my proposal. I knew my suffering would eventually lead me somewhere good. Even in my darkest moments, I've never lost hope and it's why I crawled out of that river in what I thought was a dream. I could have given in to despair and let the current take me, but deep in my gut, I knew there was more for me.

And here it is, in my arms, and it has the form of the most beautiful man I've ever seen.

"Then let's do it," I urge him. "Let's marry now!"

There are whole galaxies in his eyes, and each time I peek into them, the need to take a leap of faith becomes more insistent. I don't think I've ever wanted anything this much.

Sylvan slips out of my grasp, and I already miss his fresh smell, his warmth. Determination and focus are back on his face as he looks around. "Yes. All you truly need to do once I cover us with my shadow, is vow that you are mine, body, soul, and shadow. And mean it. But!" He raises his finger when I'm about to say these magic words, because fuck yes, I can say it and mean it. This tiny cutie owns me already, even if it's him who's mine in the sheets. "Bear with me a second, I want to do things right. Or as right as possible," he adds, exasperated, when he plucks a big red rose out of a lush bouquet on a side table. "Tradition dictates the rose should be of the midnight blue variety, but this will do."

I remember another thing he's talked about extensively and dash for the window. As soon as I pull away the curtain, we are covered in the glow of a moon larger than any I've ever seen, and for a moment I forget why I've uncovered it in the first place.

I almost feel its cool radiance, as if it were the morning sun in the summer. "It's so... so different."

"It's closer to us than the one in your world," Sylvan says and approaches me with the rose. "I hope you will be able to enjoy it as much as the sun."

"I'd rather have you than the sun." I slide both my hands under his jaw. His neck is delicate, like a bird's, and I promise myself that he will never be harmed as long as I'm around. No matter what I have to do in this strange new world, I will take care of him in ways his family never did.

He looks up at me, so full of emotion, and I'm reminded of how he grabbed a stool at the grimsmith's to reach my lips for a kiss.

"Would you like to be higher?" I point to a large chest he could stand on, but he stops me when I try to move.

"No. I want you to see me as I am and choose me still," Sylvan says with all seriousness, as if he had warts all over his face, not skin smooth as porcelain, sweet pink lips, and a compact body I imagine naked whenever my thoughts drift off.

I nod, eyes pinned to his earnest expression. "Of course I choose you. How could I choose anyone else now that I met you?"

I feel like the biggest sap when my eyes start stinging, but the words come straight from my heart. My brothers always mocked me for my interest in pretty twinks, but they don't get it. I have a soft side I can only show to someone who isn't like me. Sylvan's personality might be all jagged edges on the outside, but they fit mine like we're two pieces of the same broken vase. Life has dragged us both over the gravel in different ways, and to him, I can be important, special. Not just because of my shadow. I sense in his touch, in his kisses, and in his words, that he needs to be taken care of.

He can handle himself. Hell, he was the one to lead us here, to get his collar off, and to kill a man who stood in his way. But he's so fragile in places he shows no one else but me. He seeks my hugs and attention like an abandoned kitten, and I'll never betray him. He might be a prince of the Nocturne Court and some shadow wielding mage, but I can give him the safety and affection he craves. If this is all some elaborate scheme at manipulating me, then so be it.

I gasp when his pale shadow rises off the floor behind him like a silent ghost. "Don't be afraid," he whispers when I flinch, but when the shadow expands and settles over us like a widow's veil, a strange sense of peace overcomes me.

"So now, I grab this rose by the stem," Sylvan explains, and I'm about to stop him at the sight of sharp thorns, but it's too late. He closes his palm and squeezes it with a hiss. "And now you put your hand over mine," he says, holding the rose between us.

I spot a droplet of blood sliding down his hand and hope this ritual doesn't involve any more pain on his side. I want to grab a piece of cloth and wrap his hand, but he is the one who knows what he's doing, so I swallow my discomfort and cradle his slender hand in mine, like he told me. I tower over him in every way, yet when our eyes meet, I know he'd be as ready to stand between me and danger as I am for him.

"And now?" I whisper, afraid the sound of my voice might shatter the spell that's meant to connect us forever.

"This gesture symbolizes that even though I take your shadow, I will not abuse your trust. I will take the brunt of any injury." Sylvan is so earnest as he looks into my eyes. His hand is so dainty in mine, but he's the one bleeding, and I get it, suddenly choked up.

With my size, and the violence I so easily mete out, I never thought anyone would consider wanting to be *my* protector. I always thought that I would always be the one to give while my partner takes. Yet here Sylvan is, promising to bleed for me. I'm so touched I don't know what to do with myself, but Sylvan saves me by speaking.

"You are truly my promised, a man brought to me by destiny. I never imagined I would one day have a Dark Companion of my own, let alone one who is also my lover. I know you're leaving behind your world, and everything you know, so this is my promise that I'll make sure you never regret choosing me. I would have not been able to save you from the River of Souls, and yet a twist of fate sent you my way. You give me courage, you make me believe in myself, you make me laugh, and you touched parts of me that no one ever has."

Sylvan shoves me gently when I smirk. "I don't mean *those* parts!" He takes a deep breath and goes on while my insides turn into mush. "I love you, and I will never abuse my position. I will trust you, I will cherish you, and if you ever find yourself in darkness, I will be your moonlight. And as I promised you when we met, my body is yours."

It might be cliche, but I really do feel at a loss for words as he makes his declaration in a voice trembling with emotion. So I swallow and lean closer as the warm glow of the moon's rays caresses my face. Nobody has ever even tried saying such things to me. I'm almost afraid that I don't deserve so much love, that Sylvan's belief in me is misplaced. But as joy bubbles in the middle of my chest, I find the strength to chase away doubts and tell myself that whether I am worthy of trust or not is up to me, and the very idea of disappointing this sweet man, who's picked *me* over others makes me ache.

I clear my throat, noticing that my silence is unnerving to him. "I... I don't know such pretty words. I would write a poem for you, if I could, but since I don't know how, I want you to know this: I will *always* be in your corner, okay? If you jump down a cliff, I will follow. You're the one who makes plans, and I'll help you fulfill your dreams, because being at your side already fulfills mine. I will do my best so that you're always happy and so you never regret bonding to me."

My lips dry as I squeeze his hands more firmly. I know I can never satisfy his poetic heart, but maybe I don't have to? Maybe all he needs from me is what I *can* offer? "I love you."

"Hawk..." Sylvan whispers, and a tear slides down his cheek.

I kiss it off his skin. I want to always be there to dry his tears. "Is this... Are we married now?" I ask, giddy like a kid offered a ball of cotton candy bigger than his head.

Sylvan snorts, looking just as happy as I feel. "You still need to say *the words* and mean them."

"Ah yes!" I got so overwhelmed with my vow that I completely forgot about it, but I still remember the sentence he told me earlier, so I repeat it to him, full of excitement for what this next chapter of my life will bring. "Sylvan Goldweed, the most handsome elf ever, I promise you that from now on I am yours, body, soul, and shadow."

Sylvan gasps, and his pupils dilate, but I feel it too.

The connection that was only a thread before, no thicker than a single strand of hair, barely noticeable, becomes a stream. Invisible, yet so clear. I am squeezing his hand over the rose, but I swear I can sense his heartbeat against my chest.

No. Inside me. That's how close he is.

Sylvan's lips tremble, and when his pulse quickens, I sense it under my skin. He drops the rose and it falls into what looks like a pit of darkness under our feet. It's so black and endless my instincts scream for me to leap away to the carpet. But Sylvan is standing on this shadow too, so I stay.

He's struggling to catch his breath, so I slide my arm around his waist to steady him.

"There's... there's just... so *much* of it," he utters in amazement, leaning into me.

I give a short laugh, even though I'm emotional as if someone has injected me with pure adrenaline. "So I've been told."

Sylvan laughs louder than my joke deserves, but it's the sweetest sound. So carefree and full of delight. His heart is racing as if he were on the verge of orgasm, and it's kinda making me horny. Does this early bonding mean we get to have an early wedding night too?

He places a hand on my chest, fingers splayed, and when he pulls it away, thick black goo is stuck to it like chewing gum.

Sylvan glances up at me with a grin. "Hawk, I promise, I would have loved you regardless, but *this* is amazing, and I've not even scratched the surface. The things I will do with this..." He arches up to kiss me like usual, but then, just as I'm about to pull him in my arms, the shadows under his feet grow and lift him so he can reach my lips with ease.

I suck in warm air straight from his mouth, elated and somehow even more in tune with his body. I sense sparks wherever we touch, and when he plays with my liquid shadow, twisting it in his fingers, it's almost as if he were touching me on the inside. Not physically, but somewhere beyond that. In my... soul.

It's corny, yeah, but how else can I describe something so far beyond my experience?

My toes curl. My lips tremble, and as he stretches the black threads between his hands, I lean forward and capture his mouth in a kiss. I cannot take this strange contact-no contact moment where it's my shadow being touched instead of my flesh, but he responds with a soft moan, and his knee slides up the side of my leg, as if he were trying to climb me.

Sylvan looks back at the door. "M-maybe we could..." He licks his lips, and I know exactly what he wants. I pick him up and carry him to one of the lush red couches with one thing on my mind.

Of course that's the moment the door opens and Fenren steps in, closely followed by the tailor who worked on my clothes. "No! Why would you spoil the fun for yourselves and your guests?" he asks as if I or Sylvan had any reason to care about the opinions of random elves, who happened to stay at the same inn. But the moment of passion's been disrupted, and when my man scrambles to his feet, I know fun time is over.

I'm guessing the King of Smugglers won't be as easy to dismiss as the tailor was.

Sylvan clears his throat and spreads his arms. "It is hard to stay away from my beloved."

"I have brought some grooming supplies," the tailor says, while all I can focus on is Sylvan and the new, unfamiliar bond between us.

When my *husband* reaches the doorway, he turns, kisses his hand, then blows me that smooch in the form of a small heart formed from shadow. It floats my way like smoke until it lands on my cheek.

I have never felt so loved, and I cannot wait for everyone to witness our union.

CHAPTER 25

Sylvan

I've read about the magical bond entwining a shadow-wielder and their Dark Companion. In the past, I didn't believe myself capable of forging one, and a part of me hoped the much-celebrated connection was being exaggerated. I have no more doubts. An unbreakable thread ties my soul to Hawk's, and even when we're apart, I sense his presence at the very center of me.

If either of us were lost, the other could find him.

If melancholy were to take hold, I could warm my heart with the glow of the love he feels for me. For he wants me the way I am, and I know I couldn't have picked a better Companion even if Hawk's shadow was as pale as mine.

If that one day means my downfall, then so be it.

Elves can lead long lives. An eternity, if we make that our goal, but our desires, our curiosity, or our fury are so intense they often lead us to a premature death. The old me would have called my current actions foolish, but while baring my soul to someone else is a great risk, I can't regret it when I sense my lover's precious heart beating for me whenever I reach out to stroke the shadow thread that now connects us.

I thought I wanted power.

But while I have it now, it seems so insignificant in the face of Hawk's vow. His love. His devotion to me.

A part of me wishes my family were here to witness our union, but what for when we get to celebrate with strangers who have already been much kinder than my blood ever was?

All the lights are off as I await Hawk in the main room of the tavern, and I'm so nervous I'm glad I had a sip of wine when it was offered to me.

The wedding guests gathered around me take a silent breath when the door opens. My beast towers over Fenren, who urges him to lower his head so he doesn't hit it on the doorframe. Hawk is wearing a blindfold, because I wanted to keep that bit of court tradition in the ceremony, but he would have probably struggled in the dark anyway.

It's been less than an hour since I last saw him, and I've sensed his presence nearby through our shadow bond. The connection is still so fresh I can barely cope with being parted from him. It's as if I was expected to function without my right hand, but my other half is here now, and all will be well.

My Dark Companion's eyes are covered, but he must sense my proximity too, because his heartbeat quickens.

The elves gathered around us do their best to stay quiet, and a soft cough coming from the corner cannot spoil this moment for either of us. Fenren leads the way, but the long, confident strides my beloved takes prove how badly he wants to join me.

A breeze that must have entered through an open window carries his earthy scent toward me, and I take a lungful of it, no longer nervous or plagued by doubt. When Hawk is close enough for me to see his handsome features in the glow of the single candle I'm holding, Fenren pulls off his blindfold.

My face will be the first thing he sees, because I am his flame in the night. His protector. His guardian in the Nightmare Realm. No one needs to know it's Hawk who lights up *my* sky when our eyes meet.

Hawk smiles, and so do I as our hands entwine in front of all those strangers. I regret my Companion won't get the pomp of a court wedding, with a lush ball to celebrate our union. He is the best thing that's ever happened to me and deserves to be presented as the jewel he is, clad in the fine moth robes customarily worn by Dark Companions during a royal wedding.

But my Hawk is no dainty moth. He's a bull. Affectionate yet powerful, and delicate fabrics and bejeweled wings wouldn't suit him. I don't need him to fit the mold of the many Dark Companions who came before him when he is perfect just the way he is.

As we stand under the antler chandelier, it's clear to me that such trivialities don't matter. He and I have bonded for life, and nothing can come between us.

The flame balancing at the tip of my candle turns his eyes into pools of gold, adding warmth to their usual green.

"Let me lead you through the dark," I whisper the words a royal would say to their promised during the ceremony. No one needs to know that we've already made our bond with the Moon as our witness. My heart is suddenly so full I have to hold back tears.

Hawk swallows, and I see the muscles of his jaw twitch as he watches me with eyes so soulful I can't understand why I initially rejected him. Our meeting was written in the stars, and I have almost missed a connection so powerful and deep his presence takes my breath away. When Hawk blows out the candle, symbolically confirming his trust in me, I close my eyes and smell the burning wax, joyful about the many days and nights we shall have together.

Swamplights come to life all around us, and several dozen elves erupt with loud cheers while tavern servers appear with huge trays full of drinks and snacks. Our guests are more interested in free food than our happiness, but I can't hold that against them, because all the pats Hawk is receiving make his smile grow ever wider.

I was never fond of all attention being on me, so I'm glad Hawk is such a beacon for wide-eyed elves. Most of those gathered have probably seen a human or two, since I've got no doubt lots of them work with Fenren, but Hawk is truly something else.

So tall he has to watch his head constantly, wide in the shoulders, and handsome, he's like a warrior from ancient ballads. He's the kind of man you'd imagine capable of slaying a leviathan with his bare hands, or wielding the Frostblade, which hasn't even been picked up in centuries, let alone used.

I'm so proud to call him my Dark Companion.

"I bet you're hungry," I say, squeezing his hand and pulling him toward the overflowing buffet set up in the corner. It features a whole roasted Goldbeak as the centerpiece, and while I already know I won't be eating many of the foods on offer, the sight of its crispy skin makes my mouth water. Maybe back when I still lived at the Nocturne Court, I would have seen the food here as plebeian, but after long weeks in the world of humans and eating soft bread for almost every meal, the offerings laid out in front of me are a feast for the ages. No wonder the sight of all the rolls, roasted meats, cheeses, and mushroom dishes is making Hawk's eyes shine.

"Wow. Yes. I am extra hungry, with a side of hungry," he says and frowns, picking up an open sand clam, dusted with salt and the bright green shassel powder. "What is that?"

I explain to him how to eat it and wonder whether I should wait for someone to serve me the meat, but as the crispy skin starts to disappear on people's plates, I join in the uncouth ritual of ripping some off.

I'm very aware of people stealing glances at me or outright staring. I have been humbled by my experience in the human world and don't feel as out of place in this tavern as I would have before my banishment. After all, am I not also a criminal as no doubt many of the elves here are? We might not be *exactly* the same, since I am no ordinary cutthroat, but I do feel a certain camaraderie with those people.

Hawk sucks the clam from its shell, and I grin when he shakes at the flavor spreading in his mouth.

"What? Not to your liking?"

"It's so... fizzy. I never had anything quite like that," he tells me before grabbing one of the legs of the roast bird and tearing it off.

Two musicians choose this moment to start playing in the corner, and I flinch when the whole inn shakes with the thumping of feet as the guests stomp with approval. I'm shocked to see my Hawk jump up and down to join them, but then again, this is not the palace, and actions that would have made one the laughing stock at court seem perfectly acceptable in this tavern.

Maybe I actually like not being judged for enjoying myself.

"Oh, and this tastes just like that chicken we had at the gas station!"

I bite into the crispy skin and grin at him. "It does! What was it... thyme? That's what it's called?"

Hawk laughs. "They used a herb from my world? How luxurious! Wait, you've got some grease—" he leans in and wipes my chin with his sleeve. It's so ridiculous to be doing this in public, but I don't even mind anymore.

I stroke Hawk's clean-shaven cheek. "Thank you. I need to be presentable for my husband."

Hawk stalls and leans into my touch. "You know when I find you most presentable? Naked," he says with a grin, then drops the bone remaining in his hand into a bucket, and before I can stop him, wipes his hands on the tablecloth. My first thought is that I'll need to teach him many things once we're back at court, but when he grins and takes a goblet of cherin for each of us, my initial embarrassment fades. He is altering his whole life for me. It's only fair I don't force him into conventions he doesn't seem to care for.

"Is it wrong of me to also await our wedding night with bated breath?" I ask since the music is so loud I doubt anyone could overhear us.

My companion is satisfied with that answer and wiggles his brows before handing me my cup and knocking his against it. "Our wedding night and every other night to come," he says and guides me to the wall, where he can so easily entrap me with his firm body. I know the others are staring at this blatant display of desire, but I don't care enough to push him away.

Let them see that I am an object of lust for this amazing man. That I don't need to be taller or have wider shoulders to make him wild for me.

"I want to get drunk. And dance. And act as if all those people are my personal friends. And then I'll take you next door. You think you'll be able to keep your voice in?" he teases, whispering in my ear.

I drink from my cup, and I have to admit that it's some intensely potent cherin. Then again, maybe this drink always bites the tongue and the back of the throat. I wouldn't know, since Mother forbade me from consuming liquor due to my weak constitution. But she isn't here, and this is *my* wedding. Why shouldn't I enjoy myself? I'm back from banishment, and I have a Dark Companion whose shadow is so endless it will be spoken of in legends. I can't even begin to imagine the things we may achieve together.

"Maybe I won't, maybe I'll need your hand on my mouth." I meet his gaze with my heart beating to the rhythm of the fast melody around us. "For now, let's make your dream come true." I say and pull him toward the dancing crowd.

A tall elf with two long dark braids and a scar on his cheek steps in our way.

"I challenge you to arm wrestling," he says, and I know what this is about as soon as I spot two women giggling over cups of wine.

Hawk inhales, ready to agree, but he stalls and shoots me a glance, only saying yes once I give him a shallow nod. It makes me so happy to know he considers us a team. By the time he sits at the corner table and slams the challenger's hand down, winning the weaponless duel, I cheer louder than anyone else. He wins the next four matches, and then we end up getting our ears pierced, as local tradition dictates.

The earrings are a pair of small silver tears, which might not be suitable for a royal and his Dark Companion, but they do suit *us*. When Hawk lifts me up as he attempts to participate in a country dance, I don't regret the bloodstain on my shirt, nor the throbbing in my earlobe.

The rich, sweet cherin flows in my veins, making me flush when my Companion, my *husband*, squeezes me tightly and twirls in the middle of the room.

I've never laughed this loudly, and I don't know if it's the alcohol, or if I'm drunk on my beloved, but it doesn't matter. He's so happy to be dancing and eating, and drinking after the years he spent in prison that all I want to do is indulge him.

I'm not the most accomplished dancer even when I know the steps, but I laugh even though I'm making a fool of myself, because with Hawk, it's fun to just *be*. We twirl, we drink more, not caring about time, because our vows have already been said.

I might have gotten carried away and explained my thinking in far too much detail to a man serving me a tart beer. I don't remember that part very well. Only that as I was finishing my thought, Hawk arrived at my side to take the man's hand off my forearm.

I think they argued. But I can't be sure.

But what I do remember is that Hawk never left my side, that he told me about places in the human realm where men who desire the company of other man can dance and have fun. Apparently, during his first night in such a place, he ended up slipping on the slick floor and injured his head. I'm positive the ghost of a scar remaining from that occurrence is still visible at the side of his forehead, and I kiss its general location when he picks me up and moves us to a comfortable booth in the corner.

People come and go, eager to exchange a few words with one of the few humans they've ever met. Even those who visit the human realm to smuggle goods are interested in spending time with my tall, handsome spouse, but while Hawk enjoys the attention, he does nothing that might fuel the green fire of booze-infused jealousy inside me. He keeps including me in conversations, he always keeps at least one hand on my body, and whenever there's an opportunity, he drags me back onto the dancefloor, proud and joyful that I'm the one in his arms.

When someone laughs that it would have been easier for him to dance with someone taller, Hawk takes such great offense I have to break up a fight. It does give me quite some satisfaction that I get to use Hawk's shadow to do so. Though while I was intending to force the rude traveller back, I end up pushing a shield of shadow too hard at him, and he falls into the shadowild. I didn't even know I had access to the shadow realm, as my own powers have always been far too flimsy to even attempt entering that space. But after the initial panic, we manage to pull him out and all is good again.

Hawk then shows off just how easy it is to dance with me by carrying me all the way through a whole song while whispering filth into my ear. Once he puts me down, I'm so overheated it's as though I'm blushing all over my body, and I can't even make myself protest when he sneaks his big, strong hand under my shirt, exploring the plains of my skin with snake-like swirls. I'm on the verge of letting him go farther and get the pesky garment off me, right here, in front of all those people, but Fenren announces another game, one that needs to be started by the newly married couple.

Ivy and one other girl drag me into a small room and shut the door, explaining I'll need to recognize Hawk's knock among many others. The catch? I'll need to kiss the one I open the door for, whether I like it or not. As pleasant as the laziness brought upon me by cherin is, my drunken state is getting me worried, because if I lock lips with someone else, Hawk is bound to break a nose or two.

A part of me doesn't mind, but I do not want any more blood on my clothes.

My mind is scrambled, and I'm not all that confident in my choices when I say 'no' to the first two people knocking. Relief fills me when the third person taps in the rhythm of a song we heard all too many times on the radio during our car trip to Boston.

I belt out the lyrics and open the door, laughing. What a stupid game. And yet I'm so happy to have won I climb Hawk and let him hold me up for a kiss. He tastes of wine and something sweet, smells like heaven, and I now wish to bed him sooner rather than later.

"I knew you'd recognize me," he whispers, moving his lips to my ear as one of the musicians playing in the background slips, failing to hit the right note. Such things never happen with professional music masters at court, but it doesn't matter, because the amateurs gave me more joy than any ball I've attended at the Nocturne Court. This one is celebrating me and my mate, and that makes it special.

I press my forehead to his and close my eyes as he carries me through the stormy waves of dancing bodies. His heartbeat pulses against my ear, his shadow is practically a part of me now. When I dip my fingers into the shadowild in the crevice between our bodies, the sense of absolute contentment it offers makes me fantasize about curating my own pocket dimension, just for me and Hawk. Anything is possible with a shadow like his.

Just as I kiss him to yet more hooting and clapping, the main door bursts open, kicked in by a heavy boot. I look over Hawk's shoulder, dazed, only to meet the amber gaze of no one other than my damn *cousin*.

Prince Tristan Bloodweed. Tall, dashing, with long hair like waterfalls of red wine, and leather boots made to emphasize his muscular thighs.

Otherwise known as Thorn In My Side.

I'm too drunk to think straight, overwhelmed by the avalanche of problems I imagine this will cause. But my mind is so thoroughly soaked in cherin I struggle to come up with a plan.

My heart sinks when something glistens at me from his chest and I finally recognize the crest of the Nightcloaks—a gate wrapped in thorns. They're the wardens of the realm and deal with the safety of its borders.

Which means he's here for me.

CHAPTER 26

HAWK

Sylvan is almost too drunk to stand on his own feet, so I'm in the middle of carrying him to our wedding suite when the music comes to an abrupt stop and all the elves go so quiet their silence rings in my ears like a scream. Danger crawls up my back, a scorpion about to attack whether I pay attention to it or not. I know this feeling way too well.

I look back, narrowing my eyes when a cool breeze combs back my hair. It brings the scent of forest and steel, and by the time I zero in on two soaring figures standing at the entrance to the tavern, one of the men, a broad-shouldered yet lanky elf with long golden tresses speaks up in a clear baritone.

"Sir Lorsen Gloombane, captain of the Nightcloaks. Prince Tristan Bloodweed, my second," he adds, gesturing at a muscular elven man standing to his right. "We're here to investigate the disappearance of an exile. Cooperate, and you will soon be able to return to your present activities."

A raid can't... be good. Especially as I'm holding *an exile* in my arms.

I do a one-eighty and head for the stairs in the hope that we can slip out the window and disappear in the dark, but then the blond elf calls out a familiar name, and a whole chain of quiet curse words drops from my lips.

"The Grimsmith, Tassarion, is missing. He is an elf with ears mutilated to look like a human's."

Relief floods my muscles when I realize it's not us they're looking for, but then Prince Tristan calls out for my new husband, and Sylvan jerks in my arms, demanding that I let him go. If he wanted to be discreet about it, that did not work out, since the *thud* of his boots hitting the wooden floor is loud like a fire alarm in the night.

Tristan shouts his name again, but Sylvan's already grabbing my hand and dragging me toward the stairs, as if he thinks we can walk out without a confrontation. I don't fight him, since that would only result in more commotion, but the loud creak erupting behind us tells me I better look for a weapon, and fast.

We're halfway up the stairs when the red-haired elf in shiny dark armor appears on the landing, staring at us as if we were two children caught stealing fruit from the neighbor's garden. I'm confused to see him there, because he was behind us moments ago, but then I realize that the broad, elongated shadows extending from his back aren't a trick of the light.

This man has wings and is hovering two inches above the floor.

Despite having an obsidian-like sheen, they appear light as wisps of smoke, and I'm left staring, because what else do I not know about this world?

"Can... *you* do that?" I ask Sylvan.

He whips his head around and scowls. "Whose side are you on?"

Behind us, the voice of the golden-haired elf comes from way too close for my liking, and I squeeze Sylvan's fingers before glancing over my shoulder to spot *Sir Lorsen Gloombane* at the bottom of the stairs, cutting our only way out of this mess.

"Sylvan? Sylvan Goldweed? Your cousin, whom Lord Kyran banished merely two months ago?"

Cousin?

I don't see any familial resemblance between my pocket-sized elf and Tristan, who's built like a wildcat in its prime, but I only care about their connection if it can help us wiggle out of this mess. My hopes are dispersed the moment the redhead speaks.

"The very same. We should have been alerted about his crossing by the sigils on his collar, but looks like he's not wearing it."

"Interesting that the man we're looking for is one of the few who could remove it." Gloombane says, unsheathing a long, curved sword in a silent threat.

A drop of sweat rolls down my back as I note five more Nightcloaks with chest plates bearing the symbol of a gate. They're standing down for now, but their posture tells me they're ready to step in the moment their captain commands them to. One can fly and could hunt Sylvan down like an eagle capturing a chihuahua for dinner, so how can I possibly defend my man?

But Tristan can't hear my inner monologue and lands on the floor, folding his wings. "Look, Sylvan, you might be a traitor, but you did save my life once. I don't want bloodshed. You are the last Goldweed of your generation. Please, stand down and follow us outside along with your... your human." He frowns, taking me in as if I was a pet, not Sylvan's spouse. "We both know you can't win this."

Sylvan's sweaty hand twitches in mine, and something pulls at the very core of me, somewhere beyond flesh. "How dare you? You have no idea what I'm capable of!"

I stiffen when the stairs creak, and a glance down the steps tells me one of the soldiers is climbing our way with a rope so matte and black it looks as if it's made of coal. We're surrounded, and the noose tightens around us, leaving little breathing room.

"You know it's true, cousin," Tristan insists when the soldier dashes our way, spinning the rope in her hands as if it were a lasso. I step between Sylvan and her, ready to protect my man as the rope flies our way. Obsidian spikes rush from behind me, transforming the cord into dust at first contact. The shadow tendrils then leap toward the soldier and soften to the consistency of flesh, slamming into her. The railing breaks when the black tentacle shoves her off the stairs and into the nearest wall. Her fall is met by stunned silence, which then transforms into panic as all our wedding guests and tavern workers fling themselves at the exits.

I'm frozen, unsure what's just happened until I realize that it's Sylvan who controls the dark force behind the tentacle.

One of the other Nightcloaks dashes to his fallen comrade, but raw fear put its claws into every single person around us, even Tristan, who pulls out his own sword, watching us, wide-eyed. "What did you—" His voice chokes when he stares at the black expanse at Sylvan's feet, then sees where it originates. "That shadow..."

Something pulls deep inside me again, making me lightheaded as the black goo covering the floor simmers.

"Out of my way!" Sylvan slurs, shaking off my hand, and dashes forward so abruptly his tall and muscular cousin recoils like a wolf that might have met its match. My husband's footing is unsteady from all the booze he's drunk, but he's not letting that stop him and claws much longer and sturdier than the ones that killed Tassarion erupt from his fingers toward Tristan.

I'm about to follow him and ensure he doesn't end up impaling himself on that stuff when an icy fog settles around me. Gloombane is a faint shadow below, but he too disappears, with a coppery flash in his eyes. My jaw drops open when I realize I can't spot the railings anymore. Even my own hands remain obscured by cold gray mist. How am I supposed to fight *magic*?

Just as I'm about to head forward, Sylvan's voice echoes from the wrong direction. Could it be that I'm lost without any visual clues to go by? Or is this mist made to confuse my senses?

Squawks resonate everywhere around me, as if I'm surrounded by a maze full of hungry mice. I turn once. Twice. Thrice, because my sense of danger is ringing in alarm, but I can't spot anything in this fog. My heart thrums. My back is damp, but just as I'm about to blindly run forward, the gray cloud around me disperses, creating a bubble of clear air. Huge bats smash against the translucent shield protecting me from the fog one after another until the smoke disappears. It reveals Gloombane scowling from across the room. He must have been the one causing the fog, so the only logical conclusion is that Sylvan shielded me with his new powers.

I'm in way over my head.

The tavern spins, then rocks like a ship during a heavy storm, and I find myself dropping to my knees. Blood drizzles to the wooden floor and it takes me a moment to work out where it originates. My nose and gums. I can taste iron, but a little nosebleed isn't enough to stop me. I've survived drowning, an overdose, two car crashes, and a stabbing. This shit is nothing. When I look up, Sylvan is a blurry figure three steps above, but at least I can see him again. I summon my strength and drag him back to me.

"The kitchen," I whisper, wiping my bleeding nose on the sleeve of the coat that was carefully tailored to my size not that long ago. Sylvan's eyes are bloodshot when he glances my way, but at the top of the stairs Tristan is picking himself up from whatever happened while the fog kept me blinded. We both stumble down the steps, because we either flee or confront *all* the Nightcloaks, and I'm definitely not up for fighting men who can create rabid bats out of smoke.

Gloombane stands in our way with two of his men at the flanks, but the floor below them turns black, then burns like paper around a fallen ember, and all three elves fall into the void. Are they dead? Trapped like that poor wedding guest was earlier? Can't pretend that I care, but another bout of weakness forces me to grab the railing for support as I stumble. I couldn't have drank *that much*, could I? My eyes remain open though, and I watch the hole in the wooden planks turn dull before retreating under Sylvan's feet like a matte oil spill sucked back to its source.

"Captain!" one of the remaining wardens cries. His face is stiff with tension, but the moment he raises his sword and charges, Sylvan's arm transforms into a fat tentacle, which slams the man into the nearby table. The thin wooden legs break from the force of this freaky magic, the floor cracks, and we make a dash for the open kitchen.

The level of destruction around us is pure madness, but I'm too exhausted and shocked to do anything other than grab Sylvan's shoulder and let him lead. Surrounded by dust and the remnants of the gray fog, we're about to reach our destination when Tristan Bloodweed's formidable form lands in front of us. This time, he's ready and lashes out at Sylvan, who stumbles over his own feet, saved from his cousin's blade by my quick thinking. I pull him to my chest and spin around, alarmed by a *clang* of metal behind me. A dusky shape looms in the magic mist, and I blindly slam my fist into it, hitting metal, bone, and flesh.

The last Cloak collapses with a dull cry as pain flashes up my forearm, replaced by tingling heat. I fall over as a giant force rips Sylvan away from me.

"Stand down! I don't want to hurt you," Tristan cries, standing over Sylvan's petite form like a monster about to feast. I scream out, dragging myself back to my feet, but my voice dies when an invisible force sucks the air out of me. All at once, I'm nauseated, dizzy, and tired. *So,* so tired.

I stare at my swelling fingers and follow the black inkblot of shadow over the floor, all the way to Sylvan, who rises off the floor, levitating. He throws a punch at his cousin. I fear he might hurt his delicate hand, but then obsidian claws erupt from his fingers and tear through Tristan's wing.

The red-headed soldier shrieks, even though his cut appendage turns to dust before it can hit the floor. Shell-shocked, Tristan takes a step back, but Sylvan doesn't hesitate. A massive shadow tentacle emerging from under Sylvan's feet slams Tristan down, and then twists, pulling the other wing out, as if it were a single feather.

His pained cry rings in my ears as I crawl forward, focused on Sylvan, who collapses onto his ass and... vomits.

Shit.

Braving the lightheadedness making every move a fight, I reach him just in time to offer him my coat as a means to clean up. I don't know if Sylvan's this drunk, or if using those powers has such a detrimental effect on him, but I'll worry about that later. With Tristan knocked out and the others gone, I need to seize the opportunity to disappear.

"Let's go. Your shadow is... *amazing*," Sylvan mumbles when I scoop him into my arms and stumble toward the kitchen.

His words make me slow down, and while I get with the program and dash into the stew-scented rooms that should lead me to some kind of back door, my mind spins with questions. I noticed that he was manipulating my shadow to fight off the Nightcloaks, but is that why I'm so lightheaded and exhausted? Why my legs shake and my nose bleeds?

The way he fought Tristan, recklessly as if he wanted to prove something rather than just get us out of trouble, didn't show any care for my wellbeing. When he first tried to convince me to start our arrangement, he claimed the exchange would happen at no real cost to me. Was he... lying all along?

Cold dread pools in my gut as I rush into a room full of dirty dishes, using the wall to support one of my shoulders. I'm panting with the effort of propelling both myself and Sylvan forward, but despite the ache in my chest, I remain desperate to get him to safety. Whether his intentions toward me were pure or not remains to be seen, but *my* feelings remain unchanged, and I would not abandon him.

I reimagine my dainty prince as the sea witch from *The Little Mermaid*, and saying, "It won't cost much, just your *shadow*."

I gasp at the sight of a narrow wooden door leading into the moonlit yard on the other side of the room, but before I can dash toward it, a wardrobe opens and Fenren whistles at me from behind the curtain of aprons and tablecloths.

"Follow me," he whispers, and I don't bother considering whether he's a friend or foe. He's not a Nightcloak, and in my book that's more than enough.

"Thank you so much. I don't know where I am," I say when Fenren shuts the door hidden in the back of the wardrobe and picks up a torch.

His gaze scans me, then Sylvan passed out in my arms, and he shakes his head. "I'm only doing this because your groom ruined my tavern, and dead debtors don't pay. You two better reimburse me once this is all over."

So much for kindness and pleasant smiles.

I don't have the strength to answer and follow him down a passage not built with someone my size in mind. But that is the least of my worries. The man I've banked my whole future on was flippant with my shadow—my health and life—all because he wanted to show off his newly acquired power. Is that really the boy I fell for so hard? The boy I decided to take so many dumb risks for? Could it be that... my family was right and I once again put my trust in the wrong person?

Going to prison for someone is one thing, but this strange parasitic arrangement? The truth is that I don't quite know how the shadow bond that felt so good earlier works. Could he drain me at will? Keep me weak? Dispose of me when he's bored?

Am I only my shadow to him...? After that vow of undying love?

Maybe three days really is too little time to get to know a guy?

CHAPTER 27

SYLVAN

My head feels like a pot being beaten by a metal spoon over and over again. But maybe it's my stomach that's the pot, because it's overflowing, boiling, and I'm vomiting again. I'm half-lucid, and barely remember fragments of what I did at the inn.

Did I really grab Tristan, who is one of the strongest shadow-wielders I know, like a puppet and smash him into a wall? Did I rip his wings off? Fortunately for him, they're shadow, so he'll manage to nurture them back to their right form eventually, but still.

"I feel so bad…" I mumble to Hawk, desperate for pity.

We're in the swamps, the moon is setting as night nears, and the scent of damp earth and leaves, while fresh, does nothing to relieve the violent nausea. I don't remember how I got here, but Fenren informed me that my new husband carried me all the way from the inn. At least now I can be sure he's serious about the whole *till death do us part* vow humans use.

The bench we're sitting on creaks when we move, but it remains solid, and I'm glad I can use the wall of the cabin to lean my back against.

"Why did you drink so much if you can't handle it?" Hawk asks, watching the ruins of an ancient aqueduct sink in the murky waters. The moon now appears even bigger than it had midday, but soon enough its eye will disappear beyond the horizon, leaving us all in the dark, at the mercy of beasts.

I look up at him, ashamed of my state. We're outside a cabin in the middle of a swamp. This remote place functions as a safe house for Fenren and his gang of smugglers. The hut is small, damp, and far from what I could at a stretch call 'charming', but it has stone walls and it can protect us from most of the wild creatures roaming the area. At least the frogs outside are providing interesting background noise.

"Um... that's harsh," I mumble, looking away from the bucket I'm cradling. I must not appear very princely right now. Is it possible that Hawk is rethinking his choice of husband so soon?

He shrugs and covers himself with the threadbare blanket our host offered him earlier. Both our gazes follow a trail of bubbles emerging on the algae-covered surface of the swamp, but while it initially comes our way, the creature creating the disturbance changes direction.

"I'm just surprised," Hawk says after a moment of silence that feels strangely tense.

Fenren emerges from the hut and huffs with exasperation as he lifts a torch and moves it in a circular fashion. When nothing happens, he utters a curse and returns indoors. We could have gone way farther from the inn, but his daughter needs to catch up with us first, and now it seems inevitable that we will all need to share the tiny dwelling tonight.

I sigh and lean my head against the wall. "I just wanted to let go and be happy at our wedding celebration. I never really drank before, so I thought I was having a reasonable amount."

He frowns, watching me while the frogs and insects grow ever louder, as if they were warning each other about the upcoming night.

"Are you... a minor here?"

"A minor... what?" I ask, unsure about the change in conversation direction when even talking about the weather feels like a strain on my mind.

Hawk clears his throat and takes a lungful of the cool, root-scented air. "Since elves live so long... are you still too young to have alcohol?"

I groan. Not this again. "No, but I was advised by my mother that because of my stature, it could have an adverse effect, and that I would make a fool of myself. Guess she was right."

Hawk exhales, and I shudder, because it's difficult not to interpret the sound as agreement. "You should start slow and get used to it gradually. But I get it, that milky booze was very tasty."

But something else is on my mind when I notice that one of his fingers is red and swelling. "What happened?" I grab his hand to examine it.

"It's broken," he says, flinching when I prod the flesh. "Fenren helped me push the bone in place, but now it'll take time to heal. Maybe I should find a stick to keep it safe?"

"One of my books features a great recipe for—" I stall, only to shoot to my feet so fast the world spins around me. At least I might be done emptying my stomach for now. "My books! We left everything at the inn, even the m—"

Relief covers me like a warm blanket when Hawk pulls my hand to his chest and I sense the Sunwolf Crown under his coat. "Figured I better keep it on me, since it's so important," he says before once again obscuring it with the blanket.

I lean in to hug him, so happy I could cry. I might be able to still recover some of my items from Fenren, but losing the mask would have been a disaster. Our future at court hinges on it just as much as it does on Hawk's bottomless shadow.

"I love you so much right now."

He remains quiet as Fenren bursts out of the cabin and cups his hands at his mouth before releasing a strange cry. I've seen something similar done during royal hunts, when beast masters imitate the calls of creatures the party is after, but surely, that cannot be Fenren's goal?

A series of taps resonates over the water in response, and his body language relaxes. "She's here," he says and gestures at us to follow him inside. "Come, I brewed some tea."

Hawk is stiff in my embrace and is quick to untangle himself from it. Did I... do something? I don't want to ask with Fenren within earshot, so I turn to greet Ivy, who emerges from a nearby thatch of bushes in the same dress she wore at the reception, though right now the lush skirt has transformed into pants with the help of a long cord and some knots.

"Uh, finally!" she groans and stretches her back. "I've had to hide inside a barrel for two hours!"

"Is your wife coming with us?" I ask, getting to my toes to see if she has company.

"My wif—" Ivy's face twists into a scowl. "I really don't have the patience to play this game anymore. There is no wife. I just wanted you to go through with the wedding."

Hawk's presence next to me feels even colder.

I look up at him in panic. "I was *not* reconsidering it!" But then I turn back to Ivy, crossing my arms on my chest. "How could you have lied in such a perfidious way?"

She rolls her eyes, joining us on the porch. "Oh, *please*, like it actually matters to you whether I'm happily married or not."

My ears heat up and twitch. "That's not the point!"

"I think I'll stay outside for a bit longer. Really need more air after... all that happened," Hawk says and steps away from the hut just as Ivy enters it, leaving both of us outside.

Something's not right, and, like the research-driven person I am, I will find out what. "I will join you two later as well," I say, but Ivy shuts the door in my face before I even finish speaking. I clear my throat and turn to my husband. "I hope the Nightmare Realm has not proven overwhelming?" I ask, following Hawk down a short pier and leaning against the banister next to him.

The expanse of swampland in front of us is new to me, even though I've read about it and can name every frog, insect, or plant thriving in this environment. I both dread the beasts lurking beneath the surface of the dark water, and wish to touch every flower I can spot, just to learn its texture. There is lots of beauty in those marshes, especially now, with the moon halfway gone beyond the trees, but areas like this are considered dangerous, and no royal in their right mind would risk their life venturing into such treacherous terrain.

Which only shows how low I've fallen.

"It's... not quite what I expected," Hawk mutters and leans forward, massaging the base of his nose.

"Has the alcohol affected you negatively as well?" I stroke his arm. "It was so noble of you to carry me all the way here despite feeling unwell."

I freeze when he pushes my hand off him and meets my gaze with his lips in a thin line. "No, it was not *the alcohol* that affected me. Don't you remember anything?"

I step back and force my mind back to the fight at the tavern. My memories are jumbled, like torn pieces of paper I can try to arrange into a coherent picture. I freeze, recalling the moment Hawk's nose started bleeding, and him stumbling against the banister on the stairs.

I run my fingers over the wood separating me from the murky water he surely wants to throw me into.

"Oh, I... um... I wasn't aware I took so much." Which is stupid of me, since I can sense him through our bond, and I know how much shadow I used to have for my use. Very little. Hawk's feels like a full well, but the truth is that it's not bottomless, and if I take too much, my Dark Companion will be depleted. He will ache, he will be out of breath, he will bleed, and if I choose to take even more, I could crush him.

Did I... lose control and hurt him, on the very same day I vowed to never do such a thing?

Shame is like a spiky ball growing inside my heart. I don't know what to say and just watch him contemplate the moon.

"Do you care?" Hawk asks.

"Do I *care*? There's no one in this world or yours for whom I care more." Yet I don't dare touch him, afraid of being rejected again. Memories from the fight now punch me with their intensity. I wasn't just drunk. I was drunk on *power*, and I took, took, took, stopping only when there was no one left to fight.

"It didn't feel like you cared when you summoned giant spikes, tentacles, and broke the floor just to show off in front of your cousin," Hawk tells me, pinning me to the pier. Is it me, or have the frogs gone silent, eavesdropping on my moment of shame.

Fuck. Tristan. We lost the advantage of making our arrival a surprise.

I take a step back, pretending I'm admiring the smelly algae on the water. "He always teased me about my size, my lack of strength and my faded shadow. Is it really so wrong that I wanted to show him I can best him for once? That his wings are not as impressive as he thinks?"

I flinch when the railing creaks in Hawk's hands, as if it's about to break from the strength of his grip, but then he pulls away and kicks it so hard the wooden barrier cracks and falls into the water.

I get the sense it was either that or me.

"So you decided that it's fine to hurt me just to show him what a shadow you're now packing?" Hawk growls, and when he glances my way, for a moment I'm certain there's a red glint in his eyes.

"I can see how it might have sounded that way—"

"It didn't just sound like it! That's what you did! Like it was all about you and your petty revenge."

I swallow, and while I'm sure he won't feed me to the array of slimy, razor-toothed lizards hiding in the water, I still step farther from the edge of the pier. "We had to escape..." I say weakly, but the truth is I did lose control. I wasn't paying enough attention to how much I was taking, or how it affected Hawk. In that moment, it was all about presenting my new power to a man who's belittled me in the past.

Hawk makes a bitter snort and shakes his head. "You told me I won't be giving anything up, but now that you have me entrapped, turns out you injure me every time you use my shadow? Was this whole Dark Companion thing ever about *me*, or am I only a convenient attachment to my shadow?" he asks, glaring at me in accusation.

I know it doesn't look good that I'm spending time thinking about it, because yes, I do *love* him, but I'd be lying if I claimed his shadow didn't matter when I chose him. "You and your shadow are part of one whole. There is no one without the other. I cannot tell where you end and it begins. On the night we met, I was as entranced by it as I was by your body and the way you treated me. I... do not wish for you to feel trapped."

"But I am," Hawk says. He's no diplomat and won't bother covering a dirty table with a clean cloth. "You lied to me, told me it's safe and costs me nothing, so you can gain access to my shadow. But now I can't back out of this agreement until one of us dies."

I clench my fists until my nails dig into my palms, but it doesn't help me calm down. "I promised you my body. That was what you wanted, and it is not *nothing*."

Hawk sucks in a lungful of air, spreading his arms like a bird about to strike its prey. "And I would never use this promise to hurt you. I would never demand *my rights* if you didn't actually want to be with me, but you just took, and took, and I was powerless to stop you!" His voice chokes, and he turns away, walking back onto the shore.

I wrap my hands at the back of my head, at a loss about what to do. Am I really this bad at dealing with people? Just seeing Hawk so somber and disappointed makes me want to hug him and beg for forgiveness, but how would I even know if my touch is still welcome?

All I know is that I must make amends.

I bite the inside of my cheek to keep from crying. I am not the victim here, and I don't deserve to feel sorry for myself. I might not have understood how much my actions were affecting Hawk, but now that I do, it's my responsibility to prove to him that I can be trusted with his shadow.

"I'm sorry," I choke out. "This power is new to me, but that is no excuse. I am so ashamed to have let you down on the night I promised you protection. I vow to you, that it will not happen again. I will only use the surface of your shadow, never more. I will not hurt you again." My heart beats faster, and it shames me that he might sense it through our bond. My feelings are my responsibility. "Please give me grace," I dare extend my hand to him so that it is his choice whether to take it or not.

Hawk exhales and glances at me, so tall and strong, yet now so vulnerable to my power over his shadow. I've only ever seen this exchange from one side. Never once did it occur to me how frightening the sensation of having one's life force drained must feel to a Dark Companion, how much trust it must require. I can't turn my gaze away from that anymore, because my husband would never forgive me if I did.

"You know, I've been fucked over so many times," Hawk whispers, grabbing handfuls of his hair as he stares into the darkening sky. "The reason why I was a wanted man in the first place was because I fell in love with a boy who made me feel sorry for him."

"I also promise not to drink again," I add and let my hand fall to my side, rejected. "It has not aided my control over the situation."

Hawk nods, and when the weight of his warm hand settles on my shoulder, I'm devastatingly close to crying. "Talk is cheap, so I'll believe it when I see it. But thank you for... trying."

My heart is bleeding all over the wood, yet no amount of regret can take back time or my choices. I fucked up, and he doubts me. I have to live with that.

I slide my fingers onto his hand and look into his soulful eyes. "Please do not consider fleeing. It's not safe, not only because of the swamp beasts, but also because my cousin has no doubt alerted the Lord of the Nocturne Court of my arrival."

I'm tense but breathe in relief when Hawk squeezes my hand. Maybe not all is lost after all.

"I don't run," he says, only to scratch his head. "Actually, I did run from prison, and from my family, *and* from that soul river of yours, so watch it. I'm good at escaping."

Nerves coil in my stomach but I nod because I meant my vows and promises, even if I managed to break them so fast. I will not give him a reason to regret his choice of husband.

"Hopefully we will both be, if need be?" I offer him a shy smile, even though I don't think we're *there* yet. I want to be loved by him so badly it makes every bone in my body itch.

Hawk's mouth quirks, and he strokes my hand with his thumb. "I can be your escape teacher. But just so I know... *how* wanted are you really?"

"Well... I'm a fugitive in all of the Nightmare Realm, really. Bounty hunters might want to seize me anywhere, though the farther we go from the Nocturne Court itself, the safer we will be."

Hawk takes a deep breath. "But isn't that exactly where we're headed?"

My shoulders sag. "Yes. That is correct."

CHAPTER 28

SYLVAN

I've never been as tired as after the dreary three days in the swampland.

Fenren and his crew have safe houses along a route known only to them, but in order to reach the subsequent hideouts before nightfall, we needed to keep up a punishing speed. As a prince, I never had to lower myself to physical labor, and any trip beyond the bounds of the palace warranted a well-kept steed or carriage. Yet now I'm expected to keep the same pace as people with legs much longer than mine as we traverse treacherous terrain, often ankle-deep in water.

The rocky path is slippery, the smells of the swamp are at times unbearable, though navigating a conversation with Fenren is the trickiest part of the whole ordeal. I need to give him enough information about my return from banishment so it doesn't feel as if I'm hiding something, while most definitely *hiding something*.

He wants to know about the Nocturne Court, about my mother, about the Lord's new Dark Companion, and even why I don't enjoy hot soup. His never-ending questions are giving me a headache, and stifle my conversations with Hawk.

At night, we have to sleep on damp floors with threadbare blankets, but at least Hawk is by my side and embraces me, even though we haven't even kissed since the fight at the inn. I don't know if I love lying in his strong arms or if it makes me miss physical closeness with him so much I'm on the verge of madness.

Until last week, I had not been intimate with a man and had no prospects for it. I'd even venture that I was at peace with solitude being my lot in life. But now I have tasted my beloved's lips, I know what it means to be one with him, and for his greedy hands to roam all over my body. How am I to live with the uncertainty of whether my *husband* still craves intimacy with me?

Has my use of his shadow affected his trust so deeply that he no longer desires me? The injured hand, which Ivy secured with two pieces of wood and a string, is a physical reminder of my failure to protect him. And while I keep offering him help, it doesn't seem to be enough to make our relationship as intense and carefree as it was before.

Despite boots protecting me from the water, all the wading still leaves my feet cold, and I'm grateful when Fenren leads us back onto dry land, and under an ashen willow as big as a house. There's one in the palace gardens at the Nocturne Court, but it's not nearly this size, so I gawp at its impressive vines, which cascade from branches high above like a cloak made of purple flowers.

"Short break," the King of Smugglers decides before settling on a thick root protruding from the ground. He pulls out the same stale potato bread we had to endure in the morning, and bites in like it's a delicacy. It's not even crispy on the outside, just... old.

Hawk is too hungry to care, so I offer him my sandwich with gooey mushroom paste and sit down at the edge of the water to give my poor legs some relief.

While it is a moment of respite, I'm stuck mulling over the conversation I had with Hawk three days ago. I go over what I said wrong, what I could have said differently, what I could have omitted altogether.

It's not helpful.

At least my husband isn't avoiding me anymore and settles next to me, chewing his food loudly as a kelpie. It used to annoy me, but now I'm happy he feels comfortable around me. "This is like a better version of hummus. My ex used to eat that stuff all the time, and it was good. But *this*? Amazing," he concludes before offering me a flask of tea.

It's gotten lukewarm by now, so I take a sip. "I'm glad you enjoy it. You might need the strength when my legs fall off and you will be faced with the choice of carrying me or leaving me behind," I say grimly and throw a stone into the water.

Hawk chuckles and leans back, turning his face toward the moon high above us. It's still quite full, and its silver glow makes his face shine as if he were covered with a thin layer of dust made from mother of pearl. "That's a bit dramatic, isn't it?"

I pout. "Well, taking into account that we are still at least three days away from the Nocturne Castle, no, I think it is a valid complaint. Wait— Is that...?" I jump to my feet and strain my eyes. "Wait here!" I say to Hawk and run over to Fenren and Ivy, because I swear I saw a spyglass in his pack.

"Would you mind lending me that?" I ask, pointing out the object dangling from his belt.

Blue eyes peek at me as he chews his bread. "Your Highness, I believe your husband has a perfectly usable appendage."

I'm so stunned I just stand there as hot and cold flushes hit my face. "How insolent!" I choke out in the end. "You have overcharged me sevenfold for our wedding celebration, and now you insult me further? Give me that!" I reach for the spyglass at the same time as he does to protect it from my clutches, but even without Hawk's shadow, I'm able to create a barrier that stops him. His surprise gives me enough time to snatch it, but just as I grab it, Fenren's fingers close on my forearm, and he winks at me, shaking his red mane.

"That's a bit forward. My child is right there," he says.

Ivy sighs before rubbing her cheeks. "Don't bring me into whatever's going on there."

I take a deep breath, because I don't want to start a fight with the man leading us out of this maze of hidden swamp paths.

"Please," I groan. "I will return it swiftly."

Hawk turns to us. "Everything all right there?" he asks with his mouth full.

"Yes! I'm just borrowing something!"

"A bit of innocent flirting, don't you worry," Fenren says, making me see red. The last thing I need is for this goddamn rogue to convince Hawk that my eyes wandered, but my husband shrugs.

"You wish, smuggler. He likes them way taller than you are."

Fenren assesses me from head to toe. "How does it even fit?"

I raise my eyebrows. "How do you know *I'm* not the stud?"

Fenren snorts, but finally releases his hold on the spyglass. "Fine, fine, you got me there."

I ignore him and run back to Hawk's side. I bounce with excitement as soon as a peek through the spyglass confirms that I correctly identified the clusters of tiny white flowers on thick leaves floating in the water.

"I knew it! Marroweed," I say to Hawk, already assessing how far it is. "Those white flowers over there," I point them out and pass him the spyglass. "You can mash them into a pulp and put it over the skin. As it dries, it creates a cast. When it later turns gray, you know the marrow has been absorbed."

Hawk swallows his food. "...What?"

"Bone marrow. Hawk. For your finger. It will heal your broken bone."

He looks down on the contraption attached to his right hand, then at me. "Are you sure?"

It hurts that he doesn't trust me, but then again, everyone keeps warning him about every single thing in this goddamn swamp. For good reason. There are creatures here that would gladly eat the tasty morsel that he is, but one has to make bold choices to achieve great results.

"Well... yes. I just need to get there. I could use shadow to weave a path over the water." I touch his arm in excitement, and its warmth reminds me how much I miss his touch. I want to do this nice thing for him so badly, especially since his hand aches to the point of him struggling to hold heavy things in it. When he recoils, the fire of my enthusiasm is extinguished.

"I... no, there's no need. It'll get better on its own," Hawk says and pulls his hand to his chest, as if he expects me to grab it.

I lick my lips, unsure how to approach this gentle subject, but I'm not letting it go, because the marroweed is *right there*. Why should he suffer for no reason?

"Hawk, please. I promised to use barely the surface of your shadow. Not only will I not overuse it, I will not need to even consider such an option. It will feel like but a tingle in your palms, but my own power is too weak to hold my weight. Let me help you."

Hawk rubs his face and takes a sip from his flask. "No. I really... don't want to feel that sensation again," he says, lowering his voice. "It's like having fuel siphoned out of me."

I huff in frustration. "That's only because I used far too much too fast. Do you not trust me?"

Ivy whistles. "Woo, trouble in paradise? That was quick."

Hawk ignores her and meets my gaze. "That's not the point. This whole thing makes me feel like I'm at your mercy, and I fucking hate that. Five years in prison, and I'm really fed up with being chained up."

I turn to Ivy in frustration. "Stuff that sandwich in your mouth and be silent!" I take a deep breath. "Hawk, this is unreasonable. You are thrice my size. I am at your mercy at any given time, and I accept that because I trust you. I accepted the risk even before we sealed our bond. Look." I draw a piece of his shadow to my hand, then flatten it with ease so it resembles a leaf. I blow at it, and it falls into place on the water several feet from us. All my years of blood, sweat, and tears to reach a reasonable level of shadowcraft, and now, with the depth of power hidden in his, every skill and trick is easy like kneading dough is for a royal baker.

I point to the leaf. "See? Did you even feel a thing?"

He's quiet as he moves his gaze to me. I know he's not happy even before his mouth opens. "You took it, even though I told you not to? What the hell, Sylvan?" he asks, scrambling to his feet, ready to march off.

"I promised to use barely the surface and that's what I did! I bet you didn't even feel it at all." I stand my ground, because he's being obtuse.

"That's not the point," Hawk snaps, but as I step toward him, already holding my index finger ready to poke his chest, water sprays us both, and massive black teeth close on the shadow leaf, taking it back into the depths.

We both go still, unsure what this was, but Fenren and Ivy are already on their feet, dashing away from us.

"Run! Run, run, run!" the King of Smugglers yells, and I know we're fucked.

CHAPTER 29

HAWK

Wrestling an alligator would have been preferable to dealing with the beast chasing us. The truck-sized crocodile has two heads, two tails, sharp black crystals growing out of its back, and madness in its yellow eyes. Algae clings to its dark gray scales as it crawls onto the patch of dry land we've just vacated, and its two mouths utter asynchronous hisses that make the birds and frogs go eerily quiet.

I'm about to take Sylvan onto my back and run when Fenren passes us both, dashing back toward the monster. Air is trapped in my throat as I watch our guide toss a black ball toward the water, luring the creature away from a little brown bag he left behind.

I don't know what could be important enough for him to risk his life like this, but I grab Sylvan's hand when one pair of the giant's eyes notices the elf. Like its cousin from my world, the reptile appears heavy and slow, but when it twists its body, snapping its long teeth in the very place Fenren's left a moment ago, it's clear we're all in mortal danger.

Roaring like a failing engine, it charges after the smuggler, but instead of getting cornered by the thick trunk of the willow, Fenren grabs one of the lush vines and climbs the tree with the ease of a monkey. His feet slip when the reptile slams into the tree, but his hands remain tight around the vine, and as he unsheathes the weapon attached to his hip, the beast thrashes under him, attempting to leap up and collect him like a ripe fruit.

Sylvan digs his heels into the mud, refusing to let me lead. "He's got a blackblade! No... what is this creature doing so close to the Nocturne Court?"

It's only then that I notice the strange darkness surrounding the long dagger in Fenren's hand. He stabs at the creature once it rests its front claws on the trunk, but the attack angers rather than frightens the monster.

"Bassals are drawn to shadowcraft!" Sylvan cries, refusing to move, even though the behemoth could reach us within seconds. "Don't use the dagger!"

I've had it with this bullshit, so I grab my boy, sling him over my shoulder, and *run*.

Ivy's dusky red cloak flashes close to a lone hill with a thatch of bushes growing at the top. Its side is a steep cliff, as if the slope that previously existed has crumbled long ago enough to allow for the growth of moss and small plants. Eager to hide and wait out the damn... bassal, I run so fast my feet barely touch the dirt. As I dash behind the mound, I hear the monster coming our way.

The ground shakes as though we're on the verge of an earthquake, and the splashing of water brings to mind a horde of charging elephants, but I do the only thing I can—hold onto Sylvan's legs and use my three remaining limbs to crawl up the steep incline that might either offer us salvation or leave us even more vulnerable to the beast.

Its thundering cries resonate in my ears by the time I roll onto the overgrown hilltop and cover Sylvan with my body in an attempt to make us both flatter, less noticeable between the grasses and shrubs. But somewhere below, the bassal keeps up its violent thrashing. I open my eyes and spot Ivy curling up behind a fallen tree. She's tense and covers her mouth with both hands, which prompts me to press my finger to his mouth, to ensure Sylvan's quiet, and then crawl toward the girl.

She glances my way but seems ready to snap at any moment, and I can't blame her when I peek through the leaves and see her father leaping away from the giant reptile like a flea. He's still holding the dagger, and it's only when I see him against the backdrop of the moon that I notice the dark vapor surrounding the blade. It disperses into a trail of pale dust, and the bassal follows it as if it was a cocaine addict desperate for even the smallest particle of the drug.

"He needs to throw it away. Now," Sylvan hisses, crawling closer to join us at the vantage point, but neither of us wants to attract the monster's attention. Still, we all gasp when Fenren stumbles over something hiding below the surface and narrowly avoids the charging animal. He is losing speed, tired of the chase, and as agile and strong as he might be, he has limits like anyone else.

Rolling away over the bright reflection of the moon above, Fenren manages to throw a rock at the bassal, but it just bumps off the armored back.

"It's the most precious artifact he owns," Ivy says, but Sylvan shakes his head.

"That creature eats shadowcraft. Fenren's running around with a lure in hand!"

It might be dark, but I still notice the girl go pale. Her eyes dart between us, then beyond the bushes, but in the end she screams, "It's after the blade!"

One of the beast's heads is drawn to the noise, zeroing in on us with its golden eyes, but my initial need to run far, far away is drowned by terror when the other head clamps its jaws around Fenren's legs.

Ivy shrieks when the cold-blooded monster's other mouth seizes Fenren's torso. The heads tug in opposite directions, and in the moonlight, the elf's body opens and stretches like an accordion of guts.

With a cry of anguish, Ivy rolls away from us, out of the bushes, and toward the back of the hill, where the monster can't see her. With her father gone, she feels no loyalty to us, nor any responsibility for our survival. It occurs to me that I could do that too—convince Sylvan to use his shadowcraft and run. He'd likely die in the confrontation before he drained enough of my vital power to make me faint, and I'd be free to live out my life in this fantastically terrifying world. But as the girl disappears from sight and both of the bassal's heads have their fill of meat, I grab Sylvan's hand.

"We should go," I whisper, trying my best to not let fear take over and bring me to my knees. I didn't survive prison and escape the cops all the way to a different world to die in the stomach of a two-headed dragon... thing.

Sylvan nods and crawls toward me, his hand on my shoulder as if he wants to communicate the depth of his trust. Behind him, the monster swallows the blade with a satisfied bellow, but instead of calming down like I expected it to, it turns all four of its eyes toward our hill.

I freeze, ready to turn into a rock and avoid moving until this thing loses interest, but its gaze flashes, and it bolts our way with terrifying speed. The hill is slightly higher than I am tall, and reptilian talons dig into the ground next to my leg moments later.

"Goddamn it," I shout, capturing Sylvan's gaze as we both roll away in different directions.

Sylvan is closer to the beast, and I scream in terror when the bassal's heavy tail slams into him so hard, Sylvan's thrown several feet away. My focus narrows when I see my fragile prince hold his shoulder, face twisted in pain as he struggles to get up. His eyes dart around, as if he's lost his sense of direction, and I dash toward him.

I grab him and run up the hill. We will worry about his shoulder if we manage to survive this. As much as I despise the idea of having my energy drained, this is one of those situations that warrants it.

"Use it!" I yell. "Use my shadow!"

The bassal is on our trail, roaring to announce its hunger for flesh and shadow. As the toothy mouths open, blowing out the sharp odor of rot, a pull at the pit of my stomach tells me what's about to happen. That beast's gonna rip us to shreds.

Claws shoot from both of Sylvan's hands and pierce two of the monster's eyes. The injured head drops down the creature's chest.

"Get behind me!" Sylvan says, and my world flickers as I follow his command. The air around us trembles and I can only hope he's creating a shield around us, like he did for me at the tavern.

A feral cry resonates over the marshland and makes my ears ring as if it were a fire alarm. We're knocked down by a shockwave so powerful that for a moment I worry I may never rise again, but Sylvan is already back on his feet. He between me and the monster, so small and yet so very powerful.

Pride fills my chest alongside guilt when I realize I scolded Sylvan for using a powerful weapon that could have saved Fenren's life, if used without delay. But this isn't the time to mourn bad decisions, because the air around the bassal shimmers, and my man sends his sharp claws at the remaining head. I'm ready to cheer our victory, but the dark spikes that so easily cut into the beast's flesh earlier break as they hit an invisible barrier.

Shock overpowers Sylvan's features, but the monster shakes, and a black goo reminiscent of the liquid shadow I've seen Sylvan play with, oozes from the cracks between its scales. A tentacle shoots from the pool of shadow at our feet and attempts to strike the creature from the back, but it's all for nothing, as it's now protected by some kind of force field.

When the bassal jerks up to descend on us with its thick paws, I pull Sylvan back, saving him from talons that could tear through rock. The beast roars, but as the small body in my arms tenses and the shadows around us thicken, the invisible barrier around the reptile jitters, and the tentacle pressing on it from behind penetrates its bounds.

Heat blooms on my face, because this might be our only chance. I'm faint again, but it doesn't matter. As powerful as my shadow might be, it's not an unlimited resource, and we need to strike while the iron is hot.

"Kill it," I shout into Sylvan's ear as the creature turns its one functional head to see where it's been injured. "You just need more shadow. Take it!"

His eyes flash in the dusky fog around us. "No! I've already taken too much. I can't—"

I shouldn't have been so prissy about his mistake. He *was* drunk and was only taking baby steps in this whole shadow-borrowing business. Now I made him afraid of doing it even in a situation that warrants it.

I'm such a shithead.

"Doesn't matter!"

The tentacle twists, stabbing at the bassal where it's penetrating the barrier, and when the creature rolls off the hill with a cry of agony, Sylvan stares at me, pale as a sheet. "We'll just run and hide."

My eyes sting. Have I really suspected this boy of manipulating me? He's so desperate to avoid hurting me again that it's making breathing near-impossible. But both he and I know there's no running from the two-headed gator, so I meet his eyes and speak as clearly as possible.

"You know we can't. Even if I faint—"

"You could die," Sylvan cries, and a tear rolls from his sapphire eye. I want to kiss it away, but who has time for tenderness in the heat of battle?

"I should still have a few lives left. I want you to survive this, baby. Even if the worst happens, we don't need to *both* die."

He blinks, squeezing my hands. Time stops, and for a beautiful moment we're just two men who found one another in the unlikeliest of circumstances, but as the bassal shoots up to the hill, roaring with fury, Sylvan shoves me away.

"We don't need to both die," he repeats. Black goo climbs his form, soon covering his entire body. It makes the beast freeze. Hunger shines in its yellow eyes, and the moment Sylvan leaps off the hill, creating tiny steps out of shadow, the creature charges after him, hungry for more shadowcraft.

He's making himself bait.

It's like an ice pick stuck in my brain, and as I drag myself to my knees, terrified by the narrow distance between predator and prey, it's clear to me that I only have two options. I either run away or follow Sylvan, letting the bassal devour me too.

Suddenly, a new thought pops into my head and radiates life all over my body. Because there is one more choice I can make.

My hands shake when I reach under my clothes and pull out the Sunwolf Crown. I now know magic is real, and that it can warp my body beyond recognition, but I've already made up my mind. I was dead serious when I put that ring on Sylvan's finger, and I'll either protect him, or die trying.

I hear every detail of my last inhale, but then I slam the mask against my face and scream. It's like being drizzled with boiling gold.

CHAPTER 30

SYLVAN

I'm covered in shadow from head to toe, and I materialize levitating platforms in front of my feet in my mad dash toward doom. The power needed for this feat barely skims the surface of Hawk's darkness, but it's enough to draw the bassal's attention to me.

Just three months ago, I was too afraid to face the monster my brother died chasing away. Now I know what it feels like to have someone worth dying for. I might be petrified, but I will *not* falter. I vowed to never take more than Hawk can give, to never hurt him, and I will prove to him that my words were true, even if it means my own demise.

My only regret is that he will be left to fend for himself in the Nightmare Realm, but that gives him a fighting chance. He deserves that much after what he has been through.

The bassal grunts right behind me, and I smell its breath, so my plan of luring it away is working. But if that's the case, why is Hawk screaming? It tears right through my heart. Could it be that there are more of these beasts around and my efforts are futile? Or is he insane enough to try attracting the bassal's attention to himself?

I'm about to yell at him to stop it, but when I look over my shoulder, words die on my lips.

I expect to see the bassal's yellow eyes right behind me, but a golden creature smashes into the black body of the overgrown lizard. It's like a shooting star crashing into the surface of the Darkmoon.

I don't understand what's happening, but the bassal roars in fury, and any interest it had in me is gone, replaced by the fight for survival.

The two creatures tumble into the shallow water, distorting the perfect reflection of the moon as they spin together like the Yin and Yang symbol Kurt has shown me back in the human realm. Only that the pale half of what I'm seeing isn't just white. It embodies the very meaning of radiance, shining so bright I have to shield my eyes as I drop onto the branch of a tree. Only when I grab it do I realize how much my shoulder hurts.

The smell of burning meat teases my nostrils as the bassal shrieks, thrashing under the weight of its opponent. Smoke coils into the air when the beasts thrash in a ball of limbs and claws, but when the reptile breaks free and swings both its tails, as if it isn't sure whether it wants to bolt or fight, I get to see the other creature for what it is.

A crown of several horns shoots out from its head, framing the bare skull. The rest of its agile form is covered with fur so pale it's difficult to decide whether it's golden or flecked with sparkling particles. The head is golden polished bone, eyes like volcanic stone, and diamond-sharp teeth reflect the light it radiates with.

No matter how much I want to deny it, I know what this is.

The Sunwolf.

My stomach drops, and the shadow I'm covered with evaporates. I could have a dozen shadow tentacles right now, and the bassal would still only be focused on the Sunwolf, because it's fighting for its life. I struggle to comprehend the implications of Hawk's change, too amazed by the sight in front of me.

The golden canine the size of the huts we've slept in in the marshland, rips out the bassal's front leg with a primal growl, blood staining its crystal teeth. It's like watching the mythical fight between the sun and the moon, only that this time, I have no doubt it's the sun that will win. Even when the bassal yields, focused on survival, the Sunwolf doesn't let it go. With its leg still between his teeth, the wolf lowers its skull and slams the horns into the remaining head of the bassal.

With one last piercing screech of agony, the reptile collapses.

The fight is over.

I'm speechless. Too stunned to utter a word or even think, so I watch the massive wolf shake off whatever discomfort it's been feeling, and then walk away from the gored reptile. The glow it produces adds a new dimension to the hues around us, and the murky darkness of the swamp becomes a whole array of greens and golds reflecting off the surface of the water. Lilac crystals appear to grow on some of the trees, and every time insects flee the Sunwolf, tiny sparkles seem to erupt in the air around their wings. It's only now that

I realize the dead reptile has changed color in its death, now a dull gray rather than the intense black from before.

Hope creeps into my heart, so I glance toward the hill, which is now marred with talon-shaped grooves in rock, and broken bushes, but I cannot see Hawk anywhere. He must have—he must have really...

The pain in my shoulder hits me so hard I slump to my ass on the branch, staring at the shiny beast. I have a general idea of what happens to an elf who puts it on, but a human? Is he even still sentient?

Thoughts of losing the Sunwolf Crown are only the buzzing of a fly, because nothing worries me more than Hawk's safety. Fenren's dead, Ivy is gone, and we're in the middle of a swamp, still far from the Nocturne Court. If I lost Hawk, all has been for nothing.

Why would he have done something so stupid? I warned him the mask wasn't something to be trifled with, yet he still put it on, and now... now I don't even know if he's the one behind those empty eyes.

With a heavy weight in my chest, I watch the wolf walk through the water, a top predator that doesn't need to be afraid of anything, but as I inhale, ready to get its attention when it comes dangerously close to the line of trees, it turns back and heads toward me.

Despite watching it rip a bassal to shreds, and seeing the blood staining its horns, I have no fear in my heart as the Sunwolf approaches. It's not just that I sense no ill will, or that its body language is relaxed. I must have exhausted my limit of terror on the fight with the reptile, and have none left in me. I've never considered myself brave. In fact, my mother always taught me bravery is stupidity in another guise. But when I made myself bait so that Hawk could escape, something changed in me. I discovered myself anew, and I liked the man I found within.

I feel like a polished diamond. Sharp, clear, and impossible to shatter. But can I avoid breaking if the man I chose to sacrifice everything for is no longer with me?

I remain dead quiet as the creature approaches, terrifying in its radiant beauty, but when it meets my gaze and sits with a soft whine, my heart leaps, because there is no doubt that he recognizes me.

The part of me that cares about proving my worth to everyone at the Nocturne Court, screams with fury, because I told him to never use the mask. But my heart is stronger, and I stroke the beast's smooth forehead as I try to ignore the throbbing pain in my shoulder.

It opens its jaws, and several clusters of marroweed fall into my lap.

"Thank you." I sigh and gather the flowers into my bag. I then force myself to slide off the branch and onto the muddy ground. I'm so torn between mourning the loss of the excellent bargaining chip and being elated by the presence of this mythical beast. I don't know what it means for Hawk and me yet, but I pet Sunwolf's fur. It's soft as down. Hawk's bony muzzle pokes at my hip, and I give in to the weakness in my body, putting my arms around the wolf's neck. It's purring, and now that I recognize that it's a sign of contentment, fear, and tension leave my heart, allowing me to feel every consequence of the standoff.

My muscles ache. My shoulder's broken. My head is spinning as if the bassal trampled me after all.

"We need to leave this area," I say, exhausted to my core. "It's not safe here. See those stars?" I point out the twinkling red constellation called the Blood Serpent. "Let's go in that direction. With you like this, we should be able to cross without relying on Fenren's winding paths."

Hawk's eyes might be dark and matte like polished stone, but I know he's looking straight at me when he gives the faintest bark and then jerks his head, causing my hand to touch his back. I have no idea what he means until his elongated form lowers, and his stomach touches the ground.

"Are you sure?" I ask, but I am so exhausted nothing sounds more inviting than a bed of fur warm as the sunshine I used to despise.

I decide to take Hawk's little whines as an invitation to climb him. It's not the easiest of tasks for a man with a bad shoulder, but he doesn't complain when I have to pull on his fur to do so. I straddle his nape and lay forward with my cheek buried in his warmth.

"Follow the red stars," I mutter, suddenly exhausted, as if I've inhaled the spores of a Cerulean Puffball. After days of travel, his fur and closeness are like a cocoon of safety, and for once I don't have to be alert and in charge, because the Sunwolf can keep me safe.

Hawk can keep me safe.

It doesn't feel like riding a horse. The beast under me is hotter to the touch, even with the thick padding of fur, but also broader, taller, and softer. As I relax, sinking my face into the thick hair, a voice deep inside tells me to let go. To close my eyes and let the tide wash over me.

Is this how souls feel just before they disintegrate in the river that takes them away from their world? There's no fear, only the deepest contentment.

Back in the realm of humans, I detested the sun, but as Hawk moves, carrying me away from the scene of the fight that almost ended with our deaths, I can't resist the comfort of the warmth he's radiating, not after the nights we've spent in the swamps. He even smells like sun-parched rock, but for once the crispness of that scent is pure comfort.

I must have fallen asleep in my spot between his shoulder blades, so I'm not sure how much time passed, but the pain in my arm catches up with me eventually.

I moan despite clenching my teeth to avoid alarming Hawk. Fortunately, I've got the marroweed, so maybe my suffering won't be endless. I rise to my knees and look around.

We're not in the swamps anymore. I can tell even before spotting bright blue flowers between the trees and bushes thanks to the fresh scent of ferns. For a moment, I'm confused, because the moon must have set by now, but I realize it's Hawk's bright fur that brightens the night.

Sensing that I woke up, he makes a little bark, and I stroke his back to let him know I'm fine.

I feel that I recognize this forest, but most importantly, it's time to deal with my injured shoulder and work out what's happening to Hawk. Once he stops walking, I slide off his side, biting my lip to stifle a groan of pain when my shoulder presses too hard on his flank.

The huge bulk of the wolf seems almost too large for the narrow, mossy clearing, and when his long, bushy tail smacks against a tree, several shelled nuts fall to the ground, making so much noise Hawk tumbles, trying to get away. He lands on his side and stiffens, glaring at the offending tree as if it were guilty of bearing fruit. He growls at it and finally settles, grinning at me with teeth like the purest crystal.

"Do you understand me?" I ask, looking into his obsidian eyes. When he nods, I sigh in relief, but it's short-lived when I face reality. "I don't know what to do. I've not read anything about what happens to the bearer of the Sunwolf Crown. The risk was yours, I don't begrudge you for the choice you made, as otherwise, I would have been dead and unable to use the mask anyway, but how will we go on?" I ask and stroke the golden skull he has for a head.

Hawk gets back on his feet and shoves my chest with his muzzle. I bite back a moan of pain when he pushes too hard, but this is an attempt to comfort me, so I keep my mouth shut and stroke the smooth surface of his skull. I no longer see any bloodstains on the horns, which means he must have dunked his head in the water sometime on the way.

He moans in sympathy, and something tugs at the mystical connection we forged merely days ago, when I took him as my Dark Companion. My stomach drops at the realization that even that has changed, almost as if there is a thick door separating us, and I can only hear him scratching at it. So I allow him in.

A gateway opens in my mind, letting in the light. And with it, his voice.

[*Sylvan, I'm okay! I'm still me,*] Hawk tells me, and his thick, warm tongue laps at me so hard it pulls up my shirt and tickles my stomach.

I stroke him above the teeth, looking deep into eyes like two voids. "You're not 'okay', my darling. This is a big, *big* problem. What if we never find a way to change you back? You're massive and shiny. You will be hunted."

Hawk blinks and cocks his head like one of the many dogs I've seen in the realm of humans, but before I can say another word, his form erupts in white light and prompts me to close my eyes. I fear it might burn me, but moments later, a big, warm hand squeezes my own, and his sweet, raspy voice strokes my ear.

"Sylvan?"

He's there. In human form. I go straight in for a hug, but then back away with a hiss when my arm once more throbs with pain. My eyebrows rise at the sight of his face. His eyes are the first thing I notice, as they are like black rock filling in for eyeballs. And then there are the dark gold markings on his face, a symbolic wolf skull etched in skin. At least he's not glowing.

"How did you do that?"

Hawk is so exasperated by my reaction to his touch that he blinks, watching me with a frown. And while the person in front of him speaks in his voice, has his personality, and his face, I cannot help the fact that I find the dull black of his eyes unsettling. It's as if he's charred from the inside.

He doesn't notice my hesitation and shrugs. "I... just *did*. It felt as easy as moving my hand," he tells me and waves.

I'm about to pull him down for a kiss when I spot the outline of a castle above his shoulder. Far away, perched on a hilltop beyond the trees, the tallest towers of the Nocturne Palace reach into the sky with their jagged rooftops.

I point it out to him. "That's it! The Nocturne Court. Which means we're in the royal forest. It might not be a safe place, but I actually know my way around here."

Hawk offers me a bright grin of sharp teeth and moves as if he were about to squeeze me... only to stop before touching my injured shoulder. Instead, he presses a kiss to my forehead. "Yeah! So we're almost there? Amazing. Can't wait to sleep in a bed again. Do they have beds my size, or will I need to use doggie ones now?"

I shake my head. "It's not funny. And I have no idea how we will be greeted now that you're wearing the Sunwolf Crown. We will need to sneak in, but I know several secret entryways."

Hawk frowns and touches his face. "I... don't have the mask."

I stroke his cheek, wishing I had a pocket mirror, though I doubt he'd see much in this darkness anyway. Unless the change has also affected his vision. There are still so many unknowns.

"You do. It is now a part of you. Remember how I told you that they cut it off the face of the last Sunwolf? We don't want that to happen, do we?"

He freezes, then touches his face, attempting to sense the bone and metal the crown was made of before attaching itself to its new host. "What do you mean? It's just my face."

"No, my love. You have the markings of the Sunwolf on your face now. And your eyes... How well do you see now in the night?"

Hawk frowns. "What night?"

To be fair, *that* does have its perks. I clear my throat and pull out the dagger I took with me from Tassarion's forge. I unsheathe it so he can see at least a vague reflection in the metal.

Hawk leans in, and his long hair cascades down his shoulder as he blinks, staring at the polished blade. I see the exact moment he realizes I'm not joking, because his face falls, and he taps his open eye with one of his fingertips, as if he needs to make sure it really is that black. "Fuck... I look... like a monster."

I sigh and hug him with my good arm. "It's not looks that make a monster. You put it on to save me." I place my hand over his heart, even though I feel like crying at the loss of our greatest asset. Whether we want it or not, Hawk will now end up forever entwined in court politics. "We will handle it. Once I have access to the Nocturne Court library, I will learn everything there is to know about the mask, and maybe one day I will find a way to take it off you. For now, we still have your shadow to show up with."

I glance to our feet, where even in the darkness of the night—
"It's gone," I utter. "You have no shadow."

CHAPTER 31

SYLVAN

I dip my fingers into my shadow, trying to convince myself that Hawk's darkness isn't *gone*, but that I just can't see it.

But it's not there.

I drop to my knees and pat the ground under his feet despite the agony in my shoulder.

"No, no, no, no, no..." I whine even though I've never been one to deny reality.

When I think about it, it makes perfect sense that the Sunwolf would cast no shadow of his own, that it would disperse under the force of Sunlight inside him. I just don't want to believe it, because the implications are my worst nightmare.

I cover my face and sob.

It's a shameful moment, which not only lays bare all my insecurities and weaknesses but also once again punishes the man I love for having the audacity to risk his life for mine. I should suffer in silence. I should cover my grief with a smile and offer my gratitude, but I cannot bring myself to do it. The wound is so fresh, and it already festers.

Hawk doesn't move. Doesn't speak. He's silent, as if I've struck him in the face while I let myself mourn a future that will never come.

"Sylvan?" he asks after endless moments, so quietly I barely hear him over the dull thud of my own heart.

"Everything is gone. The mask, your shadow..." I utter through tears and sit at his feet. I'm almost angry the carpet of moss and clover is so soft under me, because I deserve to suffer for the mistakes I made. It's all my fault. Why did I insist on picking the marroweed for Hawk, if he didn't want me to? "This whole endeavor has been for nothing."

Hawk exhales, and I watch him sit cross-legged only two paces away. He combs his fingers through the undergrowth between us. "I didn't want this to happen."

The black hole that opens up inside me is darker and deeper than Hawk's shadow was. I have no strength left to fight my tears. "Of course you didn't. You only wanted to save our lives, but it doesn't matter that it's not your fault. I didn't plan this well enough, I took the opportunities that presented themselves, and now here we are, with no leverage at court, and you're still attached to *me*, a banished prince who has no right to be here. It means that you will be hunted just as I am, and I can't protect you because I am now useless.

"For but a moment, I had a power so pure, so primal, it felt endless. It was at my command, even if I still needed to learn how to truly wield it. Now I never will. I'm back to being nothing. You'd be better off with me dead."

I once more hide my face, because my tears are too embarrassing. I am and have always been a shame to my family. Now, I am also a burden to the man I love.

I flinch when he touches my shoulders, because he deserves so much more than what I, the last disgraced blood the Goldweeds, can offer. But then he's close, pushing his chest against my face, and I cannot deny myself the comfort of his presence. That new note in his scent—like hot rock and fresh air—soothes my tattered soul, and I let him cradle me.

His heart beats even faster than mine, and I relish its comforting rhythm, which is already so familiar, even though we made the shadow bond only three days back. I jerk my head up, staring into the pots of black his eyes have become, and relief loosens some of the knots inside me. I feared our bond would be gone along with his shadow, but I still feel his presence at the core of my being.

I don't know how, and I don't even know if it's a good thing, but I still grab onto it like a lifeline. Its presence means I can never have another Dark Companion, and I will never know power again, but I won't say it out loud to avoid hurting Hawk again. He is my forever Companion for better or worse, and the only way our bond can be severed is through death.

"Don't say such bad things about yourself," Hawk tells me in a tight voice. His palms slide up my neck and clasp my face in a tender gesture.

I shake my head, but look into his eyes, no longer ashamed of my tears. "It's true, and I have never been one to deny reality. You are bound to an elf of very little value, and because of the mask, you will have a target on your back. You could have gone to Canada and started a new life, but I dragged you here."

I mourn the loss of his deep green eyes too, but his face remains expressive, twisting into a scowl as he gives me a gentle shake. "That's for me to decide, isn't it? I did not get together with you because you're a prince. You're still the same guy."

I shrug, then wince in pain. At least the physical discomfort is there to distract me from the hole in my heart. "I just don't have much to offer you now. I promised you a place at court, protection, and position. I can provide none of that as a vagrant with barely any shadow."

Hawk rubs his face with his injured hand and laughs. "Well, at least now I won't feel guilty over being wanted myself. We're officially in the same boat. And, by the way, you're still much smarter and more knowledgeable about this world than I could ever be. Your value to me isn't in what you can *provide*."

I remember the marroweed flowers and pull them out of my bag. "At least we can heal your finger now."

Hawk shakes his head. "No, we should start with your shoulder. If there's any of that flower left, we'll use it on my finger, but you are my lifeline here, and you need to be okay."

With Hawk's help, I take off my shirt and jacket. I can't believe I got married in those just days ago.

"You now hold the power of the Sunwolf," I say. "I am a burden with a bit of useful knowledge and barely any survival skills." Still, I gently tug on our bond, hoping he can sense it too. It's still like a thread of my darkness, but now, in some mystical way, instead of being tied to his shadow, it feels attached to his very soul.

Hawk lets out a wolflike huff and rubs his cheek against mine. "I wouldn't have that power if it wasn't for you. Hell, if it wasn't for you, I'd either be rotting in a cell by now, or dead! It doesn't matter to me at all that you don't have much shadow magic, or that you no longer are *someone* at court. Your family's taught you to hate yourself, and I will *make* you unlearn it," he says, stroking my cheeks with both his thumbs, as if he's trying to wipe away all my worries. "I knew I wanted you the moment I saw you, and the more I knew you, the more urgent the need to stay together became. You're smart, and different, and speak so beautifully I can just listen for hours. You're so strong but also so gentle. You're sweet, even if you don't want people to know. You're funny, and brave, and so determined.

You *chose* me. No one's ever chosen me. When I'm with you, everything seems so fucking bright, even when there's no light. I never want to lose that."

It's as if he's sending heartbeats down our bond so I can feel just how much he means it. I've never been this soothed. Not even as a baby.

"I love you. We'll survive this as long as we're together." I want to believe it. Hawk is my anchor, and maybe if we stick with each other, he won't get lost at the bottom of the sea, and I will not be left adrift.

He nods and kisses me. Even if I didn't have the benefit of our magical bond, the sincerity of the way he touches me says everything I need to know about his feelings. I appreciate that about him. There are no double meanings to his words, no secret plans or attempts at manipulation. With Hawk, what I see is what I get, and I cannot even describe how much peace this gives me after living out my life in the viper nest that is the Nocturne Court.

Somehow, he managed to bring the same out in me.

"We will," Hawk agrees, grinning.

I stall at the sight of his teeth, because they're all sharp now, like those of a predatory beast. But this is still my husband, my Dark Companion, and such details don't matter, so I let him kiss my forehead and whisper sweet nothings.

"Whatever happens, you can always count on me. Now show me," he says, pointing at the marroweeds.

We don't have the proper tools, so I show him how to crush the flower petals in his hands, then roll them to release the oils. We fall into an easy rhythm of me picking the petals off the flowers, and him crushing them before spreading the white goo over my shoulder. The numbing effect brings instant relief.

I can't believe how at peace I am. Just moments ago, I was in absolute emotional and physical agony, and Hawk somehow manages to heal both.

I am *not* nothing. My handsome beast would sooner risk his life than see me perish. He put on the Sunwolf Crown without knowing how it might change him, all because I am important to him. Because he loves me.

"I missed your touch," I say as he's finishing up with the marroweed cast stiffening on my shoulder. I secretly kept a flower in my bag so there's enough for his finger later. He didn't question how much we utilized on me and applied a thick layer of the paste, just because he cares.

I'm so lucky to have found him, and while I still mourn his shadow, it no longer is at the core of our relationship. Maybe it never was.

Hawk licks his lips, leaning over me with a soft sigh. "I missed yours too. I was angry over you making a mistake, and between having company and being so exhausted every day, we never got to clear the air. I'm sorry."

I stroke his cheek and look into his eyes, even though they're a little frightening. It's still my Hawk, and I have nothing to be scared of. As long as he controls the Sunwolf within, I don't have to worry about him devouring my shadow.

"I understand. I've been brought up in a snake pit, but I trust you, and I never want you to doubt me either. I'm sorry you had to go through so much, and in an unfamiliar world at that."

Hawk stretches next to me, resting on his side and using the heel of his injured hand to support his head. He bites his lip, contemplative as his fingers trail over my naked chest. "I've been duped many times. Worst of all, I killed for someone who lied to me because he thought I was too naive to notice. He used me. But not everyone is like him. I don't want to stay bitter. And you, you will be my reward."

An hour ago, the depth of my sorrow was so great I thought I'd never be able to feel happiness again, but he washed away all the grime and showed me that I am still whole.

Hawk's lips twist into a sly grin when he presses his hand more to my chest. "Anything you missed about me most?"

I glance at him, feeling shy, but still put my fingers over his. "Hawk... since you awoke my body to being touched, not an hour passes by that I don't think about the warmth of your skin."

He trembles. I can not only feel but also see it, and by the time his lips touch mine, I'm so damn ready for him too. Those three days without his touch were like a lifetime of thirst.

"You were a *very* eager student, baby," he whispers, moving his lips to my temple, then down to my jaw.

"And we missed our wedding night..." I gasp and slide my hands over his shoulders with my heart beating faster. I smile when he slides his leg between mine, because it's clear we both want to reconnect.

"Don't you worry," he whispers into my sensitive neck. "If there's any dangerous beasts out here, I will kill them for you. From now on, I will be your loyal pup."

I snort. "The Sunpup." I lost so much today, yet disappointment is draining out of me by the minute, and I'm shedding my past worries like a caterpillar about to become a moth.

His excitement feeds mine when I run my fingers under his coat, touching the broad, sturdy back that feels like a barrier between me and the cruel world that hurt me so many times. His flesh is much hotter now that the Sunwolf is burning within, and I'm already falling in love with how it feels on my skin.

"Let's be careful with your shoulder, hm?" he asks, stroking my chest in slow circles as he showers my neck with kisses and scratches it with the sharp pins of his stubble. "Don't want all my hard work wasted."

"Yes, be careful with me," I purr, finally accepting that I deserve to be coddled a little, that my man can offer me the safety I always craved. "I guess I just have to lay there as you do all the work," I grin and stroke the small of his back as my dick hardens against him.

"Such a shame, got myself a pillow prince," he tells me, again showing off his sharp teeth. I long to find out how they'll feel against my skin. I open my mouth to speak as a dragonfly lands on the tree above, watching, but then his tongue moves lower, to my nipple, and I choke on air when I sense a needle-sharp edge.

My hand flies to his hair, ready to pull him away. It's instinct. I know he wouldn't hurt me. "Be gentle."

He worships my body with every lick and bite. When I'm with Hawk, I don't have to worry about my size, my shadow, or my status. In my man's eyes, I'm not just *enough*. He made it clear many times that I am exactly what he craves, and so I relax, because while under his protection, there will be no knives in the back. Just pleasure.

He hums in agreement and laps at my skin, squeezing and rubbing my sides, until his chin reaches the tip of my erection, which strains the front of my pants demanding attention. I grunt, opening my legs wider, but Hawk is already in his element and rubs his face against my covered shaft.

"Oh moon and stars!" I exclaim, breathless and so eager for his touch I spread my legs wider. I look at his face, marvelling at the beauty of how the golden markings of the beast enhance his natural features. "I'm insatiable for you."

He roars, and while I should be scared of the unnatural noise at the back of his throat, when he rips my pants off, dragging them all the way off with a single tug, all I can think about is the heat spreading over me like wildfire. I'm now naked in the middle of the woods, under the dome of trees, and I'm about to be ravished by the rarest of creatures.

Hawk licks my cock from the base, then flicks his tongue against the slit, and despite knowing how sharp his new teeth are, when he takes my cock in, all I can do is pant like a doe dying of *thirst*. I'm not afraid of Hawk's sharp edges. They're there to protect me.

I'm so aroused I tighten my grip on his hair, flushed and overheating. My cock throbs in his mouth, so hard and needy. I want to buck my hips, but he presses them down to show me he's in charge. I let out helpless moans, hoping no lost hunter happens to stumble upon this meadow.

"So good," I whine, curling my toes.

"My favorite meal," Hawk rasps when he comes up for air, leaving my wet cock to cool on my stomach, but I'm so impatient, so needy that I push him down, wordlessly begging for him to give me head. Now.

"Please," I mumble, rocking my body as Hawk covers his teeth with his lips, to protect me, and lowers his head, sucking me into the now-dangerous depths of his throat.

"Oh fuck, oh fuck...!" I yelp, though it's the possessive way he squeezes my thighs that pushes me over the edge.

My eyes roll back, I arch my spine and stare at the stars high above while he swallows my essence. I'm floating on the waves of pleasure, up into the sky as I stroke my lover's hair. I needed this so badly and didn't even attempt to last longer. We can always go again if we feel like it.

I'm still gathering my bearings when Hawk pushes my thighs wide apart and mounts me by pressing his erection to my groin. His grin is that of a wolf's about to take his satisfaction, and I offer myself to him, breathless as I stare into his handsome face.

When he moves, a soft heat rocks me too, and I bite my lip, trying to stay quiet, because we're in the middle of the forest, and I want him to finish on my skin, not fight off bears.

"So good. You feel so good," I whisper, hugging him with one arm and wrapping my legs around him. He makes me feel tiny, and for once, that's not a bad thing.

His rock-hard cock slides over my skin, and I swear it's even hotter than it used to be. It pulses with his need to come, and I give myself to him, hoping he will never bore of me. That I shall always remain the center of his universe. His movements are fast, jerky, and I can't wait for the next time we have a more sensible, private place so he can thrust like that *into* me.

The friction between our bodies is exquisite, and while it's becoming uncomfortable, the burn enhances our pleasure, and I squeeze Hawk's meaty pec with one hand, causing him to shiver and speed up. He stares straight at me and breathes through his teeth, as if he's already thinking about the things he wants to do to me next time.

"Mine. Tell me you're mine."

One look into those black depths, and I fall in. Or do I leap? The endless darkness in his eyes doesn't scare me in the slightest. I run straight in, welcoming its embrace.

"Yours. Forever yours. Yours to love, yours to fuck, yours to come in." I'm breathless all over again as I drag my nails down his pec, on the verge of scratching my way into his heart.

His black eyes appear glossier now, and he thrusts against me hard and fast, fueling himself with my words. "Yes. Fuck. We're in this together. I've got you," he finishes with a hiss, and liquid heat erupts on my skin.

I glance between us, greedy to see the next spurt of cum land on my stomach, but I also want to see his handsome face flushed with ecstasy. His brows are gathered, and a drop of blood rolls down his chin from where he chewed through his own flesh.

"Am I yours, or are you mine?" I murmur, licking it off.

He laughs, releasing a beautiful, raspy sound. "I might call you mine, but really it's you who has me," he tells me before resting his head on my chest as he catches his breath.

We rest in each other's arms, happy to be alive, appreciating that we have one another. I eventually reach inside my bag for the only disposable piece of cloth I have—my handkerchief with the Goldweed crest. I clean us with it, because we should get going, whichever direction we choose.

Am I disrespecting my family name? Maybe a little.

But it no longer matters.

CHAPTER 32

HAWK

Loud panicked shrieks scratch at my brain as we approach the steep cliffs towering over the sea. Jagged rocks hang over water so dark it might just be squid ink, but the dramatic scenery doesn't help me ignore the calls for help coming from the River of Souls.

We've left the Nocturne Court behind us, but since the nearest city where we can regroup lies farther along the shore of Grief Ocean, Sylvan decided we ought to follow the coastal path. We travel through the woods, of course, to minimize the chance that the glow of my animalistic form attracts unwanted attention, but apparently the harbor close to the palace is the sole port in dozens of miles and the coastline itself is sparsely populated, due to the activity of dangerous sea creatures.

According to Sylvan, we should encounter more people once we travel past the Hannal Straits, but while we will have to survive on simple travel rations and make do without a warm bed until then, at least we won't have to worry about being hunted down.

Then again, my pretty prince won't need a bed, since he has my soft warm fur to sleep on. He's currently enjoying a ride on my back, and I swell with pride that I can provide that for him without effort. He did his best during the three-day trek through the swamps, but his legs are short, and therefore, covering large distances costs him way more effort than it does someone my size.

Being able to change into a different creature still feels like a dream. Like the werewolves from *Twilight*—No. I'm *not* like the werewolves from *Twilight*. Then again, what do I know? I only watched the movie because one of the guards in prison was obsessed with it and brought us a copy. It beat staring at a wall for three hours.

Sylvan's upset about losing the mask *and* my shadow, but I'm rather excited about all the things I'm discovering about this new form. My senses have sharpened, I don't get cold, like, at all, and ended up lending Sylvan my coat, because the harsh coastal winds no longer bother me. I expected the drawback of ripping my clothes every time I grow, the Sunwolf form, but it seems to grow *around* me somehow, which leaves them intact.

Other than witnessing Fenren's gruesome death, it's been kind of a good day, at least until we approached the River of Souls and noticed the insistent howl coming from the fjord ahead.

[*What are those voices?*] I ask telepathically, because that's something I can apparently do now.

Sylvan strokes my nape with his gentle fingers. I love him so much I have the urge to wag my tail every time he does that. "It's... the souls carried by the river. If you want, we can climb down and see it from up close, but it's not a pleasant place."

I miss a step but regain my footing, saving us both from tumbling to the black moss under my paws. Memories of choking, oily water, of floating without purpose, and the growing sense of doom flood back, and I shake my head. But a part of me still wants to see the place where I could have ended up, so I approach the cliff and peek past the edge, at dark, dark waters rolling forward and pouring into the ocean to our right.

A shudder goes along my back, but I don't avert my eyes, and try to recognize human-like shapes below.

[*What happens to them once they reach the ocean?*]

Sylvan hums. "We believe they are consumed by Heartbreak, the monster from the deep sea. But I doubt they are conscious at that point. Their darkened hearts fuel the beast, and every time it gains enough strength, it approaches the Nocturne Court. We do not know its true origin. Whether it is a hateful creature with a mind of its own, or an event comparable to a violent storm, remains a mystery. I've been studying alternative ways to fight it, trying to find out what else it could be vulnerable to."

I look away from the river below and seek another way past the chasm. Once I spot a stone bridge with torn flags floating in the air on either side of the fjord, I trot along the cliff, eager to leave this cursed place behind me. [*Is it really so difficult to pull out a soul?*]

"Oh, they are all desperate to get out, but have you ever tried saving a drowning man? They are so overcome with the need to save themselves they will pull you in if you are not strong enough. Many have tried using rope and the like, but no alternative method proved effective. You need to catch the soul with your bare hands. And that's why my sister died. She overestimated her capabilities and chose a soul that easily overpowered her. I've heard of elves getting lucky in their attempts, but oftentimes, other souls will hang on to the one you're trying to free. Let's just say, I never even considered attempting the feat myself. Yet all royals, even those without Companions, are expected to fight Heartbreak when it approaches. And I... I fled. I brought shame upon myself while my brother died defending innocent lives."

I sense his grief and shame so deeply it tears a howl from my throat. Poor Sylvan does not deserve to blame himself. [*What's the point of facing an enemy you can't compete with? You would have died for nothing.*]

"At least I would have not dishonored my family. My mother thinks honor is for fools, but she finds it important we maintain its facade in public. I failed. I think..." He squeezes my fur. "I think she's angry I'm the one who came back instead of my brother."

I whine. [*That's terrible! Your mom is even worse than my family, and you've met them!*]

"I see it." He sighs as we travel under the cover of trees. "Since I met you, all I could think of was that your presence at my side would force her to respect me in some fashion. Then, I obtained the Sunwolf Crown to further put myself into the annals of history. After years of being constantly laughed at and demeaned, I craved the taste of victory, but should spite really be the point of my existence? Your approval, my darling, is worth more than even the crown of the Nocturne Court." He leans down and kisses me between the ears.

I'm overcome by a wave of joy and leap up as soon as he pulls his face away from my skull. I now understand why dogs enjoy being scratched there, because it's *the best*. [*That's their loss and my gain. You are so smart, you know all those alchemy things, and about animals and places. You can do anything you put your mind to,*] I communicate to him as we reach the bridge. It doesn't appear to be used or frequently maintained, but nothing happens when I cautiously take my first step over the chasm, so forward it is.

Fortunately, there are walls on both sides of me, which block out wind and at least some of the noise coming from the river.

Sylvan shifts and grips my fur harder. I kinda love that I get to feel his ass and thighs all the time when he rides me. It's kind of pervy, so I won't comment, but it is what it is. Soon enough though, we're on the other side, and my prince speaks again.

"I've been thinking about something." He strokes me again, and I wag my tail so hard it smacks a bush and several birds fly out of it with a screech. Sylvan just laughs. "Watch it! They might have eggs in there."

I howl in apology, but I don't think the birds take it the way I mean it. They're small, pale blue and, as Sylvan told me, people call them mourners, because they come in several pastel shades, which in this reality isn't a color scheme every little girl wants in her bedroom, but shades people wear to funerals.

Sylvan has shown me so many interesting things since we started this journey. Somehow, he knows the names of all the flowers, herbs, and little critters we encounter, but also stories related to each and every one. I appreciate having him as my guide through the Nightmare Realm.

[*Tell me,*] I demand as we leave the bridge behind.

"I realized I was so focused on my goals and how you fit into them, that I forgot to ask what *you* want, my love. We are at a metaphorical crossroads. My past hopes and dreams might be in ruins, but we get a fresh start, and I don't want to make plans based on my own vision. I want a life to satisfy both of us."

I twist my head as we follow a stone-paved road with numerous weeds growing between the cobbles. As dramatic as the views of the coast are, it's a relief to step out of the cold wind and be once again surrounded by thick trees covered with vines shimmering like glitter.

I'm touched that he wants my input, that my needs are so important to him. He is the sweetest creature I've ever met.

[*I... want us to be safe and comfortable. Where would be a good place for us to settle?*]

Sylvan chuckles and points to a tall, partially crumbling tower above the tree crowns, not that far away from us. "I don't think we can count on safe and comfortable tonight. See those ruins? Three centuries ago, a pack of werewolves used to live there, and my ancestor led the fight to get rid of them. You'd think that's a good thing, since they were a nuisance to the elves in the area. But it turns out, they kept worse monsters at bay. The bassal kind. In their absence, the forest has become even more dangerous, and this castle has not been inhabited since. We will be safe once we reach a city."

It's like he's waving a treat in front of me, and I turn because I just *have* to see those ruins. I speed up, mindful not to throw off my rider, but the closer we are to the tower, the faster my heart is beating. Soon enough, we dash along a crumbling wall and reach a gate that hasn't been closed for decades. Only one of its wings is still present, partially buried in the damp ground and rusting, but what counts is that nothing's stopping us from entering. I carry Sylvan down the rocky path leading to a garden overgrown with thorny bushes.

The place is like something out of a gothic fairytale, but I already have my prince.

"What is it?" Sylvan asks as I smell one of the many blood-red flowers dangling from a wide tree.

[*I'm just curious. I wanted to come and see this place. Your whole world is so new to me, and everything is exciting. And werewolves? Makes me think. Am I a werewolf? Should we look for them? Would they accept me?*]

Sylvan chuckles. "You are *not* a werewolf, Hawk. If you wish, we could track down a pack of werewolves, but I do not think it wise. It's best no one knows about the return of the Sunwolf. We are hunted because of my crimes, but while the Lord of the Nocturne Court can ignore my existence, he cannot afford to do the same if he finds out about you."

The garden is denser close to the tower, as if the forest around us has managed to leave its mark on every single structure. When the stone walls of the castle finally emerge from beyond the trees—two floors with rows of empty windows and foliage crawling up every surface, I'm struck by the wild beauty of this place.

It's like finding the ruins of some lost civilization.

[*If werewolves exist, does your world also have vampires?*] I ask, remembering the themed room at The Burning Corpse. [*Are they natural enemies?*]

Sylvan laughs, and I just love that sound so much. I might not see his cute face right now, but I imagine it with ease. "Where did that idea come from? Yes, vampires exist in the Nightmare Realm, but I have never met one, and I don't really know where they might reside. Or maybe they've gone extinct? Some say they live on the Darkmoon." He leans over my head and points to the sky. "Others say that they retreated to some far-away land beyond the Grief Ocean."

I look up so fast Sylvan has to grab my horns to avoid falling off. [*They live on the moon? What?*]

"We can find out more, if that's your wish. But first we need to find safety. And I have to admit, I worry how we will survive the journey to the nearest city. We lost close to everything during our journey, even your redpole. In fact, we will need to forage for our meal tomorrow. Elven settlements may be safer than the wilds, but we will be paupers. I was not prepared to have to earn my keep."

[*I could work as a pack animal,*] I point out, placing my paw on the mossy steps leading up to the main entrance into the castle. A crest is carved above the door, but vines have obscured it too much for us to spot any details.

Heat flashes through me out of nowhere, making my heart beat faster, but I shake my head, and it passes as abruptly as it overcame me.

Sylvan laughs. "Don't be ridiculous, Hawk. I just told you we need to lie low. Even the markings on your face might get us unwanted attention."

[*Okay, but I could keep you safe in the forest, you know so much about all the alchemy thingies. You could gather the expensive shit, and then we'd sell it. Easy. And in no time, you'd have a little shop, we could live above it, and... whatever else you'd like to do between fucking and eating crispy delicacies from all over the Nightmare Realm.*]

Sylvan strokes my neck. "Actually, that doesn't sound like such a bad plan. I love to learn, you know? I'd love to have time to read, research, find out more about the creature you've become. And maybe find those vampires for you, if you're so keen."

I yelp in agreement just as we face the damp-scented doors, and my call resonates through the hall ahead as if it were an oversized megaphone. Several purple shapes emerge from the building, floating through the air in jerky, rash movements. They screech, and I turn my head after them as my stomach growls.

Sylvan sighs and slides off my back, his gaze following the bat-like creatures now perched high in the nearby tree. With long ears and powerful hind legs, they look like winged hares, but their purple fur and beady eyes make it clear they aren't of my world.

My coat is so long on Sylvan, it drags over the stone floor as he steps forward. "I used to love them. Hot, crispy, salty wings. An absolute delicacy. But since Lord Kyran's Dark Companion, Luke, has adopted one and treats it like a baby, the court is banned from consuming bats. At least, since I was banished shortly after that ridiculous decree came to life, I didn't have to bear it for too long. Imagine having to smuggle them in." He laughs and stretches his body. I'm glad to see he can make light of the situation.

I don't get the desire to eat bats out of all things, but he stares at the flying critters with such longing I wish I could catch them all for him. [*Then we'll have to find a place where they're a cheap, popular snack.*] I want to tell him more, but the strange heat dashes through my body again, and I groan, lowering myself to the cool stone.

Is that what the hot flashes my mother told me about feel like? Could it be that my hormones are changing because of the transformation?

"Everything all right?" Sylvan asks and kisses my skull, just above the hole I have instead of a nose. "I have some ideas as to which cities we should consider settling in. I only read about them, but unlike vampires, I'm sure they still exist."

[*Tired,*] I say, and as a burning ring closes around my chest, I shed the wolf skin. Moments later, I open my eyes with my forehead pressed to a patch of moss.

Sylvan scoots down to me, and the touch of his cool fingers on my nape is such glorious relief. "Of course you are, you carried me all day. I slept on your back, but you barely got any rest. Let's see if it's safe inside. The dungeon used to hold werewolves frenzied with bloodlust, but I doubt any could have survived since this place was abandoned."

His smile is so bright when I look up at him that despite the fatigue and the damn heat inside, all I feel is love. "Or we could have a small house in the woods close to the city. We could trap those bats and then sell them from a little stall in the market."

Sylvan grabs my hand and leads the way, unafraid of what might be lurking inside the ruins. "I like that. You would have an easier time sneaking away to roam if the Sunwolf needs to stretch his legs. We will take a boat and leave these shores behind. I know of an elf that could take us across the water. She's usually moored not far from here."

He turns to kiss me as we enter the cool mansion, and for once, I don't miss the sun. In fact, I welcome the chill of the abandoned castle.

CHAPTER 33

SYLVAN

The old me would have said I lost everything I've risked so much for—my position, my Dark Companion, even any chance for a meaningful future. But as we leave the mossy walls of the werewolf castle, I can't stop laughing at the stupid prank my man pulled on me when he hid behind a door and gave me a scare. As much as I miss some aspects of my old life, I am not the same man anymore, and Hawk is the reason. He is why I smile so much my cheeks hurt, why I always feel warm, and why the future, difficult and unknown as it might be, does not feel bleak anymore.

Despite spending a whole night at a ruined castle that's rumored to be cursed, I wake up in high spirits. It might have something to do with the fact that I got to sleep on the best of beds—Hawk's fur. We settled in a relatively clean and dry room on the first floor, but while the building was overcome by icy, damp air, I felt warm and safe when tucked against my man's side. We even found an unopened bottle of wine. I refused to drink it due to my new vow of sobriety, but Hawk got to enjoy it while we explored the abandoned structure.

The dungeon where werewolves used to keep their brethren during fits of rage remains locked behind a huge round door. I was curious what hides beyond it, but when Hawk started kissing my ears, my desire for him won out, and we retreated to the room we picked for the night.

In the morning, we stumbled upon raspberry bushes, which supplied us with breakfast. The last stretch of our walk toward the cove where I hope to board a boat that will take us past the straits and out of the lands ruled by my cousin Kyran, Hawk decided to walk in his human form. It's for the better, since an oversized wolf radiating golden light is difficult to miss, and the last thing I want is for the Nocturne Court to find out about his existence. If Kyran discovered the Sunwolf was on the loose, he'd hunt us down like he had Heartbreak, and I refuse to let anything happen to my husband.

I meant every word I told him during our wedding vows, and if protecting him means foregoing any rights I might have as a royal, then so be it. He is and always will be more precious to me than titles, finery, and comforts.

Despite it being a chilly day, and the wind blowing at us constantly, he's not only offered me his coat, for additional warmth, but even took off his thin shirt, and has been walking bare-chested for the past two hours.

I do remember reading that werewolves tend to have a much higher body temperature than elves (or humans), so maybe his new body acts in a similar way? Not to mention that my sister Vinia, who had the rare power of Sunlight, tended to run hot too. This issue will require more research. Hopefully, once we settle, I will have access to a library of some kind, or at least to decent book vendors.

That is something to worry about in the future though, as now our priority is to leave the Nocturne Coast and head for the shores of Ravanzia. And since we can't risk boarding a legitimate vessel, we're making our way down a path known solely to those who might need alternative routes of travel. Just like with the grimsmith, I do have to begrudgingly admit my mother has equipped me with knowledge of people and places that might come in handy if I ever needed to flee the Nocturne Court. Or return to it for that matter, though my familiarity with secret passages allowing to enter the castle unnoticed will never again be of use.

It's a clear day, and while the moon only presents us with the larger half of its face, it emits enough light to make the waves ahead glint like quicksilver. The lines of the rocky slopes on either side of our way into the cove look sharp enough to cut into flesh, and the caverns around it might make perfect hiding spots for bandits, but I fear nothing as long as Hawk is holding my hand, so we joke around and tell each other stories. His are less bloody, though I do appreciate the one which features women cutting off chunks of their feet in order to fit a crystal shoe and marry a prince.

That's the kind of message I can get behind.

Mid-laughter, Hawk stops to take a deep breath and leans against a seaweed-covered rock. "Gimme a sec, babe," he says, and then proceeds to take his shoes off so his feet touch the cool sand.

"While I appreciate that werewolves might need to be more in tune with nature, please make sure you don't step on a crab," I say.

"Well, if it cuts off my feet, I will be shorter, and kissing you will be easier." Hawk gives me a faint smile, which... has me a little worried.

"Are you all right, my dear?" I ask, as we walk out onto a rocky beach. At this time of day, the waves have receded, which makes reaching our destination much easier. I even spot the large white skeleton of a leviathan emerging from the dense sand not far away. A reassuring sign that we're in the right place.

Hawk looks at the stars with a grimace. "I just feel so damn hot all the time. And it's like when a fever won't let you think."

I touch his forehead, suddenly worried, and he is, in fact, burning up. "Oh, my love, let's cool you down before we go any farther. I'm sorry we cannot rest just yet. The boat trip will take several days, so maybe you will recover *en route*."

I pull him along the beach and to the skeleton of the elongated sea beast. Strands of seaweed hang from its bones, and maybe their touch might provide the respite Hawk needs.

The wet sand, usually weighed down by tonnes of water, is easy to walk on, and soon enough, Hawk is assessing the leviathan's sharp teeth while I lay the cool seaweed on his back, creating a weave that should help with his plight. I spot more of the cooling strands past the skull, between the skeleton's ribs, so I grab Hawk's hand and lead him in that direction.

One moment, we're headed for the seaweed, the other, Hawk tugs me back with a growl that sends a shudder down my spine.

"Watch it!" he snarls.

I turn to see my man hunched forward and holding onto his forehead while blood spills from between his fingers. It doesn't take a lot of brain power to conclude he must have hit himself on a bony ridge, and I step closer, trying to soothe him with my touch.

The noise he utters then comes from deep in his chest. It's low and animalistic, and when he opens his black eyes, they are angry voids. I take a step back, suddenly aware how tight the spaces between the ribs are. My stomach drops and my instincts scream in warning, as if I'm a fox that let a hungry wolf corner it between tall rocks.

But also... I'm confused. He's never been this snappy. Is it the illness that makes him short-tempered?

"I'm sorry," I say and stroke his arm. "I'll just get the seaweed myself. Wait here."

I hate the fact that not hearing his footsteps follow me is a relief. Anyone's allowed to be in a bad mood sometimes, and Hawk's been through a lot in the past week, but there was something strange about the emptiness in his eyes. I shake off the unreasonable anxiety, but by the time I'm back, his eyes, while black, reflect the silver moonlight. It seems I've been spooked by a trick of the light.

He stands still as I place the leaves on his chest and abdomen, and only speaks once I'm almost done.

"Are you angry?" Hawk asks.

I hesitate, unsure what emotion has curled in my chest. "No. I'm just a pain in the ass when ill. All that matters is that you will soon be able to rest. Come." I give him a kiss, and I have to admit that even his lips are hotter than usual.

"But I snapped. I don't snap at my partners," Hawk tells me and brings my hands to his boiling forehead. "Did I scare you? You looked scared."

I swallow, but he deserves the truth. "A little. You are a man of substantial size." I smile at him to sweeten my words. "Which will be a boon for us when we meet Captain Lepearl. I have heard she is fearsome, so I feel better knowing I have you at my side when we face her."

Hawk nods, but he leans down and clasps his arms around me before lifting me up. His blazing face slides under my shirt in the process. "It won't happen again, baby."

I stroke his hair to comfort him, even though the fact that he has a sense of guilt over his actions is welcome. "I'm just sorry you are poorly."

We end up walking along the beach with our hands entwined, and he does seem to have cooled down. The seaweed even has a fresh scent, similar to mint. Mingled with the smell of the ocean, it reminds me of nights back at the Nocturne Court, when I would escape my siblings to a roof above our bedrooms and read by the moonlight, with only tea as my companion. Now, I have Hawk.

We approach a rock with the letters *ML* carved into it, which tells me we are almost at the cove where the captain is either currently moored or where we will have to await her return.

"I will handle everything," I tell Hawk. "But if securing passage with her proves impossible, we will travel down the coast. Captains communicate with each other, so it is better if we do not cause problems. I'd rather not be blacklisted."

"Right," Hawk says, squeezing my hand as we walk ever faster. "You think me being a human might be a problem? Maybe I should cover my head?"

I sigh and stroke him with my thumb. "I'm afraid you're memorable either way."

"Maybe I should stay behind then. You'd get on the boat, and we'd meet in Ravanzia. I'd travel in the Sunwolf form, through forests, hunt on the way. Just tell me the direction, and I'll figure it out."

I frown at him, shocked at such a suggestion. "Hawk. No. We either go together, or find another way to reach our destination."

He licks his lips, staring at the waves crashing onto the shore. "I don't want them to turn you away. You are in danger."

"And as my Dark Companion, you are too, even if they don't know you're also the Sunwolf. We are in this together, just as we promised in our vows." I show off the ring I've ended up wearing on my thumb. "We do not leave each other behind."

He swallows, and his nostrils flare as he exhales. Moments later, his arms are around me, his lips at the top of my head, breathing me in. "I won't let anything happen to you."

I melt into him, wishing we didn't have to continue this perilous journey. The seaweed on his skin has already dried so much it crunches when we hug. I just hope the cool breeze of the ocean will help once we're on the boat.

Not far from the rock with the initials, the wide mouth of a cave opens in the cliff towering over the beach. With my heartbeat in my throat, I lead us inside.

The resident doesn't attempt to hide her presence, as I can see swamplight torches from the entrance. I suppose not many people would end up here by accident, so I pull Hawk along, walking deeper into the hideout. The air smells of salt and adora smoke, which the captain must often use for it to be so pervasive, but those musings evaporate from my mind when we turn the corner and see the back of the cave.

Furniture worthy of a royal family is set up on top of carpets, along with colorful textiles and items that are as expensive as they appear. Beyond them, in the green glow of the torches I spot a small ship as white as bone. No, actually, it *is* made of bone, and I find myself stilling at the sight of the pier next to it, and the three people lounging there over a game of cards.

Two men are stretched on fancy chaise-lounges, one of which is suspiciously reminiscent of the piece of furniture that apparently sank on the way to the Nocturne Court before Lord Kyran's ascension to the throne. But neither of them look like the type of gentlemen who can afford such fine pieces.

Both of them are wearing leather pants that don't even reach their ankles. In the moonlight, their pale bodies seem almost as white as the bone vessel behind them, while their long black hair falls in messy streaks down their backs. I see enough resemblance to assume they're brothers.

But while they are a mystery to me, I'm sure the woman sitting on a barrel next to them must be Captain Margaux Lepearl, as her mane of curly blonde hair beneath a hat fashioned out of the skull of a Skyshark is a distinct feature my mother told me about. As we get closer, I realize she's dressed just like her companions, and wears nothing beyond a pair of leather pants, leaving her breasts bare.

As soon as the crunch of rocks under our feet alert the group, three pairs of eyes turn our way and Lepearl grabs a shirt to cover herself.

I raise my hands when one of the men grabs a crossbow. "Greetings, Captain Lepearl!" I say to signify I know what I'm doing, even though confidence drizzles out of me the moment a bolt is aimed at my heart.

She frowns, and her feline features grow even more angular as she raises her chin. "Who's disturbing my peace? I do not know you."

Behind me, I sense the faintest vibration, as if Hawk is growling deep in his throat, but he remains still, as I asked.

The other man drops his cards with a frustrated sigh. "Can you not come back once we're done playing strip poker? I was winning."

Judging by his state of undress, I'm not sure if by winning he actually means losing.

The captain jumps off the barrel and puts on a flamboyant jacket embroidered with a pattern of spider crabs in black and red. As I step on the pier, I'm secretly glad to see she's no taller than me. Well, maybe if it wasn't for her hat.

"I am sorry to disturb you, but I come with an urgent matter. My name is Prince Sylvan Goldweed, and I have been told you used to work for my mother."

Lepearl squints at me. Her eyes are like two rubies surrounded by kohl dust. "*With*, not 'for'. So what can a banished prince want from me? You do know there's a bounty on your head, right?" she asks, but does glance at Hawk next. If news of Hawk and what we've done at The Burning Corpse has traveled, people might assume we're more dangerous than we are.

I clear my throat. "Passage to Ravanzia. As I said, urgently. My mother will pay." I'm bluffing, but my family name is the only bargaining chip I have left, unless the bag of fresh raspberries attached to my belt counts.

Lepearl sighs and grabs an apple from a golden bowl. She doesn't bite into it though, almost as if the fruit is a wax prop. "How much is her blood worth to her?" she asks while the two men relax. One of them pulls out a pipe and packs it with dried adora, which explains the herby, sweet scent lingering in the air. The other puts down the crossbow with a deep sigh. Is he upset he doesn't get to use it?

"Everything," I say without missing a beat. Another useful thing my mother taught me. Don't hesitate when lying. "I am her only remaining son."

When the man behind Lepearl lights his pipe, I get a good look at his blank eyes. They have no pupils, just empty sclera in a watery shade, and it hits me where I've seen a gaze like his before. The royal coachman at the Nocturne Court, and every single kelpie in his care have eyes like that . But how can these two stay in elven form? Who enchanted them? And how does Lepearl keep them disciplined when kelpie are known to be rowdy and violent creatures with a knack for cruel games?

The captain taps her pale lips. "Let's say I agree—"

"No!" One of the kelpie gets up and spreads his arms. "We just got back yesterday!"

I frown. "I am speaking with your captain."

Lepearl cocks her head at me. "Kick and Bite will be the ones making sure we have a safe journey, so you don't want to disrespect them, and if they say they're tired, then we're not going anywhere until tomorrow."

Kick and Bite? Seriously? I glare at the glorified horses, but when I take a deep breath to speak again, Hawk steps in front of me.

"Listen, lady. We don't have the time. His mother will pay, and we will be the best passengers you've ever had. Hell, I can row if you want. But we need to leave *now*."

She glares at him, buttoning her coat, as if to let him know this is not a game. "My crew said no. You can stay in the cave until tomorrow, but don't push your luck."

Hawk steps farther onto the pier, and I follow him, unsure how I should act in order to calm the situation. "You can't be serious! You'll get paid extra if we go now."

"I have enough money," Lepearl says, her face growing colder. "You're welcome to swim on your own, though I wouldn't recommend it."

Hawk lets out a growl. He takes another step forward and some of the dried seaweed falls off him. "You need to get him on that ship, and to Ravanzia or I will rip you all to *shreds*! That's the deal!"

My stomach plummets, and I want to pull him back, but it's too late. I have no idea why he's being like this when we could just wait until tomorrow.

I don't know whether it's Kick or Bite, but one of the kelpie steps in front of Lepearl and shifts in front of our eyes. Within seconds, his pale body turns tar-black, only the head remaining bone-white since it's a skull. The imposing horse beast stomps its hoofs on the creaking pier. This must be Bite after all, because he lunges forward, teeth-first, but Hawk doesn't fall back.

He punches the kelpie right on its bony muzzle.

"No!" I yell, because this mess is about to get even messier.

Bite collapses to the wooden floor, making the pier creak in warning, but as he falls, so does Hawk. He shrieks in panic, grabs Bite's neck with his unprotected hand, and his fingers get stuck to the kelpie's coat. The need for clothing made out of octopus leather meant to prevent situations like this has been drilled into me before my first kelpie-riding lesson. But Hawk is ignorant to what's going on and drags Bite over the pier in an attempt to get free.

Lepearl stares in mute shock, and leaps to the end of the pier when a flash of light radiates from my man. He starts glowing, as if there were demons attempting to free themselves from under his skin.

"Fuck! Don't! Hawk! Don't!" I yell, but take a step back, afraid that in his fury he might take a bite out of my shadow.

To make matters worse, Kick turns into his animal form too, and moments later, the Sunwolf stands on the pier, no longer stuck to Bite.

"Wh-what is that?" Lepearl asks.

Hawk lowers his skull-head with a growl as the kelpie back away. They could easily leap into the water, but I'm guessing they want to stand between the golden beast and their captain.

"No one fight!" I put all my princely authority into my voice. "We can resolve—"
The pier crashes under the combined weight of beasts and elves. With a panicked yelp on my lips, I fall into the dark water.

CHAPTER 34

HAWK

I let myself float in the gentle waves, along with all the wooden debris. But then movement sends bubbles of air my way, making me open my eyes in time to see the weird horse's hindquarters morph into a twisted fishtail. It resembles the creature featured on the collar we had taken off Sylvan. A merhorse. A... kelpie.

I can't explain how I went from hanging on to Sylvan's advice about not interfering to white-shot anger that made the smugglers hostile. It's ended up with the pier destroyed, and everyone floating in cold water. When I emerge to take in air, the dampness on my face and shoulders evaporates, creating a white cloud of steam that prevents me from seeing the details of my surroundings.

I'm boiling up.

I just want to...

"Sylvan! Where are you?" I ask as soon as my brain is no longer an overheated mass of goo.

"Here!" he yelps, struggling to keep his face above the surface. He's splashing about like a puppy dropped into water for the first time, his lips wide open and facing the rocky ceiling of the cave. I reach him before he can disappear beneath the surface, and steel myself, in case I need to prevent him from attempting to climb me like the last person I saved from drowning had.

But he's calm and holds on to my shoulder as I scoop him up with my arm before setting off to where the shore is a mild slope. Both the kelpie and Lepearl are already there by the time we exit the water. I can't help but stare at the majestic creatures that nevertheless would not be out of place in a gothic horror movie. They're back to being four-legged animals, but it's hard to miss features that would be unusual on a regular horse, like the translucent film covering their hooves. Or the fucking *skulls* they have for heads.

Lepearl glares at us as she takes off her fish bone hat to twist salty water out of her hair. "I don't know what you are, and frankly, I don't care! Get out! I don't want to fight, but if you step anywhere near my ship, I will!"

A tremor passes through Sylvan, but his lips are set, and he nods. "I understand. May I just ask you not to mention this to other captains?"

"Ha, only the ones whose ships I don't want at the bottom of the ocean," she shouts back, and that is that.

I let out a howl as the heat within starts once again rising. Alarmed, both the kelpie stand between me and their captain, a direct challenge to the demon inhabiting my blood. But before I can make another mistake, blinded by the fever burning out the insides of my skull, Sylvan grabs my hand, and I relent, like a dog brought to heel.

I want to apologize, to try to negotiate a safe passage for my husband at least—all he did was try to stop me—but when Sylvan tugs on my arm, I follow, leaving the cave with my tail between my legs.

The silence between us is inflamed and uncomfortable like an ulcer developing deep under the skin, but every time I inhale, about to speak, the absolute resignation painted on Sylvan's face stops me from attempting to excuse my behavior. He doesn't deserve what I'm unleashing on him. When I remember how I growled at him, the sense of despair inside makes me want to cry.

It's Sylvan who speaks first once we're on the coastal path, walking toward fuck knows where. Unlike my rapidly drying clothes, Sylvan's are soaked, and he trembles from the cold no doubt piercing his flesh even more pervasively now that we're back at the mercy of the wind.

"Why would you do that? I had it. I was negotiating," he says, refusing to look my way.

I'm not a stranger to disappointing others, but his quiet resentment makes me long to crawl into a hole and disappear.

I've failed him.

I've failed my husband by letting this unnatural anger take over, and he's the one who'll have to live with the consequences. My teeth grind when a hot spasm shoots up my back.

It's doing something to my mind, demanding things so terrible I'd rather die than comply. Suddenly, I can smell the smoky aroma of Sylvan's shadow with such clarity I dash to the rocky shore and dip my head in the salty water.

I'm heaving by the time I lift my head, but a degree of clarity is back. Sylvan is scooting next to me and puts his cool fingers on my hot back. I want to press my whole body against him so he can calm me. But I'm not worthy of his care.

"Hawk? What's going on?" he asks with uncertainty in his voice, the earlier demands and anger gone.

He deserves to reach Ravanzia safely, not get stuck caring for me while I lose my mind. I know he should leave me here. Still, I push my head against his chest and claw at his damp clothes, taking whatever care he's willing to give me after the stunt I've pulled.

"I'm sorry. I— I think there's something wrong with me."

Instead of getting annoyed, as most people would, he holds me close. No one has ever shown me this much patience. Sylvan slides to the sand, and at least I can hope I'm warming him up with the heat burning me from the inside as if I had the sun for a heart.

"Oh, no... Hawk. What is it? You must tell me at once." He strokes my hair with tender fingers I want to kiss all over.

I've already done so much wrong today. I hate that telling him the truth will only add to his worries. I wish I could shield him from what is happening to me, but he needs to know. For his own safety.

"It's... it's as if my brain is boiling," I whimper and squeeze his hand, even though deep down I feel seeking comfort is making the situation more difficult for us both. Being in my presence is putting him in danger. I can't allow myself to rely on him in this situation. Still, he needs to be aware of what's going on. "I think it's the Sunwolf. I get so irrationally angry it's like molten fire in my blood."

Sylvan's gaze is so soothing, even when he frowns with worry. "Fuck. This could be caused by a dozen of different reasons. Because you're human, or because you weren't a shadow-wielder and still used the mask. The Sunwolf might be trying to take you over. We will deal with this, Hawk. You should have told me sooner, but that doesn't matter anymore. I brought you into my world, and I *will* find a way to help you."

I stall, meeting his gaze as guilt and shame spread through my body. Maybe this would have been a rational option in another situation, but we are out here on our own, and if

I snap, there will be nothing to stop me from hurting him. "No. You need to go on the boat. Please," I beg, grabbing his hands as I hang my head and push it against him.

Understanding dawns in his eyes. His pupils widen, and what's left of the ice blue seems to darken. "I'm not leaving you. I made a vow." He takes a trembling breath and strokes my face. "Listen, it seems that the water cools you down. I will go to Lepearl, plead with her. I know I'll find a way for her to take us—"

I shake my head and squeeze his thighs with a cry of anguish. "No. No. No. You have to leave me. I'm... I'm not myself. You can't be trapped with me in the middle of the ocean!"

Sylvan goes so silent I can only hear his heartbeat and the hum of the ocean. He's thinking. He's not given up yet. But he *has to*. He has so much heart, but he's also smarter than anyone I know. He has to see that I'm right about this.

"If I leave you, and you overheat again, you will go to the ocean. Those waters are dangerous, deadly even at the shore. You must at least let me take you somewhere safe. Even if you turn feral, maybe one day I will come up with a cure, and then I'll know where to find you."

I hate that he's considering putting himself in danger for even a minute longer, but it's impossible to say no to that last glimmer of hope.

Because I *am* afraid.

More than after my first kill. More than I was of a bear that once accosted me in the woods, more than of prison, and of death itself. I have been close to finished several times, but somehow this slow agony and the fear of becoming something else seems so much worse than a sudden end.

I shudder, nodding as his palms slide up and down my back, giving me comfort I haven't earned, but which I'll gladly accept. "As long as you're safe. It would kill me if I hurt you."

"I understand, but I'll be safe. Especially now that I know what to watch out for." He gets up, fists clenched with new determination. "Is it agitating for you to change into the Sunwolf?"

I shake my head, following him to my feet. "No, it's actually soothing, more body for all the heat inside me. I think. Or it's just trying to entice me into that form by making it feel good."

Sylvan nods. "I'm only asking, because our travel will be much quicker that way, and we can't waste time. We will go back to the werewolf castle. Remember the dungeon? It has access to a cold stream where they handled frenzied werewolves. You will have water but remain away from the dangers of the ocean."

I want to protest, but as our gazes meet and I focus on the dark blue galaxies shimmering in his eyes, I give up on arguing. He's right. The castle is not that far, and maybe there is in fact something that could help me? I need Sylvan to be safe, but I don't want to give up on myself either. I didn't survive six almost-deaths to do that.

"All right."

I allow the sunlight within me to expand, and shift into the Sunwolf as he's asked. The relief is instant, but deep down I know it's a slippery slope that will lead me to losing myself. For now, I just focus on the fact that I will be able to keep Sylvan warm on the way.

"If it worked on feral werewolves, it might work for you," Sylvan says while I'm speeding up. "No one can track you down in the dungeon."

After five years in prison, that sounds dreadful, but if the thick walls keep me from hurting my lovely prince, I'll take it.

CHAPTER 35

HAWK

I try not to think about the future. That's what always kept me going when things went sideways, but while the form of the Sunwolf lets my thoughts clear, each passing second feels like a step toward the inevitable. My senses sharpen, detecting sounds, smells, and flavors I've never before noticed, but even with the abundance of animals in the forest, I feel like the most delicious morsel of all is on my back.

Sylvan's shadow is faint, pale, and smooth like whipped cream with just the right amount of sugar and spice that's so uniquely him. A tiny snack, really, when compared to the magnitude of the shadow making up Tristan Bloodweed's wings, but I want it all the same. Its touch makes my skin tingle, and I long for its essence in the blood pumping through my husband's small form.

It scares me how easily I can imagine myself diving my muzzle into his open rib cage, and lapping its insides as if it were a cup of yogurt, not the body of the man who I—

A frantic yelp leaves my throat as I shake off the image my mangled brain sees as both horrifying and enticing. He's not safe with me. Not the way I am now.

"It's all right, my love. We're almost there," Sylvan says, unaware of the dangerous thoughts crowding my mind. I try to remember each time he speaks to me this way. It makes me feel like I'm truly special, someone worthy of being chosen, and I let it be my comfort.

Would he run from me if he knew? Or would he have stayed despite it? I'd rather not test that in what might be our last hours together.

I wouldn't call the castle 'familiar', but at least it's a place I already know. We explored it a little last night, so we know that it's abandoned.

Then again, tonight, it might become my home, and a place of doom for any elf foolish enough to cross the threshold. I dread to think about spending the rest of my life stuck in yet another prison, but it's the loneliness of it that truly terrifies me. If my consciousness isn't consumed by the Sunwolf, then I might go mad because of the isolation. I've never been someone who likes spending a lot of time on his own. Even if I'm not talking all the time, I long for touch and company.

Another thought hits me as I transform in front of the gate.

"If you lock me in there, what will I eat?"

Sylvan strokes my hand and pulls me in. "As the Sunwolf, you will not need to eat material food."

I want to whine and complain that I *like* to eat *material food*, but hearing that is the last burden Sylvan needs.

I dash inside the castle, and then down two flights of dusty stairs. We were down here last night, but the huge circular door facing us now was the limit of our exploration. My vision is quite decent even now, but the swamplight flickering to life inside a lamp attached to the wall reveals the deep grooves marking the huge entrance. It's an artwork—a depiction of wolf men dancing under the moon.

The unbearable heat returned the moment I regained my smooth skin and fingers, but that only means I need to act fast. The door doesn't seem to come with any handle though, and I growl, smacking my palm against it. The thing is so damn thick we barely hear any echo inside.

I'm about to complain when something clicks, and I put my ear against the cool surface.

"Does it work?" Sylvan asks, prompting me to look back his way. I haven't paid attention to anything beyond the door itself, but far away from it, by the stairs, is a mechanism embedded in the floor. Sylvan puts his entire body weight on the lever attached to it, and the sharp noise is back.

I want to kiss him.

"That's it! That must be the way to unlock the dungeon!"

"Come over. I need some of that superior strength." He smiles at me—for the first time since the disaster with Lepearl and her kelpies.

Pride fills my chest, and I join him by the device, intent on moving the lever. When raw strength doesn't do the trick, he admits he carries a bit of oil, to aid our lovemaking, and we use some of it on the mechanism. The process still takes a lot of effort, but the vault door finally cracks open, its lock released after at least a hundred years of inactivity.

Sylvan's instinct is to crawl through it, but I keep him back and widen the gap leading into the dungeon before settling next to it and letting myself inspect the hidden space.

It's cold and damp, but there is no life I can sense, just fungi, moss, and old bones.

Sylvan follows me, his cool fingers sliding into my hand. My whole being knows he belongs at my side, and yet he will leave me in this cold prison. He has to. I want that for his own safety. Every minute he's still here feels stolen.

I need him as far away from the Nocturne Court as possible, so he can live a good life, and maybe sometimes think back to me, smiling.

The massive chamber has a tall, vaulted ceiling, and Sylvan slips out of my grasp to light all the swamplight torches by the rows of cells. Behind thick metal bars, corpses have long been devoured by time, leaving behind only bones and chains. I can't help but stop to stare at the skeleton of a creature with a canine skull and a humanoid body.

Will this be me in two hundred year's time?

Sylvan grabs a torch and walks across the stone floor, all the way to the end of the long corridor of cells.

"There should be... Aha! Hawk, you need to see this!"

Just as I walk up to him, he lowers the torch, and a massive firepit lights up with green flames, revealing what's at the very end of this dungeon.

A mosaic covers a whole wall, depicting men and wolves. Some chained, some cowering under waterfalls. In the center of the image is a large pipe in the shape of a dragon's head.

"And down here," Sylvan says, leading me to a part of the floor covered with a round slab of metal roughly the size of a small car. "Is where they brought feral werewolves. Help me open it."

Unlike the vault door to the prison, this covering isn't that hard to lift, and what's revealed is a three foot-deep, rounded hole. The mosaic here is colorful, and not stained by years of dust the way the walls are. If this small pool wasn't located in a dungeon, it would fit right in at a luxury spa in my world. At least that's how those places look in the movies. The closest to a spa I've ever been to was the gay sauna in Boston, and that had... a bit of a different atmosphere.

I exhale and stare at the metal covering. "Do you... want to lock me in here?"

He frowns, as if I hurt him by even voicing my question. "No. First, we will turn on the water to cool you down," he says and puts the back of his hand against my arm. "Then—"

I meet his gaze. "Then, you must leave. I'm not joking, Sylvan. If I hurt you, I will never forgive myself."

He's silent for a while, so beautiful with the green light dancing on his skin. "I *will* leave. I will lock the vault door behind me. T-to not starve, you will need to turn into the Sunwolf," he mutters.

My lips quirk into a smile despite the hole inside my chest. I know this will be for the best, even if spending an unpredictable amount of time on my own, underground, sounds like torture. But if my mind gives in to the creature I've invited inside me, it won't matter any longer.

I've had a pretty good run after all.

"Yes. Thank you, babe. For... everything," I add softly, despite the fire inside me climbing my throat.

Sylvan gets to his toes and cups my cheeks. Maybe I've only had so little time with him, but it was worth everything I'm going through now. He's my perfect prince. Beautiful, with the heart of a lion.

"Don't give up hope, Hawk."

He believes it. Even now, he believes there's a future for us. So I will entertain that too. For him.

My gaze seeks a way to fill the pool, and when I notice a valve on the nearby wall, I head toward it and give it a little nudge. Like the cover, it's not nearly as stuck as the door lock has been, and moments later, a gurgle echoes in the walls around us. Then, the pipe at the very bottom of the pool spits out water.

"It comes from a nearby stream, so it's clean, and not salty like the ocean," Sylvan says, but I'm already taking off my pants because I'm dying to cool my skin.

The pool is filled halfway when I slide in naked and scoot down to sink in at least to the neck. The relief is instant, and I let my head fall back onto the edge before glancing up at my sweet boy.

We didn't get nearly enough time together, but for him I am ready to be martyred. "This is... so good."

Sylvan's expression is pensive when he kneels by the pool and dips his hand in. "You're so hot it's warming up the water."

I lick my lips, drawn to his soft scent. I know this is the moment I ought to make him leave, but thinking about a forever without him makes my heart so heavy I end up squeezing his wrist. "Stay for a bit longer. Be with me."

My lovely elven prince swallows, knowing exactly what I'm asking for and after a moment's hesitation, sheds his coat.

My heart leaps with joy, and I brush the back of my hand over the tip of his boot. He is the most charming man I've ever met, and the purest soul. I might have not led the best of lives, but one thing I *don't* regret? Meeting him.

I wouldn't turn back time to avoid ever putting on the Sunwolf Crown either, because we'd both be dead if I hadn't. This way, at least, he has a fighting chance in this strange world of merhorses, werewolves, and elves. Our time together was short, but I have never known the kind of happiness I feel when he smiles at me, approving of some small thing or another. I imagine that setting him free was my purpose from the very beginning, that I was born for it, and that our meeting at Best Burger Bonanza was far from accidental. Maybe that's why I survived all my brushes with death? After all, Sylvan seems to believe in destiny.

"I love you," I whisper, as he sheds his clothes, revealing his lithe form.

My romantic feelings for him are tender and mushy, but when I see his naked body, there's no denying I also *crave* his flesh. I still don't understand why someone like him would ever be self-conscious, because he has the glow of moonlight and all the stars put together. An ethereal beauty with eyes like precious sapphires, dainty feet, soft hair, and a delicious cock I itch to feel against my skin.

"I love you too," he says, dipping his bare toe into the water. From down here, he is a god I want to worship, so I grab him by the hips and pull him into the warmed-up water, determined to make this ancient dungeon our personal paradise. Even if just for a little while.

Our bodies coming together is bliss. "Thank you. For everything," I say and enfold him in my arms, lowering myself to one of the steps making up the edges of the pool.

He straddles my lap, and the initial tenderness soon transforms into a more visceral need for him. I run my hands up his spine with a low groan.

"Did you just... get even hotter? Maybe I should leave after all." The little smile on his lips tells me he doesn't mean it, but I still pull him closer, until he crosses his ankles behind me and his soft hair tickles my neck. This will be the last time I hold him, and I want to remember every detail.

The water keeps bubbling around us, cooling my feverish body as I explore his smooth skin. He smells of his shadow, so mild, sweet, and intense it's making my head spin, so I bury my face in the crook of his neck, lapping at the shade there. The wolf in me wants to devour all of it, until my man is a burned-out husk, but all *I* want is a taste.

"Maybe I did. Maybe I'm burning for you," I whisper, nuzzling at his flesh.

Sylvan gasps when I suck in his skin. "Oh! I can *feel* that," he murmurs and slides higher up my thighs, until his cock presses against mine.

It's almost too much, and I grab his ass with a low growl. He's so soft, so smooth, so warm in my embrace. I want to be inside him so badly, and not even the Sunwolf can take this moment from us.

Hugging him is like sinking into a land of impossible dreams where pain or sorrow don't exist. I want to forget reality for a bit longer. I can't keep him forever, but as our blood grows hotter, I know we'll be left with memories to last a lifetime.

I want to connect. Be inside and outside him. To brand this moment on the backs of his eyelids, so he can never forget me. I hope he can love me even when I'm gone. Selfish, I know, but I won't get much more time, and I need this.

My middle finger rolls up and down his opening, exploring the wrinkled skin. He shivers, and his perfect moans caress my ear, sending sweet sensations down my back.

"I want to feel you inside me," he whispers, offering me the little bottle we used to open the vault door.

I nod, rubbing his cheek with my stubble. "Of course you do. My needy treasure. My sweet boy."

The old me would have called out my own words as pure cheese, but I mean each one, and if we are to part, I need him to know how much he matters. How very grateful I am for his love. How it's changed me, and gave my life the meaning I was searching for.

I get up, taking him with me, and moments later he's stretched on the tiled floor, with his hips on the very edge of the pool. Blinking, he reaches for me, and I rub my face against his beautiful chest. The scars left behind by the failed attempt to remove his collar are still there, purple dots like a new constellation made for him only. I kiss each one as he cradles me between his legs, as if there's no rush.

"Hawk... I... I never met anyone like you. I would have been proud to introduce you at court as my Dark Companion." Sylvan's voice is filled with emotion when his slender body arches under my touch.

It hurts to know that we're at the end of our journey, but I've always sought my fortune wherever I could. It no longer matters. All I want is to be with him for a few moments longer, so I kiss his chest and stomach as I take some of the oil onto my hand. The white-hot noise that feels more primal than my usual desire for Sylvan prickles at the back of my neck. I ignore it and tease him, circling his hole with my slick fingertip.

"Just... be with me now. The future doesn't matter," I whisper and push the digit in.

A sudden tug on my heart makes me still, but Sylvan smiles, raising his hips as he rides my hand. "Feel that? We still have our bond."

I still for half a second and let myself experience it fully—the magical connection that links my soul to his. His heartbeat quickens, and so does mine as they dance together like two butterflies.

Tears sting my eyes when I think about being apart—maybe for good—but I would do anything for him, and what he needs is for me to let him go. But not yet. I want to keep him for a bit longer. To make my mark and keep his scent in my memory.

There are no words to describe the depths of my feelings for him. Maybe the English language is simply not good enough to provide them?

My cock throbs as I rut against his thigh, fingering his tight hole. I want this to go on forever, so that we never have to part, but the beast in me demands satisfaction, and I enter Sylvan in a single thrust, following the sweetest of moans.

His cries resonate under the vaulted ceiling, and he reaches for me, lost without my kisses. I suck the tender flesh of his neck, leaving marks that will stay with him that little bit longer, and he holds me close, as if he too longs for our bodies to become one, so we never need to part.

The heat inside me grows, gripping my mind with its red-hot claws, and as we move together, the call of the beast becomes near impossible to silence. Our skin sparks where we're connected. When I catch the smoky whiff of his shadow, my hands find his hips, and I hold him in place, thrusting into his delicious heat over and over.

His eyes are two skies full of starlight, and when he reaches his climax, they all fall. I make a wish on every single one.

With my fingers buried in his golden hair, I too find my release, and we slide back into the water, sharing those last few moments together.

I'm afraid.

So very afraid.

But that is not what he needs to hear, so I summon all my strength and whisper, "Be safe."

Sylvan holds me tight, running his fingers over my nape in a calming manner. I wish he could stay here and pet me like this until I lose my mind, but that wouldn't be safe for him.

"You have my heart, Hawk," he says when he untangles his limbs from mine.

"And you have mine," I tell him, sinking into the water, all the way to my jaw. "I will turn. But this is how I want you to see me when you leave."

"Magnificent?" he asks with a sigh and gives me a kiss before rising to his feet.

My heart feels as if it's falling apart, and while I've been through so much shit, no pain ever felt this intense. But I don't let any of that show, because he needs to focus on getting to safety, not comforting a man who'll inevitably lose himself.

"That too," I say, snorting. "Handsome, and tall."

The smile falls from Sylvan's lips as he dresses in the damp black clothes that no longer look very refined. "Hawk... please stay in that pool once I leave. Turn the water on, so you have a steady cooling stream."

I nod and rest my chin on the tip of his boot, clinging to the chance to touch him once more. "You know what's best."

But when he lets out a sob and turns to hide his face, I *have* to get out. The need to comfort him is stronger than my sense of self-preservation.

"I don't want to leave you," he whimpers when I pull him into my arms.

"You must," I insist, burying my face in his damp hair. Nothing was ever as hard as letting him go, but there is no other way. I pick up his backpack and lead him toward the heavy door, because this will be easier for him once he can no longer see me.

His heavy inhales weigh on my heart. When I usher him to the other side of the vault door, it feels like leaving a kitten out in the rain.

"This can't be happening. Not right after I found you," Sylvan utters, grabbing my hand, but he must know what is about to happen, because he doesn't try to come back in.

Overcome by a wave of grief, I give his hand a quick kiss, and then shove the door back in place before either of us can change his mind. It's only then that my tears fall, but I wait, holding the door until the lock finally clangs.

And still, he speaks, his voice like an echo through the thick metal.

"Hawk? What if we—"

"No, Sylvan. You need to promise me you will leave."

Silence.

"You need to promise!"

An eternity later, he says, "I promise."

My legs give up, and I curl into a ball on the cold, dusty floor, trying to contain the anguish tearing me up on the inside. But I got what I wanted.

Now, I can waste away in peace.

CHAPTER 36

SYLVAN

So I fucking lied. I only made the promise to Hawk so he stays put. And I would lie a hundred times more if it meant saving Hawk's life. I would lie, beg, steal, and kill if need be. Maybe it means I'm no good, but I've not been brought up to be *good*. I'll leave that to the *heroes*.

The promise I made at our wedding was way more important, and I intend to keep it. I understand full well that he wanted me to leave for my safety, that he cares for my life as much as I do for his. That's why he put on that damn mask in the first place. I *would* honor his sacrifice if there was no other way, but I am not giving up on him when there might still be something I can do.

Our bond tells me he's still alive, and I will fight for him for as long as I can sense his heartbeat, no matter how faint.

It might be a shot in the dark, but there are artifacts capable of containing the power of Sunlight. Were he a shadow-wielding elf, he would stand a chance against the force radiating inside him, but because he is not, he needs something to do that for him.

There are collars that suppress shadowcraft, like the one I wore during my time in the human realm, but the treasure vault of the Nocturne Court contains one capable of blocking Sunlight. A long time ago, a grimsmith fashioned it for his daughter out of a rare metal mined on the Darkmoon. He embedded it with sunset gems, and it was used a few times to aid royal children born with the power to wield both shadow and Sunlight, until they learned to cope with the two forces tearing them up from the inside.

The Umlaris Band.

Could it save Hawk? There's only one way to find out.

I need to steal it from the Nocturne Court.

I'm the prey about to dash toward the hunting party, but I've grown up at the castle and know several ways to sneak inside. My mind fizzes with the many plans and options, but I can only make them happen if I reach my destination safely. And fast, because I have no idea how long Hawk's soul has until it is burned to char.

So even though I dread meeting Lepearl and her crew again, I make my way back to the cove where they are still hopefully moored. Her vessel is small enough to get close to the Nocturne Court without being spotted, and with two kelpies tugging on the boat, it should take merely hours, unlike the perilous journey I'd have to make on foot.

Whatever Captain Lepearl might want, I'll give it to her, as long as it brings me closer to my goal.

The moon is high when I walk into the cave.

All three pairs of eyes turn toward me from the shore where the smugglers have gathered the wood from the broken pier.

"You've got some nerve, *Your Highness*," she says through gritted teeth, and both her crew members glare at me with their watery eyes.

It's not a great start, but I have been raised among snakes and politicians, and here I don't feel as defenseless as I did against a bassal.

I raise my hands so they know I'm not armed. "I know. It's pathetic, but I am desperate. I am wanted, I am banished, and my beloved ruined your pier while attacking your crew. Still, I come here to throw myself at your mercy. Hawk never meant harm or destruction. He is... cursed with the form that all of you saw. There's only one way I can think of to help him, but I need to get to the Nocturne Court as swiftly as possible. I have nothing but my mother's promise, but I vow—"

"What is that?" Lepearl asks and steps closer. She grabs my hand and eyes the ring on my thumb. "I wouldn't say you have 'nothing'."

I swallow, torn between saying it's my wedding ring, a piece of sentimental value, so that she leaves it alone, and inflating its cost with my words so she's greedy for it. My choice depends on what outcome I wish for. If I lose Hawk, this ring will be the one memento I have of him and our love. But if I don't use it, Lepearl might not want to help me. I'd give my hand for a chance of saving Hawk, so what is a ring? Material possession won't matter if I can't save him.

I take it off. "It is my wedding ring. A human tradition, and a token of my husband's love. The piece itself was made by the legendary grimsmith, Tassarion, and features a diamond, a ruby, and a sapphire set in titanium. A diamond for the longevity of our bond, a ruby for the blood we shed for it, and," I smile shyly as I lie through my teeth, "a sapphire in the shade of my eyes. I... as you can imagine, I struggle to part with it."

She comes closer, reaching for the ring, but I squeeze it in my hand and take it out of her reach. A flash of annoyance passes through her gaze, but I stand my ground. "I need to go now. Deliver me to the Nocturne Court, discreetly, and it shall be yours."

She licks her lips as I try to keep a cool head and avoid blurting out something that might expose my lies, but she glances at her crew. Moments pass, and when the kelpies harrumph, unhappy with the prospect of needing to venture out on top of all the work they've already done fishing out the broken chunks of the pier, I open my mouth again.

"Surely, you can discipline your crew in order to finish the day with something this precious," I say, once again, showing her the ring, which isn't nearly as valuable as I presented it. Not to her, at least.

Bite growls but stops when Lepearl pats him on the chest, as if he were in the form of a kelpie. "Calm, my sweet."

I hide my surprise at the endearment. The kelpie is... her lover? I'm not one to judge, but I still wonder about the legitimacy of such a union.

Kick throws a piece of wood to the pile with an exasperated sigh. "How much do you want it?" he asks Lepearl, and the fearsome pirate captain smiles, turning into a playful coquette.

"It is so very pretty..."

Bite glares at me. "Maybe I'll just take it then."

I stare right back at him. "Try me. You must have heard what I did to the Nightcloaks at The Burning Corpse." A bluff, since I no longer have Hawk's shadow, but that's my life now.

Lepearl sighs and gets to her toes to kiss his jaw... just as she reaches for Kick's hand.

I feel very confused. And uncomfortable.

"Wouldn't that be a bit too easy? Sometimes, your captain wants to see you're willing to put in the effort," Lepearl says as her fingers entwine with Kick's.

The kelpies share a glance, and Bite growls before letting out a low snort.

"Fine."

"Fifteen minutes," Kick adds, walking off toward the boat of bone.

I bow to him as if he deserves such a courtesy. Nothing is beneath me to get what I want. As the kelpies walk off to prepare the ship, I watch their pale, muscular bodies, long black hair streaked with seaweed, and I have to admit they are quite fine men. But it's confusing to even think of them as *people* when I've been *riding* a royal kelpie so many times. I suddenly feel self-conscious about it.

I clear my throat as I stand next to Lepearl who is stuffing her pipe with adora.

"If you don't mind me asking... are they not dangerous? They're not from the Nocturne Court, so they must be wild kelpies. Even if they wear elven skin, are you not worried about their violent nature?"

She glances my way and rubs two of her rings together, creating a spark to light the herb. "Oh, there are ways to tame wild kelpies. I'm surprised they're not known at court, considering what I heard about royal... exploits."

My cheeks heat up at the suggestion, but in truth, the kelpies have only ever been a means of transport for me, and I never spent excessive time at the stables.

"I'm not sure I understand the meaning. Are you saying there is a way to break them?"

Lepearl scowls, watching her crew set up the ship. They rush around, almost as if they were in competition with each other. "Break them? Such an ugly way to put it. They are amazing creatures, the kelpies, extremely loyal once they bond. Like with many things, you'll get more with sugar than with salt."

His philosophy is definitely *not* what I've been taught all my life, but I can see its merit. "Please, let me clarify, are we talking sugar cubes, or—"

Lepearl stares at me like I'm stupid and inhales some adora smoke. "Fucking, Your Highness, I mean *fucking*."

My ears twitch, turning as hot as my cheeks. "Oh, and... um... *both* of them?"

She smirks. "Yes, both. How is that so shocking? I've heard of royals at the Nocturne Court who have both a spouse and a Dark Companion."

It's not something I am interested in pursuing, but I have to admit she has a point. "I suppose I was taught I need to dominate others to command respect."

Lepearl spares me a glance telling me all she thinks about an elf my size dominating anyone, but I'm not offended. Thanks to what I've been through with Hawk, I know my worth isn't tied to the force I can exert.

"I used to be part of a big crew, worked my way up by proving I can be as ruthless as anyone else on board. But then I met my match, and it wasn't even in a brawl. Instead, someone whose name doesn't even deserve mentioning, rallied others against me with lies and shit talk. I got left in the middle of the ocean in a boat no bigger than a bathtub. When Bite and Kick appeared, I tried to fight them at first, but every time I hit them with a paddle, they'd come back, curious about me. Instead of dragging me to the bottom of the ocean, they brought me food, and hauled my boat to an island. When I stopped trying to exert dominance and befriended them instead, I realized that so far I've been going about my life wrong. So no, I didn't need to 'break' them. If anything, it was them who showed me I don't always need to be cruel to get what I want. Just like in the ocean, you have to follow the waves. Sometimes, you have to surrender to reach your destination."

I ponder her words as the kelpies drag a little boat to shore. If it were just me, they'd probably make me wade through water to get to the ship, but since they want to treat their captain, I'm lucky to also step aboard with dry shoes.

As much as I see Lepearl's point, and I'm more open to making friends than I used to be, I can't justify the risk of letting guards take me to Lord Kyran and throwing myself at his mercy.

Once I obtain the Umlaris Band and save Hawk, I'll consider what to do next. Until then, my plans must remain carefully concealed.

I know an entrance into the palace, but I cannot just break into the vault. If I obscure myself with whatever shadowcraft I possess and reach Lord Kyran's chambers, I might use the Cerulean Puffball spores I have collected before reaching the tavern to put him and his Dark Companion to sleep. With the human as my hostage, I should convince Kyran to hand over the Umlaris Band without much fuss.

Will I be making an enemy for good? Most likely, but that is a matter to worry about later.

With the salty wind on my face, I feel hope in my heart.

CHAPTER 37

SYLVAN

I assumed I'd need to risk leaving the boat and swimming into the labyrinth of caves below the Nocturne Court, but once the moon disappeared from the sky, darkness allowed Lepearl to let me out by the rocks at the shore. Kelpies are deep sea creatures, and their senses proved vital in navigating the jagged coastline without colliding with rocks hiding under the surface.

The imposing castle is like a giant black octopus, with many sprawling wings for tentacles and sharp, tall towers jutting into the sky like spikes. It sits atop a cliff, so it can overlook Grief Ocean, but that is its weakness. A vessel as tiny as ours could fall prey to the many predators in the sea, but thanks to the kelpies, we can avoid those as well and arrive at the shores right below the castle.

Guards patrol all around the Nocturne Court, but I could see the swamplight in their hands from very far away. If I were to light my own torch, I'd no doubt end up spotted by one of the watchmen stationed on the ramparts, but I have spent my childhood at this castle, and while years have passed since I frolicked on this beach, I still know it like the back of my hand and carefully make my way into the caves, guided by touch.

The familiar song of the shark skins drying in the salty wind above is like a welcome home, but I still watch out for the bats that inhabit this cave. They usually avoid elves, but in the dark a swarm can get confident enough to attack. I only hear the occasional screech, so most must be sleeping, which is a welcome strike of luck. While I might be partial to crispy bat wings, I don't want to hunt them myself.

My path through the caves takes me deep under the castle, and up stone stairs so winding I have to touch the damp walls now and then to stop my head from spinning.

The night is my ally, as by now, most inhabitants should be long asleep, yet I keep being distracted by thoughts about Hawk. I wonder if he's keeping his body cool, if he's in pain, and whether the water will be enough to preserve him the way he is. How long does his mind have? Hours? Days? Years? It's the uncertainty that is the worst.

I open the door hidden behind a painting and step into the corridor, cloaking myself in shadow. It might not hide me from talented shadow-wielders like Lord Kyran or Prince Tristan, but if I stay focused, my disguise should fool the average elf. I'm glad a servant passing me in the Hall of Lords doesn't as much as look my way, far too occupied with dusting one of the many portrait frames.

I pass the many depictions of Lords and Lordesses with their Dark Companions, and it strikes me that I don't care about having a portrait with Hawk painted so it hangs in this castle, marking my contributions to the Court. I don't need a crown, the power to pass judgment, or approval in the eyes of royals. I don't care to show him off, even if I'm proud of the man he is. All that matters to me is that he is safe. If we end up hunted for stealing the Umlaris Band, for him being the Sunwolf, or even for my illegal return from banishment, then so be it. We will deal with it, and we will deal with it together.

I sneak through endless corridors adorned with the finest artwork, expensive furniture from all over the realm, and precious textiles. Here at least, a rare lamp remains lit, creating deliciously dense shadow for me to sink into. I never learned how to enter the shadowild, but the presence of shade allows me to remain near invisible as I climb upstairs, to the Lord's private chambers.

There are wards against shadowcraft in the entryway, past the backs of the two women standing guard tonight, but while my family was aware of an alternative route inside for over two hundred years now, it was considered too risky to utilize. After all, to effectively usurp the throne, one needed to appear powerful, not a petty royal who sneaks into his enemy's bedchamber at night like a coward.

But I'm not here to murder the Lord of the Nocturne Court, or his Companion, and I no longer care that my actions might throw mud on what remains of my family's good name. Only Hawk counts now, and I am ready to be bold in my actions, if this ensures I save him.

The way past the magical wards starts at a beautifully fashioned ventilation grate. The passage was created after one of the Dark Companions in the past wished for artificial fog in their bathroom. Their flight of fancy that is now my way in. I crawl down a shaft occupied by dust and pretty spiders. A whole family of them crawls over me as I twist my body in order to move past a bend, but I am in no mood to play with the babies. I fear getting stuck here and rotting within the walls of the castle while my beloved howls for me, but the desire to free him from the curse overcomes fear, and soon I open the other end of the narrow passage with utmost care.

Sweat beads above my lip as I reach out of the tunnel and grab the wall on either side, pulling myself out. One look around tells me I'm in Lord Kyran's bathing salon. The tiles on the wall make up the Nightweed Family Crest above a tub big enough to contain the Sunwolf. Its size does not surprise me in the slightest, since I've heard long baths are Luke's beloved's pastime. Oh, how I wish I could also give my Dark Companion all he could ever wish for.

I hold up the small vial of Cerulean Puffball spores, ready to open it and put my victims to sleep. No one is speaking on the other side of the bathroom door, and no moans of pleasure reach my ears either, so with my heart in my throat, I push the door open, hoping it doesn't creak.

The vast bedroom is illuminated by stars, but I see well in the dark, and the two shapes resting in the huge four-poster bed remain still, curled together under the thick comforter.

All I need to do is get close enough to sprinkle the spores in their faces. This will offer me enough time to tie them up.

The floor gives the faintest creak under my weight, and I still with my heart in my throat, but nothing happens. The waft of musky perfume reaches my nose as I continue my careful journey through the bedchamber. I can see the couple more clearly now, and my chest tightens at the way Kyran cradles his Dark Companion, as if he wants to stand between him and all the danger in the world. Hawk holds me this way too, even during the long trek through the marshland, when we barely spoke, rattled by what I've done with his shadow at The Burning Corpse, he was there to support me. I shall free him from the Sunwolf's clutches, even if it's the last thing I ever do!

My lungs are tight as I lean close, listening to two breaths, two heartbeats, and I'm about to make my move when something shuffles in the corner of the room. And then—

Loud shrieks cut through the silence, followed by metallic clacks that sound as if a rat were trying to free itself from a cage, and I drop the precious spores, because the larger of the two men on the bed is already rising.

I cannot see his eyes, but his gaze feels heavy nevertheless. Before I can think or act, or... do anything, a shadow tentacle rushes up my body, locking around my neck. My stomach protests when it tugs, but by the time my knees hit the floor, a lamp comes on, illuminating Lord Kyran, who stands over me like the personification of the Darkmoon, about to pass judgment.

Fuck.

CHAPTER 38

Sylvan

I try to speak, excuse my presence in the royal bedchamber, but as soon as I open my mouth a tentacle made of shadow smacks my face. It then stuffs itself into my mouth, gagging me.

"How dare you?" comes out of Lord Kyran's mouth in a low growl.

No matter how much I resent him, I have to admit that he is an impressive elf. Tall, wide in the shoulders, muscular, and since he's wearing nothing but a pair of dark green silken pants, two shadow eels are visible on his pale chest, like moving tattoos. His long dark gray hair is like the waves of Grief Ocean during a storm, and I half-expect his mane to rise in the charged air.

"I've shown you mercy! Banishment instead of execution, and you invade my home with poison?" He points to the vial on the floor. "You are no better than a rat."

Behind him, Luke leaves the bed. "What's going on?" he asks, frightened. He might be much shorter than Kyran, but is still bigger than me, which fills me with frustration as I writhe in binds stronger than steel. Pale, with messy brown hair dyed green at the bottom, he is so plain he had to put a ring in his nose to feel special. And yet, unlike me, he is celebrated at court.

Luke slides his feet into a pair of slippers and rushes over to the cage where the critter that gave me away resides. It didn't occur to me that someone would keep their *pet bat* in their bedroom. I loathe this creature that stood between myself and victory.

Kyran scowls and gestures toward me, as if I'm a stain on his carpet. "My wretched cousin, Sylvan, attempted to attack us in our sleep. I don't know how he moved past the guards and sigils, but I will not just leave this!" He turns to me, and dark shadows dance in his gray eyes. "You know I have the right to kill you? The only reason you're not dead yet is my husband's sensibility."

"It's okay, Flap," Luke says, pulling the bat out of its cage and hugging it like a child as it whimpers, pushing its ugly face against the human's chest. In the long black nightshirt decorated with lace at the bottom, he is strangely reminiscent of a young parent tending to their child at night. The purple bat has a matching outfit.

His gaze lands on me, and even though there is no love between us, I do try to plead with my eyes. If only I can speak up before I lose my head, I'll be able to at least try to convince them that they need to help me for their own benefit. Because I doubt they would do so out of the goodness of their hearts.

Luke glances at his husband as he strokes the bat's fur, which peeks out from under the black costume it's wearing. "Kyran, he looks... haggard."

"Of course he does, my love. What else could we expect from a rat who illegally escaped banishment, murdered one of my grimsmiths, and now made an attempt on our lives?" Kyran says, pacing in front of me, as if he wants to flaunt how perfect of an example of a noble elf he is. "Perhaps you should return to bed? I will deal with him."

Luke attempts to tidy up his brown-green hair. To no avail, as he has to hold the bat with one arm. "No, I need to know what's going on. I know firsthand that Best Burgers Bonanza is a shitty place to work at, but is that worth dying over?"

Kyran shakes his head, and if glares could kill, I'd be dead. "Oh yes. He is *that* petty. He thinks that just because he found himself a powerful Dark Companion, he can come here to challenge me? Nobody can challenge me. I am the Lord of the Nocturne Court, Ruler of the Shadowild and Protector of the Nightmare Realm. I saved our shores only months back, while you *ran*, Sylvan."

I mumble in denial, but it's no use with the damn gag.

I despise Luke for the pity he exudes when he looks at me, but he is my only hope. Kyran's so bull-headed, he'd sooner rip my head off than let me speak. So I stare at the human without blinking, and beg with my eyes. I don't have any shame left.

Luke frowns and strokes Kyran's arm. "Where is his Dark Companion then?"

Kyran stalls, capturing his husband's gaze. His large, graceful hand finds the head of the bat and scratches it between the comically long ears. Doubts pass over the handsome features, but then the shadow tentacle retreats from my mouth.

"This might be your only chance to speak ever again, so answer my Companion."

"I have found the Sunwolf Crown!" I blurt out immediately, because appealing to Kyran's selfish interests has a chance to hook him so that I can plead my case.

Luke has no idea what this is about, but Kyran leans back, as if the beast were already coming for him. "Do you... have it?" he asks in a steady voice, then answers instead of letting me speak. "No, your Companion must have it. That was how you decided to ensure your safety in case something like *this* happened."

The human pets the bat's black wing when it whimpers again. "What is that? What crown?"

Kyran strokes his head, and I can't help but miss Hawk's touch when I see their easy affection. "I will explain it to you soon, my starshine. But I must know what is going on first."

I take a deep breath. "My plans have long been thwarted, and none of them included your death. All I wanted was to return from banishment, and I thought I found a way to do so in a man with the most potent shadow I've ever seen. We stumbled on the Sunwolf Crown, and I wished to bring it to you as means of buying back my place at court. But in our travels through precarious swamps, my Companion put on the mask, as it was the only means to save us from death."

Kyran blanches, and a sob tears from my throat as I think about my beloved suffering in that cold dungeon, all alone while the Sunwolf slowly takes over.

"Is he at large?" Kyran asks, keeping his voice even despite understanding the implications of such bad luck. Even the Lord of the Nocturne Court cannot be safe from the Sunwolf.

"No. I locked him away for his own safety, but you don't understand." I point to the vial with my chin. "That is no poison. I simply meant to put you to sleep to have more leverage when you awoke. My Dark Companion is the reason I am here. I now admit freely that I intended to steal from you. The Umlaris Band is my only hope of containing the Sunwolf within him. He isn't feral, his soul yet survives, but I don't know how much time we have left. And if you don't care to help me, I beg you, save *him*. Put me in the dungeon, lock me away in the human realm forever, or slay me, but show him mercy." I hang my head as tears streak down my cheeks when I think of the impossible position in which my beloved is in. "He will be a loyal servant of the Nocturne Court if only he gets a chance to keep his mind."

My heart overflows with sadness. Grief Ocean is just beyond the window, I can hear its waves crashing against the cliffs, and I feel like I'm drowning in its depths.

My vision's blurred with tears, but I can see Luke's feet turning toward Kyran's, his toes even gently stepping on his husband's.

"Oh, that's... soul-crushing," Luke says. I've seen that fragility within him since he first appeared at court, but while it used to disgust me, right now, his support is my only chance.

"He and his family attempted to murder me," Kyran grumbles.

"And now most of them are dead. If you save his Dark Companion, he will be forever in your debt."

I nod, too beaten to look up. "I never cared for the scheming of my siblings, and never sought power. I know my place," I say to appease him, but then immediately sob again, because my place is at Hawk's side. If I don't save him, if he perishes within the Sunwolf, there will be no place for me to call home ever again.

Kyran exhales, but when Luke all but climbs him to whisper, I know the Lord's resolve is crumbling. Even great men have weaknesses after all.

"For him to return to Court and flaunt his Dark Companion's shadow? Luke, he ripped Tristan's wings off!" Kyran exclaims, but I grasp those words despite having to reveal another of my tragedies.

"He has *no* shadow! The Sunwolf Crown burned it out of him." I look up, in hope that this news can sway Kyran's mind.

He cocks his head as though I'm a curious creature from the deep sea. "You have a Dark Companion without a shadow, and still, you want him back?"

I nod, too choked up to speak. Luke gives him a meaningful glance that must have something to do with what he whispered moments ago.

Kyran sighs and approaches a bell that calls in the guards. I know, because I used to have one just like it in my own chambers. Moments later, the doors open, and the two women I noticed outside enter, both slowing down at the sight of me.

"No, I don't know how he got past you either," Kyran says as the guards pull me back to my feet, the shadow tentacle retreating under Kyran's feet altogether. But then his gaze meets mine, and he shakes his head. "We will venture out at moonrise, when Prince Tristan returns with the hunting party. For now, take him to the tower."

The two guards share an uncertain glance and one of them speaks. "Your Highness... With all respect due, I have heard of the new power Prince Sylvan possesses. Should we bring the right kind of chains first?"

Kyran shakes his head, staring me down. "That won't be necessary. His shadowcraft is once more... insignificant."

A cruel slap to my face, but I'll take it and ask for another if it means I have a shot at saving Hawk. "But we will use the Umlaris Band? Or at least attempt to?"

"*I'm* not stepping near the Sunwolf, but yes, I will give you that one chance."

Kyran's voice is filled with contempt, and I'm well aware that my actions will be scrutinized, but he's giving me more mercy than I deserve.

Even when I'm put in chains, my heart feels a bit lighter.

"Thank you, Lord Kyran," I bow right before he slams the door in my face.

CHAPTER 39

SYLVAN

I thought I knew what loneliness was. My whole life until Hawk, I had to remain guarded at all times and never got close to anyone. But it's only now, when he's been taken away from me, that I understand what loneliness is.

It doesn't matter that I'm in the tallest tower of the Nocturne Palace, not a prison cell deep in its dungeons, or that I have a comfortable chair and a selection of crispy snacks on a silver tray. I'd rather sleep on the bare floor in the werewolf castle and live on wet bread if it meant Hawk was safe.

His absence is so obvious I feel like alternating between curling up on the bed and screaming at the empty sky. Kyran did say we'd leave at moonrise, and it seems that time will never come.

If it wasn't for the promise I made to Hawk, I'd drink the whole bottle of wine left for me on the table. Instead, I've bitten several of my fingernails until they bled——a nasty habit that always comes back when I'm nervous. Every time I recall what lying under him felt like, what warmth and comfort his arms provided, I want to leap from the balcony just to be closer to him. He's the only person who *listened* to me, who accepted me even when I lashed out, and gave me the kind of love I wasn't ready for. The kind of love I couldn't comprehend until I experienced it myself.

If I by some chance survive this whole ordeal and he doesn't, I have no doubt I will never be loved again the way Hawk loves me.

Selflessly, all-encompassing, with the brightness of a thousand suns.

His kindness leaves no room for lies, doubts, or hidden meanings.

I've cried so much already it's embarrassing, so when I feel the stinging in my eyes, I grab the silver fork left with my food and stab the center of my palm.

I breathe through the pain and focus on what needs to be done instead of wallowing in more self-pity.

Everything will be fine.

I will put the Umlaris Band on Hawk.

I will save him.

We will have a future at court.

A rattling of keys at the door interrupts my inner chant so abruptly I drop the fork. The moon is still nowhere to be seen, not even a glow at the horizon, but stand, ready to leave if Tristan's back to tell me they wish to depart sooner.

Tall, slender and sharp as a hat pin, my mother enters the room instead. I didn't recognize her at first, since she's dressed head to toe in mourning white. Her dress is like cascades of moonlight, the decorative corset reminiscent of armor. Her long, pale hair has the same golden sheen as mine, her eyes are just as blue. She is my blood, so I hope that despite our differences, she came here to offer me some solace.

As the door closes behind her, she dips her fingers between her breasts and into her corset. She then pulls out a long, transparent... horn? No thicker than two fingers, it's reminiscent of an icicle made of frosted glass, and I have no idea what I'm looking at or why she brought it here.

"I don't have that much time, Sylvan, but if you want to prove you're worth something, this is your chance," she says, presenting the item to me.

I'm too stunned to process it all at once. I've changed so much since we parted, and now her voice sounds as if it's coming from behind a wall. She is speaking to a Sylvan from three months ago, and while what she's suggesting still stings, I frown and straighten up.

"Explain, Mother," I say, already disliking the way I've stepped into the shoes of the person I no longer am. Cold, calculated, focused on the deadly games of the Nocturne Court to make sure I never end up hurt.

She shakes her head as if there was no merit to my question. "I'm no longer allowed at high court, so I cannot get anywhere near Lord Kyran, but you can. I have heard all about your exploits, where they have led you, and what you will be partaking in at moonrise. You will be at his side. With this dagger—"

My eyes grow wide. "What is this? You've heard a tiny part of what I've been through, and you came here just to use me as your weapon against Kyran? That's the only thing on your mind after all our family has been through? Killing him?"

She's taken aback but squeezes the strange dagger. "Oh no, this will be much worse. Using this will injure his shadow. The disease will spread over time—"

"Do you hear yourself?" I ask, crossing my arms over my chest.

"He murdered your brother! I am sure of it. Anatole was smart, he would have sooner retreated than fallen to Heartbreak! If you'd gone with him, he might have been alive now." Despite the gentle white makeup around her eyes, her features are like an unsheathed blade, dangerous and sharp. "You *must* avenge your brother. If not for me, not for yourself, then for your sibling to come." She places her hand on her abdomen, and I suddenly need all the wine I can get.

I run my fingers through my hair, so stunned by the lengths she's willing to go to in order to manipulate me that I initially can't bring myself to respond. She could have treated the deaths of her children and the banishment of both me and her past husband as an opportunity to reassess her life, take stock of the mistakes she made in raising her children. But instead she brings me a dagger, a suicidal task, a promise of a new sibling, and not even a hint of an apology.

I am her pawn. A weak piece, but the only one she has left, so she'll play it anyway.

Talking to her is enough to throw me into the same old hell I've lived in before my banishment. She doesn't understand that I've moved on and changed, because she's been back here, plotting and scheming as she has for years, while I got the chance to experience a world without her boot pressing on my neck. In a way, the banishment has been the best thing to ever happen to me.

I spread my arms. "Who did you even get pregnant with? You know what? I don't care. Unless you know of something that can help me save Hawk, you might as well leave."

"Hawk? The human." Her eyes get that detached coldness I'm so intimately familiar with. As the least talented of her offspring, I've often borne the brunt of her disappointment and anger. Even now, I hold my breath, even though I'm no longer a child. She is still physically bigger than me, and I hate the echoes of fear it evokes in me.

"My Dark Companion. My husband."

"What kind of Companion is he? I've heard of the feats you were capable of just days ago, but I don't see even a hint of his shadow anymore. He is lost to you. You should kill him and—"

I grab the bottle of wine and throw it against the wall to relieve some of the rage boiling inside me. My mother must have not expected that from her meek, obedient son, because she makes half a yelp and steps back, but the flood of red still stains the bottom of her dress.

"I will not harm my Companion! I love him. And you can't possibly understand, because you're incapable of sacrifice. If stabbing that dagger into Lord Kyran's eye could save Hawk, I'd do it, but since it won't, I will be aligning myself with the man who can actually help me."

She steps aside to avoid the puddle of wine, her lips in a tight line. "I hoped you could still make something of yourself and elevate our family, but if you don't want to do this," she shows me the dagger, "then you are proving yourself to be as useless as all of the Nocturne Court believes you to be."

I let out a sad laugh, because what else is there to say in the face of such contempt? "I don't care."

"Have two months in the human realm ruined you so completely? You've lost all ambition." Mother cocks her head at me, and I see it for what it is. Yet another tactic to guilt me into doing what she wants.

"My only ambition is saving Hawk. Once I succeed, my deal with Lord Kyran will stand, and you will be *dead* to me." I stare her down with the cold glare I learned from her. "No. You already are."

She shakes her head but slides the dagger back into her corset. "I will bear another son. One who is worth something, and one day, you will regret what you've just done."

"I will not. And your future child? You will crush them with your dark dreams just like you did all of us!"

Mother squints, but she's turning away. "Of course a weakling would say that. You should be guided by the greater good, not just emotion—"

I see red. "Guess what? *Anger* is an emotion too, and you're full of it. You stew in helpless fury, and I hope you drown in it. I will let my love for Hawk guide me instead. I am my own man, and will live by my own rules, not yours!"

She stares me down. "You're biting your nails again. It's unbecoming."

"Leave!"

She doesn't even look back. The bottom of her dress leaves a long red smear as it drags over the floor. She slams the door to my cell so hard I fear the tower will topple, but nothing else happens, and I'm left in such blissful silence I collapse into an armchair to enjoy it.

I had no idea how much I needed this. Our umbilical cord is finally cut.

Guided by a surge of unreleased tension, I walk out into the balcony and scream at the top of my lungs. I scream until I have no more breath, and only then do I fall into bed.

Sleep doesn't come, because every time I close my eyes, all I can think about is Hawk, alone and convinced he'll live out his days in the dungeon. I pass the hours by imagining his cocky smiles, and the warmth of his arms around me.

There's a knock on the door I can't open myself anyway, but it gives me a second to sit up. I spot the first rays of moonlight through the window as Tristan steps in. His temple is adorned by a purple bruise, and he squints his golden eyes at me.

"Hey, little shit. We're going hunting. I need a new fur coat."

CHAPTER 40

SYLVAN

I've never shared my sibling's love for the kelpies, but being back in the saddle, mounting the tall, powerful creature with seaweed in its mane makes me feel a bit more like my old self. I even got to change out of the rags I was wearing and into a fresh riding outfit that includes sleek gloves made of octopus leather, which will keep me from sticking to the beast if I accidentally touch it. In defiance of my mother, I opted for a fully black set, without the customary blue of the Goldweeds. My victory or defeat will not be in my family colors nor crest. My blood has forsaken me, and the only loyalty I owe is to my Companion. My Love. My Hawk.

The guards follow my every move, as if they expect me to take off at any moment, but I came here of my own free will and shall be the picture of dignity. Though my dealings with Lepearl and her crew of rowdy kelpies make the fact that I'm sitting on one's back slightly awkward. How sentient is the creature under me exactly, if it's been reared on land? I prefer to leave that unanswered. All that matters is that Octo might be my one ally if the situation calls for a swift retreat with Hawk at the front of my saddle, so I made sure to feed him more sugar early that morning.

We left the castle at moonrise, bathed in the glow of green torches, and the journey has already taken over three hours. Nothing in comparison to what it would have been on foot, especially that we're now traveling through the royal forest, taking main roads without fear, but I still feel disempowered by the length of our journey. We've left behind the River of Souls, but the faint echo of the wailing wretches is still carried by the breeze. It reminds me of the misery my life has been before I met Hawk.

Each moment away from him feels like hours, and I attempt to focus on the bond connecting us, just so I can feel that bit closer to him already. It's faint, but I sense his heartbeat on my breastbone, as if we were resting chest to chest. It pains me to imagine him alone in the dark, limbs twitching as he fights the new nature invading his mind.

I can only hope we reach him before the change is irreversible.

Lord Kyran rides nearby, his expression pensive, and he's lost in thoughts so I dare not speak to him without reason. As long as the Umlaris Band remains attached to his saddle, I won't do anything that could make him change his mind about helping Hawk.

Resentment toward the Nightweeds has been instilled in me since the cradle. As the ruling family, they have access to a level of privilege my own blood does not, and for years I have accepted the lie that the Goldweeds deserved a chance to sit on the Nocturne Throne too. But as I sneak glances at Lord Kyran, taking in the smoky hair cascading down his back like a cape, the breastplate bearing the Nightweed crest, and his regal profile, I have to admit he is the right person to wear the crown. Even the fact that he gave me a chance to plead my case instead of striking me down the moment he saw me in his bedroom speaks a lot of his character. My brother wouldn't have shown such mercy.

Flanking me from the other side is Prince Tristan Bloodweed. His long red hair is braided for battle, and his black armor with red accents—polished to perfection. Today, he's not here as a member of the Nightcloaks, but the Lord's entourage, as is custom whenever he is back at court. He hasn't yet acknowledged the way I attacked him at the tavern, so I worry he might try and stand between me and Hawk when the time comes. For now, he jokes around as if he isn't at all bothered by the callous way I butchered his wings, yet I have seen my share of betrayal growing up at the Nocturne Court and refuse to put my trust in words. I did wipe the floor with him at the Burning Corpse for all to see, so he might take his revenge if a chance for it presents itself. And if not, hopefully he can take joy in the fact that with Hawk's shadow gone, I will never be able to best him again.

Dozens of guards and hunters surround us from all sides. They are like black wolves with their dark garments accented by glints of silver. These men and women are armed with several weapons each. Some are tall and in heavy armor, others only a little bigger than me and dressed in leather from head to toe. A medic travels in a small carriage at the very back, with their own escort.

In my mind, none of this is necessary. Once we arrive at the ruined castle, I will go to the dungeon, where I left Hawk. He will be still conscious thanks to the pool of cool water staving off the heat, and I will lock the Umlaris Band around his neck, making him go back to normal. I don't love that doing so will tie us to the Nocturne Court permanently, but it's not a magical bond, only a promise, and, as we have already established, my sense of honor has one allegiance—Hawk. If necessary, I'll use the collar and attempt an escape.

"What I'm wondering," Tristan starts what is surely another one of his quips, "is how you got a man with a shadow like that to bond with you in the first place?"

Here we go.

Kyran doesn't add to the question, but he glances our way, eager for gossip as any other man.

"You might be shocked to find out that not all men crave your muscles," I say in a level tone, to not show how much the question really bothers me. I've made enough of a spectacle of myself on Kyran's bedroom floor.

Tristan whistles. "Look at you trading like a—"

"That's enough," Kyran cuts into what was surely another insult coming my way.

Tristan rolls his eyes but doesn't shut up despite dropping the earlier topic. "Did you bed him in his Sunwolf form? Would that even be considered 'bedding'? I hear the Sunwolf is as big as a house and therefore wouldn't fit in a bed."

My cheeks go up in flames at the idea that my cousin is imagining my Companion mounting me like I'm a bitch in heat, and I can't hide my shock. "How dare you! What kind of question is that?"

Tristan shrugs. "What? I've heard of elves seeking all sorts of pleasures."

Kyran growls. "Tristan, *do not* bring up the kelpie incident. It does not matter that they're sentient. That man is long gone from court."

As they bicker, with Tristan pulling Kyran's leg and the Lord remaining dead serious, my thoughts return to my lover, on his own in a tomb of cold stone.

It is when I spot the faintest hint of the spire at the top of the tallest tower of the werewolf castle that the steady rhythm I've been sensing from afar quickens so rapidly, my own heart skips a beat to match it.

"What is it?" Kyran asks.

"The castle. We're almost there," I point out the ruined building. "But his heartbeat has sped up. Could it be due to my proximity?"

While usually I would keep all secrets to myself to hold more cards, I need to share everything for Hawk's sake. If there is anything Kyran knows about the bond that I don't, he might use that information for all our benefit.

Tristan chuckles. "Prince Sylvan Goldweed, makes men's hearts race even from afar."

I want to respond with a biting retort, but when the echo of my husband's heartbeat makes my chest ache and my head spin, I press on my breastplate, fighting for air. Petty rivalries don't matter in the face of my husband's suffering. I flinch when Kyran gets close enough to touch my back.

"Sylvan?" he asks, brows knotting above his regal nose. Ah, how I hate that he really is the right man for the job.

"May we add haste?" I ask, and Kyran gestures at the guards without a word.

The kelpies are taller than regular horses, but I still need to stand in the saddle to see the ruins better as we stampede down the track.

"I haven't been here in ages," Tristan says as we emerge from the forest and approach the crooked gate. Despite his carefree attitude, he makes sure his sword is ready. I shoot him a sharp glance as the soldiers spread out in a fan-like pattern in front of the steps leading inside the building. We dismount, and the moment my feet hit the ground, the unrest in my heart becomes yet more urgent. I cannot sense Hawk's closeness despite being right by the castle. Can it be that the thick walls are somehow muting our connection?

"We will not fight him!"

"That depends on you though, doesn't it?" Kyran asks and unpins the Umlaris Band from his saddle before tossing it to me. "Put it on him. We shall wait."

I try to catch it, but I'm not the most agile of elves, and in a moment that will haunt me for the rest of my life, the collar slips from my grasp. Someone sniggers, and then, just as the Umlaris Band is about to drop into the mud, Tristan catches it with a long vine of his shadow. He lifts it and dangles it in front of me until I grab it in frustration.

He raises his brows. "Maybe don't drop the priceless ancient artifact?"

"Maybe it shouldn't have been thrown," I grumble.

"*Maybe* you two can stop bickering," Kyran adds, imposing in his spiked pauldrons as he looks around, tense despite the veneer of calm he's trying to project.

Tristan smirks and extends his hand to me. "I can go collar him if you're worried about dropping it again."

Kyran's gaze zeroes in on the hulking Bloodweed menace. "You're not going anywhere. The Sunwolf is a deadly threat to any shadow-wielder. We're *not* risking your darkness."

His words stab me so deeply I can feel them bleeding my heart. Of course, my shadow doesn't matter. Measly as it is, from the perspective of a powerful user of shadowcraft, my power might as well not exist at all. Humiliation is like a rope around my neck.

"You're risking his. You think I'm less brave than Sylvan fucking Goldweed?" Tristan growls, visibly offended, even though Lord Kyran is just looking out for him.

"Your wings are still regrowing. And it's not your mate who is afflicted."

Tristan shakes his head. "What's it matter? If the Sunwolf is feral, he needs to be put down, and *he* will not do that." He points to me, and this is the one comment I can't let go.

I may not even reach his shoulder, but I *will* stand my ground for Hawk either way. I approach and shove his chest, putting my whole shadow into the push. It might not be much, but Tristan wasn't expecting the attack and is forced to take a step back.

"You will not touch a hair on his body! The only way you're getting to him is through me."

Tristan sighs theatrically, and before I can stop him, pats my cheek with his massive hand. "Go on, cousin. Get your man."

Blood boils in my veins and only Kyran's level stare stops me from unleashing my claws on Tristan's mocking smile. It doesn't matter.

As the guards part to make room for me to reach the stairs, Kyran speaks.

"Remember that you shouldn't even be back in the Nightmare Realm. Officially, you are a fugitive with a price on your head. But collar him or kill him to get me the Sunwolf Crown, and you will have a place at my court."

I don't acknowledge his words, but they ring in my head like I'm inside a giant bell. I don't want a position at the Nocturne Court if it comes at Hawk's expense.

What matters is that I came to these ruins for Hawk and now that I'm here, nothing can stop our reunion. I sense many eyes on me as I walk up the moss-covered steps, but I hold my head high, because I shall come back out holding my Companion's hand. The future remains murky, subject to Lord Kyran's whims, but nothing will be impossible once I'm reunited with my love.

I'm worried about slipping and embarrassing myself in front of all the soldiers, but the burden inside doesn't ease once I'm out of their sight, because Hawk still feels distant, even though his heartbeat has slowed to a more manageable pace.

Bats fly above my head in erratic patterns, but I pay them no mind and descend the stairs with a swamplight torch in one hand and the collar in the other. The Umlaris Band is known for its beauty, but while I sense the engravings on its surface with my fingertips, I only care about what it can do for my Companion. My mouth dries when I approach the circular door on the lowest level of the castle, because this is my final trial. I can put the collar on Hawk and preserve his sanity, or die, ripped to shreds by sharp teeth, my shadow devoured like a juicy delicacy.

There is no other path.

The lightheadedness I was feeling since my foot stepped inside this cold, drafty building makes my vision blur, so when I face the entrance to the dungeon, I initially don't want to believe what I'm seeing, but dread coils inside me as the swamplight reveals the machinery I used to lock my love inside.

It is now painfully clear why I could not feel him in close proximity.

The thick vault door has been ripped off its hinges and hangs half-open.

I know what it means, but I deny it and step inside, hugging the collar to my chest.

"Hawk?" I call out into the empty dungeon, but I'm answered only by the echo of my own voice and the sound of dripping water.

Hope is still a bright presence in my heart when I approach the pool at the very back, but it dims, the closer I get.

Empty.

Hawk's gone, and the long grooves on the door tell me he didn't leave this place a human.

CHAPTER 41

SYLVAN

I didn't spend much time in the dungeon, but every wall reminds me of the moments my beloved and I have stolen here. I should run upstairs and warn the shadow-wielders that the beast is on the loose, but my feet first take me to the pool. I dip in both my hands, hoping that some of Hawk's essence still lingers.

But he is gone, and unless I reach him first, Kyran will have his soldiers hunt down my husband as if he's a rabid animal.

My chest overflows with fear and grief. Soon, so do my eyes, but I cannot waste precious time feeling sorry for myself. Hawk is somewhere out there, frantic and hurting, and each passing moment lessens the chances that the man I fell in love with is still asleep somewhere within the Sunwolf.

I force my legs to move despite wishing to cry as I curl into a ball. The winding stairs make me dizzy but I speed up the closer I am to the top. My heart gallops in my chest as I think over everything I can still do to save Hawk. I don't even know if the collar will work, or how to approach the Sunwolf with it. I've had the most basic training a prince needs in hunting or riding a kelpie, but this is way beyond my skill level.

By the time I emerge from the building, I'm panting.

All eyes turn to me expectantly, because they see I'm still holding the collar.

"I... He... He's gone," I choke out between one breath and another, and a hum goes through the ranks. The elves have started preparing food, but my emergence makes them all still. At the bottom of the stairs, Kyran shakes his head before jogging up to join me.

His features are clouded as he and Tristan stand before me, but neither of them is out of breath, as if the universe wants to show me proof of how inferior I am to them both.

"Are you certain?" Kyran asks, and Tristan unsheathes his sword, lovingly stroking the flat of its blade.

"Gone feral, like we expected."

I'm nauseated when I think of the dark metal edge anywhere near Hawk's body. I push it aside, fighting tears.

"He can still be collared!" I raise my voice, because I can't pretend to be calm any longer when Hawk's life is at stake.

Tristan frowns, and the moon behind him adds more dimension to the strands of blood red hair that have come loose from his braid. "He's no longer a person! He's a threat to every shadow-wielder in the realm, and you're hardly a warrior!"

"That's enough," Kyran says curtly, but Tristan won't be silenced.

"Before you spell that out, yes, I am angry at him for attacking me. But that is not why I want the beast gone. Sylvan's not trained for fighting. If he goes after the beast, he'll die for nothing. We've had our differences, but he's still my cousin, and I don't want that to happen. Reluctantly, I'll even say he's the most tolerable Goldweed I ever met," he adds with a frown.

I take that in but find it hard to focus on anything but Hawk's plight. "Am I not at risk of execution anyway? If there is any chance that Hawk is still inside the Sunwolf, I must try to bring him back. The collar offers me that chance," I finish meekly, because it's all in Kyran's hands. If he chooses to imprison me right now, I won't be strong enough to fight him.

His thick, elegant brows lower as he takes in his men, who listen to our exchange, no doubt ready to set out the moment he says the word. It might be Hawk who is to be hunted down, but I sense an invisible noose around my own neck too, because without him my own life will no longer be worth living.

I'm shocked when that thought crosses my mind, but right after comes the realization that it's not a dramatic exaggeration. I would survive without Hawk. In fact, my life might even return to its pre-banishment state, but how could I forget everything I've lost after finally tasting the bond I never expected to forge? It would be a life without purpose, without meaning, drained of the one true joy I've ever known.

I need to reclaim Hawk and I'm ready to die trying.

"You do realize a loose Sunwolf threatens the whole Realm? We need strong shadowcraft to defend ourselves," Tristan says.

Kyran exhales and meets my eyes. "I'll give you an hour's advantage. Then, I'll send the hunters after him." He gestures at the biggest of the hunters, whose armor is likely heavier than my whole body. "Dame Lorena, you will accompany Prince Sylvan to make sure he doesn't flee when faced with the beast."

I should consider that an affront, but I just grab Kyran's hand, then bow to kiss a ring on his finger. "Thank you for the opportunity. I will not fail, My Lord."

There's a brief moment of silence before Kyran speaks. "Good luck. May the sun never burn you."

I have no reason to feel touched. It's just one of those things people say, but there's something about the raspiness in Kyran's voice that makes him sound genuine. I squeeze his hand and touch it with my forehead before straightening my back. I planned to respond with resolve, but my throat feels tight and raw, so I nod at him, then at Tristan, and finally meet the gaze of my guardian.

The giant woman in front of me squeezes her gauntleted hand into a fist and places it in the middle of her chest, knocking on the breastplate made up of dozens of scales. "Lorena Sheerwhisper of Ocalot Deep," she says, introducing herself to me before focusing on Kyran. "I shall do as you command, my lord."

I wait as she receives the same customary blessing I have, and moments later we head for our mounts, watched by dozens of eyes. The knight pulls back her dark hair and mounts the large horse capable of carrying both its mistress and her armor while I use a discreet ladder to reach the back of my kelpie, Octo.

I'm dizzy, as if I've had my skull bashed with a club, but I can't push back the inevitable by excusing myself with a headache. Considering the danger the Sunwolf poses to shadow-wielders, Kyran's decision to offer me a whole hour to find Hawk is an unexpected kindness. He is offering me more mercy than I deserve, given that my family attempted to assassinate him not long ago, and I shall not squander this chance.

I lead the way out of the improvised camp, through the overgrown gardens, and past the open gates of the abandoned castle, but once I'm no longer distracted by the curious soldiers and their noise, I stare into the dense trees ahead.

"Can you still sense him?" Dame Lorena asks, stopping her mount next to mine.

I blink, surprised she wants to speak to a traitor like me at all. I know her face, as I've seen her at court, and in the nearby villages, but this might be the first time we are interacting. After all, the fighters, even the low born, knew the lackluster extent of my shadowcraft. I have once overheard a group of guards discussing it over wine, and their claim that I'm not worthy of my birth stings to this day. But Dame Lorena's eyes don't hold any resentment, as if she's content with her lot in life and doesn't wish for anything beyond it.

I wonder if there's perhaps an unusually large amount of human blood in her line. She's not Hawk's size, but almost as tall as him, and broader in the shoulders than most of the male elves I've seen. It's no wonder Kyran sent her out with me. If she can wield the massive sword attached to her back with the same ease she guides her horse, then hers might be the blade to end Hawk's life. If I fail him. Which I will not.

"Yes, I can sense him, but he deserves a chance. Don't harm him," I say, sliding my gaze over the thick grip of her weapon.

She regards me with the emotionality of a statue. "I shall do what needs to be done for the greater good. If he doesn't recognize you—"

"You wait," I tell her firmly and raise the Umlaris Band in my hand. "The real him might still be in the Sunwolf."

"I cannot let him harm a member of the royal family."

"Have you never loved?" I ask as worry and frustration grow in my chest like a tide, but my words make her avert her gaze, as if I've struck the right chord. I don't need her to answer. Whoever she had feelings for is no longer with her, whether they're alive, or dead.

"What happened to them?" I ask.

She exhales, looking north, toward the ocean. A shadow passes over her features before she speaks. "Heartbreak. He died when the monster attacked. He did his duty and protected the people. And so will I."

My lips go dry, because the tragedy is still very fresh. Memories of the dreadful day three months ago pass through my mind in a whirlwind of terror. I ran and lived. Her lover stayed and is with us no longer.

Guilt creeps up my chest, because she must know of my shame, but time is ticking. "Then understand that I am ready to give my life for my Companion. I don't care what happens to me, but give him a chance. Do not protect me."

A band of iron locks around my chest as she chews through my words. In the end, her gaze meets mine, and she nods. "I won't."

"Thank you," I tell her in a soft voice. Emotion makes my head spin again, but I have wasted enough time already. The wind carries the ghost of a familiar scent, and I close my eyes, sinking into moonless darkness as I seek my Companion's heartbeat. The smell curling around me does not belong in this realm. It's dry, warm, burned in my heart with the heat of the sun rather than fire.

The Sunwolf.

My beloved.

I lean forward in the saddle, and as the breeze dances around us, I realize Hawk is straight ahead. His heart beats calmly, as if he were resting, and maybe it's just a miscalculation on my part, but he doesn't *feel* far away.

I open my eyes and nudge my kelpie, releasing a sharp cry. Octo leaps forward, turning the dry ground muddy wherever his hooves strike it, but as I lead him past a thatch of black raventalon bushes, we emerge on a path of trampled greens and broken branches. The fresh odor of plant blood tells me the destruction was recent.

Joy spreads in my veins when I realize Hawk has been through here, and I follow, riding my kelpie faster than I've ever dared. The newly formed passage through the woods lets me spread my wings, and dash forward like a shark cutting through the waters of Grief Ocean. I vaguely hear the *thump* of horse hooves behind me, but I'm not going to wait for my escort and chase the sensation of delightful familiarity induced by the scent of sun-kissed rock.

He is so close, my Hawk, I just know it. My man. My husband.

A choked laugh tears from my throat when I circle a cliff, and once Octo heads in this new direction, a warm glow shimmers beyond the trees ahead.

Sunlight.

I feared its power when my younger sister Vinia used it to diminish my shadow-craft further. I still fear it now. But its presence means the Sunwolf is here, and I tighten my hold on the Umlaris Band, ready to do whatever it takes to get my love back.

For he is my everything. My starshine. The only moon in the sky above me.

I duck close to Octo's thick neck as he jumps, cutting through the trees, but then we're in a clearing, and I lift my head to stare at the stream cascading down a series of steep drops. The waterfall flows into a pond, which then drains into a narrow river that carries on all the way to the ocean, but I have but one focus.

The Sunwolf rests on a pile of rocks under the falls. His golden fur emits a glow I find familiar after three months in the world of humans, and as his light shines through the rushing droplets, fantastical patterns are cast everywhere around him.

"Hawk? Can you hear me?" I ask, hoping he answers me through our bond like before. When nothing happens, I reach along the thread that connects my soul to my Companion's and call out to him.

No answer, but the Sunwolf lifts its monstrous head and pushes it through the waterfall. I ignore the hoofbeats of Dame Lorena's horse catching up to me, and instead lead Octo down the slope and to the river.

He recognizes me, I'm sure of it. My kelpie isn't happy to come this close to an unknown beast, but I pat his neck to calm him.

"It's me, Hawk. I know I promised to forsake you, but I would not," I say, staring into the onyx voids the Sunwolf has for eyes.

But the calm I felt at the sight of him drains out of me almost immediately, because there's nothing there.

No understanding. No connection. No soul.

My heartbeat speeds up as the Sunwolf bares its crystal teeth.

I open my mouth, unsure what to do next when an arrow swishes close to my ear and hits the beast's leg.

"No!" I scream out before even the Sunwolf howls with fury.

"He is lost," Dame Lorena cries, riding along the clearing. She's keeping her distance from both me and the beast, but it's clear she's going for the kill.

Terror seeps into my bones, and I snap the reins, making Octo fight through his reluctance and dash straight at my man. "Stop! I command you!"

The knight ignores me. Another arrow flies the Sunwolf's way and misses, but as Dame Lorena gets closer to the bristling creature, she grabs her sword and pulls it out of the long sheath on her back. Octo's hooves hit the water, but I can't use the collar for as long as my supposed protector interferes.

If she won't stop when commanded, I will *make* her. I pull up all the shadow I have at my disposal and create a dark wall right in front of Dame Lorena's horse. I scream from the effort I feel in every muscle and tendon. It would still not be enough to physically stop a galloping horse, but the illusion it creates is enough for the animal to rear as soon as its muzzle pushes into the barrier. The knight tries to hold on to the reins, but with the sword in her hand, she's off-balance and topples to the ground with a yelp.

I look back to see that she's down when her spooked horse bolts between the trees, then turn toward the Sunwolf, but his dead eyes don't look my way. They're focused on the barrier I've created. It's no longer needed, so I huff in exhaustion and let it slide into the water. This is my chance. The Sunwolf wants to hunt down my shadow, and while I'm terrified to lose what little power I possess, I'll be the bait, if it means getting Hawk back.

I smack Octo's backside so he gets close to my beast, and I climb to stand in the saddle in a feat I didn't think myself capable of. But if I am to put the collar on his neck, I need to move fast. I reach to my side and unclasp the straps holding my breastplate in place, then shrug it off, ready to leap.

Black eyes widen as the wolf opens its jaws. His glow brightens, making me narrow my eyes to protect them, and I tighten my hold on the collar, focused on the creature keeping my man hostage. I'm about to jump off the kelpie's back when the Sunwolf lets out a growl. Octo steps aside, then bucks, and I shoot out of the saddle before I get to make a controlled leap. The brilliant, rainbow glow of sunlight shining through water spins around me as I fly through the air, unable to confirm where the ground is anymore.

Colliding with the stones is a painful affair, and I grunt when something in my recently injured shoulder moves, blinding me with pain.

Yet I get to my feet. I try to work out where I am when the Sunwolf comes at me. His massive jaws filled with sharp teeth open... and close on my leg.

I scream out when pain rips through me like lightning, but I barely have time to process the torment when he pulls me up in the air as if I'm merely a plaything. And even though my bones are getting crushed like twigs and hot blood splashes my face when he swings me from side to side, all I can think of is that I'm close to where I need to be.

"Hawk! Please! It's me!" I yell, half-gone with the agony in my leg.

I will die here. That thought hits me when I sense my shadow dissolving on his tongue. The only reason I'm still alive is because he wants my shadow first.

So I give it to him. All I want is to hold him one last time.

Panting, I grab the hard edge of his skull head and look into the void of his eyes. My stomach muscles burn, and my crushed leg is numb, but I grasp the connection between us, so strong and alive despite shadow being drained out of me along with blood.

I let him feel my heartbeat.

"My love," I choke out and stroke the golden bone. "Let me do this for you. Let me give you the safety you wanted."

A soft grunt comes out from deep in the Sunwolf's chest, and I'm lowered to the moss. The beast lets go, then pushes its bloodstained muzzle under my tunic, pushing up the fabric. Hot air dances against my skin as he smells me, and I float in the shimmery blur where everything has soft edges. The pain is gone, and all I feel is warmth so intense I wish to strip my clothes.

My eyes are about to close when I realize the Sunwolf's throat is right above me, so I open the Umlaris Band and push it up, into the thick coat. Each inch forward is like a separate battle, but I know I can do it, and when the dark collar locks with a soft *click*, I can finally rest.

CHAPTER 42

HAWK

Dreams have always escaped my grasp, dispersing the moment I woke up, but as I curled up in the dungeon, trying to forget that I might stay there forever, dense waves of fantastical images carried me away from the shores of consciousness and straight into the depths.

There was no regret there, nor pain, just cozy warmth that brought me back to my childhood and the delicious Summer mornings in the woods. I used to stretch in the moss, pick fresh berries straight from the bushes, and enjoy the sun on my skin, half asleep and content.

Going back to that state is like coming home.

Time does not matter.

I have no obligations beyond staying put so I don't endanger anyone.

My consciousness drifts on the surface of the calmest of oceans.

Then, in a flash, an icy stream washes over me, taking my breath, and carries me away from the nothingness in the middle of the ocean, back toward the beach of sharp rocks. It's going too fast. I see the pink clouds above turn an angry red shade, and lightning tears the sky in half as blood rain falls, splashing my cheeks and filling my open mouth.

As the wave clashes with the shore and sharp gravel tears into my skin, the dream fades, gone like an old memory.

I taste blood and iron.

Sylvan is stroking the sides of my head. Oh, I would recognize his touch anywhere.

Has he returned to me?

No. He shouldn't have. He promised. I must still be dreaming.

"Let go of him!" A female voice yells.

The world around me is a blur, but I spot a bright red light where the woman is. She's... on the ground? Shooting a bow into the sky?

I'm so confused when the arrow with a bright red tip flies up in a sea of colorful smoke, but the edges around me sharpen, and I sense it on my tongue again.

Blood. So much blood.

I'm surrounded by Sylvan's scent, but it's not quite right. Coppery, sharp rather than warm, as if it were coming from the very center of him. The smoky aroma of his shadow is gone too.

I can hear his frantic heartbeat when I spot sapphire eyes watching me from an unnaturally pale face. Reality clashes into me with the force of a freight train, and I let go of the mess of meat and bone in my muzzle.

A horrified whine leaves my throat when everything falls into place. Then, a howl.

No. No. No. No.

Crying wordlessly, I crawl on top of him in an attempt to give him some of my warmth, because he's shivering, and it's all my fault.

When an arrow flies over my head, grazing my ear, I look up with a snarl, because it might have hit Sylvan, but I spot the knight struggling to get up. She's screaming at me to get off *"the prince"*.

I'm so frantic about Sylvan's state I can't think straight, but I have to focus if he is to survive. All it takes to change back into a human is the desire to do so. The Sunwolf's form around me sparkles with sunlight, blinding me for a moment, and then I'm kneeling at Sylvan's side.

I'm covered in blood, and there's so much of it I struggle to work out where he's most injured. It only takes one look at his leg though to realize what I've done.

From the hip down, it's bent out of shape, bone ripping through his pants in at least two places. I must have crushed it in my jaws.

Me. I did that. I hurt him in this unspeakable way.

I have no memory of doing it. I don't even know how I got from the dungeon to this clearing in the forest, but I am soaked with his blood, and there's no denying reality. I wail. Then sob. Then scream at the top of my lungs, but Sylvan's no longer conscious, the beautiful eyes I've fallen in love with shut, his slender form broken.

I tear off my shirt and rise, wrapping it on his upper thigh in an improvised tourniquet, even though I'm not sure if I'm doing it correctly. Everything is a blur. He's so fragile, so small, and already lost so much blood.

"What's happening?" I yell to the knight who is crawling our way on all fours at the pace of a snail.

I hear hoofbeats and yelling. A whole group of people is approaching fast, and all I can think of is that maybe one of them will be able to help Sylvan. My connection with him is fading, his heartbeat slows. It's like a piece of gum being pulled on, and soon enough, it will become thin enough to break.

"Help! Help," I call out at the top of my lungs as horse riders enter the clearing in armor polished to perfection. I tighten the knot around Sylvan's leg and rise on my knees, waving to draw the attention of the knight riding at the front of the party. He's tall, with skin that shines like the surface of a pearl, and a presence so regal I know he is important before he even speaks.

"Healer!" he demands, looking down at us from up on his unusually large and dark mount with a skull for a head. It only takes one glance to know this is not a horse at all, but a kelpie. The creature is dripping, as if it's just ridden through a waterfall, but the man in its saddle remains dry.

Someone dashes through the ranks, followed by a small team in identical red coats. Despite begging for help, my first instinct is to growl as the elf squatting right next to Sylvan touches him without asking first, but then a smoky dome forms around my mate, and at once I feel his heart calm.

"Will he live?" the dark-haired elf on the kelpie asks.

The medic puts their hands through the barrier surrounding Sylvan and rests them on his chest. The elf seems young, but for all I know, they could have hundreds of years of experience, so I have to trust them no matter how much I want to hug Sylvan's shattered body and protect him.

"I stopped the bleeding, but I cannot say for certain, Your Highness. He must be taken to the castle at once. His heart might not take it," the medic finishes in a quiet tone.

I barely contain the sob rising in my chest, because this is not about me. I don't know how it happened, but I've mutilated Sylvan. I have turned into a monster, just like I feared, and now he might lose *everything*.

Why? Why has he come back when I told him to leave me behind? Or was it me who hunted him down? I have no idea how much time passed since we parted. What if it's been years?

Prince Tristan, who's still sporting a bruise on his face, jumps off his own kelpie. I'm a big guy, but Tristan is imposing in his armor, and he is headed straight for me.

"What did you do to him?" he roars as he pushes my shoulders so hard I fall over.

That's when my self-control ends. Tears fall from my eyes as I howl, hiding my face in my palms. "I'm a dangerous monster. Please... please help him!"

I'm inconsolable, but the punches I most definitely deserve don't come.

"Enough of this self-pity," the dark-haired royal says, sliding from the back of his kelpie. He might be clad in full armor but walks as if it didn't hinder his movements at all. "Time to take responsibility for your actions."

I attempt to focus on his words, because I know he's the one making all the decisions, but my attention still drifts to Sylvan, who's being moved to a stretcher. When Tristan steps in to help, I initially want to stop him, since he might be inclined to exact his revenge when my husband is at his most vulnerable, but the red-haired knight picks him up with tenderness and familiarity.

The dignified elf pulls out a sword blacker than the sky and puts the very tip at my chin. I don't even attempt to get up. "I am Kyran Nightweed, Lord of the Nocturne Court, and Protector of the Nightmare Realm. You are wearing the Sunwolf Crown, which belongs to my family. You will either pledge yourself into my service, as Prince Sylvan promised me you would, or you will die." His eyes are so intense that I have no choice but to focus on him.

"B-but... I'm a danger," I mutter before gesturing at my lover's body as it's transferred, along with the shadow dome. "I don't remember hurting him. What if it happens again?"

Kyran shushes me and reaches to my throat. I expect him to squeeze it in warning, but instead he grabs something I didn't even realize was locked around my neck, and gently pulls me forward. "Not for as long as you wear this collar. Sylvan put it on you, at the risk of his own life. Do you deny the commitment he made in your name?"

"No! Of course not, Your... Highness," I blurt out as Kyran lets go. "Please, help him, and I will be loyal like a dog. I will do whatever you want from me."

The tiniest smirk appears on his lips. I have no doubt my future at his court won't be easy, but all I care about is Sylvan's life.

"Good. That's what I expect from my loyal Sunwolf." I half expect him to pat me on the head, but he doesn't, and, to my relief, pulls away his sword. "Is your... bond with Prince Sylvan still there? I saw that you drained his shadow dry."

I can't bear that I took his power away, and I bite my hand, trying to contain the pain eating me up inside.

But his serene presence, and the slow, yet steady heartbeat I can hear alongside my own are still there, so I nod.

Lord Kyran scoots down like I'm a child in need of comfort. I feels ridiculous to be treated that way by a grown-ass man, a stranger. But right now, I do feel like some pauper wishing for nothing more but this royal's grace, and assurance that all will be okay. That Sylvan will be taken care of if I just do as I'm told.

His gaze is much softer than before when he meets my damp eyes. "You can no longer be his Dark Companion," he says, and I can't help the sob escaping my lips. I never cared for that title, but Lord Kyran's statement feels like a knife stabbed into my heart. He cups one side of my face and lifts it. "From now on, you will be his Bright Companion."

Tears fall again, and I wipe them off with the back of my hand. "I hurt him. And I promised to keep him safe."

Kyran sighs and places both his hands on my shoulders. There's such comfort in their weight I find myself sobbing again. "He knew the risk of approaching a feral Sunwolf, yet he thought you were worth it. Be there for him in turn."

I nod. "Yes, Your Highness."

When he gestures toward a large black carriage with doors thrown wide open as the men in red coats carry Sylvan in, I crawl toward it on all fours, exhausted, scared, yet so very desperate to watch over him.

Tristan grabs my arm and hauls me up. I expect violence, but he pats me on the back and allows me inside the carriage.

The medic glances my way, their bright green eyes hopeful. "Sit here," they urge me as Tristan shuts the carriage door behind us. "I do think we caught him in time. The state of his leg is questionable, but he will live."

Whether Sylvan can still stand my presence once he wakes up, or not, I will be there to offer my aid. In any capacity he wishes.

I take hold of his lovely slender hand and place my nose and lips inside the cool, sweaty palm, hoping that a part of him will be aware of my presence. I promised loyalty to the Lord of the Nocturne Court, but it's my tiny prince who truly has all of it.

CHAPTER 43

SYLVAN

My mind is filled with fuzzy darkness, but it's pleasant, like a comforter filled with warm wool. I can hardly feel my body, sunken into a bed so soft—

I sit up with a gasp, my eyes flying open.

"Hawk?"

Everything around me is a blur, but when a large, dark shape moves at me, and warm arms smelling of sun-kissed rock close around me, I know I've succeeded.

"Sylvan! You're awake!"

My body is quite numb, but I hug him back as much as my limbs allow. I smell him, kiss his shoulder as my eyes regain focus.

We're in an unfamiliar bedroom, but the massive moon is high up in the sky, and the blue-black decor tells me we are most definitely in the Nocturne Palace. The bed I'm in could fit three elves, the canopy has kelpies frolicking in the waves embroidered over dark green silk, and a table next to me is filled with vials and boxes used for salves.

I kiss the side of Hawk's face, too overwhelmed to comprehend it all. "I lived?" I ask, but Hawk only hugs me tighter. He's shaking so much I feel compelled to comfort him, even though it's me who's in a sickbed.

"I'm so sorry! I don't remember any of it. I didn't want to hurt you."

"I know, my love. But you recognized me. It was enough for me to help you." It's all coming back to me, and I'm dazed when I remember that I didn't flee from those crystal teeth. I've never considered myself brave, but now I know that for Hawk, I'd be ready to do anything. Even sacrifice my shadow. All it takes is a gentle pull of my fingers to confirm that I have none left.

Hawk kisses the top of my head, exhaling as he rocks us back and forth. "Your cousins, they helped you, like I asked," he tells me, and I take in the rest of the room. It's not nearly as refined as my old quarters, but if we are to stay, there will be time to decorate the place up to our combined taste. Wherever this room is, I just hope it is far away from my mother's residence.

I let myself melt into Hawk's warm body, resting my cheek on his shoulder. "I... can't feel my leg," I choke out, afraid to look under the covers.

Hawk's face reflects pure terror, and he lifts the comforter. I remember flashes of the crunching noises, and the pain that came with them, but when I open my eyes, I realize my leg is still attached to the rest of my body.

Hawk shifts on the mattress and flicks my toes where they stick out from the black cast. "They're not cold. Maybe you just need to change position," he offers before leaning down to kiss my foot.

I laugh out loud, even though there's nothing funny about my situation. I run my fingers over the cast, understanding the salves under it must be making my injured limb numb. Which is for the better because I would be in a world of pain without them.

"No, I think it's just the cast. I... thought I lost my leg," I say with a sigh of relief. "How about you? Are you not hurt? Are you no longer overheating? How long have I been out?"

Hawk stretches his body alongside mine and kisses my face so tenderly that if I were in any pain, it would have been instantly diminished. "You're crazy! You promised you'd get yourself to safety. I almost killed you! I—I could have *eaten* you along with your shadow," he tells me as his voice trembles. But he doesn't seem angry that I broke my vow and once again kisses my head. "Your leg won't be the same. The medics did what they could for the bones but not all of them healed right. You'll need to use a cane. But I'll carry you wherever you want to go."

I have to take a deep breath to absorb the unfortunate news. "What matters is that we both live. I couldn't leave you. Not when I still had hope. You are where I belong, my only future. Though it is a shame that I'll no longer be able to join the circus as vault master." I don't want to make light of the issue with my leg, but Hawk needs this. I don't want him to feel guilty over something that wasn't his fault.

He grumbles and gives my arm a gentle slap. "Very funny." But he does smile and curls around me, with his head on my chest, as if he desperately needs the comfort of my forgiveness. "Everyone's worried about you. Luke Moor was here with his husband, the Lord, and their bat baby."

I curl my fingers into fists. "That fucking thing! I would have gotten away with my plan if it weren't for that meddling bat. I managed to sneak into the Lord's bedchamber, but the creature alerted him of my presence."

Hawk frowns. "Flap actually licked you. Maybe there were berries in the salve they put on you."

Hawk laughs at the face I make, but I don't find it funny at all. "I understand the Lord honored his word? We get to stay at court? Me and my Dark Companion?" I kiss the top of his head, trying to forget that I have been *licked* by that creature in lace.

Hawk nods, and as he entwines our fingers, I focus on the soothing warmth of his breath on my skin. "He told me I'm your *Bright* Companion now."

I bite the inside of my cheek at the sudden urge to cry. "He did?" It feels... special. Something just for me and Hawk. Suddenly, even my lack of access to any shadowcraft is meaningless. "I've not had any time to think about a future for us. I based a lot of my research in shadowcraft, but since I have a Bright Companion, I shall devote myself to figuring out everything I possibly can about the Sunwolf."

I look into his black eyes. Perhaps I should be frightened, but I sense so much love and warmth in his strange gaze. Nothing scares me about Hawk. Not the sharp teeth, nor the golden tattoos on his face.

"Should I... tell them you're awake?" Hawk asks, but I shake my head and wrap my arms around his thick biceps, just enjoying the warmth of his body.

"Not yet. Give me a few more moments with you in silence. We have all the time in the world."

Hawk nuzzles my ear with a shivery sigh. "You are my forever."

EPILOGUE

Sylvan

One year later

My mouth is dry as I watch the sunset gem twitch in boiling water. When it glimmers, Peregrin, my apprentice and assistant, takes a step back, worried the flask might explode, but I stand firm, knowing the steron mask will protect my face if the worst happens. Moments later, the small bead, procured at no small expense, stabilizes, and I continue watching the condenser. It's full of moisture, but the receiving bottle is starting to fill.

My new laboratory has many windows, as tall as they are wide, and while the use of artificial light is still necessary when I'm performing more precise tasks, the glow of the moon is more than sufficient for now. Lord Kyran spared no expense once he understood the importance of my research.

The sputtering of the apparatus evens out, and I glance toward Peregrin, my smile not visible behind the protective gear. He's wearing a mask of his own, as well as a leather robe with fireproof padding.

"I—I'm sorry," he chokes out and joins me close to the large wooden table housing the equipment I use most frequently. Vials, devices, and materials take up all of the available space on wide shelves and inside heavy coffers, and for the first time in my life, I'm helped rather than hindered in my research.

"Even the simplest and most routine of alchemical operations might prove dangerous. And it's even more so with experimental procedures. You'd do well getting rid of that fear," I tell him, licking my lips as the distilled liquid fills the flask.

"I'm sorry," he says again. He has a habit of apologizing for everything all the time, but in the grand scheme of things, it's not the worst quality in an assistant, so I just ignore it.

I light the small lantern filled with Sunlight, an object I needed a special permit for and which I'm required to keep in a safe box whenever it's not in use. Once it illuminates the flask, Peregrin's already large eyes go wide behind the thick glass of the protective mask, and his heart must be skipping a beat the same way mine does.

The tiniest particles glimmer in the liquid. Some are golden, others an intense orange.

"What are they?" Peregrin whispers as if he feared his voice could shatter the glass.

"I... don't know actually. Which means we'll get to do much more research. Next week, we will get right back to testing their qualities," I say with my heart beating faster.

Peregrin dares to step closer. "Why not tomorrow?"

My curiosity is like an itch, but I put down the flask. "I'm afraid I have plans with my husband."

His shoulders sag, but he nods. "I'm sorry for pushing."

I stop myself from rolling my eyes. "It's fine. I appreciate the enthusiasm. In the meanwhile, letting the flask just sit there for a week can be our first experiment. When I come back, we will see whether they're still floating, or if they sink to the bottom of the container."

Peregrin's eyes widen, and he removes the mask as I kill the fire underneath the vial holding the sunset gem. "Is there anything in particular you'd like me to work on while you're gone? My knowledge of herbs still leaves a lot to be desired, so if you don't require me to do any preparation for your experiments, I shall dedicate myself to my studies."

I give him a once over as I take off my robe. While he could indeed spend more time studying, my year with Hawk has taught me personal connections are just as important as knowledge, and Peregrin lacks them. "You rarely have time to socialize with other alchemists. Maybe it's a good opportunity to do so while I'm away. Exchange notes," I add so he feels there's an important scientific purpose to this advice.

His chest rises as he inhales. "Of course. I shall... do just that then," he says.

But my attention slips when I recognize the familiar rhythm of thick and heavy paws. "You're dismissed."

Peregrin clears his throat and looks past me just as I hear my husband enter. We had a huge wooden flap installed in the laboratory, so he can get in and out without the need to transform into a human when he doesn't feel like it, and it falls shut behind his towering form as I turn.

"I'm sorry, I know I said I won't be long." The irony of apologizing to him after mentally chastising Peregrin for the same thing is not lost on me. "But we've had quite the breakthrough," I add, approaching my golden Sunwolf when the door closes behind Peregrin. Hawk, ever forgiving, gives a happy yelp before pushing his skull face at my chest. His hot breath tickles me through my thin shirt, and I laugh, scratching him behind the ears.

[*That's all right. I lost my sense of time chasing after a bird. Never seen one like that before. It had feathers as blue as your eyes!*] he tells me, wagging his tail so rapidly I'm worried about my equipment, so I urge him to sit.

He's found so much joy in being able to transform into the Sunwolf, and I love to listen about his exploits in the forest. I've also heard gossip about him giving rides to children in the local village, but I dare not confront him about it, as I'd have to urge him to stop. As long as I pretend not to know, I don't have to take a stand.

"You're just adorable. Did you make sure to avoid crossing Dame Tallin's patch? She wasn't pleased that you stepped on her vegetables last time." I give the golden bone he has for a face a kiss to soften the tone of my question.

Dame Tallin is a good friend of my mother, or as close to a friend as she can have, and while I don't speak to my family anymore, the last thing I need is the two of them having a new reason to badmouth my beloved.

Hawk grunts. [*It's a shortcut.*] But moments later, I'm blinded by light. By the time I'm able to open my eyes again, a naked hunk is kneeling in front of me, with both arms locked around my midsection.

My face flushes. "Hawk! I told you not to transform naked! What if there's an emergency that requires you to shift in front of others?" I stifle the need to cover his shoulders with a blanket and kiss the top of his head. He's so impulsive, but I can't help but find that quality attractive. On the upside, our rooms are next door, so it's not like he'll be strutting through the palace without any underwear.

He shrugs and offers me a cocky grin. "Kyran said he doesn't mind. And who's to argue with him?"

Typical Hawk. Talking about the Lord of the Nocturne Court, the protector of the realm, as if he were a friend from the tavern. Who could *not* love this man?

"Well, I imagine *Kyran* would not be happy if you walked around naked in front of his husband. He's known to threaten men for lesser transgressions. But come, my love, let's not waste time," I say yet still give him another kiss before pulling on his hand.

Hawk grunts. Moments later, I'm in his arms and holding on as he carries me past the door, and then upstairs, to the chambers that have been so graciously provided for us. In the past, I would have considered quarters so far away from the Lord's an affront, but the location is convenient for both me and Hawk, who enjoys the relative freedom provided by the small lodge in the Nocturne Gardens.

"You worry too much. He knows I only have eyes for you."

I wrap my arms around his shoulders as I look into his eyes. I've learned to love their darkness, as it's a part of Hawk now, like the golden tattoos on his face and the sharp teeth. All those features are a testament to the sacrifice he was ready to make for me.

"Are you saying you've been *talking* to the Lord about such things?"

Hawk shrugs. "Nah, it just came up when we talked about the wedding anniversary."

He is impossible. And I love it.

"Speaking of which, get dressed. We need to be at the port by moondown. Have you fed Bloodgore?" I point out the red frog in its grand terrarium. We may have lost the redpole from Tassarion's disposal, but I gifted Hawk a new one not long after we settled in here. It's been growing since, and is now the size of his fist. I dread to think how big it will still get, but my man loves it, so I'll just deal with what comes accordingly.

Hawk nods, but his pitch-black eyes widen as he puts me down in our front room, which is filled with books and the games Hawk had me import from the human realm. One of those caused a week of strife between Lord Kyran and myself. A board game called A Game of Thrones. The night when we both played it with our respective husbands got unreasonably heated as we argued over the rules, the betrayals, and then over who won. Hawk hated it, since he lost his army within the first hour of the match. He ended up dozing off but my violent argument with Lord Kyran woke him up. I'm not proud of my moment of madness. In the end, we had to agree to a peace brokered by Luke, which involved a Nocturne Court-wide ban on the game.

I turn on the lamp Hawk helped me construct out of numerous glass vials. It's a more elaborate version of the lava lamp I owned in the human realm, as that one couldn't be recovered and is no doubt being passed on the black market. I don't even mind, as while a nice memento of our troubled journey, it doesn't work without electricity anyway.

"Where are we going?" Hawk asks.

"It's a surprise, but one I'm pretty sure you will appreciate."

I grab my cane as he dresses. I wish my leg could have healed better, but despite the efforts of the best medics, I've been left with a bit of a limp. But it's a price I was willing to pay for Hawk's safety and happiness.

He's not yet had to take anyone's shadow. One day, the Lord of the Nocturne Court will call upon him, and he will need to be the executioner to someone's shadowcraft. All I can hope for is that the punishment will be just when it's required, so Hawk's conscience can remain clear.

I've had his luggage packed for him, which he seems delighted by as he grabs our coffers and leads the way outside. By the time we're boarding the ship, the moon's gone from the sky, and the swamp lights are burning all around us as the crew adjusts the sails. The darkness beyond is absolute, but my husband doesn't seem bothered and unpacks the snacks I purchased for him in the town closest to the castle. A woven screen is stretched across the deck to afford us privacy while we settle on a low sofa at the prow and glance at the sails bulging above. A member of the crew calls upon the wind.

"This whole magic thing is so useful. People used to get stuck in the middle of the ocean when there was no breeze," Hawk tells me, pushing a stuffed bird into his mouth. The delicate bones fracture the moment he bites down.

"At least they aren't at risk of being swallowed whole by a leviathan," I jest, but Hawk's eyes open wider, so I pat his arm. "We will be fine. This is a royal vessel, the captain knows these waters like the back of his hand, and will not endanger us, even if it means turning back."

Hawk shrugs and eats another bird, crunching with every bite.

"The vendor knew your name. You should have told me to order more snacks for you." I smirk when he opens the cherin. The smell alone reminds me of our wedding day, and I choose to only remember how happy I felt before the Nightcloaks crashed our party.

He frowns and takes a swig straight from the bottle. "I have a fast metabolism."

"You'll need all that energy where we're going, as there's no laboratory there. I will require a lot of your attention." I smile and sit closer, patting his belly.

Hawk's mouth stretches into the goofiest of smiles, and he leans in to kiss me as the wind tousles our hair. "Come on, surely you can tell me where we're going now that we've boarded the ship!"

I pinch his cheek. "No! It's a surprise. All I can tell you is that the trip there will take several hours, and required me to obtain a special permit."

He grunts and pushes his hands to my flanks. I stiffen, worried he might try to tickle the truth out of me, but he pulls closer, and our lips meet in the sweetest of kisses. "I also have something for you," he whispers and reaches into his pocket.

My breath catches in my throat, and I get choked up at the sight of the ring in his fingers. A sapphire, a diamond, and a ruby set in titanium. "Hawk... It's like the one you gave me on our wedding day! How did you get one just like it?" I sigh as he slips it on my finger. Unlike the one I had to leave behind, this one fits just right.

He clears his throat and kisses first the ring, then each of my knuckles, and this display of tenderness makes my chest tighten. "Remember that time I disappeared and you yelled at me for two hours once I returned?"

My ears heat up in shame. "Was I that bad? I just got really worried..."

He stops me with a gesture and smiles. "I'm not mad. Of course you were worried. But if I told you I was headed to Lepearl's hideout to buy the ring back, this would not be a surprise."

My breath catches as I stare at the ring. "It's the same one? And you even had the size adjusted?" I have to bite the inside of my cheek to fight the tears stinging my eyes. "You are a marvel, my love. More than I could have ever dreamed of."

Hawk swallows, hesitating, but then he's pulling me close, and I curl up against his broad chest. Oh, how I love the scent of him. There is nothing more soothing in this world. "You must be joking. You're literally a prince from another world, and *I'm* the 'marvel'?" He chuckles before pressing a kiss to the top of my head. "You made me into an immortal wolf, I live in a castle, and rub elbows with royals. I still sometimes wake up and wonder if it's all just a dream, but you're more beautiful than anything I could imagine, so you must really be mine."

Moths flutter their wings in my stomach when he kisses me. I have never felt more wanted and at peace. "I love you. And I..." I said that I wouldn't tell him, but now I'm itching to see his reaction. "I thought that if there's something you miss from the human realm, it's sunshine. I have arranged a sunny retreat for us. Though I warn you that I will most likely spend a lot of time in the shade."

He blinks, leaning back, and stares at me as if he were waiting for me to tell him I'm joking. Alas, I am not. "Like… to the human realm?" he chokes out, attempting to control his breathing.

"Yes! And I made sure to confirm that it'll be safe for you there, as we are going to a remote beach in the Land of Tay."

When he frowns a little, I wonder if I said the word correctly. "Luke has assured me you would know of this place. Teyland?" I try again, and his eyes grow wide.

"Thailand? We're going to Thailand?"

The excitement is so clear in his smile I sigh in relief. "That is the name."

Hawk presses his hand to his chest. "Oh shit! I never even had a passport! Wow!"

I have no concept of what a pass-port is, but after a moment's thought I figure it must be a permit to cross the border between different lands. Who knew humans can rival us in terms of bureaucracy?

Hawk gets to his feet and pulls me up with a single tug, and before I know what's going on, we're dancing. "Fuck, I love you so, so much, Sylvan. You always think about my needs. But I promise I'll bring you the best mai tais to your shadowy corner!" When he sees the question in my eyes he clarifies, "Cocktails. Sweet alcoholic drinks."

I smile at my giant. "Will we make that the exception to my no drinking vow? An allowance in the human realm?"

He winks and slides back to the sofa, before bringing me into his lap, which happens to be my favorite place. "Don't you worry. I'll make sure you don't drown."

The End

Would you like to find out how their vacation in Thailand goes? Read the bonus scene here:

http://kamerikan.com/freebies

Thank you for reading our book! If you enjoyed it and want to find out what happens to Sylvan, Tristan, and the others next, follow us on Amazon and join our Facebook group, the K.A. Merikan Playroom

For more extra content, swag, Q&As, ARCs, and exclusive fiction, join us on Patreon: http://patreon.com/kamerikan

Please, remember to review the book on your favorite platform, as it helps us out a lot :)

TAKEN
BY THE LORD OF THE
NOCTURNE
COURT
K.A. MERIKAN

TAKEN BY THE LORD OF THE NOCTURNE COURT

DARK COMPANIONS #1

"I am yours, and I can be your prince as well as your beast."

Luke

I'm your typical small-town loser stuck in a dead-end job. Single, because dating is for well-adjusted human beings, not traumatized gay boys with trust issues. All I want is to leave my past behind and finally start living.

My wish comes true in the most bizarre way imaginable. One evening, a beautiful man with pointy ears and flowing dark locks appears out of nowhere. He proclaims I am to be his 'Dark Companion' based on some stupid deal I made in a dream. Oh, and apparently he's an elven prince, the Lord of Shadows, Protector of the Nightmare Realm and Knight of Grief Ocean.

Which is a weird way to ask me out, but okay.

It's a hard no from me, but this absolute psycho abducts me to his palace in a moonlit realm populated by vicious beasts and backstabbing courtiers.

If I am to ever get back home, I need to adapt, because our full moon wedding is approaching fast. I can't allow myself to buy into his seductive kisses, poet shirts made of spider silk and bouquets of sapphire roses. They hide poison and deception. A gilded cage is still a prison.

But...

What if I just never realized that what I need is a man with a cruel smile and a sword dipped in midnight? A man with secrets, and scars, and smoky eyes, and a past filled with darkness, and... have I mentioned he has a big d—

"Taken by the Lord of the Nocturne Court" is a standalone, scorching hot, dark gothic M/M romantasy filled with snark and dark humor, but also violence, peril, jealousy, and angst.

The book is a darkly romantic escape into the shadows where love and destiny collide. Dive into the pages to discover if a gilded cage can become a home when shared with a seductive elven prince devoted to his Dark Companion's every wish.

Themes: abduction, enemies to lovers, size difference, fake relationship, dark humor, snark, jealousy, hurt/comfort, afraid to commit, obsessive hero, forced marriage, isekai, fantasy elven prince, gothic castle, childhood trauma, shadow magic, monsters and fantastical creatures, fish-out-of-water, secrets, portal fantasy

WARNING: This story contains scenes of violence, abduction, offensive language and morally gray characters unafraid to burn the world down for their beloved.

Available on AMAZON

TAKE MY BODY

K.A. MERIKAN

TAKE MY BODY

K.A. MERIKAN

***Freaky Friday*. But Gay.**

Gunner. Big. Butch. Bully... Secretly submissive.
Caspian. Tiny. Weak. Nerd... A Dominant at heart.

Caspian might be rich and destined for a life of privilege, courtesy of loving parents, but he's far from happy. Short, frail, and hung up on his physique, he's never built up the confidence to be the dominant man from his dreams.

But when he clashes with his old high school bully - Gunner Russo, reality becomes stranger than either of them could imagine.

Gunner is Caspian's polar opposite. Tall, muscular, tattooed, he oozes testosterone, and violence. Caspian hates him with all his heart, yet he couldn't be more jealous, so when they **swap bodies**, it's everything Caspian ever wanted.

Only that it isn't.

Because Gunner is dirt-poor, unemployed, lives in a trailer with his toxic ex, and has drug dealers for friends.

Gunner on the other hand, wakes up in a body that is nothing like the hyper-masculine mask he'd perfected, and in that new form, he feels free to explore his submissive fantasies without consequences.

Only that the man whose body he now occupies isn't about to let him sleep with just anyone. Caspian wants to experiment too, and if they both found themselves in this crazy situation, why not do that... with one another?

Dirty, dark, and delicious, "Take My Body" is a gritty M/M dark romance novel with magical elements and a happy ending. Prepare for violence, intense arguments, and scorching hot, emotional, explicit scenes.

Themes: body swap, enemies to lovers, magical bond, revenge, poverty, body dysmorphia, past bully, masculinity, coming out, size difference, opposites attract

Length: ~130,000 words (Standalone novel)

WARNING: This story contains scenes of violence, offensive language and morally ambiguous characters as well as sensitive topics of child abuse, body dysmorphia, and bullying.

Available on AMAZON

ABOUT THE AUTHOR

K.A. Merikan is a duo of queer writers who don't believe in following the well-trodden path. In their books you can dip your toe into dangerous romance with mafiosi, outlaw bikers and bad boys, all from the safety of your sofa. They love the weird and wonderful, stepping out of the box, and bending stereotypes both in life and in fiction. Their stories don't shy away from exploring the darker side of M/M romance, and feature a variety of anti-heroes, rebels, misfits, and underdogs who go against the grain.

Be prepared for shocking twists, dark humor, raw emotions, and sizzling hot scenes.

e-mail: **kamerikan@gmail.com**
http://kamerikan.com

More information about works in progress and publishing at:
Facebook: https://www.facebook.com/groups/1817541075240882
Patreon: https://www.patreon.com/kamerikan

www.ingramcontent.com/pod-product-compliance
Lightning Source LLC
Chambersburg PA
CBHW030553170726
48283CB00002B/304